W9-BNC-769

PRAISE FOR TOM DEITZ'S

WINDMASTER'S BANE

Other Avon Books by
Tom Deitz

WINDMASTER'S BANE

FIRESHAPER'S DOOM

a tale of vengeance

TOM DEITZ

AVON
PUBLISHERS OF BARD, CAMELOT, DISCUS AND FLARE BOOKS

AVON BOOKS
A division of
The Hearst Corporation
105 Madison Avenue
New York, New York 10016

Copyright © 1987 by Thomas Deitz
Cover illustration by Tim White
Published by arrangement with the author
Library of Congress Catalog Card Number: 87-91601
ISBN: 0-380-75329-4

First Avon Printing: December 1987

for all the folks of Madoc's Mountain
once and future
near and far

and for Maggie who made the buttons

ACKNOWLEDGMENTS

Jared Vincent Harper
Gilbert Head
Margaret Dowdle Head
D. J. Jackson
Adele Leone
Chris Miller
Klon Newell
Vickie R. Sharp
Brad Strickland
Sharon Webb
Wendy Webb

FIRESHAPER'S DOOM

Prologue: The Horn of Annwyn

Tir-Nan-Og, where Lugh Samildinach rules the youngest realm of Faerie, is a bright land—brighter by far than the dreary Lands of Men that float beneath it like a mirror's dull reflection. Its oceans shine like liquid silver; its deserts sprawl like lately molten gold. The very air imparts a gleam to field and forest, man and monster. Even the Straight Tracks take on a sharper glitter there—at least those parts that show at all as they ghost between the Worlds like threads of tenuous light.

But a thousand, thousand lands there are, linked by the treacherous webs of those arcane constructions. And some are less idyllic.

Erenn, that mortal men call Eire, is one such country. Finvarra holds court there in his ancient rath beneath the hill of Knockma, king of the greater host of the Daoine Sidhe. Erenn's sky is much more sober; its air not nearly as clear. It rubs along the Mortal World at an age more distant than its fellow to the west, yet the smoke of human progress still seeps through at times to grime the Faery wind with soot and the smells of death. Sometimes, too, the awkward, eager clatter of some man-made invention breaks the Barrier Between to haunt the Fair Folk at their feasting. Finvarra smiles but seldom.

And there is Arawn's holding: Annwyn of the Tylwyth-Teg, which humankind name Cymru. If Tir-Nan-Og is early morn, and Erenn afternoon, then Annwyn is twilight. By day the sun looks veiled and dusty; at night lamps made by druidry shine brighter than the moon. Shadows tend toward purple there; the sky ofttimes takes on the hue of blood. The wind is not always gentle. And the borders are not clear—for in spots the very ground simply fades until it will support not even a spider's passing. Many of the Straight Tracks end in Annwyn, or else lead into places where even the Elemental Powers merge and fragment endlessly like the dreaming of the damned.

1

* * *

"Will you go with me to Annwyn?" Lugh asked Nuada Airgetlam one morning. "If we do not visit Arawn's court ere the Mortal World unfreezes, we may find no chance again for many ages."

Nuada's dark eyes narrowed with suspicion. "And what has fueled this sudden haste, my master? What difference can *their* weather make to us? The Walls Between the Worlds make cold no danger; and as for the Road, no ship of man can pass there, whatever be the season."

"Leif the Lucky has beached his boats near the red men's north-most holding," the High King told his warlord. "Winter may hold them yet awhile, but spring will bring them south and westward. Tir-Nan-Og is safe at present, for my Power is great, and the glamour I have lately raised is strong. But I fear our time of peace will reach an ending, once word of Leif's good fortune spans the ocean. Soon, I think, we must set watch on our borders!"

Nuada sighed his regret. "I too fear men's coming and the tools of iron that always travel with them. But it is a thing that was bound to happen. You are right about Annwyn, though: if we would leave Tir-Nan-Og unguarded, we must start the journey eastward very shortly."

And so, on a day when snow sparkled bright on the Lands of Men, and Leif the Lucky sang of Vinland and the kingdom he would carve, Lugh Samildinach and Nuada Airgetlam took the Golden Road across the sea and came to Arawn's kingdom.

The Lord of the Dim Land received them well and feasted them for many days. Deep grew the bonds among the three, and diverse were the pleasures the three lords shared—in hunting and in trials of arms, in the savoring of song and poetry and subtle arts of women, and most particularly in the study of wondrous objects strangely fashioned.

"There is one thing left in Annwyn I would show you," Arawn said one evening. "But I would not reveal it here."

"And what might that thing be?" Lugh asked his host.

"We will ride out on the morrow," Arawn answered, and no more would he tell them.

And so, in the shallow light of dawn they journeyed forth: Lugh astride his great black stallion, black hair bound by a fillet of gold, black mustache stirring in a west-blowing wind, gold silk surcoat shimmering loose above tight black leather; and fair-haired Nuada beside him in white and silver, his left arm clothed in creamy satin, the other a shoulder-stub forever cased in shining metal; and showing them the way, Arawn himself, in dark gray velvet and blue-tinged bronze. No banners flew above that riding, no trumpets marked its passage. Arawn's squire alone went with them: a sullen, tight-mouthed Erenn-lad whom the Dark King had in fosterage. Ailill was his name, though some already called him Windmaster—and in bringing him along that day Arawn was very foolish, though how much so would not be clear for nearly a thousand mortal years.

They rode all day, and at dusk were riding still.

At sunset they found themselves on a cold, black-sanded plain, so near the tattered fringe of Annwyn that even a nearby Track showed as nothing more than a smear of sparkling motes, like brass filings strewn across the ground. A solid sheet of clouds hung low above them; before them was a country Arawn liked but little and the others not at all. A dead-end, blind pocket of a place, it was; open to nowhere else save Arawn's kingdom: an ill-lit land where gray mist twisted in evil-smelling whirls among the half-seen shapes of stunted trees and shattered, roofless buildings.

It was a place of mystery and rumor, shunned even by the mighty of the Tylwyth-Teg. Powersmiths lived there: the Powersmiths of Annwyn, some folk called them, though they did not name Arawn their master, and Arawn was not so bold as to set any claim upon that race at all.

But the Powersmiths made marvelous things—things the Sidhe could neither craft nor copy nor understand, and it was just such an object that was the cause of the riding that day.

Arawn drew it from his saddlebag and held it out for Lugh's inspection. A small hunting horn, it seemed, wrought of silver and gold, copper and greenish brass. At its heart was the curved ivory tusk of a beast that dwelt only in the Land of the Powersmiths and was near extinction there. Light played round about it, tracing flick-ering trails among the thin, hard coils that laced its surface. Nine silver bands encircled it, the longest set with nine gems, the next eight, and so on: nine black diamonds, and eight blue sapphires, seven emeralds, six topazes in golden mountings, five smooth domes of banded onyx, four rubies red as war, three amethysts, a pair of moonstones. And at the end, on a hinged cap that sealed the mouth-piece: a fiery opal large as a partridge's egg.

"It is the most precious thing in all my realm," the Lord of Ann-wyn told them. "Most precious and most deadly." His gaze locked with Lugh's, and he paused to take a long, decisive breath. "I would make you a gift of it."

"A gift—but not without some danger, it would seem," Lugh noted carefully.

"You are a brave man," Arawn continued. "But you are also prudent, much more so than I. It would be best that you have mastery of this weapon."

Nuada cocked a slanted eyebrow. "Well, if there is more to it than beauty, then it keeps its threat well hidden."

Arawn nodded. "The Powersmiths made it. One of their druids set spells upon it—and then he died. It was meant as a pledge of peace, but now I dare not trust it."

"It does not look much like a sword," Ailill interrupted. "Does it hold some blade in secret that perhaps I have not noticed?"

"It cuts with an edge of sound, young Windmaster," came Arawn's sharp reply. "But perhaps it is best that I show you."

The Lord of Annwyn gazed skyward then, to where a solitary eagle flapped vast wings beneath the red-lit heavens. "Behold!" he whispered, as he thumbed the opal downward, raised the horn to his lips, and blew.

No sound resulted—or at least no sound that even Faery ears could follow. But their bones seemed at once to buzz within them, and the hair prickled upon their bodies. The solid flesh between felt for a brief, horrifying moment as though it had turned to water. For an instant, too, the air seemed about to shatter in the wake of that absent noise.

And then the air *did* break, cracked apart in a file of jagged angles that snapped closed again quick as a flash of lightning. But not before a series of shapes had leapt through, to congregate in a milling, hairy horde around the legs of Arawn's stallion.

They were hounds, or at least they looked like hounds: great rangy beasts with shoulders near as high as the horses' bellies, and narrow heads almost as long as a tall man's forearm. Their hair was a remarkable white like sun-bleached bone, and where that hair grew longest—upon their backs and in fringes on their tails and the hind sides of their legs—it looked less like fur than feathers. Four parts alone held any color: their claws were iron black; a deathly gray their tongues; their eyes glowed a startling green. And their ears, up-pointing like those of a wolf, showed red as a warrior's blood. They swirled among the legs of Arawn's horse like the pale, foaming waves of a cold and greedy ocean. The sound of their breaths was like thunder.

Arawn's face froze; a line of moisture condensed upon his brow.

One of the hounds—the largest one, the one with the greenest eyes and the reddest ears—looked up at him.

Arawn took a ragged breath and pointed toward the eagle that still floated against the sky. Somewhere a cloud stretched thin enough for a single ray of dying sunlight to paint the plain beneath with brazen glory.

"I would have the life of that bird," Arawn said, as though he named his own destruction.

The pack bayed then: one cry. And there are no words in the tongues of the Sidhe, or the Tylwyth-Teg, or of men, either, to give image to that howling. But two centuries later it still echoed sometimes in Airgetlam's dreams, so that the Warlord of Tir-Nan-Og awoke into darkness with a sweat upon his body, his single hand reaching for his sword.

And then they ran, those dogs that the horn commanded. They ran upon the earth, yet no dust rose at their passing, and the sand where they had stood displayed no padded prints. And then they ran into the sky, describing a tight-coiled spiral that twisted upward with more speed and purpose than the fastest hawk might summon.

The eagle circled once in abstract interest, for never had it been challenged in its own realm by any less than Arawn's folk themselves, when they put on other forms to frolic there. But these were not the Tylwyth-Teg, whatever shape enwrapped them, and the eagle felt uneasy. It straightened its glide, flapped its mighty wings, then folded them to dive. But by the time it had dropped twice its own length, hot breath fanned its feathers, and in one length more fangs sank into its body. Not even a drop of its blood escaped those dogs to spatter the ground before Arawn's staring company.

"It is a hunting horn," Arawn told them grimly, "of a sort. But the hounds it masters are no beasts born of Annwyn. Even the Powersmiths do not know whence they come, or else they do not tell us. The hounds always catch what they pursue, though it flee through all the Worlds. But one must take care when he sets them on a quarry, for once they are loosed, they must have a life. And"—his voice darkened—"they can devour both the body *and* the soul."

Lugh's face was as grim as the Lord of Annwyn's, but he took the horn from Arawn's fingers. "A gift like this shows trust beyond all measure, for with it one could master whatever land might please him."

"He would have to be careful, though," observed Nuada. "For it could also make him many enemies—and many false friends besides. And," he continued, with the first shudder any there had ever seen upon him, "has one of you considered what—if the Powersmiths cast off such things of Power—they hoard in secret for themselves?"

The Dark King did not answer, and the Bright King was also

silent as he tucked the Horn within his surcoat, though his eyes held great misgiving.

Arawn faced his squire then, and his face was hard as stone. "None of this has happened, young Windmaster. *None of this at all.*"

But Ailill had thought already of a lady who might listen.

PART I

TINDER

Prelude: A Sending

(Tir-Nan-Og—autumn)

On a beach of black sand in the south of Tir-Nan-Og, Nuada Airgetlam sat astride a white horse and gazed eastward across the ocean.

Water spread before him, and all of it was gray—gray, that is, save where it was silver filigree stretched thin across the towering fronts of monstrous waves, or the froth of ragged ivory lace atop them.

Or gold where the Straight Tracks threaded through them.

But it was not the healthy sun gold that told of easy passage; it was the weak, shifting color that told of danger and the perilous way. For the Circles of the Worlds turned out of track this season: the suns rose against each other in the Lands of Men and Faerie; the moons added each their contentious influences. And in the skies of the Mortal World was a hairy star that wrought its own disruption.

And so all the seas of Faerie ran high, and not even the ships of the Tuatha de Danaan could sail upon them. Storms raged in the High Air, so that those same ships could not skim above those seas, nor birds any longer fly there. And the Tracks between the realms were so weak and fickle that no foot or wheel dared pass upon them, as had not been the case in five hundred of the years of men.

"Lord, you may not pass. You would not return," said the border watch. "The way is sealed, no one goes that way, except to lose himself forever."

"But what of my ravens?" Nuada asked. "I would set them a-traveling: word must be sent to Annwyn and Erenn of what passed at the Trial of Heroes. Nearly a month that word has waited, and it can wait no longer."

But wait it did, for almost a change of seasons. It was summer in the Lands of Men before the eastward Road reopened.

Chapter I: Mail

(MacTyrie, Georgia—
Friday, June 21)

David Sullivan—Mad Dave, as he had somehow come to be called during the previous school year—had what his mother would have termed in her Georgia mountain twang "the nervous, pacing fidgets."

Except that he wasn't exactly nervous—just impatient, which was generally worse because it was usually somebody else's fault. And except that he wasn't, for the moment, pacing—but only because Alec McLean had just asked him, quite forcefully, to stop. For the fourth time in twice as many minutes he flopped down in the window seat snuggled beneath the dormer of Alec's second-floor bedroom and took another stab at reading the page of *New Teen Titans* he had likewise commenced four times before.

And once again was not successful.

Before he knew it, his gaze had wandered away from the comic to survey the neat, odd-shaped room beyond his cubby. An aluminum-framed backpack dominated his view, bulging lumpily atop the double bed at his left like a blue nylon hippopotamus. And just beyond it, David knew, lay the very heart and center of his impatience: a pair of half-empty suitcases.

"*Well*, McLean," he growled. "Do you think I'd be out of line if I asked you if you could maybe, possibly, you know, like *hurry* just a little? I've been sitting here like a knot on a log 'til I'm about half-way mildewed."

A tall, slender boy straightened from where he had been thumping around on the floor of the closet in the opposite wall. He aimed an exasperated glare at David, one hand snagging a pair of shiny black ankle boots, the other grasping a pair of wrinkled burgundy ENOTAH COUNTY 'POSSUMS sweatpants. He rolled his eyes with the tolerant resignation of the much-put-upon.

"Give me a break, Sullivan," he retorted sourly. "This packing for two trips at once is a real bummer. Camping overnight with the M-gang and staying six weeks at Governor's Honors with the brightest kids in Georgia demand fundamentally different logistical and aesthetic approaches."

"Ha!" David snorted at his friend's attempt at high-flown language, which he didn't have the patience for just then. "Didn't take *me* all day."

Alec gave the sweats a tentative sniff and wrinkled his nose distastefully, but nevertheless stuffed them into the backpack. The shoes thunked into one of the suitcases. "Well, considering that *your* entire wardrobe consists of holey T-shirts, scruffy jeans, scuzzy sneakers, and sweaty red bandanas, I'm not surprised." He turned around and began rummaging in his chest of drawers.

David sighed and glanced down at his current attire, which indeed precisely reflected his friend's assessment: plain white T-shirt stretched tight across a chest that had thickened considerably in the last year; cutoff Levis beltless around a narrow waist, their side seams ripped almost indecently high; Sears second-best sneakers loose on sockless feet. He raised a black eyebrow into a tossled forelock of thick blond hair—shorter now than he had ever worn it, though still nearly shoulder-long in back. "I resent that, McLean! I've got two pairs of cords and—"

"One of which I gave you for Christmas."

"—and a paisley shirt."

"Which *Liz* gave you."

David flung down the comic and stood up, stretching his fingertips to the dormer's ceiling—at five-foot-seven, it was nice to be able to touch a ceiling somewhere. He began to pace again: four steps along the narrow space between the front wall and the foot of the bed, and four steps back. "Just move it, okay?"

Alec frowned, unloaded a stack of white Fruit-of-the-Looms into the closest suitcase, and snapped it closed. "It was your idea to try to fit in a last-minute camping trip before we leave."

"And yours for us to head straight to Valdosta from camping."

"Thereby saving me at least an hour of Mad Davy Sullivan and the Mustang of Death."

"You may *think* so," David said, flashing his teeth fiendishly. He paused at one end of his route and hefted the backpack experimentally. "Good God, McLean, what've you got in here—lead?"

"You should know. You've been watching me like a bloody hawk ever since I started."

David drummed his fingers absently on the shiny metal. "Negatory, my man, you had this thing half full before I ever got here. All you've put in since then's a pair of stinky britches."

Alec ran a hand unconsciously through the soft, neat spikes of brown hair he had affected lately. "Well, if you've got to know, it's full of extra clothes, among other things. I have a way of needing them when we go camping. It inevitably rains, or somebody spills beer on me, or worse. I figured if I packed stuff that was dirty to start with, maybe my luck'd—"

"Damn!" David groaned loudly and slapped himself on the forehead. "Damn! Damn! Damn! I *knew* there was something I forgot—I didn't raid Pa's beer stash. I— What're you grinning at?"

Alec patted the backpack meaningfully, his face fairly glowing. "Figured you would—forget, that is. So let's just say that what you so frivolously referred to as lead is—how shall I put it?— a little bit more liquid and a hell of a lot more potable."

"You didn't . . ." David began dubiously, his eyes growing wide as Alec nodded and raised two fingers. "You *did!* Two six-packs? Oh lordy, lordy—at the ripe old age of seventeen Dr. McLean's only boy finally becomes a rebel!"

He sat down on the foot of the bed and fell backward behind the suitcases, giggling uncontrollably.

"That's not *quite* the reaction I expected," Alec responded with forced dignity, but the dour facade dissolved as his gaze met David's and a new chorus of giggles erupted. "Snagged a bottle of bubbly while I was at it, to toast the quest with," he added with a smirk.

David levered himself up on his elbows, his face still flushed. His eyes glistened. "What quest?"

"For the Holy Grail of Knowledge, fruitloop." Alec dipped his head toward the two suitcases. "Or more accurately, the Holy Shrine of Our Lady of MTV and Saint Shopping Mall."

"That assumes they have MTV in Valdosta, and even if they do, that they've also got it at the college where we're supposed to be staying. We ain't roomin' at the Ritz, after all."

"Well, it *is* in south Georgia, but that doesn't mean they're entirely uncivilized—"

"It also assumes we can leave campus once we get there."

"God, Sullivan, you're starting to sound like me!"

David flung a convenient pillow at Alec, which he dodged neatly. "No need to get insulting."

Alec turned to face him, hands on his hips. "Look, if you think I'm gonna spend six weeks just sitting in a classroom with a bunch of other geniuses, while the whole material world waits across the highway, you're crazy."

"The rebel rears his head again," David chortled. "Can cigarettes and leather jackets be far behind? Or maybe a Porsche Speedster? Now *that's* an idea I could go for."

"If it'd get me out of here, I'd consider it," Alec shot back. "But just think, Sullivan: seven hours away from Enotah County. Seven hours from my dad screaming at me to read more of the classics, and yours yelling at you to 'git outta that bed and into the sorghum patch.'"

"Too true, too true." David laughed, then glanced at his watch and started to his feet in alarm. "Jesus, man, we have *got* to boogie!"

Alec stared at him for an instant, then checked his own timepiece. "What *is* this, Sullivan? It's not like we've got a deadline or anything."

"Well, if you've got to know, I want to check the mail one more time before we leave the county." He picked up the abandoned comic and stuffed it in his right hip pocket.

Alec shrugged. "So check it in the morning."

"But that would be out of the way," David observed. "And thereby lose you most of your precious reprieve from the Mustang of Death."

"Well, David, my lad," Alec sighed, as he closed the remaining suitcase, "I may be wrong, but I suspect there's a woman at the bottom of this. And I just bet I know what her name is."

David's response was to wiggle his eyebrows like Groucho Marx, flick the ashes off an imaginary cigar with one hand, hoist the backpack with the other, and stalk toward the doorway.

Alec tugged his seat belt a fraction tighter and dared a glance at the highway ahead. Nothing had changed: the white dashes of centerline were still disappearing beneath the expanse of red Mustang hood far too rapidly for either his nerves or his stomach's liking. A quick check through the window showed the staccato pattern of flashing pine trees that was common to much of rural north Georgia. The current batch masked any sign of the looming mountains. "Ride of the Valkyries" thundered from the cassette player in harmony with the rumble of dual exhausts.

"I really miss Liz," he shouted above the music, as gee-forces pushed his right shoulder against the black vinyl door panel.

In the driver's seat beside him, David reached over and turned the volume down a fraction. "*You* miss Liz? How do you think *I* feel?"

"I can't imagine."

"Why'd you bring it up, then?"

"*I* miss her because of the unseemly haste her absence seems to provoke in you at the most inconvenient moments."

"God, you sound pompous, McLean. Too much *Masterpiece The-*

ater's rotted your mind. Either that, or yo' papa really *has* managed to corrupt you."

"That's beside the point."

"The point *is*, fool of a Scotsman, that I need to get to the Post Office before they close, and I've got"—he checked his watch—"three minutes and twelve seconds to do it in."

Alec gulped as the Mustang hit a straightaway and picked up even more speed. "Thought you guys were on the route, man. You're not looking for anything in *particular*, are you?" He cocked a knowing eyebrow.

David cleared his throat uncomfortably. "Well, I was sort of expecting a package from . . . from Liz, as a matter of fact."

Alec's eyes glittered wickedly. "I'd be interested in knowing what term you intended to place in that moment of hesitant reconsideration I thought I just detected. The one right before 'from Liz.'"

David glared at him. "Okay, Alistair, stuff it."

Alec nodded and folded his arms in smug satisfaction. "Yep, I *figured* your lady was involved in this somehow."

"Somehow I doubt she'd appreciate that, Alec. Nobody owns Liz Hughes but herself, and I'm not even sure about that!"

"Well," Alec replied pragmatically, "if you don't get off your butt and do something, what to call her may not be a problem too much longer. I mean, you may be the only guy in Enotah County that fills her prescription, but what with her living down in Gainesville with her dad for the last nine months or so, she's had a bigger drugstore to shop in lately. You might not measure up."

"Watch it!" David warned, suddenly only too aware of how close Alec had come to one of his own secret insecurities.

Alec would not be swayed. "Okay, okay. Now granted, she's not exactly been available," he continued. "But still, she's not been what you'd call inaccessible, either—especially not to somebody with a car and a tendency to run the highways."

"I've seen her, Alec, you know that: Christmas, my birthday, Easter, Memorial Day, the weekends she doesn't have to work, which isn't very many."

"At which times I'm certain you've unburdened your soul in preference to your hormones," Alec inserted quickly. "Which I doubt is really satisfactory to either of you."

David slapped a hand on his friend's denimed thigh and started squeezing. "You know that for a *fact*, McLean? Been spyin' on me, *boy?*" The grip tightened on every word.

Alec gasped and turned pale. "I'd prefer you kept that on the *wheel*, kiddo."

David's voice softened into an exaggerated meld of mountain twang and coastal drawl as he went on obliviously. "Spyin', huh? Betrayed, more like it. Betrayed by mah closest friend. I knowed them flatland ferriners in MacTyrie'd ruin you."

"I don't have to spy," Alec gritted. "Because, number one, I know you, and I know you'd have told me if anything happened; you'd have been unable to resist. And, two, I know Liz—and while I doubt she'd relay such intimate details to the likes of me, I think I could tell anyway, just by the way she'd look."

David removed the hand to further soften the music—which had begun "Brunhilda's Immolation." "And how might that be, sir?"

Alec grinned and punched David's shoulder in a quick one–two. "Like real happy-like."

"A lot *you* know about it."

"More than you think, Sullivan; I got eyes and ears. But don't try to change the subject. Liz won't wait forever. And besides, you've got less than a year before you reach your sexual peak, and then it's all downhill. You'll have wasted—"

"Bunch of crap."

"Use it or lose it."

"I *do* use it."

"Not, however, as the Lord intended."

"You should talk. You're the only person I know whose right hand complains of headaches."

Alec stared at him askance, his face deadly calm. "I haven't noticed any signs of atrophy in *your* nimble fingers, either, Mr. Sullivan. But as I was saying," he continued more lightly, *"you* should talk. To Liz. Soon, and then often. And not about the weather."

"Real hard to do when she's in California," David observed sullenly.

Alec nodded in sympathy. "It really is too bad she couldn't make it back before we headed out."

"Yeah, and that really pisses me off, too. I mean she *said* she'd be back from Gainesville at the beginning of summer—but is she? Hell no! It's out of Lakeview Thursday night, and hop a jet for a month in Frisco Friday morning."

"Well, she really couldn't afford to miss the opportunity."

"Oh, sure." David sighed. "I understand—rationally. But dammit, we'll be graduating in another year and who knows what'll happen then."

"Yeah, I know, man. But you've got to admit that logically it was the best thing for her, and she's basically a logical person. Lakeview's a lot better school than Enotah County High, and for photography, it's no contest. She'd never have won the award she did by hanging around here."

David frowned and sucked his lips. "I know that too, Alec. But she *knew* we'd be gone to Governors Honors most of the summer. Surely to goodness she could have put off California by one bloody day."

"She didn't make the plans, as I recall. It was a graduation present from her aunt one year early."

"Well, damn her aunt, then."

Alec braced himself and pointed through the windshield. "Better damn that traffic light up there instead— 'cause if it turns red, you're in trouble."

"No way, man!" David laughed as he floored the accelerator and flashed through the light at about twice the posted speed limit. It was the only one in Enotah County and easy to forget—especially as only a month or so had passed since the familiar caution light had been replaced with a full-fledged red/yellow/green. *One more intrusion of so-called civilization into the mountains,* David thought.

The black glass cube of the Enotah Municipal Post Office was a block off the main square, right between the prickly mass of ancient Gothic courthouse—abandoned now, though thankfully not slated for destruction—and the bold planes and angles of the brand-new one. Old Mr. Peterman the postmaster was coming through the front door when David screeched into the parking lot. He looked up, smiled, and shook his balding head. A ray of stray sunlight reflecting off the polished surface behind him gave his remaining hair the appearance of a wispy halo.

"Hey, Davy, what's up?" he asked as David bounded up the two stone steps from the sidewalk.

David found himself unexpectedly out of breath. "Am I too late to check the mail?" he panted. "What about packages—you got any packages? I'm leaving tomorrow for six weeks, so do you think you could, like, check and see if anything came in the afternoon stuff? It wasn't sorted when I was by on my way to MacTyrie, and I'll be gone before it runs tomorrow."

Behind David's back Alec shot the postmaster a conspiratorial wink.

The old man pursed his lips, but his eyes twinkled merrily. "Five o'clock, boy."

David checked his watch. "Four fifty-nine," he countered, with his most ingratiating smile. Suddenly he felt very foolish.

Mr. Peterman pointed to his wrist. "Government issue. Never wrong."

"Oh, come on! Couldn't you just check?"

"How long you been living here?"

David vented an exasperated sigh. "Seventeen years."

"And how long has the Enotah Post Office closed at five?"

"How should I know?"

"Longer'n that!"

David's face fell. "No package then?"

The postmaster reached inside the door and picked up a large flat parcel from behind the glass front wall. "Not unless it might be this'un." He grinned triumphantly and started to hand it to David, then at the last possible instant whisked it from the boy's eager fingers, staring at the address label like a mischievous child. "Wait a minute. This says, 'David Sullivan *Esquire.*'" He cocked his head sideways. "You ain't no 'esquire,' are you?"

David rolled his eyes desperately.

"Well, that's what it *says* here," Mr. Peterman went on guilelessly, thumping the package with a stubby finger. "Must not be you after all. Reckon I'll have to put this back inside." He started to turn.

David was bouncing from foot to foot. "Give me a break, man!"

"Okay, so maybe it is you. You don't know any L. Hughes in California, do you?"

"That's Liz Hughes, my—" He shot a glance at Alec. "My friend."

"Well, if you're *sure* . . . I *guess* I can pass this on."

David reached once more for the package, but the old man stuck it quickly behind his back, forcing David to dodge first left, then right. On the second left feint David snagged it.

"You knew I'd be by, didn't you?"

The old man shook his head. "Not really, but I knew you were leaving tomorrow, so I thought I'd just drop this off at your house on my way home. Glad you saved me the trouble."

"Yeah, sure," said David. "Thanks a bunch!"

"Right on, boy, no hard feelings, hear?"

Alec poked David in the ribs as they returned to the car. "Did he just say 'right on'?"

"Hell if I know." David shrugged as he lowered himself into the seat, leaving the door open as he attacked the package. Within the brown paper was a second wrapping of white, and within that a file-folder box. David pried off the lid and examined the contents: a somewhat stained and dog-eared book at least two inches thick, bound in dark blue fabric; a fat white legal-sized envelope almost the same thickness; and a pair of beige T-shirts bearing a more or less circular design from the *Book of Kells* silk-screened on the front in bright, rich colors and perfect registration.

"One for each of us, I'd imagine," Alec observed over his friend's shoulder.

David fixed him with a level stare. "You imagine a great deal, sir."

"Well, they're different sizes, for one thing: a medium and a small. What's the book?"

David fished it out and studied it curiously. *"The Fairy-faith in Celtic Countries,* by somebody named Evans-Wentz. I've heard of it. Supposed to have a bunch of stuff about you-know-who and you-know-what in it."

"God, more of that crap. Don't you ever get tired of the Other-world, Sullivan?"

David ignored him and began flipping through the pages. "Ho! What's this?" he cried, as a folded slip of paper fell into his lap. He opened it and scanned it quickly, then read it aloud. "'Found this at the local used book store and thought it looked interesting, especially in relation to certain *privileged* information of ours. Some tidbits of folklore in it you might want to look into, and a tiny bit about Nuada. Apparently the Ailill they talk about's not the same one we know—if you can call it knowing. A bit about changelings and the Sight that ought to ring some familiar bells.'"

"As if you didn't already know everything there is to know," Alec appended.

"Forewarned is forearmed," David said. "You *can't* know too much about that stuff when your survival may depend on it."

"But—"

"I'm gonna forearm *you* if you don't hush and let me read my blessed letter."

Alec clamped a hand over his mouth and steepled his brows in feigned contrition.

And David started reading.

"So what'd she say?" Alec asked when the letter had been re-folded and tucked back into its envelope.

David smiled cryptically. "Well, most of it I'd rather not repeat: stuff about wanting to ravish my manly body, and all— Don't look at me like that, I can dream, can't I? You were right about the T-shirts. She got them at a Renaissance Fair. The small's for you."

"Little does she know."

"*Ahem,* McLean. Just cause you gained fifteen pounds since last summer."

"And three-quarter inches."

"We'll forget that."

"I won't."

"So you outweigh me now. So what? You've always been taller. But I have my own advantages."

"Name two."

"This, for one thing," David said, fishing into his shirt collar for the silver ring that hung on a silver chain around his neck. "And this, for another," he added, pointing to his eyes.

Alec yawned in obviously feigned boredom. "A magic ring and the Second Sight. Big deal."

David poked him in the ribs. "You thought so last summer."

"Has it really been that long. Almost a year?"

David frowned thoughtfully. "Close to it. It was July thirty-first when I got the Sight, and the next day—Lughnasadh—when I heard music in the night and followed it to the woods."

"And saw the Sidhe."

David began to stroke the ring. Almost before he knew it he found his mind agleam with images: a moonlit forest; a golden radiance upon the ground; a parade of men and women mounted on beautiful horses, their faces fair but far from human, their clothing from another time entirely. The Sidhe of Ireland at their riding.

He had read of them—dreamed of them . . .

Met them on a summer night nearly a year before and nothing had been the same after. The fabric of his reality had shattered in twenty-one days, and he still hadn't put it back together.

The sun slanted through the windshield, warming his face.

"David?"

"Huh? What?"

"You went off all of a sudden."

David smiled apologetically. "Sorry. But you know, if it wasn't for this ring Oisin gave me I'd almost think it *was* a dream."

"Those were interesting times, that's for certain," Alec replied carefully. "I still feel bad about not believing you when you told me about the ring."

"Well, let's face it: the idea of a whole system of other worlds overlying our own's a lot for anybody to swallow. I doubt I'd have believed it either, if it'd happened to you."

Alec's brow wrinkled thoughtfully. "Probably wouldn't have, though. Things like that avoid me like the plague."

"Unless I drag you in."

"Yeah, but I know you'd go again in a minute if you had half a chance."

"Would you?"

Alec paused, scratching the sparse line of stubble on his chin. "I don't know. Part of me would like to, but part of me's scared I'd get stuck there and not be able to get back. I think you could make a go of life in the Otherworld, but I'm not so sure about myself. I . . . I need normality, at least most of the time. I guess I think one world's enough."

"But nothing's really normal, even in this world."

"Particularly not Mad Davy Sullivan."

"Nor the fool of a Scotsman he claims as his best friend."

"At least I don't become inarticulate when discussing a certain young lady."

David did not answer. His face had gone distant and dreamy again. "You know, the thing I regret most is that business about Fionchadd," he whispered at last.

Alec stared at him, then frowned. "Get off it, Sullivan," he said a little roughly. "You can't change what happened."

"Yeah," David replied bitterly. "What's done is done, and who's dead is dead. He could have been my friend, Alec."

"Or you could have been born in Kalamazoo, and then you'd never have met."

David sighed and squared his shoulders. "Yeah, right—as usual. 'Tis just a case of the moodies sneakin' up on me," he added in a convincing brogue, though his apparent good spirits seemed more than a little forced. "Now how 'bout readin' me some o' yon massie volume, laddie?"

"You can read, Sullivan, do it yourself."

"Ah, and sure that I can, lad. But would ye have me be doin' it while I'm drivin'?"

Alec stuck out his hand in despair. "Give me the blessed thing, then."

"I was just tryin' ta take yer mind off other problems," David chided, the brogue already disappearing.

"Such as?"

David turned the key, revved the engine a great deal more than necessary, and returned to his natural voice. "Such as the two-hundred-fifty raging Ford horsepower I have just awakened!"

"I'm reading, Lord. I'm reading!" Alec moaned extravagantly.

David slipped the ring back under his shirt and shifted into reverse. "I really am sorry about Fionchadd, though," he whispered again, as though to some invisible confessor. "I still feel like I killed him."

But in a high place in Annwyn, someone would soon disagree with him.

Chapter II: Messages

(Faerie—high summer)

1: Annwyn

A single torch guttered in a circular chamber of polished white marble; the light of a thousand seldom-seen stars sparked at each arched, glassless window. A fair woman stood alone in the center of a floor mosaicked in a knotwork maze of blue and silver...

Morwyn verch Morgan ap Gwyddion grasped a bloody fistful of red-gold hair in each of her ivory hands and screamed.

The walls screamed back at her, perfectly smoothed stone mirroring sound as easily as it cast back pale, wavering images of the tall, white-skinned woman whose heavy silk gown was as red as the blood that trickled from her temples.

"Dead!" those walls cried her dismay. "My son is dead. Fionchadd of the sun-bright hair and the cat-quick hand has left me!"

She cast back her head, so that the line of her jaw and her breast and her delicate throat formed one taut curve of anger and despair.

"Dead. Dead. Dead."

Even in her anguish the words chimed like bells.

A raven had brought the message: one of Nuada's ravens, white as the cold moon of Annwyn. Whiter, even, than her own pale skin or the sharp teeth of the cat-shape she favored when her own form began to bore her. Almost she had put on that other seeming; almost she had devoured Silverhand's messenger. But that, she had recalled in time, would be discourteous in the extreme. There was her heritage to consider: her father of Faery blood, brother to Annwyn's queen; her mother of the race of the Powersmiths, daughter of a Fireshaper, a mighty man of Power in his own right, if not a king in earnest—for the Powersmiths hold no lord above their own, and among themselves no single one is master.

"The messenger is not the message," they had taught her. "Truth is beyond emotion. Wrath ill focused is wrath in vain."

And so she had made herself listen.

"Lady Morwyn," the raven had begun, "I bring you the grace of good greetings from Nuada Airgetlam, sometime Warlord of Lugh Samildinach, High King of the Sidhe in Tir-Nan-Og, and from Lugh Samildinach himself."

She had inclined her head at this, for she had little use for protocol.

"And with this greeting," it had continued, "I bring apologies for its tardiness. Nearly a year has lapsed since first these words were given me, but well you know the state of the seas and the Tracks. Only now have I been able to come here, and a year is a long time in which to contain ill tidings."

Her shape had flickered then: a warning. A ghost of furred claws danced upon long fingers.

"Very well," the raven had croaked. "This am I commanded to tell you: In the second quarter of the afternoon forty-five sunsets after Lughnasadh, the son of your body, Fionchadd mac Ailill, was pierced with an iron-pointed spear wielded by the hand of his father, and so died the Death of Iron. His soul has fled. His likeness may no longer be found among the realms of the Sidhe. Only his ashes remain, at one with the winds and waters of Tir-Nan-Og."

The raven had paused and cleared its throat. "That is the message, Lady. But more there is to follow, if you will hear it."

"Hear it I would indeed," Morwyn had replied. "How came my son in combat with a mortal man? More to the point, how came his father to be the agent of his dying? I did not think even Ailill so dark-souled as to countenance that."

"It was the Trial of Heroes, Lady. Ailill had been troubling the Lands of Men since he came to Tir-Nan-Og. Somehow a mortal boy gained the Second Sight and saw the Sidhe at their Riding. Ailill challenged him to the Question Game and the boy bested him. After that there was no peace between them. Ailill became obsessed with capturing the lad, but was forestalled. At some point, he enlisted the aid of your son—though truth to tell, Fionchadd had little heart for it. In the end, Ailill took the mortal's brother as a changeling. Lugh did not like that at all, nor was he pleased that Ailill had begun to flaunt the laws of his kingdom. And then one day Ailill dared to raise a sword against the High King himself, and Lugh exiled him."

Morwyn had felt herself growing impatient. "I would hear of my son, bird, not of his father's folly."

The raven had fluttered its wings nervously and continued. "That is next to be told, Lady: Neither Lugh nor Ailill had reckoned on the mortal's strength of will. Almost too late the lad learned of the Trial of Heroes and claimed the right to undertake it. Victorious in the

Trial of Knowledge and the Trial of Courage, he came at last into
Tir-Nan-Og for the Trial of Strength. He met Ailill there, even as that
one was being escorted from Lugh's kingdom. Ailill claimed that
Trial as his own, but Fionchadd put forth a better claim, and Lugh, as
Lord of the Trial, with the consent of the Morrigu as Mistress of
Battles, agreed. So it was that the mortal boy competed with your
son at swimming—and bested him. He was given the knife with
which to claim Fionchadd's life, and he did not—thus by his mercy
ensuring true victory. But this so enraged Ailill that he seized an
iron-headed spear from one of the mortal's comrades and tried to slay
him. Alas! Ailill missed, and the spear drank up the life of your
child."

"And Ailill? Tell me of him. Was he punished? Or does his cursed
luck stand by him?"

"Lugh's judgment has been laid upon him. Ailill hid his changeling in the form of a white horse, and so Lugh's daughter, Caitlin,
whose child Ailill had left in the mortal's stead, claimed the right to
make of Ailill a mount for her son until he be of an age to bear arms.
Ailill will live in horse-shape until young Ciarri's growth is finished."

"A fitting form, too—though one, perhaps, too elegant," Morwyn had observed thoughtfully.

"More than one voice has said that," the raven had agreed.

"Is there more news?"

"Much more, though none of it so dreadful. Would you have me
give it?"

"No. Leave me; I will see you again at sunrise. Perhaps I will set
upon you the shape of a man and we will feast together. But now—
there are rites a woman should perform when her son dies the Death
of Iron. I must be about them."

The raven had bobbed its head then, and flown away. And then
the screaming started.

At some point the torch went out; eventually the sun rose.

Morwyn raised herself from the crumpled heap into which she
had collapsed somewhat earlier. There was crusted blood on her temples and beneath her fingernails; dark, brittle lines of it had dried
upon her cheeks. Her red-gold hair was wild as the clouds of autumn.

She straightened, raised her arms above her head, and closed her
eyes.

The Power came, burning hot as the core of the Earth-heart. She
began to glow, as though her body were metal long steeped in forge-
fire. The red silk of her dress flared up and was gone in a rain of
black dust and droplets of gold. The brown flakes of hardened blood

crisped away in instants. Flames encased her in a pillar of blue-white light. It was a purification: all the anguish in her soul set free, so that one thing only remained:

Vengeance.

She banished the flames and swore: "Vengeance, Ailill mac Bobh, for the death of my son, and for the distress and dishonor you have cost me and that continues to cost me still!"

She would go to Tir-Nan-Og, she decided. And she would find the mighty Horn, of which Ailill long ago had told her. The Hounds of Annwyn would have a feasting they would long remember.

"Vengeance!" she whispered again, into a room whose walls were now black marble.

And those walls, as if fearful, gave back no echo at all.

2: Erenn

"He was still your nephew, Finvarra, your own half brother's child. Does the honor of the High Kingship of Erenn not concern you? If *you* will not act, *I* will."

So Fionna nic Bobh had begun her tirade as soon as word of the raven-borne message had reached her at first light. Now, halfway to noon, her rage showed no signs of faltering. Indeed, it beat about the chilly stone of Finvarra's high-arched feast hall like the demon-waves of a winter storm. No man was safe from it, nor was Fionna either, to judge by her appearance: Her cheeks were flushed, her black hair wild and tangled, the side laces of her tawny velvet gown undone as though she had dressed without thinking. In her blue eyes glinted dangerous red sparks of madness.

She shook a sharp-nailed finger in the handsome, hard-lined face of Finvarra, who was also *her* half brother, totally oblivious to the ten-leafed symbol of the kingship of Erenn that glittered on his black hair, completely ignoring the plain granite throne where he sat wrapped in furs and green-checked wool, with the naked blade of the two-handed sword of state shimmering ominously athwart the two high armrests.

"I *will* go into Tir-Nan-Og, brother," Fionna swore, eyes flashing as she faced the king. "I *will* have my vengeance. Not by any mortal's guile will *my* brother be dishonored. Nor by the guile of Silver-hand or High King Lugh, either! It was their doing, of that I am certain now. A plot to discredit Ailill, an insult to your sovereignty, if you would but see it—for he was your ambassador. Not for all the mortal blood in the Lands of Men would I suffer such impudence! My nephew dead by treachery. My brother—my *twin*—imprisoned in the shape of a horse, to be ridden by gutless fools! Lugh's justice? Ha! Better call it Lugh's shrinking fear—he who was once a fighter and will fight no longer. A warrior with no love of battle. A king with no right to his throne. Thanks be for you, brother, who still know how to govern. But you must act, and quickly!"

Finvarra sighed and rubbed a ringed finger across his lips. "Sister, you know I cannot."

Fionna's eyes brightened dangerously. "I know you *will* not. There is more than a little difference."

The High King shook his head and took a sip of wine from the silver goblet that rested next to the sword's pommel on the throne's right arm. "*Cannot,* Fionna. But there is another thing I cannot do as well, and that may fulfill your wishes."

"And that is?"

"While I may not aid you, neither may I forbid you to seek such justice as may seem good to you. If you were to ride the Road to Tir-Nan-Og, there is no one in all of Erenn who would lift hand or sword to stop you. Whether there is anyone in Lugh's land who might receive you is another tale entirely."

Fionna set a thoughtful fist to her mouth. "If I succeed, there may be war."

Her brother shrugged and folded his arms across his chest, tugging his fur cloak closer with one hand. "It has been a long time. If you succeed, so be it. If you do not, then that will be as happens."

"I will go," she said decisively. "And I will return. Pursued by warriors, or leading them. But with me I will bring two heads . . . or maybe three."

"*One* head will be sufficient," Finvarra told her pointedly, "if you see that it be your own. And take no warriors."

Fionna paused, stepped forward to retrieve the curious heavy goblet she had earlier set at the foot of her brother's throne. She grasped the ivory-toned cup by its thick, gold-mounted stem and raised it into the stray shaft of sunlight that broke the space between them, turning it so that the eye sockets faced her. "MacIvor's braincap is becoming worn," she observed, smiling. "The skull of a mortal boy would make a fine replacement, I would think."

"It is what the *boy* thinks that matters," replied Finvarra. "From what I have heard, his head seems to take care of itself very nicely."

Fionna turned away then, so that her unbound black hair swung like a mantle of night drawn across the trees of green and gold embroidered on her garment. "Perhaps I will leave his head until last, then," she whispered over her shoulder. "A mortal man may live a long time without his limbs. With Power cleverly applied, he might live for several hundred years—a thousand, even. Think of it! A thousand years crippled, blind, and sexless—with only his tongue left to scream as his wounds are opened daily and boiling oil poured in them."

Finvarra slammed his goblet down on the throne's arm so that the wine sloshed out to paint dark patterns upon the stone. "Fionna! Such thoughts do you no honor. An enemy worth your challenge is worth your mercy!"

"You are beginning to sound like Lugh" came his sister's sneered reply, as she swept with deadly hauteur from the chamber.

Finvarra thrust himself up from the throne, took an angry step forward. *"You* are beginning to sound like a fool!" he shouted to her shadow. His words echoed among the complexity of pointed arches above in a hollow chant: "Fool, fool, fool."

Or, he added to himself, when the sound of her footsteps had faded, *like your poor, mad mother who sundered the Silver Thread a thousand years ago and now screams alone in the darkness beyond the Borders.*

Chapter III: The MacTyrie Gang

(Sullivan Cove, Georgia)

It took David seven minutes to cover the eight miles from the Enotah Municipal Post Office to the Sullivan Cove road—and less than five seconds to turn in there. Probably he should have at least *considered* slowing down before he started pulling at the steering wheel, but what the heck? A little excitement never hurt anybody. It certainly wouldn't hurt Alec. So it was, the Mustang entered the gravel road half-sideways, with its front wheels pointing at an angle that bore no relation at all to its intended direction of travel. The tail slid wide, flirting with a ditch. A rain of small stones exploded from beneath the tires like shrapnel.

David noted Alec's sharp intake of breath. "Coward," he snorted derisively as he twitched the car onto its proper westward path and floored the pedal again.

"Yea, though I ride in the Mustang of Death," Alec began shakily, "I will . . . fear for my life, I guess," he improvised at last, grimacing at his own poetic ineptitude. Fear did things like that to him.

David ignored him. He also very pointedly refrained from glancing up the hill to his left, to his family's farmhouse glowering across its assemblage of porches at the creek bottoms they were currently traversing. A little farther on to the right, the Sullivan Cove Church of God peeked out from a mass of oak trees. David's favorite and namesake uncle was buried there. He didn't look that way either.

Nor did he pay particular heed to the weathered gray planks and tin roof of Uncle Dale's ancient dwelling in its hollow an additional half-mile up the way on the southern side.

But fortunately he *did* notice Gary Hudson when he topped a fairly steep rise and found his second-best buddy jogging happily down the exact middle of the road ahead of him—stark naked except for skimpy black nylon gym shorts and a pair of top-of-the-line Nikes.

David braked hard, felt the back tires skip sideways on the loose stones. The Mustang ground to a halt a hundred feet or so beyond the runner. David poked his head out the window as the boy materialized out of the cloud of red dust behind him.

"What ho, G-man?" he hollered, as Gary trotted up and braced both hands on the car's roof, panting heavily, though he still managed to grin his famous grin: blindingly white and accompanied by the twin dimples that accented his strong, square chin and gently arching nose. His eyes were a startling blue, his close-cropped hair a forgettable brown. He was in good shape, but even so it took him a couple of seconds to catch his breath.

"Well, G-man," David went on, *"you're* certainly not the one I expected to find bouncing along out here in the wasteland. What happened—Runnerman set you out for bad behavior?"

"Negative, oh most Mad One," Gary said between gasps. "We got to the site, found nobody there, set up camp, and decided to jog up to the highway and back. Runnerman took a wild hair about a minute ago and abandoned me."

David stifled a giggle. "Just like him, the shit."

"Well, he thinks nobody can run as good as he can."

"I can," David replied matter-of-factly.

Alec rolled his eyes. "Bloody hell you say."

David shot him a glare that should have fried him. "Come to think of it, I could *use* a quick dash—need to work out some of my cane-patch stiffness. Here, McLean, you take the M.D. on in." He stuffed the car into neutral, pulled up the hand brake, and joined Gary outside, leaving a very confused Alec sputtering ineffectual protests in the passenger seat. "You bend it, just keep on going, hear?"

Alec's lips twitched in a sour grimace. "Oh, come on, Davy, you know I never have any luck with your clutch."

"Now's a good time to work on it, then!" David replied quickly. "You'll run in the ditch before you hit anything solid."

And then he was off, pacing the much-larger Gary stride for stride and breath for breath down the Sullivan Cove road.

They had already covered nearly fifty yards before a tremendous roar and spitting of gravel indicated that Alec had finally got the Mustang moving. An instant later, it barreled past, enveloping both of them in a haze of grit that invaded their lungs and stuck to the sweat on their bodies. David couldn't help but giggle through his coughing fit when he saw Alec's look of grim distress as he passed. The wind brought them the sound of gears grinding in the distance.

David winced and mouthed a silent "Damn!"

Gary saw him. "He tried to tell you."

"Yeah, well, maybe it'll make a man out of him." He sighed resignedly and increased his pace.

"If he doesn't make scrap metal out of a perfectly good sixty-six."

"If he does, I'll just *kill* him," David replied with precise conviction.

"Sounds like fun," Gary acknowledged. "Need any help, let me know. Hey—race you to the fire ring!"

In five yards David was ahead of him.

Three-quarters of a mile farther on, the road ended in a flat, circular turnaround. Golden wisps of broom sedge lined its perimeter, and a dark stain of charcoal surrounded by a rough square of logs and low boulders marked the center, token of hundreds of illicit campfires and weenie roasts. Twenty feet beyond the gravel a finger of Langford Lake invaded the land like an accusing finger, its shore embraced by twin arcs of black-green pines that reached in from either side. David's car was parked out of the way to the right, its wheels hub-deep in coarse grass. A second series of tire tracks led northward through a couple of acres of the sedge toward the line of forest an eighth of a mile away. Dark clouds glowered to the south. They hadn't been there earlier.

The runners slowed as they approached the car. Something white fluttered in the driver's window—a piece of white wrapping paper, as it turned out. David ripped it off and scanned it quickly. A penciled line of Alec's even printing showed there: *I parked your car; if you want your keys back, you can park my gear. Trunk's unlocked. P.S.: Asshole.*

He handed it to Gary, who exploded into laughter as David lifted the deck lid.

"Here, guy, put that overblown bod to some use," David said, tossing Gary the larger of the two backpacks. As an afterthought, he added his bedroll and one of the two iron-tipped hiking staffs that he and Alec always carried with them. A quick search behind the seats produced the package from Liz. He started to bring the whole thing, then changed his mind and stuffed the T-shirts into the corner of his khaki pack. An attempt at fitting the book beside them failed, so he tucked it under his arm, checked the locks one final time, and trotted off with Gary.

It was not a widely known place that they came to a moment later, having first navigated a couple hundred feet of pine forest (David couldn't help wondering how Darrell had managed to get his van through) and then a vigorous stand of the blackberry briars that were ubiquitous to the whole southern end of the county. Fortunately, the van had dispatched the worst of them.

B.A. Beach, David had christened the open semicircle of land when he and Alec had discovered it some years before—the name signified by its initials a reminder of what he'd done to his backside the first time he'd fallen there. A layer of mossy grass covered much of the ground, and a series of rock shelves to the left overlooked a slice of beach and the lake proper. At the edge of the woods to their right, Darrell Buchanan's tan VW van loomed like a startled bread loaf, its double doors open wide, with a bright canopy staked out between them. A tiny fire smoked before it.

The camp was empty, but David could hear occasional bursts of boisterous laughter coming from beyond the trees to the north.

He and Gary deposited their gear inside the vehicle and headed toward the woods. A curtain of laurel closed in, blocking any view of the campsite. Soon they were in the peace of the forest.

A glimmer of water fifty yards ahead showed the lake, and the sound of voices had grown louder: mindless garble, shouts and protests, giggles and loud guffaws.

Clothes began to appear: a sneaker here, a T-shirt there, then a pair of white tube socks like shed snakeskins, converging a short way behind a break in the trees into twin piles—one neat, one in appalling disarray.

A raised finger quieted Gary just as he was about to speak. A nod acknowledged it. Soundlessly they crept toward the voices.

The land sloped gently uphill beneath them, opening at last onto a sheer bank maybe eight feet high. Directly beneath it was the only point on the whole nearby shoreline where diving was really possible. Silent as trees they peered over it.

It was them, all right: Alec and Darrell "Runnerman" Buchanan. Dark hair and light hair was all David could easily distinguish through the sparkle of sunlight on the choppy surface—Darrell's brassy yellow, shoulder-long in the runner's mane the Enotah County High track team affected; Alec's mousy brown darkened to near black by water.

Darrell twisted underwater, thrust up a wiry arm in salute, then sank into the depths again, reminding David of the final scene from *Deliverance*. A moment later Darrell's head broke surface. Even at that distance the flash of teeth in his foolishly handsome face was visible, stark white against his deep tan.

"Well, it if ain't the two lost boys!" he shouted cheerily, treading water. "What took you so long? Looking for Tinkerbell? Drop your drawers and join us!"

"Didn't waste any time, did you?" David called back.

"Well, it's supposed to rain, for one thing," Darrell said. "And then we remembered Hudson's cooking tonight, so we decided now'd be better than later. That way we won't have to worry about cramps."

"Or look at what we're eating," Alec added. "That's a hell of a lot more important."

Gary picked up a convenient stone and tossed it into the dark water a precise foot from Alec's open mouth.

He ducked—too late. The wave left him choking.

"So, you guys coming in, or not?"

"Didn't bring our suits." David laughed.

"So?"

"So what've *you* got on?"

In answer Darrell leapt as far out of the water as he could, then dove quickly forward, displaying a flash of bare white bottom.

David and Gary looked at each other and nodded once in unison.

"Just as I suspected." Gary snickered.

"*I* have nothing to be ashamed of," David replied haughtily, prying at the heel of one shoe with the toe of the other.

Gary knelt to remove his training shoes. "Let's just say you have nothing, and leave it at that!"

David waited until his friend was untying his laces, then leapt onto his back, wrapping his legs around Gary's waist and clamping his arms tight around the boy's bulging chest and upper arms.

"Would you like to repeat that, G-Man?"

"Do you *want* it repeated?" came the choked reply. "If you'd like, I'll tell everybody we know—in minute, biological detail, with approximate numbers and dimensions." He tensed and started to stand, completely ignoring David's weight. "If you've got Liz's address, I could even mail her a description," he continued. "Or I could take some pictures . . ."

David lost his grip and slid to the ground, bringing Gary's gym shorts down with him. He shrieked and jerked his hands away, scrambling to his feet in embarrassed horror. "Oh, Christ, Hudson, all I need to see is your furry butt staring me in the face!"

"You asked for it, faggot!"

"You guys coming or not?" Alec shouted from below.

"Sullivan might be," Gary called back. "I think he's trying to rape me."

"I'll get you for that, Hudson," David shot back as he hastily skinned off his T-shirt. The ring glittered on his chest. He paused, fiddling with the clasp of the silver chain that held it. It was just the slightest bit too short to pull over his head easily.

Gary eyed him curiously. "God, Sullivan, what is it with you and that blessed chain? Why don't you just *wear* the damned thing?"

David's expression darkened to one of deadly seriousness. *"Because*—if I wear it people get all kinds of stupid ideas, and then they start asking stupid questions, and I'm sick of answering stupid questions, *okay?"*

"So why bother with it at all, then?"

David rolled his eyes. "Because—because I like having it around—if that's all right with you. I mean it really isn't any of your business."

Gary's face darkened in turn, as the tone of David's words sank in. "Okay! Okay! It's no big deal. You never have been straight with us about that ring, though, and I'm gettin' a little tired of it."

"Not *haven't*, Gary, *can't."*

"Bullhockey," Gary snorted, as he trotted the few steps to the bank and dove outward.

The ring at last on his finger, David followed him very quickly.

"We stay in here any longer we'll shrivel up to nothing," Alec said, as David's head broke surface beside him. Darrell and Gary had long since departed.

"I think part of me already has." David giggled.

Alec looked disgusted. "Who could tell?"

David sent a miniature tsunami splashing toward him. "Would you like to be dead, McLean? I've heard enough about *that* already."

Gary appeared on the bank, barefoot and shirtless, a pair of camouflage fatigues slung low across his hips. "Hey, guys, soup's on."

Alec rolled his eyes. "Thanks for the warning."

Gary threw a pine cone at him. "No problem, McLean, I'll just pee in yours."

Alec sighed and began stroking toward shore.

David glanced toward the southern horizon, saw the clouds massed there. They'd been building steadily since he'd arrived. "I hope it doesn't rain," he said as he set off after his friend.

"Not supposed to. Supposed to go south of here, according to the forecast," Alec replied. "Christ, look at old Bloodtop over there!"

David felt an anticipatory chill race over him, even as he glanced over his shoulder.

Half a mile away a mountain rose from the surface of the lake. Bloody Bald it was called, though David knew it by another name as well. In the Faery realm that mountain bore a castle, and that castle was the home of Lugh Samildinach, High King of the Sidhe in Tir-Nan-Og. Usually it looked like an ordinary mountain—*was* an ordinary mountain as far as most men were concerned. But sometimes it was much, much more: sometimes at dusk and dawn the glamour between was stripped away and he could see what really crowned that summit. Sometimes, too, he could hear horns calling there.

But this was nothing so remarkable.

It was a simple trick of light—the very one that had given the mountain its name, in fact, for the westering sun had caught the pale silicon surfaces that slashed its vertical faces, and had lit them with its own blazing glory, painting them red from top to water's edge, so that the whole peak seemed awash with bloody fire. The mountains behind had fallen into shadow, darkened by the approaching clouds, and Bloody Bald shone like a sentinel of light before them. And then a cloud brushed the sun and the effect was gone.

"Geez," Alec said. "For a minute there, I thought I'd had a glimpse of Faerie."

David shook his head as he joined him on the shore. "Not this time, my lad; sometimes this world has its own magic." He reached for the rope they had tied there for the purpose, and hauled himself up the bank, realizing only then that he hadn't brought a towel. *Have to use my shirt, I guess,* he thought, tugging at the ring. *Soon as I put this back on its chain.*

Five minutes later he and Alec pushed through the last of the laurel and joined their friends at the campsite. The fire had been built up a little, and a pile of steaming hamburger patties was arranged on a foil-covered rack beside it. A cooler full of beer stood open by one of the awning poles. Gary and Darrell had their backs to them and were occupied with something inside the van.

"Well, smells good, anyway—" David began, his jaws clenching in sudden outrage as he saw what occupied his friends' attention. "Dammit, guys, that's personal!" he cried, dashing forward.

Gary spun around and stuffed something behind his back, then changed his mind and held it out accusingly. "Yeah, Sullivan, right. Real personal. Look, what is this shit about other worlds and all? I mean, look at this!" He thrust the note from *The Fairy-faith* straight into David's face.

David reached for it, but Gary snatched it away. "You can read, Hudson. What does it sound like?"

"Sounds like a bunch of crap, my man. Either that, or your woman's gone stark, raving bonkers."

David's eyes flashed dangerously. "Just give me the note, okay?"

"No way, man! Not till you tell us what's going on."

"Nothing's going on. Absolutely *nothing*—except that you're standing between me and my property."

Gary stuck the paper in his hip pocket and stood up very much straighter, his arms folded across his outthrust chest. "You gonna do something about it?"

David started forward, but Gary blocked him with one stiffened arm. "Dammit, Gary, don't do this to me!"

"I ain't doing nothing, Sullivan. Just trying to get some straight answers out of you. It's not like we haven't been patient."

"Like what happened to you last summer that had you so weirded out?" Darrell put in, moving to stand beside Gary, thereby blocking the entrance to the van. "Like why were you so vague and drifty all last fall? Like how come your brother and uncle were so sick, and then healed all of a sudden—in one night, so I hear."

"Yeah, Sullivan, spill it. We've waited a year, and all we've got is some weird shit your brother's supposed to have told at church about a dog talking to him, or something. And some stuff about shiny people in the woods."

"And a boy in white," Darrell added.

David's mouth dropped open. "How'd you know about that!"

Gary and Darrell exchanged troubled glances. "Tell him, Runnerman."

Darrell cleared his throat. "Well, my mom works in the hospital, see. Twice a week as a volunteer. You knew that, right? . . . Well, when your uncle was sick last year, she had to check on him every hour or so, and found him really ranting and raving a couple of times."

"You should have told me!" David exploded.

"What—and given you something else to worry about?"

David took a deep breath, trying to calm himself. "So what's he supposed to have said?"

"Talked about a boy in white, mostly. That really put the wind up her, 'cause she thought he was having one of those out-of-body experiences, or something. Only he wasn't."

"And how do you know? Those things might be for real."

"'Cause she asked him what he was seeing, asshole, and he kept saying something about the blond boy in the woods. First she thought it was you, but when she asked him if it was, he said no, it was the boy in the funny white clothes with the bow."

Gary took up the attack again: "And there's that friggin' ring you're so damned particular about. You can't tell me there's not something strange about that! Hell, man, I've looked at the friggin' thing close up and personal, and it gives me the willies, let me tell you. Handmade out of solid silver or I'm a virgin. Older'n shit, or may I never get laid again."

"What do you mean you've looked at it?"

Gary puffed his cheeks and stared at the ground. "Oh, hell—remember that time you spent the night at my house last winter? When my folks were gone and we raided my dad's bar and sat up 'til four drinking and talking, until you passed out?"

David bit his upper lip, nodding slowly.

"Well, once you were, like, out of it, I just pulled that mother out of its chain and took a look at it in the light. I mean, I know you'd let me see it before, but always kinda quick and uneasy-like. Well, I wanted me a good long look, and I took one."

"Asshole!"

"No, man. Just curious. Curious as to why one of my best friends had just spent six months acting like the cat that swallowed the canary, and the canary that had been swallowed by the cat, all at the same time."

"More like nine months," Darrell amended. "He's still doing it. An honest man'd level with his buddies."

"Right-o, Runnerman. I mean, hell, guy'll go swimming stark naked at the drop of a hat, *admits* to jacking off and God knows what all else. But ask him about a silver ring and an attitude that evidently goes with it, and he clams up tight as a nun's you-know-what. Oughta kick him out of the M-gang, just for not playing straight with us."

David had stood about as much interrogation as he could. "It's not that I don't *want* to tell you . . ."

"Oh *yeah?*" Gary cried. "Then why don't you?"

David glanced over his shoulder to see Alec looking confused and ineffectual and unhappy. There'd be no help from that quarter, nor could there be. Alec couldn't tell them any more than he could.

"Okay, Sullivan, start talking."

"About what?"

Gary almost hit him. "Anything—everything! What've we been talking about for the last ten minutes?"

"I can't tell you."

"That crap again. Talk, boy, or I'll have Darrell diddle your balls with the fire poker."

David's heart sank. He would not be able to tell them anything, though his life depended on it. It was the Ban of Lugh, the goddamn, wretched magic ban Lugh had placed on him and Alec and Liz not to discuss what they knew of Faerie with anyone except themselves. He wanted to be honest with his friends, truly he did. But he knew that he could not. It was physically impossible: his tongue would cease to function as soon as he started.

"Sullivan?" Gary warned.

"Ask him about this Nuada cat," Darrell suggested.

"Yeah, Sullivan, how 'bout it?"

Shit! David thought. *May as well try, I reckon.* "He's one of the S—" His tongue stuck to the roof of his mouth, just as he had expected. "One of the F— He's from—"

Gary's eyes narrowed dangerously. "What is this, Sullivan? Don't play games with me."

"What do you mean, Hudson? I don't do that kind of crap. I'd tell you if I could, I swear it. But I can't—I honestly, physically can't."

Gary stared at him incredulously. Something he saw in David's face, something of disappointment and failed effort and despair told him the truth of it. He relaxed. "God, man, I didn't mean to upset you."

David swallowed hard and smiled weakly. "Not your fault, guy. Truly I'd tell you if I could."

Darrell's gaze shifted toward Alec.

"Don't ask me," Alec responded quickly. "I don't know any more than he does."

Gary was staring at the ring that once more glistened on David's bare chest. He reached out to touch it.

A pulse of light flared between them, startling David as much as Gary.

"Shit!" Gary shrieked, jerking his hand away and sticking it for an instant in his mouth. "Damn thing burned me!"

David's heart flip-flopped. The ring *was* burning. It could only mean— He looked around frantically. Where was it? Was it friend or foe? Finally he saw it, perched right above them on the striped awning beside the van: an immense and very self-satisfied-looking raven, every pristine feather of which was white as snow.

Gary followed his gaze, saw the bird bob its head and fly away. "If it's that big a deal, I won't press you on it. But God, your ring just scared the ever-loving bejesus out of me." He gave David's shoulders a brotherly squeeze.

David looked at him and smiled. "Scared the crap out of me too. Maybe I'll be able to tell you about it someday."

Gary's puzzled stare spoke volumes.

"Damn," Darrell muttered, looking up at the overcast sky. "I think I just heard some thunder."

Chapter IV: Katie

(Murphy Village, South Carolina—Friday, June 21)

Lightning struck again, closer this time, fracturing the world into stark planes of black and white. Katie held her breath, waiting for the thunder. One, two . . . It came, crashing as though a fist had smashed the heavens. The pale, cheap paneling of her tiny mobile home rattled. A framed picture of Our Lord slipped from the wall and shattered. A cold breeze sailed through the darkened trailer. And then the rain returned, hammering the ceiling.

"Mother of God!" she whispered, as her gnarled old fingers sought her rosary. "Such storms we do not have in Ireland!"

She pushed aside her knitted comforter (warmth against the unseasonable chill) and reached for her knobby cane. It took her a moment to twist herself upright, a moment more to reach her kitchen.

Lightning again, blasting away at the tops of the pines. A glance outside confirmed earlier fears: a tree had split near the trailer so that one of its heavy splinters now hung dangerously close to the roof of Mrs. Sherlock's place next door. Another flash and she could see further into the night, down the semicircle of trailers nearly to the sign at the highway that identified the Traders' home place.

She filled her ancient copper kettle and turned up the flame in the stove's smallest burner. "No sleep for you tonight, Katie, me girl," she muttered. "Might as well make ye another spot o' tea and wait its passin'. Eighty years of wind and weather, yer old eyes have witnessed, so what difference makes another?"

Four flashes, then, in quick succession. The thunder tripped over itself in the wind. The trailer seemed to lift upon its skirting.

Katie hobbled back to her place on the vinyl sofa.

More thunder, more lightning—this time not as close, though the rain had not abated.

Maybe it's passin' already, she thought hopefully.

Another rumble—

A crash of lightning right outside: the whole world turned to light. She closed her eyes, her hand at her heart.

"Holy Mary, Mother of God—" she began.

Thunder rolled again.

And then there was another sound: footsteps on her porch, it sounded like.

Katie's breath caught.

A knock shook the flimsy doorframe.

She hesitated—should she open it? This was not Ireland, but America, and not by all accounts a safe place for an old woman left alone while her sons and grandsons were traveling. But still, she was who she was, and Katie McNally had never let anyone stand wet in a storm when they had sought her shelter.

"Comin'!" she called, and reached once more for her cane.

The knocking came again, sharper, more insistent.

"Comin'!"

She opened the door, squinting rheumy eyes into the gloom.

A tall man stood there, with two others crowding close behind him, slick shadows against the rain. The man's head nearly brushed the top of the doorway; his shoulders were almost as wide. He was wrapped in something dark, a heavy coat, maybe, or—possibly—a cloak. There was a strangeness about the way the garment fitted him, though, and it took Katie a moment to figure it out. The man had no right arm.

Katie had to twist her neck into an awkward angle to look into his face. His eyes met hers, burning out of the darkness: beautiful eyes. She had seen eyes like those before—once. Once too she had seen a face as fair.

"Woman, do you know what I am?" the man asked.

"Aye," she replied solemnly. "Ye be one of *Those*. I thought I'd left yer kind across the ocean. What do ye want of an agin' woman?"

"I would have the peace of your roof, Lady; for myself and two companions," the man said quietly. "I would study the ways of men."

Katie closed her bad left eye and screwed the better right one into a squint of challenge. "Be ye Christian, then?"

A ghost of sadness seemed to cross the man's sharp-chiseled features. "I walked this World a thousand years before That One's coming; how could I be such a thing?"

"Stay there," Katie warned. "I'd have me own proof o' ye."

The man inclined his head ever so slightly.

Kate's fingers twitched through her rosary, found the silver crucifix at the bottom end. With trembling hands she brought it to her lips and kissed it, then raised it almost above her head and set it against the man's chin.

She left it there for a full minute, but nothing happened, save that the man's lips curved in a smile full of infinite sadness.

"You have nothing to fear, Katie McNally."

"Well," came Katie's pert reply, "if ye be not of God, neither be ye of the devil. Come in and have my welcome."

PART II

SPARKS

Chapter V: Trysting

(Tir-Nan-Og—high summer)

The horse was black like thunderclouds beneath a moonless sky, and its gallop across the grassland was as swift and silent as a hawk at dive.

The rider bent close upon its neck and felt the wind whip through his long black hair, singing in his ears a song of joy and youth and freedom.

Lugh's palace was far behind him, an eruption of towers, walls and gardens atop a cone-shaped mountain. Somewhat closer were the forests that wrapped its lower flanks. And all about him now were flickering leagues of red-striped tiger grass.

Ahead was another wood—the one where he would meet the lady. She had promised, the lady had, to lie with him this morning. "Not until I see you tall and handsome on Lugh's black stallion will I sleep with you," she had told him.

"It is forbidden to ride that horse" had been his answer. "Only Caitlin's son is allowed in that one's saddle, and only then when calming spells are worked upon him—spells with which I may not tamper, except for young Ciarri."

The lady's eyes had sparkled with amusement. "I have heard that no man can master that horse without Lugh's intervention . . . yet a man who cannot master a horse will never be *my* master!"

There had been glamour in her voice, but he did not know it, for the lady was far more powerful than he, and had applied her skill with greatest subtlety. No one else among the Sidhe in Tir-Nan-Og had seen her, and he did not know that either, for she had not let herself be seen. Nor had he spoken about her, though he had intended to. Somehow he had never quite remembered.

Still, he had been entrusted with the means to master the four metal and four magic locks that barred the way to the black horse's stall. That was part of his duty as chief groom to Caitlin, daughter of High King Lugh. There was one thing he did *not* know, however, and that was how to command the four degrees of interlocking spells that kept another sort of binding on the stallion, for that binding itself was unknown to him. No single person knew all those spells, in fact, for it took Caitlin to prime them, the Morrigu to shape them, Nuada to fix them tighter, and Lugh himself to seal them closed.

And up ahead was the wood. Red-trunked trees twenty times a man's height tall, leaves small and lacy, almost, as fern fronds. A gray-green twilight drowsed within it.

And the lady, straight ahead, standing tall and fair in the center of the pathway. Her dress was very white, her hair exceedingly black. Her lips were red and smiling. Without a sound they shaped his name: Froech.

Froech grinned and dismounted. He flung the reins over a low-hanging limb and knotted them loosely. "See, lady," he laughed, "I have mastered Lugh's black horse, and now, it would seem, you have no choice but to let me do the same to you!"

He reached for her then, one hand already tugging at the laces of his tunic.

She smiled and stepped forward. Her white silk dress shimmered to the ground as she raised her arms to embrace him. She kissed him hungrily, ran her hands across his hard-muscled shoulders, up the cords of his neck to tickle his earlobes.

Her fingers caressed his temples—and then she called upon the Power.

Froech's eyes blanked, confused. His body felt very heavy of a sudden; his legs seemed ten leagues distant from his torso. Clumsy hands slid numbly from the woman's waist. His head pulled his neck forward as his joints folded upon themselves. A touch of Power softened the force of his fall.

Fionna picked up the pile of snowy silk and wiped her hands, then turned toward the horse. The beast whickered, danced aside a nervous half step. She frowned. "Well, brother," she said, "it does not seem you are glad to see me. I cannot say that you look well, but I will say that you make a very acceptable horse. Now come."

Her gray eyes locked with the horse's. She raised a hand toward the hopeful nose it extended. *Four locks,* she noted. *Lugh was ever a cautious one. But I am this one's sister, and against the Power of blood, the Power of mind alone can never stand.*

Sister? The question was hesitant, weak, but that it had reached her at all surprised her.

Brother! You are very far away. You have worn this shape a long time, have you not? Too long, for this form almost recalls no other. What do they do, brother? Do they make you a man again for as long as it takes to return your senses? Do they drug you then? Keep you drunk? Do you sleep away your manhood and arise again a stallion?

A . . . stallion? The mind-words whispered confusion.

She answered the thought aloud. "We must be quick. Now that I have touched your soul, the bond of blood between us will allow me to take this spell upon myself and set your own shape upon you; unfortunately it is too strong to dispose of otherwise. I have left clothes for you in the root-hollow of yonder maple. It is not far from the Track. You will hide there, regain your man's Power and your man's strength until I return for you. I will awaken the boy, and he will recall nothing of the woman who came to meet him. He will return me to Lugh's palace as though nothing had happened. But the locks that bound you will not hold me. Tonight I will join you here, and we will go to a place of waiting—for I will not rest until I have had my vengeance. And you, dear brother, I have no doubt, will find that almost as sweet a morsel as will I."

She closed her eyes, felt out the limits of the spells, began to turn them onto herself, one layer at a time. Skin, first, as black hair grew out upon her creamy flesh, her ears lengthened, eyes darkened.

And before her the horse's skin grew pale and smooth. It lost its mane; the ears shortened but retained their points.

Second layer: muscle and bone. Fionna's nose stretched. Fingers and toes merged into one. A tail sprouted at the base of her spine. She bent awkwardly onto all fours, even as Ailill stood upright.

Some pain, now, as the workings became more intricate.

Third layer: blood and nerves and brain. More pain.

Fourth layer: consciousness. Fionna felt her own thought drown in the thoughts of the other shape, as she sensed her brother's Power waken. She fought this final spell, kept it thin and diffuse, assimilating it an aspect at a time, careful to leave a gap through which her essence could withdraw when she had finished.

Fionna was a horse—a black stallion, and wasn't that interesting, she noted—and before her was a naked man. White-bodied, long-limbed, black-haired. Good to look upon. Good enough for her bed, had they not been such close relation. He raised his head toward her, eyes glazed, confused.

Brother, go now. Wait. I will return.

Ailill nodded and began to wobble uneasily toward the place his sister had shown him with her sending. A moment later he was gone.

She extended her thought toward the boy.

—And found another Power coiling there, prowling about her spell like a scavenger around a carcass.

No! Fionna's outrage shook the Overworld. The horse snorted; flames sparked from its nostrils.

The intruder gained a mind-voice. *Yes! Ailill mac Bobh is mine! You will not stay me from my vengeance!*

Who are you?

Do you not recognize me?

An image flickered across Fionna's memory: a fair woman of Annwyn. Ailill had made much of her, had gotten a child on her once. *Morwyn: the Annwyn bitch.*

Well, there is some truth in that, I suppose. For though I am but partly of Annwyn, yet it is for hounds that I have come here.

The Horn!

You know of it?

All who know of Power at all know of the Horn of Annwyn. Lugh is as careless as Arawn is cowardly. But you will not have it.

How so?

"This way, and this way," Fionna cried aloud, and began to fling the horse shape from her, setting it wavering about the sleeping boy. Her own form blurred and twisted. She struggled to stand erect, even as she felt Power lancing toward her.

"Power I will meet with Power!"

The ghost-thought that was Morwyn laughed.

Fionna hesitated. "What amuses you?"

It is common to laugh at a child at its playing.

"You call me a child?"

In the ways of Power? Of a certain!

"A child may yet withstand a woman!"

Ha!

Fionna froze, wrapped in anger. At last the spell slipped free enough for her to fully command her Power. She drew into herself then, focused it, began to send it forth.

Fire!

She was burning up. Flames licked about her in Tir-Nan-Og and in the Overworld as well. Everywhere she went there was fire. It chased her, devoured her.

Morwyn smiled, sent a thought coursing behind her. *I have no quarrel with you, Fionna nic Bobh. But your brother I am sworn to destroy, and you will not prevent me. Feel my wrath: feel the Power of a Fireshaper's daughter!*

So, Fionna thought in her terror, *that is why I cannot reach her. One cannot touch a flame, one can only . . .*

. . . quench it, Morwyn's thought laughed. *And that you cannot do, if I do this . . .*

The fires lapped hotter, and Fionna felt herself dwindling. There was only one refuge and that was deep within her. She went there: inward, ever inward, drawing away from the walls of flame that followed close behind her.

And found, there in the center, a spot of coolness.

Morwyn's spell locked tight.

Fionna felt her body spinning, stretching. Flames writhed about her, tortured her. She fell to the ground and rose again a horse— glanced about— She was trapped. There was only one way out.

She stretched her thought in that direction. Failed, and tried again.

—And was through. But it was no good, she had not strength enough to stave off Morwyn's stifling enchantment. Only one option remained.

She drew back into herself, focused her Power, then sent it arrowing forth—not at Morwyn, but at Ailill. *Brother!* she cried as she felt the spell enwrap him. *Please forgive me, but this one would have your death! Now, run! I will join you if I can.*

Somewhere in the forest Ailill started, felt pain come upon him as he lay dazed upon the ground. He arched forward.

"No!" he cried.

No! No! No!

Antlers sprouted from his head; his body fell once more onto four legs. Man's awareness left him.

Something sparkled on the ground before him, something familiar, something beautiful. He stepped upon it. Power welcomed him. And he ran, his mind awash in madness.

You have not won yet, Morwyn! his sister's challenge echoed in the empty air behind him. *I will—*

The thought broke off like a slammed door. *You will do nothing!*

Morwyn stepped out of the woods and looked at the fine black horse before her—and at the sleeping Froech. "Well, Fionna, I will grant you a good eye for boys," she observed. "Perhaps the one true talent in your keeping. It is a shame I have no leisure to sample this one, so I will simply send him on his way—on your back. But know, oh Fionna nic Bobh, that where four spells bound that shape before, now there are five upon it, and the fifth you may not sunder. You may think you have beaten me, Fionna, but I *will* find your brother. And I *will* have my vengeance."

No! a ghost-thought whimpered softly.

Morwyn smiled and began to plan her hunting. First she would have to search the Straight Tracks . . .

Chapter VI: The Crazy Deer

(White County, Georgia—
Saturday, August 3)

"Watusi Rodeo" ended, and the cassette popped from the Panasonic player hung below the red Mustang's dashboard. David snagged it neatly and flipped it sideways to Alec for refiling. "Well, so what'll it be, McLean? That was my choice; it's your go again. Amazing the amount of music you can eat up in seven hours."

Alec fumbled through the assortment of tapes in the cardboard box on the console. "Is that all it's been? Seems like years since we left Valdosta. But let's see, we've had Mr. Petty, Big Country, all the R.E.M. . . . Just finished Guadalcanal Diary. *Cat People* won't play. Aha! What about this?" He stuck a clear plastic box in front of David's nose.

David squinted at the hand-lettered label, then refocused on the road, pausing to downshift for a curve before accelerating again. "Blackwater! All right! I could get into a little Irish folk, just now."

Alec inserted the cassette and set it on rewind. "Not just Irish, strictly speaking. Too bad it's only a copy."

David nodded. "Third generation, but I'm lucky to have it at all. They never made a record, and now I hear they've broken up, so this is all there's ever gonna be."

Alec sighed. "Real bummer."

A moment later the sound of Uillean pipes filled the car with the rollicking opening bars of "Finnegan's Wake." David cranked the volume up, leaned back in his seat, and stuck his arm out the window. The hot August wind set his blond hair to thrashing wildly above his red bandana. Gentler breezes wafted across the bare arms and legs exposed by cutoff jeans and Governor's Honors jerseys. MAD DAVE, David's proclaimed: black, for communicative arts, which had been his area of study over the summer. Alec's shirt, the brilliant green of science, simply read MCLEAN.

As the second verse came around David began to sing along—off-key, as usual.

Alec rolled his eyes, but he too kept time with his fingers as he took in the landscape streaking by outside. *Great to be back in the mountains*, he thought. Nearly the mountains, anyway; just then they were cruising down the eastern side of one of the narrow valleys that slashed the upper part of White County from north to south. A small stream paced them to the left, matching the wide, undulating highway curve for curve. Beyond the tinkling water, the Blue Ridge rose in tier on tier of oak and pine and maple. To the right, where the road had been gouged from the mountains, a vertical wall of jagged, iron-colored rocks loomed close above the pavement.

A few miles farther on, the road would bend sharply upward and begin to wrap itself around the sides of Nichols Mountain. There would be a series of switchbacks and steep straightaways leading to Franks Gap at the top (site of a restaurant, now), and beyond that, home: Enotah County—David's part first, the southern end; then Enotah, the county seat; and finally truly home: MacTyrie.

Actually, Alec considered with a sigh, there was one thing he was *not* looking forward to: he would have to cross Nichols Mountain with David at the wheel.

But that was a ways ahead yet; there was still time to relax, to enjoy the lush green of the trees, the subtle tans and grays of the forest floor, even the harsh patterns of the rocks flashing by six feet away to the right.

As if sensing his mood, the music turned softer, became Nelson Morgan's mandolin showpiece, "Ghost Waltz." Alec allowed his eyes to close blissfully.

David too was content. It was late afternoon and almost tourist season, but the road was blessedly empty. He set the Mustang into a sort of rhythmic back-and-forth glide along the crests and curves. This was what driving was all about.

The instrumental ended, replaced by a livelier tune just as David braked hard, downshifted, and tugged the wheel hard left into the first switchback of the mountain proper. Beside him Alec uttered a groan of resignation, checked his seat belt one final time, and snaked a surreptitious hand down to grip the side of the console.

The first few curves were fairly gentle, but then the music changed to a yet faster tempo. David smiled gleefully, mashed the gas, and bore down on a sharp right. Tires squealed as the Mustang skittered around the bend.

"Damn, Sullivan, *slow down!*"

David flashed a fiendish grin. "But if I slow down, it'll just last longer. And if it lasts longer, you'll just be scared longer. So why not cram all your fear into a few brief moments of eldritch terror?"

"Mr. Lovecraft can have eldritch terror, Davy" came Alec's shaky gasp. "I'd just like to stay alive, thank you. Next time *I'm* gonna drive."

"Ha!" David snorted. "Not *my* car."

"No, mine," Alec shot back, "assuming I inherit Dad's Volvo."

"Humph!"

"What *are* you in such a hurry for, anyway? I mean we've already been gone six weeks. What's another couple of minutes?"

David shrugged. "No reason. No hurry. Just feel like going fast."

"Ha!" Alec's eyes narrowed. "Ever since you heard Liz finally made it back to the mountains you've been acting like a horny old tomcat."

"Will you get *off* if, McLean?" David snapped. "That's all I heard all summer."

"Well, all *I* heard all summer was you gasping and groaning across the hall when you thought nobody was listening. Think of it as a concession to the peace of the universe."

David found himself at a momentary loss for words, though he could feel his cheeks burning. He chose to thwart Alec's attack by increasing his speed, cutting curves deep and close, tires shrieking louder at every turning.

Alec hung on tenaciously, both to his seat belt and his topic: "So—you gonna try it?"

David chewed his lower lip thoughtfully. "I donno . . . Maybe. I'd like to . . . I mean I'm normal, and all. And she is mighty nice-looking."

"Good! We've established the intention, that's step one. Now to step two, the execution: When?"

"What *is* this, McLean?"

Alec's face was smug. "Scientific method: establish the problem, then proceed step by step to the solution. No task too big if you break it down into logical steps. We've established step one, now comes step two: *When you gonna do it?*"

"Better you should concern yourself with your problems."

"Such as?"

David's lips curled wickedly. "Such as what you're gonna tell yo' pappa when he sees that bodacious earbob."

Alec's fingers sought automatically for the small silver cross that depended on a chain from his left earlobe. It was the only sign of flamboyance in his usually restrained appearance—that, and the thin ghost of mustache that had lately begun to grime his upper lip.

"You gonna answer me, McLean? *You're* on the spot now."

"Well, I guess I'll take it off before I get there. Comb my hair over it, if it'll go that far. Wear Clearasil on it or something till it grows over. 'Sides, my dad probably won't notice. All *he* ever notices are my English grades."

David reached over to tweak the dangling bauble. "Dr. M. may not notice, but I bet Mama McLean does. What's she gonna say when she finds out her foolish son's started sporting an earring? If I were her I'd—*Damn!* There's another one!"

"Wha . . . ? Huh? Another what?"

"Another friggin' Straight Track, Alec. That's *four* we've crossed since we left Valdosta. Four—and I shouldn't even be able to see *one!*"

David's eyes began to water and he blinked them furiously. A soft white glow flickered briefly through his shirt from the silver ring that lay upon his chest. Almost before it was visible it was gone.

Alec twisted around in his seat, squinting out the back window at nothing. "Not even with the Sight?"

David shook his head. "Negative. I shouldn't be able to see them at all unless the Sidhe are using them. And Nuada told me that the Sidhe don't use the Tracks down in south Georgia much. They only use them anyway when they need to get somewhere in a hurry, and who'd want to rush to Macon? Mortals don't, why should the Sidhe?" His brow furrowed. "This doesn't fit at all."

Alec looked perplexed. "Nothing Nuada or Oisin told you any help?"

David shrugged. "'Fraid not. Most of what we've talked about is cosmology—the difference between the Worlds, and all that. A bit about the different realms of Faerie. Some history, the line between myth and reality. Lady Gregory was awfully muddled, for instance. And Kirk was even worse. *The Secret Common-Wealth*'s as full of holes as one of my old T-shirts . . . I've got to get that back to the fortuneteller at the fair this year, too: Xerox myself a copy and return the original."

Alec made no reply, but he regarded David thoughtfully.

David noticed that stare, though he pretended not to. He knew perfectly well that Alec could see right through his flimsy efforts at redirecting the conversation, but he knew, as well, that Alec would abide by the ancient conventions of their friendship and not press him—yet. If the topic came up again, though, Alec would spare him no quarter. He'd have no choice but to admit that the sudden visibility of the Tracks was bothering him more than he was letting on. *Should have kept your big mouth shut to start with, Sullivan,* he told himself.

David expertly shunted the Mustang around a sharp uphill right.

Once around it, the treetops dropped away to their left, suddenly revealing the gut-wrenching swoop of a steep-sided valley filled with lumps of trees that looked like the lichen and moss replicas made for model railroads. It took Alec's breath, and made David's stomach flip-flop. Heights gave him problems, sometimes.

A long straight followed, them a left, a right, and another left.

David slowed. Ahead was the worst turn on the mountain, a true ninety-degree right-hander, totally blind. Beyond it was one final straight and then the gap. He began to brake for the turn, pulling the wheel hard as he downshifted into second. The tires shrilled their protest.

They rounded the curve, entered deep shadow.

"Look out, Sullivan!" Alec yelled abruptly.

"Damn!"

There was something in the middle of the road ahead, something huge and alive and extravagantly antlered.

And it wasn't moving.

The ring awoke, sent pain stabbing into David's chest—there and gone too quickly, almost, for him to notice.

He braked hard—too hard. The brakes locked; unlocked; locked again. The steering wheel tore from his grip, spinning wildly. He grabbed at it, felt it bucking against his fingers.

Beside him he glimpsed Alec bracing one arm against the dash, his legs pressing hard on the floorboards.

The car lurched sideways.

David grabbed the wheel—twisted—

And spun.

Rocks—too close. *Too* close.

The galvanized steel guardrail swept by in that strangely attenuated time that accompanies the sudden onslaught of panic. Someone had pasted a smiley face there.

And then it was the road again. A dotted white line atop a long gray surface that had narrowed to a flat plane of fear.

He was sliding now:

The tires screamed a counterpoint to the howling of Jim Dunning's piping.

Sliding—straight for the rocks.

"Oh, shit!" Alec cried.

Impact.

Metal shrieked.

David's head jerked back and forth. From somewhere a pain came into his wrist.

The car listed to the right . . . stopped.

The engine coughed and quit.

"I just wrecked my car," David whispered into the suddenly heavy quiet. "I just wrecked my goddamn, friggin' car!"

Alec was twisting his head from side to side, fingering it gingerly. David noticed his movements. "You okay?" he asked.

Alec nodded, wincing as he did. "Think so. *Did you see the rack on that thing?*"

David rolled his eyes. "Not really. Just the guardrail. Just the cliffs. Hard things to bounce off of. No time to play boy naturalist."

"Well, we'd better bounce out of here, if we don't want to get rear-ended. One wreck a day's enough for me, thank you."

David ignored him. He bowed his head onto the steering wheel, pounded his hands on his thighs. Tears burned in his eyes.

"I wrecked my goddamn, friggin' car," he repeated. "And all because of some goddamn, friggin' deer." He looked up, snarled through the windshield—unbroken, he was relieved to note. "If I get my hands on that goddamn deer, Alec, season or no season, there's gonna be venison on the Sullivan supper table!"

Alec poked him forcefully on the shoulder. "You don't get out of this car, there's gonna be Sullivan on the coroner's table, with a side order of squashed McLean. We could get snagged from behind any minute just sitting here. All we need's a semi to come charging round that corner and knock us all to Kingdom Come."

Still David hesitated.

Alec raised an inquiring eyebrow. "I mean I appreciate you waiting for me to go first and all, Davy, but I'd kinda have to move a mountain—either that or cut a hole in your roof, and I *know* you wouldn't like that."

David sighed and reached back to unlock the door. "You sure you're okay?"

"I'm fine. Now get your ass out."

"Shit," David grunted as he pushed at the door. The Mustang had come to rest hard against the rock face with its right side wheels in the ditch. David thus had to fight gravity to open the door. Finally he wormed his way through. "Window'd probably have been easier," he observed as Alec joined him a moment later, after first tangling himself in the shift lever and then pausing to turn off the tape player, which had, perhaps appropriately, begun the first heartrending bars of "Flowers of the Forest."

"Whew!" Alec breathed, casting furtive glances up and down the mountainside.

The deer was nowhere in sight.

David stomped around to the front of the car and stepped purposefully into the shallow ditch, oblivious to the stagnant water slopping into his new white Reeboks. He squatted to examine the damage.

"Well, it could be worse, I guess," he muttered. "Lost the headlight. Fender's pushed into the tire, but it doesn't look like any suspension damage. Side's probably scraped all to hell, though. Definitely have to be repainted."

"Reckon Gary can fix it?"

"Oh sure, if I'm willing to pay him enough."

"He *is* a friend, after all. Maybe he won't stick it to you too badly."

"*He* wouldn't. But his old man would. Man trying to sell Bimmers in a county with three thousand people's bound to need a little extra. There aren't that many rich Atlantans up here—and," David added pointedly, "some of *them* drive Volvos."

He knelt in the ditch and began to probe around the curve of the tire, feeling for any contact with the fender.

"Shit!" he muttered after a moment, then, *"Damn!"* as a finger snagged a piece of jagged metal. He yanked it out, saw blood, and stuck it hastily into his mouth.

"For God's sake, Sullivan," Alec cried, stuffing a wadded handkerchief into David's good hand, "you've tried being a werewolf to no good effect, so what're you doing now? Making a start on vampire?"

David wrapped the cloth around the wound, then knelt again and stuck his other hand back under the car.

"Uh, Davy . . ."

"Take it easy, kid. I've *got* to find out if the fender's slashed the tire."

"David—"

He felt a tug at the back of his jersey.

"David!" Alec whispered insistently.

The hair on David's neck prickled unaccountably. "What *is* it, McLean? I'd like to get home sometime this year!"

"Uh, David, I hate to tell you this, but . . . it's back."

David extracted his hand and twisted around in the ditch. "What's back?" he snapped. "The tire's—"

And then he saw it, standing pale and magnificent in the exact center of the road not thirty yards uphill from them:

A monstrous stag, the size of a small horse; light reddish gray, with a vast backward-sweeping rack half as wide as the Mustang. Its legs were long and thickly muscled, its chest deep, its narrow head arrogant. Its eyes were black and moist—and looking right at them.

Intelligence showed there—intelligence or madness, David could not tell which.

Even more disquieting was the way David's eyes were beginning to tingle as the ring put forth its warning in stabbing bursts of heat and radiance. Magic was afoot.

"That's not a deer," Alec gasped, "it's an elk—a friggin' elk!"

"No," David whispered. "I don't think it's either one."

"Huh? What're you talking about, Sullivan?" Alec froze. "You don't mean it's . . . one of *Them?"*

David nodded. "I'm pretty sure."

"Well, whatever it is, it's huge—and it's looking straight at us, Davy!"

The creature took a step forward.

"Oh, God, it's gonna charge!"

David grabbed Alec's arm and dragged him toward the front of the Mustang. "Quick. Onto the car. It can't touch us there if it's one of them—steel and all."

Alec stared dubiously back and forth between the car and the animal. "What if it's *not* one of them?"

"Then we're in trouble. Now *come on!"*

They backed up quickly and scrambled onto the Mustang's hood. The elk took another step, lowered its head so that its outstretched antlers seemed to reach toward them like a cage of silver spikes. Fire blazed in its eyes. Steam—or smoke?—vented from its nostrils.

"David?"

David's face was contorted in pain. The ring was a point of fire above his heart; his eyes felt as though they were blazing.

The image before him swam, shifted in endless cycle: a horse—a deer—a man. Over and over.

It was too much, not like any manifestation of the Sight he had ever had. It was *most* like the changeling that Ailill had once left in place of Little Billy. That had been one of the Sidhe shape-shifted and wrapped in the substance of the Mortal World. Yet even then he had been able to discern a sort of shadow form upon it that revealed its true configuration—as if he had looked on a memory of a shape. But this was more complex, as though all three strove for some arcane ascendency.

In confirmation of his fears, the burning in his eyes and the ring hot on his chest pulsed out their own dire warnings: Power afoot, dangerous Power. The Power of the Sidhe.

David felt behind him, began to inch his way back up the hood, slipping up the windshield to sit on the roof.

The elk pawed at the pavement, lowered its head farther, antlers pointed straight for the front of the car.

And began to run.

There was a rumble behind them, suddenly loud—a squeal of brakes, a blast of horn.

David's gaze darted to the left, just in time to see a dark green Jeep Cherokee swish by. Yellow markings were emblazoned on its side: FOREST SERVICE. It swung wide to miss the crippled Mustang and headed straight for the charging elk.

The beasts's head jerked up; its steps faltered.

The driver was good, David handed him that, especially in such an ungainly vehicle. The tail broke loose but he caught it, flicked the wheel, and was beside the animal. Another flick, and the back end snapped smartly sideways—a little too wide, so that a ragged corner of the Cherokee's left rear fender flare snagged the creature along its lower thigh. An angry red slash darkened the pale hair.

The creature leapt straight into the air—ten feet or more, David was certain—crossed the road in two bounds, and disappeared down the side of the mountain to their left.

The burning in David's eyes, the light and heat of the ring ceased abruptly.

The rangers' Jeep shuddered to a halt at a scenic overlook a little farther up the mountain. The driver killed the motor and opened the door. A muscular middle-aged man with black hair and a lined and weathered face stepped down, followed a moment later by a shorter, younger man whose hair was only slightly darker than David's.

Somewhat self-consciously, David and Alec slid off the car and walked up to meet them.

"Hell of a place to put a deer—if that's what it was," the older man said when he came into easy speaking range. "You boys okay?" He indicated the Mustang. "That your car?"

David grimaced sheepishly. "Uh, yeah, 'fraid so. Ran off the road—was run off, actually. Deer ran in front of me. Same one you just missed."

"Stood in front of you, you mean," Alec amended.

"*Stood* in front of you?" The man's mouth hardened to a thin line. He looked thoughtful, almost troubled.

"Yeah, I know it must sound funny," David said. "But that's what happened. I rounded that corner just like you did, and there it was, just standing right there in the middle of the highway."

The ranger's face clouded. "Anything . . . special about this deer?" he asked carefully.

Dave glanced first at Alec, then at the ranger. "You saw it: you tell me."

The older man's nose twitched; he shot a troubled glance at his partner. "Uh, yeah . . . Look, if I tell you boys something fairly confidential, can you keep it quiet? Nothing really bad, we hope, but it don't hurt to be careful. It wouldn't do to upset folks right at the start of tourist season."

"Sure thing," David replied, though he personally wou!d have been glad to see something upset tourist season.

The older ranger took a breath. "Yeah. Well, I think it was what we've started calling the Crazy Deer—if it even *is* a deer—looked more like an elk to me. Anyway, there've been a number of . . . encounters, you might say—most pretty much like ours. Animal appears virtually out of nowhere. Runs across the road sometimes, but most often just stands there and stares down cars, almost . . . almost like it was *trying* to wreck them. That's what unnerves folks: that strange behavior—even more than the size and that funny-looking rack. Doesn't seem scared of people at all, or cars either. Even chased a bunch of picnickers off over near Hiawassee."

"That far?" David whispered incredulously.

The ranger nodded. "Been seen all over."

"Hey, Benj, look here," the younger ranger called from the other side of the road. They all followed him to the soft dirt beyond the shoulder, almost at the guardrail. There, amid the stray leaves and bottle caps, was a single cloven hoofprint almost as large as a man's outstreched hand. A few inches away a solitary splatter of dark blood gleamed atop a chunk of schist.

Benj's eyes widened. "Look at the size of that thing! Maybe it *was* an elk. Ralph, you check down the bank a ways and see if you can see anything, then I guess you'd better go on down to that curve and try to warn anybody you see coming this way. I'll see about getting these boys out. Can't leave that car there." He headed back to the Cherokee as David and Alec returned to the Mustang.

"I live just over the ridge," David called. " 'Bout three miles. You couldn't give me a tow home, could you?"

Benj shook his head. " 'Fraid not, son. Insurance won't allow it. But let's get you outta there and then decide. Looks to me like you might be able to drive her."

While the younger ranger kept an eye out for approaching traffic, Benj wheeled the Jeep directly in front of the Mustang.

David looked dubiously first at the Jeep, then at the disabled car, but gamely helped the ranger set a hook on the front cross-member before sliding back into the driver's seat. The winch whined, the cable tightened, and the Jeep began to inch slowly backward. There was a jolt and an agonizing grinding sound, and then the Mustang rested again on level pavement. Alec climbed in while the older man disconnected the hook.

David tried the engine—and it caught. He put the car into first and eased down on the gas, slowly releasing the clutch. The car began to creep forward, but there was a hideous squeaking from the right front, and the wheel shuddered in David's hands. He frowned and gritted his teeth, but continued grimly on. The squeaking became louder, much worse as he tugged the wheel to negotiate a slight kink in the highway.

Ahead lay Franks Gap, guarded now by the Valley View Restaurant. Only completed the previous spring, the Valley View was a low-slung series of stonework shelves and glass planes artfully merged with the surrounding landscape by virtue of the rock and heavy timber from which it was constructed. It also had a very large parking lot—mostly empty now.

A hundred feet before he got there, David heard a loud, muffled pop, and more thumping. The right front corner of the car sagged and the steering wheel jerked hard, bruising the inside of his fingers. The last fifty feet were the worst, as the tortured tire shredded itself from the wheel and he had to continue on the rim, a shower of sparks marking his passage.

"Just hope it doesn't get down to the brake disc," David muttered.

He eased the car into the Valley View parking lot, and was relieved to see the rangers turn in behind him.

"Didn't make it, huh?" Benj said. "Well, there ought to be a phone in the restaurant. Anything else we can do?"

David shook his head. "I guess not. Thanks for the help, though."

"Our pleasure—but keep quiet about the Crazy Deer, okay?"

"Right . . . uh, what do *you* guys think about it, anyway?"

The rangers exchanged glances again. "To be honest, son, we don't know what to think. Sure didn't look like your regular old Georgia whitetail, though. Nor like any deer I ever saw, to tell the truth—not moose, not elk, not even caribou."

"Well, if we see it again, we'll give you a holler," David called as the men headed back to their vehicle.

Benj paused with his hand on the door handle. "You do that, son. You keep a close eye out."

Chapter VII: Lugh's Stables

(Tir-Nan-Og—high summer)

In the cold, dim light of early morning, Tir-Nan-Og seemed an island shrouded by a veil of mist. The sun had not yet risen, and fog hung among the trees like ghostly tapestries. The empty plains were silent, the forest tracks yet sleeping. The wind was still. Even the great dome-shelled Watchers relaxed their vigilance, their tiny brains awash with dreams of darkness.

In all Lugh's realm, in fact, three minds alone were fully conscious, and only one of them was sapient.

Locked in a stall of pure white marble in the sprawl of the High King's palace, Fionna had not slept for the three days that had passed in Tir-Nan-Og (nor the nine that had lapsed in the Lands of Men) since Morwyn had trapped her in horse shape.

The first day she had been too angry either to think or to take any action. The second she had spent in consideration of her circumstances. On the third day she was ready.

Taken by themselves, the fourfold shaping spells she had drawn upon herself would have been no problem to escape. She had touched them before and knew their form and structure.

But Morwyn's binding had complicated her plans considerably, for it had insinuated itself through the layered sorceries and locked them tight around her. It had taken her a long time to find the gaps, but the enchantments Caitlin had contrived, and to which Lugh and Nuada and the Morrigu had each applied their Power, had been set to hold another body and to drown another memory. Thus they did not fit her quite precisely.

It therefore took Fionna the better part of a day to twist her thought through the innermost entrapment. It was subtle work and painful, so she worked carefully, removing the substance of the bindings a thread at a time, as one might unravel fabric and yet preserve the pattern. The first shape-spell she broke this way; the second followed quickly. The third was far more trouble, for the weaving there was tighter, yet it she breached as well, straining her Power through like water through fine linen. The fourth as easiest of all, for by then almost nothing remained of horse-thought to distract her.

By dawn Morwyn's spell alone retained its substance, like a hard layer of lacquer casing the fragile filaments of the other four. That one *had* been made for her and fitted her much better, yet it too had a weakness. In her final desperation, Fionna had sent a Shaping arrowing toward Ailill, and though Morwyn had broken off that contact, the way of its passage had left a frayed spot in her sorcery. It was a tiny thing, that thinning, yet Fionna found it, and poured her Power through.

Part of her was free now, though not corporeal. A moment later there was more. She split her Power then, and applied it to her bindings both from outside and within. There was resistance at first, but then a weakening that became more obvious as she put forth greater effort.

Suddenly Morwyn's spell collapsed, and with it the other four pooled away to nothing, like melted ice. One moment Fionna was a black horse; a moment later a fair-skinned, black-haired woman.

She smiled her exultation.

"Morwyn, your head is *mine!*" she whispered. "As soon as I find my brother."

Fionna studied the entrance of her prison. Statues of rampant stallions carved from jet-black marble flanked the opening; the double doors of the gates were a grillwork of cast brass, their junctures bridged by four hand-sized knotwork medallions wrought of gold-wound iron—human work that, and very dangerous. Those locks did not daunt her, though, for she had learned something of their workings in that part of Froech's mind she had seen when she bespelled him, and she had passed long hours since then surveying them more closely. It would be a simple matter of Power applied to the golden wire alone: just *so*—and the first lock tumbled open—and *so*, and *so*, and *so* . . .

The four magic locks were even simpler, for their pattern too she had stolen from Froech and carefully remembered. *So*, and *so*, and *so*, and *so* . . .

But what form, she wondered, when she had finished, would make her escape most certain? Not the perilous human nakedness that now enwrapped her, though clothing it would be no problem. No, it must be another shape, possessed both of subtlety and cunning, for Fionna knew that she had spent too long in a skin of other-seeming to change again so quickly and expect to retain control. No, whatever shape she chose must be able to sustain its own survival.

She cast her gaze about the stables, fixing it at last upon a disk of gold-chased silver that had snapped from some bit of harness and rolled against the stone wall opposite.

The very thing! she rejoiced, when she saw the creature graven there, and so she caused it to happen.

Her body drew in upon itself, shrank once more onto all fours, put forth again a tail. Red fur cloaked her skin, black hair marked her feet and nose and ear tufts. In ten short breaths, Fionna nic Bobh became a vixen.

She slipped through the open gates and entered the arched corridor beyond the stalls, nostrils twitching warily, seeking such odors as might presage some danger. But no scents rode the air in the High King's stables save the normal ones of horse and dung and fodder; metal, stone, and leather. Nothing told of danger, but the fresher air came from the right, and so she turned that way.

But in spite of her precautions, Fionna did not escape unnoticed, for as she picked her wary way among the scalloped shadows, two other sets of eyes espied her. She had not sensed their owners, for they had been bespelled to aid their watching. They were also the only other beings in all of Tir-Nan-Og who were fully conscious.

Silently they paced her: creatures scarcely taller than herself, with lean, dark bodies, steel-strong feline hindquarters, and heads the same as her own. One thing more there was about them, though, that gave their shadows strangeness, and that was the feathered forelegs that sprouted from their shoulders and ended in red-clawed talons more cruel than any eagle's.

Chapter VIII: Home

(Enotah County, Georgia)

It was with considerable relief that David saw the battered old Ford pickup truck chug around the last curve below the gap. He'd called home from the Valley View, filled at once with a vague, nervous excitement and considerable trepidation. There was always a chance Big Billy might answer the phone, and he was not quite ready to confront his father with news of his accident, regardless of its origin. Big Billy's response to crises was unpredictable, and he had been known to react to almost identical situations in entirely different ways. News of the wreck might send him into a rage (or what was almost worse, into a tirade about David's driving), or it might not faze him at all. But to David's intense relief, it had been Uncle Dale who had picked up the receiver in the Sullivans' kitchen and who'd said he'd be right over.

The ancient black pickup crunched onto the gravel of the parking lot. David could see two figures inside: Uncle Dale at the wheel, face shadowed by the battered straw hat he would wear all summer; and a shorter, towheaded form beside him. David's face lit up when he saw them. He hadn't realized how much he'd missed the family. Almost before the truck stopped, the passenger door scraped open and a small shape launched itself toward him, crying, "Davy! Davy!"

David tried not to smile too widely. "Heeey kid, how're you doin'?" he laughed, as he swept up his little brother and swung him around and around at chest level.

"Goooood!" Little Billy squealed joyfully, as the spinning turned his cry to ululation.

David set him down with a breathless gasp. "Gettin' heavy, kid. What's Ma been feedin' you lately? Lead?"

"Cookies!" Little Billy exclaimed. "While you was gone I got to eat all of 'em!"

"Yeah, I bet you did." David poked his brother's rounded tummy. "Shows, too."

Uncle Dale displayed more reserve, but he too seemed glad to see

62

his nephew. Grandnephew, actually; David and Little Billy's grandfather had been Dale's youngest brother. "How're you doin', boy?" he muttered through a scraggly white beard that had scandalized David's mother when he had started it the previous winter. He shook both their hands, then regarded Alec for a thoughtful moment before reaching out to tweak the taller boy's earring. Alec blushed fiercely and set frantically to removing it.

The old man stuck out a wiry arm and stopped him. "Don't bother *me* none, boy. It's *your* ear; you're the one that's gotta put up with whatever folks sez about it. If it 'uz me, I believe I'd just stick with a plain old gold ring, though; them dangly kind is askin' for trouble. Being a modern-day pirate's one thing, but I'm not sure the Lord'd like his cross a hangin' down like that. " He looked back at David and cocked a grizzled eyebrow. "Surprised you ain't got one of them doodads, Davy."

David scratched his nose. "Well, Alec kind of beat me to it, and . . . well, you know me—I never have liked to copy anybody."

"Now, *that's* the truth!" Uncle Dale agreed. "You always was an original. I always said they broke the mold when they made you—both before and after; durin' too, maybe. Somebody put in a double dose of craziness—and then felt bad about it, so they added a good-sized pinch of smarts to balance it off—that, and two or three other good things I'd best not mention. Wouldn't do for you to get the big head."

Alec couldn't resist a gibe: "Too bad they didn't put in more fertilizer."

David, who was sensitive about his lack of height, shot his friend a scathing glare. "I'll remember that, McLean, next time you want to run or wrestle or swim or—"

"Or play basketball?" Alec inserted smoothly, drawing himself up to display a clear three-inch height advantage.

"Better quit while you're ahead, Davy," Uncle Dale cautioned. "Now let's get a look at that car."

Ten minutes later they were traveling again, the four of them crowded into the cab of the pickup, with Alec in the middle and Little Billy scrunched up in David's lap. The Mustang dangled forlornly behind, its front end suspended by ropes and chains from the old truck's wooden bumper. It was a solution more functional than elegant—not that the Mustang looked very elegant, just then. Little Billy was playing with a *289* emblem he had salvaged from the mangled fender.

"Guess what, Davy!" the little boy exclaimed suddenly.

"I give."

"You ain't even gonna *guess?*"

David shook his head. "Nah, you're too smart for me, kid. Better just go ahead and tell me."

Little Billy looked a trifle disappointed. "They's guppies over in MacTyrie."

David frowned his confusion. "Guppies?" He glanced at Uncle Dale. "Somebody opened a pet store, is that it? You wantin' a gold-fish or something?"

"No, Davy," Little Billy said patiently. You know. Guppies. Them fortuneteller folks with the colored wagons and the horses."

"Oh! *Gypsies!*"

"That's what I said: Gippies."

"*Jip-sees,*" David enunciated clearly. "Short for '*Ee-jip-shun,*' supposed to be, you know—like that Bangles song."

"I don't know about that," Uncle Dale interjected. "But one of his buddies saw 'em and told him about 'em at Sunday school, and he's been about to pee in his pants to see 'em. What with helpin' your pa, I ain't had time to take him. Bill ain't too keen on him goin', if you want to know the truth, so I figured maybe you could scope 'em out when you run Alec home, an' if you thought it was a fit place for a young boy, you could take him later. Get his fortune told or somethin'."

David ruffled the little boy's fair hair; mischief sparkled on his face. "Sell him, maybe? Reckon I could get a good price for him? Wanta go halves on the profit?"

Uncle Dale chewed his lip thoughtfully. "Way he's been cuttin' up lately, might not be such a bad idea. Way he's growin', won't be able to feed him much longer nohow."

Little Billy's blue eyes had grown larger by the moment. He stared at David suspiciously. "You puttin' me on again?"

David feigned innocence. "*Moi?*"

"*Vous,*" said Uncle Dale unexpectedly, his smug yellow-toothed grin countering David's suddenly shocked expression. "I've got me a little bit of book learnin', too."

"I'll remember that."

The old man aimed a hard look at David. "Course you might not ought to go either, Davy. I've heard a tale or two about them Gypsy women. Love potions, an' all. Supposed to be 'specially fond of fresh young blond boys like you. You ain't careful, you're liable to come out different from how you went in. Come to think of it, you go messin' with the women, you almost *bound* to come out different —p'ticularly if the men catch you at it."

Alec giggled. "I've been trying to get him to take care of *that* problem all summer, but he won't listen."

David jabbed an elbow into his friend's side.

Uncle Dale's eyebrows lifted expressively. "You better watch your step, too, little Alec. However fresh Davy is, I don't allow you're any riper."

"What're you all talkin' about?" Little Billy inquired.

David tickled his ribs. "Don't play innocent, kid."

"Moi?" Little Billy replied, exactly aping David's previous intonation.

They were nearing Sullivan Cove now, putt-putting down the last bit of mountain before they came to the long straight that bisected Big Billy's riverbottom. David found himself tensing. Somewhere in here was another Straight Track—the very one, in fact, on which he had first encountered the Sidhe. The curve was in sight: the place where it crossed the highway. He held his breath, tried to focus the Sight. But there was no need, for his eyes took on the familiar tingle even as the ring warmed slightly upon his chest.

It was before him, then: a straight strip of golden light maybe ten feet wide that seemed at once to lie upon the land and to float in the air above it. Shapes slithered along its surface like the shifting arabesques oil will form on water. As nonchalantly as he could David clapped his hand across his shirtfront, fearful the ring might betray itself with a display of sudden radiance. Much to his relief, however, the prickle of heat brought no accompanying flicker.

The Track was closer—closer, then beneath, and then they were past. David saw Uncle Dale blink a time or two, Alec flinched involuntarily, and then it was over. He exhaled carefully as the truck came onto the straightaway.

Only then did he realize that he'd been holding his breath, though for what reason he had no notion. He didn't know all the workings of the Tracks—nobody did, not even the Sidhe. But he was reasonably certain this one presented no real danger. Yet the Crazy Deer had unnerved him more than he wanted to admit. He'd grown complacent about the things of Faerie, he realized, and that was very dangerous.

Uncle Dale ground into a higher gear, and the truck lurched forward a little more energetically. Something banged behind them, and David risked a furtive glance through the backlight.

"What kinda mood's Pa in?" he asked finally.

The old man shrugged and continued sawing at the steering wheel. "Bill's himself, I reckon. He'll be glad to see you and not want you to know that he is."

David braced himself as the truck slowed to turn left onto the dirty, red-brown gravel of the Sullivan Cove road. "You tell him anything about the wreck?"

The old man nodded. "Had to. Couldn't hide it. Had a word or two to say 'bout your drivin's all."

"What do *you* think about my driving?"

"I think a boy's gonna go fast till he learns to slow down. Given that, I'd rather you went fast in a car made to go fast than in somethin' that ain't. If you'd been drivin' your mama's car you'd've been off the mountainside, 'stead of in the ditch."

"I'd have been driving Mama's car, I'd still be down around Macon."

"Well, wherever you might have been, Davy," Alec observed pointedly, as they jolted up the rutted slope of abandoned logging road that was the Sullivans' driveway, "you're home now."

From where it sat high on a steep grassy hill, the faded white farmhouse seemed almost sentient, a spot of light standing guard against the dark forested heights behind it.

JoAnne Sullivan, David's mother, was waiting in the yard when they pulled up. She looked the same as ever: short blonde hair above dark tanned skin; crinkle lines showing on a face that had once held remarkable beauty and still attracted admiring glances; slender body, work-hardened and dressed in faded jeans, a sleeveless pullover blouse, and worn Sears sneakers. She gave him a hearty hug, rather to David's surprise—usually she was reserved about displays of emotion. Then, truly to David's amazement, she embraced Alec. David risked a glance at Alec's ear and was relieved to discover that the dangling ornament was nowhere to be seen.

"Looks like the flatlands agreed with you," JoAnne said decisively. "Both of you browner'n a nice plate of biscuits. Looks like you both put on a little weight, too. I figured you'd come back looking like toothpicks with fuzz on top." Her eyes narrowed suddenly. "And speakin' of fuzz, what's that on your lip, Alec McLean?"

Alec jumped self-consciously and fingered the soft growth above his mouth. He colored slightly. "Oh, nothing . . . Caterpillar crawled up there and went to sleep, I guess. Just couldn't bring myself to bother it."

"Looks to me like it died and fell away to dust." JoAnne snorted. "Now get on inside, boys—it's too early for supper, but I thought you might like a brownie or two."

David hung back, staring at his car.

His mother followed his line of sight. She wrapped an arm around his shoulder and squeezed him hard. "Too bad about your car, hon, but that kind of thing happens. It'll get fixed sooner or later. Till then you can drive mine: I've started doin' take-home piecework from that Clifton Precision plant up in North Carolina, so I don't need it but two days a week now." She released him and headed up the back porch steps.

"I'll have to be gone more often," David whispered to Alec as he retrieved his suitcase and followed her. "She ain't been this nice in ages."

A tall shape filled the doorway ahead as Big Billy pushed aside the screen and sauntered onto the porch. As was usual in the summer, he wore no shirt. David looked up at him. How could his father be so tall and himself so short, he wondered. Maybe the mailman was involved, or something. But he knew that wasn't true, for such speculation denied the reality of Big Billy's dark blue eyes and level black brows, and denied as well that under forty pounds of muscle and thirty more of flab, the cut of Big Billy's jaw and the clean angles of his nose and cheekbones were exactly the same as his son's. Only the hair was different: JoAnne's blonde had overridden Big Billy's fiery red.

An uneven grin jagged across Big Billy's face. "'Bout time you got here, boy; I been saving chores for you all summer. Ain't mucked out the barn since you'uz gone."

David's face fell. He'd expected as much, but *this* soon?

The grin altered into a rather foolish smile as Big Billy grabbed David in a bear hug and lifted him far off the ground. "Just teasin', boy. How're you doin'?"

David grinned back somewhat breathlessly, though he knew that the reference to the barn was probably accurate, and that he'd have about one day of grace before the rural life closed in on him in painful earnest.

As he dropped David roughly to the ground, Big Billy's gaze fell on Alec. "And Mr. McLean—you lookin' right healthy, too."

Alec paled a little and found something to look at on the ground. "Thank you, sir."

Big Billy raised his eyes to survey the pickup truck and the lamed Mustang. He pursed his lips and frowned, then looked back at David. "Well, car don't look *too* bad. I'm right glad to see you made it home in one piece. I s'pect you'll appreciate the fixin' money too—when you get done earnin' it." He poked a stubby finger in the middle of David's chest. *"Monday mornin',* boy. Bright and early. You and me in the sorghum patch. Dawn till we get finished, you understand?"

David sighed dramatically.

His father held up a warning hand. "None of that. You did it, it's yours to set right. Now then. Get you something to snack on, and run your buddy home. And then you hightail it back here in time for supper."

"Okay if I check out the Gypsies when I'm over in MacTyrie?"

Big Billy's face hardened. "You might as well, since I'm sure you will anyway, whatever I say. But you get on back here by supper-time, you hear that? We've still got a thing or two to discuss about your drivin'." He slapped David hard on the fanny. "Might have to converse with your backside while I'm at it, too—memory tends to last a little longer that way." He laughed, as if to prove he wasn't serious, then paused, staring at his son's downcast expression. "Well, hell, boy, don't look like that. I'm glad to have you home sure enough, and I hate to come down on you so hard so soon, but it's for your own good, and you know it. One day of grace, and then it's me and you in the fields. Deal?"

David stuck out a reluctant hand. "Deal," he muttered.

One day!

"So," Alec asked as soon as they'd cleared the driveway and swung Mama Sullivan's LTD left onto the road that would eventually take them to MacTyrie, "what do you think was up with the elk?"

David shook his head. "You've decided that's what it was, huh? Well, I have *no* idea. Absolutely zilch. It had to have been one of the Sidhe in animal shape, but I haven't a clue which one—if it's even one I know. The image kept shifting on me, from man to deer to horse and back again, so fast I never could get a fix on it, just . . . impressions. It wasn't like any manifestation of the Sight I've ever had."

Alec frowned. "Horse, you say? You don't suppose it could have been . . . you know who?"

David's eyes widened. "God, I hope not! Anyway, I think Nuada would have warned me. And besides, Ailill's got binding spells on him out the wazoo. Even Lugh can't unmagic him by himself."

"And you've got the ring," Alec added.

"Good point. But I wouldn't have wanted to bet on its protection this afternoon. And besides, those antlers could have done a job on the front of my car worse than the rocks did on the side."

"I'm really sorry about that, too," Alec said. "I'm surprised you're not more bothered."

David's mouth quirked in a smile of resignation. "I don't think it's really sunk in yet. Just wait—I'll probably wake up half-crazy in the middle of the night. Right now it's just a bad dream. And made even more unreal by that mad deer."

"Crazy Deer," Alec corrected.

"Whatever."

"I don't suppose there's any way you could go to the Sidhe and ask them what's up?"

"No, not really. Every time I've seen them the last year or so has been at their instigation. And I don't know how to operate the Straight Tracks. I could *try* to summon somebody, I suppose . . . but if Ailill really has escaped, he could answer the summons. And I tell you what, Alec: in spite of the Sight, in spite of the ring, in spite of my so-called Power, I don't ever, *ever* want to be attacked by a giant eagle again."

"That I *would* like to have seen."

"Oh no you wouldn't, fool. It was seriously scary. Blind luck saved me as much as anything—that and the maple twig I accidentally broke that summoned Oisin."

"Couldn't you try that again?"

David shook his head emphatically, his lips tightened to a thin line. "Nope. That was an absolute onetimer . . . It's *real* strange, Alec: first every Straight Track between here and Valdosta being activated, then the Crazy Deer. You tell *me* what it means."

"Some loonie escaped from Lugh's dungeon?"

"Who knows? I don't know if he's even *got* dungeons."

Alec looked suddenly wary. "As long as—"

David joined in: "—*it's not Ailill*. And now," he added, "let's see if Mom's had this thing tuned up lately."

Chapter IX: The Irish Horse Traders

(MacTyrie, Georgia)

No such family gathering as they had encountered earlier greeted them in MacTyrie. Instead, Alec's parents had left a neatly typed note on the Cape Cod's paneled front door saying they'd gone to Young Harris to hear a poetry reading by Bettie Sellers and would be home after midnight. There was supposed to be cold roast beef in the fridge. David helped Alec unload, grunting as he lugged the heavier of the two suitcases up the stairs to Alec's bedroom.

Alec folded his arms and looked at him from beside the bed. Their eyes met in knowing smirks. "Now?"

David dropped the suitcase with a thud. "Now!"

They raced back downstairs, pausing in the kitchen to grab a couple of cans of Dr. Pepper from the refrigerator.

"Any notion where these 'guppies' are supposed to be?" Alec asked.

"Well, we could always call somebody, but let's just look around first. Last time anybody like that was anywhere near here was when the Goat Man came through a couple of years ago. He hung out over at the old ballfield till they ran him off. Seems like I recall a circus setting up there when I was little, too."

"I don't."

"It was before you came."

"Breathed hard, anyway."

"Fool."

"Of a Scotsman," Alec finished as they returned to the car.

David backed down the drive, careful to avoid the ivy that flanked it on either side. "Ugh—this thing handles like a tank. Remind me to tell Mom to get a T-Bird next time."

"I think the tank might be in better keeping with your driving style."

70

"I resent that, Alec McLean."

"Shouldn't. It's just the truth—— What the——" he cried a second later as David slammed on the brakes. "Don't take it so personal, Davy!"

"Not my doing." David grinned, as someone rapped hard against the window glass on Alec's side.

Alec powered it down as Gary and Darrell stuck sweaty heads through the opening. Neither boy had on a shirt, and perspiration sheened their chests and shoulders.

"Well, look who's back." Gary grinned, elbowing his slighter companion in the ribs.

Darrell elbowed him back more forcefully. "Yeah—Fool of a Scotsman and Mad Davy Sullivan—madder than ever, I'd imagine."

David jerked the car into park and stretched an arm in front of Alec's nose to grasp the hands that were suddenly cramming their way into the window. "Well! If it ain't G-Man Gary and Runnerman Buchanan. How you guys been keepin'?"

"Keeping busy's what," Gary said.

"Look real busy," Alec observed wryly. "Looks to me like all you're doing's running. Whether into trouble or away from it remains to be seen."

Darrell slicked a stray lock of yellow hair out of his face. "Yeah, well, gaming without you guys isn't much fun. Just leaves eating, drinking, and sex as worthwhile activities."

"Not in that order," Gary inserted.

"I notice you didn't include running," David laughed.

"Running is *not* an activity," Darrell shot back haughtily. "Nor is it an option."

"Maybe not, but one of these days you're gonna run so long and hard there won't be anything left when you get where you're going but a pair of dirty Nikes going flip-flop along the sidewalk."

Gary looked a trifle apologetic and patted the mere trace of bulge visible above the waist of his shorts. "Don't look at me, guys, I'm just trying to lose a pound or two."

"Christ, he'll have us doing it next," Alec muttered.

"I like to run," David reminded him.

"So get your togs and join us. We'll wait."

David shook his head. "Can't. We're going to see the Gypsies for a second and then I gotta get back home. I wrecked my car just the other side of Franks Gap, and I've sorta got to stay in my folks' good graces for a day or two."

"God, not your car!" Darrell exclaimed. "Shit, Sullivan, how bad?"

"Good enough for Gary's old man to get a fair price out of me for fixing it, probably."

"Well, the labor's on me if you'll let me do it," Gary said.

"Gee, thanks—but what's a Bimmer dealer charge for Ford parts?"

Gary grinned evilly. "Whatever the market'll bear. Let's see, considering that the Mustang's virtually an antique—"

"A classic," David corrected.

"Right. So I figure . . . Oh, maybe a thou, or so."

"Crap!" David groaned.

"I say something wrong?"

"What you haven't said," said Alec, "is where the Gypsies are."

"Huh? Oh, right. Up at the old ball ground."

"You guys want to join us?" David asked. "Might give you a reason for running, if what my Ma says is true."

"Sorry, can't," Darrell apologized. "Mom's cooking spaghetti for supper, and then I've got a date."

"*May* have a date."

"Well, I'm gonna call again. If it blows, I guess I'll raid my old man's beer supply and drown my sorrows over Risk at Casa McLean —if it's okay with you, Alec?"

"Sure," Alec replied. "Long as my folks are gone. What about you, Davy?"

David grimaced and shook his head. "I sure would like to. I could use a good game—nor would a beer or two be bad, the way I'm feeling right now. But I've got to play it close, at least for a couple of days. Hope you guys understand."

"Well, don't be surprised if your name doesn't come up in conversation," Darrell said slyly.

"Nor Liz Hughes's either!"

"I was about to say that," Darrell added.

"And *I* have got to be traveling," David said, as he put the car in reverse. "You guys keep on truckin'."

It didn't take them long to find the Gypsies. They were indeed encamped on the north side of town at the ball field that had been abandoned when MacTyrie built a new recreation center near the half-completed bypass to the south. It was a flat area of maybe ten acres, fringed on all but its eastern approaches by a double row of pines. A small creek flowed beyond the trees at the northern side, tributary to the lake that lapped the northeast corner of the town. A low hill studded with small, neat dwellings overlooked its western margin—mostly the residences of faculty at MacTyrie Junior College.

They passed the rusty gateway and stopped in the sandy parking lot. There were a couple of other cars around; some David recognized, some he didn't: several pickups with Enotah County plates, a Mazda RX-7 from Florida, a battered brown Peugeot 504 (that would be Mr. Johnson, the visiting art prof, David decided—taking pictures for one of his books, probably), an anonymous GM sedan from neighboring Towns County. . .

And a shiny black Ford EXP that had just pulled in behind them.

And kept coming.

Getting closer and closer, until the tiny car's rubber-capped bumper nudged the LTD's heavy chrome one.

David flung open the car door and stomped out. "Who the hell *is* that son of a bitch?"

"David, wait," Alec called. "It's—"

"Liz!" David cried as the door opened and a familiar red-haired figure climbed out.

"Mind if I park behind you?" she asked brightly, green eyes sparkling with mischief.

"Liz!" David cried again. "What're *you* doing here? Where'd you get that?"

"*That* is a birthday present from my father," Liz said, as she came over to stand beside David—fairly close, he noted with some satisfaction. "He got tired of having to run me up here every time I wanted to see . . . certain people. It's called Morgan, after the Morrigu, kind of, but not exactly."

David chuckled. "One question down."

Liz raised an appraising eyebrow. "Oh—why am I here? Looking for you, of course."

"How'd you know I'd *be* here?"

"Easy. Soon as I heard there were Gypsies in MacTyrie I figured you'd show up sooner or later. I knew the day you were coming back, had a good idea of your departure time. Knew you'd have to give Alec a ride home. So I've just been sort of hanging around MacTyrie all afternoon, keeping one eye on Casa McLean and one on these folks. What took you so long?"

David developed a sudden interest in his feet. "I kinda had a wreck."

Liz raised an eyebrow. "A wreck, huh? Well, I was thinking about letting you drive Mr. Morgan, but I'm not so sure about that now."

"No backseat," noted Alec, who had been examining the car. "But a space big enough to stretch out in under the hatch. Be even better than a backseat for some purposes I can think of."

"Alec!" David growled.

Liz looked at him askance. "What've they been teaching you guys down in Valdosta, anyway? I thought Governor's Honors was to make you smart, not horny. There's enough of *that* kind in Gainesville. And as for California, well . . ." She rolled her eyes in exaggerated exasperation.

"The two are not mutually contradictory," David pointed out.

Liz sighed. "Just when I was beginning to think you two really weren't like most of the boys I met down there, I come home to this. You're no better than they are—no different, anyway."

"I should hope not." David grinned. "We've all got the same hardware."

It was Liz's turn to blush.

"So," Alec continued brightly, "here we all are again, just about to go see the Gypsies, and almost exactly a year later—well, actually it was a fortuneteller then, but small difference. Life runs in circles."

"Sure that's not Straight Tracks?" Liz giggled.

"Right. So let's away."

Alec grabbed David by the collar and hauled him back. "Uh, Davy, what exactly do we do, anyway?"

"Easy enough," Liz interjected. "Karen was over earlier, and she told me a couple of things. They're not really Gypsies, they're tinkers and traders—Irish Horse Traders, to be exact, not that there's really much difference in practice. They travel around the country trading horses, laying linoleum, and painting houses, if you can believe that. Do some music on the side. Sell crafts, stuff like that. Evidently they don't mind folks coming by in the daytime, but not after dark. Karen said they have guards posted at night. Said Mike Wheeler and a bunch of his crew came by a couple of days ago and these folks made short work of 'em."

David looked impressed. "How long've they been here, anyway?"

Liz's brow furrowed thoughtfully. "I'm not sure—week today, I think. Weren't here one evening, were the next morning. Town policeman came by to see what was up, called the mayor. Money supposedly changed hands and suddenly everything's hunky-dory. Paid in gold, so I hear."

"Well," Alec said decisively, "shall we go see what's happening?"

David nodded and flopped his arms across both sets of shoulders, suddenly acutely aware of the contrast between Alec's firm muscles and the delicate bones he felt beneath Liz's scarlet T-shirt.

"We're off to see the wizard," Alec began.

"Not funny."

"No."

There was no clearly defined entrance to the Traders' encampment. A chain-link fence that remained from the glory days of the MacTyrie softball team more or less encircled the area, weaving in and out among the pines, but it had been torn down, or had fallen down, at many points. Those parts that remained upright were shrouded in kudzu, particularly on the nearer side. The old concession stand/ticket office looked like the most promising way in. They pushed past the recalcitrant turnstile and entered the enclosure.

It was like stepping into another world: The sky above was the rich, clear blue of late afternoon, the air felt strangely damp and . . . *green*, somehow. Foliage framed the clearing on every side, almost masking any view of the rest of the town. The wagons were ahead, maybe twenty of them, drawn up in a three-quarter circle with what looked like a camp fire/cook fire in the center. Each of them was a delight to behold, painted as they were in bright primary colors with elaborate scrollwork ornaments that were either gilded or lacquered in contrasting shades. Mirrors flashed from their sides, and long, multicolored fringes decorated the canvas roofs. A closer inspection showed that every surface bore some carved or painted embellishment, and the designs themselves were disquietingly familiar.

"Celtic knotwork," David whispered aloud after a moment's concentration. "Of course. Just like on those T-shirts you sent us. Why fool with baroque froufrou when you've got the *Book of Kells* to steal designs from?"

Liz looked at him skeptically. "Oh, so we're an art critic now?"

David flicked her a sideways glance. "Hardly. But it's kind of in my best interest to know as much about Celtic stuff as I can, don't you think? And that includes their art. I mean, if I hadn't read *Gods and Fighting Men*, I'd have been in deep shit last year."

He continued his survey of the camp, noting a larger semicircle of square green tents lurking beyond the cluster of wagons. Very few people were visible, and those he could see seemed to take no notice of them. The few he could make out looked normal enough, though both sexes tended toward stockiness and red hair. The only thing at all remarkable was that every one of the women wore a skirt or dress. There wasn't a woman in pants in sight.

"I wonder where the horses are," Liz said. "I want to come by sometime and photograph them—if they'll let me. I haven't had a *good* horse to shoot in ages. One problem with living in town."

Alec gestured toward a large open area enclosed by a high fence of bolted-together planks that butted against a part of the wire fence about fifty yards away to their right. "Over there, maybe?"

David squinted in the indicated direction. "See anybody you know?"

Liz shook her head. "Negative. Not native types."

Alec wagged a discreet thumb at a particular rotund figure who stood by the enclosure gate. "Not Traders, either, I bet. I don't know much, but I'll wager no self-respecting vagabond of the road would be caught dead in flowered Bermuda shorts."

David chuckled loudly as they drew nearer.

"No, but I bet *that's* one," he replied, as he indicated a tall, fair-haired man who was leaning against the fence with one black-booted foot resting atop the lowest plank. The man was remarkably tall, in fact, and very slender; though when viewed from the rear he seemed to evoke the same sense of latent power as a rangy cat. His long golden hair was tied in a ponytail, and blinding white Levis rode low on his narrow hips. He wore a matching white denim vest over a long-sleeved plaid shirt. The right sleeve was pinned up at the shoulder.

As the group drew nearer the man turned and stared at them.

David almost froze in his steps, suddenly aware of a tingling in his eyes. His mouth gaped open. He had seen that face before, though there were subtle differences.

"Nuada!" His lips shaped the words, but his throat gave them no voice.

The tall man raised an expressive dark eyebrow and inclined his head imperceptibly, then shifted his gaze to the right as if indicating the presence of the obvious tourist. "Just a moment," he said to the gaudily dressed man beside him. "I must point these young folk in the proper direction."

"Sho 'nuff," the chubby man replied in an affable (and patently phony) Southern accent.

Nuada casually placed his single hand on David's shoulder and drew him away from the paddock with Alec and Liz in tow. He bent his head close and David heard him speak. But even as he did so, other words shaped themselves in David's brain, and it was those unheard sounds which came to him most clearly: *I see questions, David Sullivan, but this is not a good time for their answering. Come tonight, after sunset. Bring your friends and join us.*

And with that, Nuada dropped the hand and turned his back on them. An instant later he had rejoined the tourist.

David glanced nervously at his companions. "You guys catch that?" he asked, as they headed away from the camp without further investigation.

Alec nodded. "Imagine finding Nuada here with a bunch of Irish tinkers."

"I certainly never expected to see him in white Levis, that's for sure," Liz put in.

"Wonder what's up—something serious, I bet."

"Hope it doesn't involve us. I've had enough adventures."

"Shouldn't," David said, though he did not quite feel convinced. "If they'd wanted us, they knew where to find us."

Alec frowned uncertainly. "Yeah, well, that *is* a point."

David glanced at his watch and grimaced sourly. "Crap! I've got to get home!"

Alec confirmed David's statement with a glance at his own time-piece. "Right you are. Papa Sullivan won't be satisfied with one cheek now, he'll want to wallop both of 'em."

"Alec!"

"Hope that new car of yours has got soft seats, Liz," Alec went on mercilessly. "Next time you see him, David may need 'em. You see him standing up a lot, you'll know what happened."

Liz pursed her lips and looked askance at David. "Aren't you a little old for that?"

David sighed. "Well, *I* certainly think so. But Pa says that until I'm eighteen I'm still technically a child."

"'And,'" quoted Alec, "'a good whuppin' never done nobody no harm.'"

"Got any liniment?" David asked, cocking a mischievous eyebrow at Liz. "I may need somebody to help rub the pain away."

Liz's eyes flashed dangerously. "I'm gonna beat Papa Sullivan to the punch if you don't hush up!"

"Sure." David grinned as he unlocked the LTD.

Liz got out her own keys. "Eight o'clock okay for me to pick you up?"

David looked up. "I've got Mom's car, I can use it."

"I'd feel safer in this one," Liz replied. "It's got two things yours doesn't."

"*Oh?*"

Her face broke into a glorious smile. "Me as a driver—and no backseat." She giggled, and slammed the door.

"No backseat." Alec grinned as he aimed a blow at David's shoulder. "But a hell of a lot of room behind the front ones!"

Chapter X: Froech's Discovery

(Tir-Nan-Og — high summer)

A slanted shaft of morning sunlight pierced a dome of frosted opals and stretched Froech's shadow across the marble floor before him. Yet the darkness that pooled on the snowy tile was as nothing to the despair that burned in his heart. Dread was a fire within him: such dread as he had not felt in all his five hundred years. But there was no denying it.

He stared at the gated archway, at the black stone horses that flanked it, twin lines of ruby eagles sketched thin and glittering upon their incised bridles. At four medallions of gold-wound steel that now hung as broken and useless as the teeth of an ancient hag. And at a white marble stall in which no trace remained of a certain jet-black stallion.

I must go and tell Lugh, he realized, *even if it mean my death.*

Chapter XI: Discussions

(Sullivan Cove, Georgia)

"But you *said* you'd take me!" Little Billy insisted passionately from beside the refrigerator. He glared at his older brother, small hands fisted on his hips, red cheeks puffed in outraged indignation: the very image of six-year-old fury.

David glared back at him, aping his pose exactly. "I *know* I said I'd take you—but I was there this afternoon and it's just not the kind of place you ought to go. You wouldn't have any fun. Trust me."

His voice rang harsh and loud against the kitchen walls. He continued to frown at the little boy. Things had been happening too quickly during the last few hours and he hadn't quite got his bearings yet. It was making him irritable, he knew, and he was sorry about that, but there was nothing he could do to remedy the situation until he had some time alone to sort things out. The whole afternoon had been an insane series of crises and chance encounters. Coming home was like putting on clothes you hadn't worn in a while: they didn't always fit, and sometimes you found things in the pockets you'd forgotten.

"Okay?" David added hopefully.

Little Billy was adamant. "But why not?"

"Because there's nothing there for a kid to do!"

"Then why are *you* going?" Little Billy countered.

David blinked back surprise. "Because I—"

"Because he ain't got no sense," Big Billy interrupted from the hallway door. "Always running after craziness."

David's fist slammed the enameled wall beside him. The telephone rattled.

"Better that than running after nothing at all!" he flared, feeling his eyes go wide as he realized what anger had betrayed him into saying.

Big Billy's mouth snapped shut. He took a step into the kitchen, bare chest swelling like a sunburned sail as he sucked in air.

"Bill!" JoAnne warned from the shadows behind him. A slender hand brushed her husband's departing shoulder as he strode to the refrigerator and wrenched the door open.

Little Billy looked smug and danced expertly sideways. "Whip 'im, Pa!"

"More craziness," Big Billy muttered as he pulled out a can of Miller beer. "Craziness and shit! I thought we'd settled this at supper!"

David's gaze flickered frantically from parent to brother to parent, but found no sympathy anywhere. He took a deep breath, forcing calm upon himself. Things were going badly—had been since the subject of the Traders had first arisen half an hour before. It had been like day and night: glad to see him that afternoon, but as soon as he introduced an alien element into the conversation, things had returned to normal—the same old contentious normal. It was too bad his folks hadn't seen a few of the sights he'd seen. *That'd* give them a different outlook on a lot of things.

"Look, Pa," David said carefully, hoping to defuse his father's rising anger. "I never said I'd take Little Billy. I said I *might;* said I'd scope it out and see if he ought to go. And I did, and I don't think he should. But Liz wants to do some photography, and the Traders told her she could. And there's supposed to be a *ceili* later—that's a sort of music festival. That's mostly what I want to go for. And I don't want to have to keep up with a fidgeting six-year-old."

His mother took a swallow of tea and peered intently at David from beneath lowered brows. "I've heard some bad things about them Gypsies, David. Real bad things: thievin', cheatin', dope . . . *whorin'*. Heard they beat up on some local boys."

David stuffed his hands in his back pockets and flopped up against the doorjamb. "Yeah, well, it was Mike Wheeler and his gang that got into trouble, and you know how *they* are. Most likely Mike and company tried to cause a ruckus and got more than they bargained for. And for another thing, they're not Gypsies, they're Irish Traders. They don't like being called Gypsies, in fact. They don't read fortunes or anything."

"And how do *you* know so much, Mr. Smarty Pants?"

Exasperation traced furrows on David's forehead. "Look, Ma, I read a little about the Traders in the Sunday paper a couple of years ago. They're not bad folks. Used to trade horses and mules, now mostly itinerant painters and rug layers."

"Sounds real exciting," Big Billy muttered sarcastically. "So why you want to go see a bunch of painters?"

Behind him, David's hands plucked nervously with the spring that held the screen door closed. "I told you, it's the music. That's the thing."

His father's face was like the red-lit sky before an evening storm. "I don't like them folks," he rumbled. "I just don't like 'em. I don't like you messin' around with 'em, either; just want you to know that. Somebody's gonna call the law on 'em yet, you'll see. Somebody'll run 'em off."

"Pa—"

"You get into any trouble, don't come crying to me."

"When have I *ever* come crying to you?"

Big Billy's face became dangerously still. "Watch your mouth, boy."

"Physically impossible."

"That's it, mister. You're staying here."

Gravel crunched in the driveway, a car horn sounded.

"No, I'm not!" David said with deliberate control, matching his father glare for glare. "I know what I'm doing, and *you're* not gonna stop me."

And with that, he slammed the door behind him, leapt off the back porch, and sprinted across the dusty haze of backyard.

He was pounding on the car door even before Liz got it unlocked. "Quick, let's boogie," he gasped. "Pa and me just had one god-awful fight. Gotta get outta here before he comes out."

Liz hesitated.

"Stand on it, Liz!"

She frowned and shifted into reverse, then gunned the engine. Gravel showered from the front wheels.

Liz glanced at David's troubled expression. "That bad?"

David nodded grimly. "That bad. Didn't want me to go without Little Billy. And I couldn't give him a good reason why I shouldn't take the little pest."

Liz wrenched the EXP onto the Sullivan Cove road. Pebbles pattered against the floorboards.

"You could have told him we had a date."

David's mouth gaped foolishly. He stared at his freshly cleaned Reeboks. "Suppose I could," he whispered, nodding. "I never thought of that. *That* he'd understand."

Liz flashed him an appraising glance. "Yeah, that's the trouble. You never think of things like that."

"Liz, I—"

"Don't say anything, Davy. Just think. Think for once before you talk."

"Liz . . . Would . . . would you *like* to make this a date?"

"Doesn't matter what I'd like," Liz replied glumly. "We can't. Gotta pick up your number-one shadow. Gotta see Silverhand. Where the Sidhe are involved, people don't count. Not with you, anyway."

"Good God, girl! You know *that's* not true."

"Davy! You . . . oh, never mind!"

A heavy, awkward silence entered the car and rode with them for several miles. David spent the time stealing covert glances at Liz. She was taller than he'd remembered—almost as tall as he—and a tiny bit rounder in all the right places, though still slender as a willow staff. Her nose still tilted at the same impudent angle, though, and her green eyes still sparkled with the same unforgettable fire. She was wearing her hair shorter, too, and he wasn't sure if he liked that or not. For the first time he noticed she had pierced ears.

Finally Liz took a long ragged breath and spoke again. Both her face and her voice had softened considerably.

"You're right, David. I shouldn't have said—what I said. I know what you went through last year, for your brother, for Uncle Dale. For me and Alec. That was the good side of David Sullivan. Davy the selfless hero, and I mean that. . . . But sometimes I wish you could be like that all the time."

David sighed and slumped down in the seat. "Sometimes I wish I could too."

Chapter XII: In the Green Tent

(The Traders' Camp)

The tent was square and made of green canvas, and maybe fourteen feet on a side. A brass pole supported the center, and anchored to it were four pie-shaped sections covered with nylon mesh through which a trickle of fragrant white smoke escaped. A bank of thick, stubby candles illuminated the space inside, erupting like stag horns from between two facing crescents of elaborately embroidered cushions. A red-and-gold rug of fabulous richness covered the floor from corner to corner. Woven tapestries glowed upon the walls, and beneath them low tables held bread and cheese and fruit—and a honey-golden wine as cold and clean-tasting as winter ice, but with a sparkling bite like fire.

Six people sat cross-legged on the silken cushions, sipping that wine: David and Liz and Alec; and facing them, Nuada and a man and woman of the Sidhe—Cormac and Regan. In spite of their prosaic dress—jeans, plaid shirts, and knee boots for the men, a long-sleeved white blouse and blue denim skirt for Regan—none of the older three looked remotely human.

The door flap rustled and a man entered, shorter than any there except David and Liz. Knotted muscles bulged under a layer of fat; his face was florid, his hair red as the candle fire before him. He cast a glance at Nuada, cocked a shaggy brow in inquiry. "Lords, is there anything else you'll be needin'?"

The woman shook her head. "Not Lords," Regan corrected softly. "Not in this World. Gods never, Lords no longer. Rarely even memories now."

The man swallowed awkwardly. "Maybe not, Lady, but the Traders remember. Bridget, or Saint Bridget. Words don't change what is." He turned to leave.

"Oh, but they do," the woman replied. "Ask about 'God' or 'sin'

84

or 'evil' in three houses of men and see what answers come back to you."

"As many as there be men alive," the Trader said. "I'll be right by the door if you need me." He closed the flap behind him.

David took a bite of bread and cheese and looked at the man across from him: Nuada Airgetlam, called Silverhand. Warlord to Lugh the Many-Skilled himself. Once David's unseen protector; now, possibly, his friend.

Candlelight flickered on Nuada's features, setting the angles of nose and cheek and jaw in harsh relief—harsher still because of the assumed mortality that was like a pall stretched thin across eternal youth. He sipped from a pipe at intervals; a white clay pipe, filigreed with silver, and as long as his single forearm.

That was disturbing: that single arm. To see such a man—such a perfect face and body—thus disfigured; the loose, flopping sleeve pinned carelessly to the shoulder like a sign of some dishonor.

Nuada followed David's gaze.

"The arm is a thing of Faerie," he said quietly in response to the unspoken question. "It cannot remain in this World for any great length of time; nor can I, for that matter, unless I wrap myself in the substance of the Lands of Men, which, as you see, I have done."

"I was wondering about that," David noted. "But I sure wouldn't swap a Faery body for a mortal one."

"Nor would I, if there were any choice," Nuada replied, "for the change is indeed both a blessing and a curse. There is the wielding of Power to be considered, for instance: human bodies have little strength for it, which can certainly be an inconvenience. In order to perform more than the simplest enchantments we must once more put on the stuff of Tir-Nan-Og."

David shook his head. "I don't understand."

"It is a thing difficult to explain to you who have but little Power and only one substance to wrap it in. But imagine if you can a thread of infinite fineness joining my form in this World with the very stuff of Tir-Nan-Og of which my true body is a part. Think of it as the link between body and place that memory provides—though it is more physical than that. As long as the linkage exists, we may draw on the full Power of our homeland and switch between the stuff of the two Worlds at will. Yet were we to draw on that Power while in man's substance, it would almost surely destroy us."

"And what happens if the thread is broken?" asked Alec.

Nuada's face clouded. "If the Silver Thread be severed while we are in man's flesh—which few things in all the Worlds can accomplish, or I would not be telling you, you may be sure—we would be doomed to roam the world as men, and to die the death of men at the ending."

"And if you were in your *Faery* bodies?"

"We would have to take up the substance of whatever World we were in, for our homeland would start to call us if we did not. It would be tolerable at first—a mere annoyance—but it would quickly grow worse, until we had either to return or go mad. The call of our World is like music, now: a tune playing in the back of our minds, but the longer we stay away, the louder the music becomes. And just as music played loudly enough can bring on deafness, so it is with the Call, except that the result is madness."

"That doesn't sound too good," Liz interrupted. "But you said something about advantages too."

"That should be obvious," Nuada replied. "The primary one is simply comfort, for the reason I have just stated: to resist the madness prolonged separation from our land engenders. While we wear man's flesh, the Call of home is weaker, no more than a fond memory of a pleasant song once heard. And as for the *other* advantage, watch and find out."

And with that, Nuada casually reached into one of his high boots and drew out a narrow-bladed knife. The naked steel sparked in the candlelight as he touched the blade to his fingertip.

"Iron!" David cried. "You're touching iron!"

Nuada nodded almost smugly. "We could not hope to avoid it in this World; man's flesh can wield what Faery flesh denies me. But in this form it can also wound me beyond any power to heal. When I lost my arm to a blade of iron in the Battle of Mag Tuired, even Dian Cecht could not grow me another. For that I must die and be reborn again. Send my spirit into a womb at the moment of quickening."

"But . . . with immortality, couldn't you do that?" Liz asked tentatively.

Nuada shook his head. "The joy of continuous living is greater to me than the shadow of pain in the arm."

"In other words," said Alec, "you're afraid you'll miss something."

"Exactly," Nuada replied. "But this is not why I asked you here."

"I was wondering when you would get to that." Cormac sighed restlessly. "Soon everyone will know our secret."

Nuada looked up. "Not everyone, Cormac, only those who need to know. These three, at least, are owed an explanation, for we have met before. They have seen much of the arrogance of the Sidhe; let us now show them our hospitality."

Cormac inclined his head a little less than graciously.

Nuada fixed him with a momentary stare, then turned back to the three friends.

"I see one question on every human face before me," he said. "And the question that I see is, why do the Sidhe now seek to pass among them?"

"May I speak to this, Airgetlam?" Regan said. "It is a matter dear to me."

"Yours may be the telling, Lady."

The woman looked at David then. "You and your friends are no longer alone, David, in knowing of Tir-Nan-Og. The Traders, too, number those who remember us. We met them a scant few weeks ago, and a lady among them knew us. She was the mother of one of these folk. Fresh from Erenn, and she knew us for what we were as soon as she set eyes upon us. She promised to help us with our watching."

David's brow wrinkled thoughtfully. "But what do you hope to gain by that?"

Nuada set aside his pipe and took a taste of wine. "It is as Regan said: we are observing. For a very long time it has been my thought that the Sidhe have grown too much apart from men. Once we traveled freely between the Worlds, but as the years passed and men's minds turned to other Powers, we found less and less reason to meet with them. But now, as well you know, the works of men encroach upon Faerie everywhere. I fear a confrontation may be inevitable unless something be done, and quickly. Yet there are things we dare not do. We could reveal ourselves to your leaders, for instance, but with the knowledge of Tir-Nan-Og would come the knowledge of the Powers of that land, and Power is a thing with which few mortals may be trusted. So I have come into the Lands of Men with two chosen members of my household. We will watch your people, learn what we can of the ways of men. Assess what manner of threat you may embody. And in a year I will return to Faerie and tell what I have learned to the High King."

"Know thy enemy," Alec muttered.

Nuada grimaced. "I do not deny it, but neither do I call mortal men my enemy—not yet. I hope that day will never come. Lugh hopes the same. Even the Mistress of Battles would not see blood spilled between the Worlds, and battle is her glory."

"But," Alec said, recalling the books David had lent him during the previous year, "isn't that what your whole history consists of? One war after another?"

Nuada's face clouded. He took another sip of wine. "Mortal and

Immortal are not by nature foes, young McLean. More often, in fact, we have been friends, where there have been dealings between us at all. You have suffered no harm from our meetings, have you?"

"I'm not so sure about that," David interrupted slowly.

Nuada snapped his head around. His eyes glittered with sudden warning.

"Would you have me strip them from your mind then, David Sullivan? I could do it. I could *make* you forget. Burn away the Sight, make you *normal* again. Say it, and it will be done."

Suddenly a long-fingered hand was poised inches in front of David's face.

"Shall I?"

David could not reply.

"Shall I, *mortal?*"

"No," David said quietly. "Never!"

"Then guard your tongue."

David gulped. "I'm sorry, I'll . . . I'll try to be more careful. But," he added, "there are a couple of things I kinda need to ask you, and some stuff I need to tell you, too—stuff you folks really ought to know."

"Oh?" Nuada replied somewhat distantly.

"Yeah," David said carefully. "Like why can I see Straight Tracks all of a sudden? I must have seen four—no, *five* of 'em on my way back from Valdosta. And I shouldn't have been able to see any at all, should I?"

Nuada shook his head. "Not unless Power has touched them."

"Power?"

"Most of what the Sight sees is Power. When the Tracks are awakened by the touch of Power, their own Power increases."

"But how else *can* they be used, except by you folks traveling on them?"

"Any number of ways," Regan answered. "Mind travel, the sending of messages, exploring the Worlds, maybe. But the hairy star disrupted all roads Eastward until lately."

"You said something about exploring," David noted. "Could that be like somebody searching for something—or someone?"

The lady pursed her lips thoughtfully. "It is possible. Why do you ask?"

David cleared his throat. "Well, there've been some problems with . . . what *looks* sort of like an elk causing trouble in our World. I saw it, almost wrecked my car because of it . . . and I think it's one of the Sidhe. In fact—I'm afraid it might be Ailill. I thought somebody might be using magic to look for him."

Nuada frowned. "Grievous news that, if true; but not likely. My last message from Ard Rhi Lugh was this morning, and at that time he was watching Ailill be put through his paces with Caitlin's son, Ciarri, on his back. Now, if I have allowed for the difference between the Worlds correctly, that would still have been after you saw the Tracks—or the animal. Also, the bonds about Ailill are very strong. I myself must be there to break them."

"Yet something may be amiss in Tir-Nan-Og," Cormac observed. "For what your young friend saw seems certainly a thing of our World."

"Faery creatures often wander onto the Tracks," Regan noted. "But they do not usually stay long, nor do they venture far from them, for the call of Tir-Nan-Og is very strong. Usually the drawing is so strong they cannot help but return."

"But this wasn't necessarily an animal," David protested. "Its shape flickered between three forms: man and horse and deer. I wish I could have got a better look at the man."

"Boredom is the chief curse of our kind," said Nuada finally. "And our folk sometimes run the Worlds in forms of other-seeming. Lugh does not like such things, but he cannot watch every man and woman, every half-grown child with a taste for stretching his Power. It could be anyone."

"Even Ailill?" Alec asked pointedly.

Nuada shook his head emphatically. "If Ailill were loose in the Worlds we would know, of that I am very certain. Now, there are other things I would discuss with you: affairs of the Lands of Men. I have many questions that the Traders cannot answer."

They talked then, for a very long time. The walls of tension that had briefly risen quickly fell away. Many subjects they discussed, many questions raised and answered, but at last it was time to go.

"Farewell, David Sullivan," said Nuada at the border of the camp. "But come again tomorrow. And bring your brother. He will be safe here, I promise."

"Right," said David. "You got it."

Chapter XIII: The Wrath of Lugh

(Tir-Nan-Og—high summer)

"Escaped? Windmaster has *escaped?"*

Lugh's shout of rage echoed around his bedchamber like a clap of thunder.

The High King of Tir-Nan-Og slammed his goblet down upon the long wooden table before him. The stem buckled slightly between his fingers. A chip of pearly inlay flaked from the table's edge and fell into the thick white fur that lay beneath his feet.

Beyond the table Froech bowed his head, not daring to face the wrath that blazed in the eyes of his overlord. He was already kneeling. Perhaps he would be crawling next. Perhaps he might be crawling for several centuries, given Lugh's penchant for shape-spells as punishment.

Lugh's hand tightened on the heavy gold chalice. A ruby popped free.

He stared at Froech with a terrible calm anger in his dark eyes that the youth found far more frightening than the threats and rantings he had feared.

"And how was this escape accomplished, boy? Four metal locks there were, and four magic, am I correct? And four binding spells as well? Were they not sufficient?"

"It was the Lady, Majesty," Froech managed to stammer. "It must have been the lady. I . . . I meant to tell you about her."

Lugh drained the wine. "Froech, look at me."

The youth raised his head.

Lugh's gaze locked with his and would not release it. He closed his fist around the goblet. A panel of silver scrollwork was pressed into ruin. A second ruby fell as the High King tightened his grip. Finally he opened his hand and flung the mass of twisted metal against the floor a handsbreadth away from the cowering boy.

"Would you rather that were your *head,* Froech? It *will* be if you do not tell me everything."

"My Lord . . . I . . ." Froech's eyes widened. He sought his voice but could not find it, searched his memory and found emptiness waiting there—that and the image of a dark-haired woman whose face he could not bring to focus. Perhaps he had lain with her. But he could not remember.

Lugh's eyes narrowed; he rose from his heavy carved chair and paced around the table, the fur trim at the hem of his black velvet robe swishing across the stone floor.

"Stand up!"

Froech did, though his legs almost failed him. His breath came in shallow gasps.

"Look at me!"

Their eyes met again: Froech's guileless, fearful emerald pale before Lugh's fierce, dark blue.

Lugh's stare reached beyond the boy's eyes, pierced his memory. Froech felt his touch there, fought it to no avail.

Lugh saw everything. Hopes, fears, battles, trysts—lots of those —but no deceptions. And another thing, an image that fled elusively as he pursued it.

But he was the Ard Rhi, Lugh Samildinach, the man skilled at every art, even that of chasing wayward memories. He followed that image though it ran, found it though it hid, ripped it from Froech's mind and read it like a page of illumination.

Froech gasped at the touch of the High King's Power. His entire memory seemed ablaze: five hundred years of life exploded into fragments and swirled around a center of pain like ashes wind-whipped before a firestorm.

"So that is the way of it," Lugh whispered to himself. "That woman I know, I think, though she seems to have gone far down her mother's path to madness since our last meeting—and her brother's way to treachery as well, it would appear. She must have freed Ailill and set herself as his replacement."

He broke the contact then, ignoring Froech's cry of pain as the youth staggered against the table.

"Well, boy, it seems to me that, though foolish, you truly are no traitor."

Froech dragged his head up. "No, Lord."

Lugh twisted absently at a strand of sweeping mustache. "That is a good thing, Froech, for I have a task for you. Ailill must not be allowed to escape my judgment, and I fear what he might do if he reaches the Lands of Men. It may be that he is still in my realm, or it may be that he has passed beyond into the webwork of the Tracks. The former choice I will deal with myself, but the latter I entrust, in part, to you: Go and seek Nuada Airgetlam, who currently travels in the Mortal World. Order him to cease his watching there and commence a search for Windmaster. Now, go!"

Froech managed a shaky bow and turned toward the high bronze door.

Lugh's brow furrowed thoughtfully. "Wait!" he commanded.

Froech spun around.

Lugh's fingers tapped a certain rhythm on the pattern of the table-top before him. A panel opened. He reached forward and drew out two elongated objects masked by matching scabbards of white leather: a dagger and a sword of identical design. Both had gently curving blades and graceful S-curved quillons. Both had ivory hilts rich with jewels and banded gold that exactly continued the curvature of the edges.

Froech's eyes widened in wonder. "They are beautiful, Lord."

Lugh nodded grimly. "Aye." He picked up the sword and balanced it across the palm of one hand as though its weight were nothing. "Take this to Nuada. He will soon grasp its implications."

The youth took the weapon gingerly, then squared his shoulders, bowed stiffly, and clipped the scabbard onto his gold-linked belt.

Lugh waved his dismissal. "Go now and summon the Morrigu to me; then hasten on your errand. Take the fastest horse you can find, or put on the fleetest form your skill commands. But travel quickly, boy, for my wrath will blow behind you, and if it catch you, you may be consumed."

Froech left the room at a run.

The bronze door boomed shut behind him.

Lugh began to stalk the chamber. Sparks leapt from his fingertips whenever he paused to touch an object. The fur trim on his robe crackled ominously. His dark hair lifted beneath its golden circlet. He came to a high-arched window and stared briefly across the empty plains and forests of his kingdom, before his gaze was drawn to the large blotch of map that hung on the wall beside it.

Worked on the thin tanned hide of a golden wyvern, which shape it still bore approximately, Oisin had made that map for him in the days before his blindness. It showed all of Tir-Nan-Og, with the Tracks worked in fine ribbons of beaten gold and the lakes and rivers of quicksilver cased in a film of glass so thin it could be bent like paper and not shatter. Forests were marked by a crust of pounded emeralds, and deserts by ground topazes. A twelve-pointed star of faceted diamonds indicated the palace itself.

Lugh wrenched the map from the wall. He rolled it roughly under his arm, and strode from the room, only pausing at the table to snatch up the dagger he had left there.

Fourteen flights of stairs coiled around him before he reached his throne hall.

The room exploded about him in a thunder of light and color, of white piers and distant silver arches, and windows like frozen fire or burning water. Artfully placed mirrors caught the sun's rays and sent them shooting here and there among the piers and pylons, filling the whole vast chamber with a textured web of light.

There was no movement anywhere, nor any sound except the purposeful slap of Lugh's boots against the mosaicked floor.

At the center of the room was the throne: made of plain, squared stone, as were all royal thrones in Faerie. High-backed it was, and high-armed, cut from the bare rock of the land on which the palace was built. Not apart *from* the land, but a part *of* the land, its roots were one with the roots of the mountains.

Lugh seated himself. "And now, Ailill Windmaster, we will see how clever you really are—and how brave."

He unfolded the map, placed it on the throne's wide left arm, and laid his hand palm-down upon it.

With his right hand he drew forth the ivory-handled dagger and unsheathed it. It gleamed in the morning sunlight. Somewhere a bird called. The only other sound was Lugh's breathing.

He closed his fingers about the hilt, raised the weapon—and stabbed across and downward.

The blade pierced his hand, but he did not cry out, for he felt nothing, so keen was that weapon's edge. It pierced the map of Tir-Nan-Og, and it pierced the stone beneath it.

Lugh left it there, felt the pain awaken.

Blood oozed forth from his palm; he could feel it now, trickling out like cold fire. In a moment it had soaked through the vellum.

Lugh felt the Power start to rise: the Power of the Land and the Power of the High King joined by metal in a bridal bond of ever-increasing pain. He closed his eyes and sent his Power outward.

He did not allow the blood that now crept from between his fingers to pool in random patterns. Rather, he set it to tracing the lines limned upon the map, following them outward toward the border.

It was begun, then: his seeking and his sealing. If Ailill was anywhere in Tir-Nan-Og, the Power Lugh had just unleashed would discover him, and if he had escaped into the Lands of Men, either Nuada would, or else the dark Faery would find himself forced to put on the hated stuff of the Mortal World, or face the ever-increasing strength of the Call, which if unheeded led to madness. Hopefully he would give himself up before that happened—that was the plan. Ailill had sworn himself to Tir-Nan-Og, had joined with it for the time of his service there, was now much more a part of it than of Erenn. And now Lugh had cut him off. The High King could endure the pain—but could Ailill endure the Call that could destroy his mind? It was a gamble, a game of bluff and counterbluff. The waiting had begun—and Lugh was very patient.

At the far end of the hall a lofty door cracked open. The shape of a woman showed there, darkness cut out against light. Tall she was, and dressed in red, with a crow perched on her shoulder.

"You sent for me, Lord?" the Morrigu inquired.

"I have sealed the borders, Lady of War," Lugh told her. "Now, this is what must happen . . ."

Chapter XIV: By Moonlight

(Sullivan Cove, Georgia)

It was just past eleven-thirty when Liz eased the car onto the Sullivan Cove road.

"I dread going home," David sighed, noticing that the lights were still on at his house. "And I *really* dread what Pa's gonna say when I get there. I wouldn't be surprised if he weren't waiting for me belt in hand."

"You two should try not to fight so much," Liz said. "I know you care about each other, you just don't like to show it."

"Yeah, well, it just kind of happens, you know how it is—*Hey, you just missed the driveway!*"

Liz was continuing out the road, her eyes focused straight ahead with deliberate concentration. The headlights picked out a pattern of split rail fences laced with weeds, and fields beyond those fences, with mountains looming above them all like waiting beasts: dark, watchful shadows in the night.

"Liz?"

She grimaced momentarily as the surface roughened, then flashed an amused glance at David. "Well, you said you didn't want to go home yet, and *I* certainly don't want to go home yet, and we're both enjoying the conversation, so I thought I'd see if I could find a good place to finish it. Reckon B.A. Beach'd do?"

"Sounds good to me," David agreed. *Very good*, he added to himself, if it meant what he thought it might.

In a moment they had reached the turnaround, the line of steel gray lake now glimmering under the first stars. The moon was almost full. The best thing, though, was that the place was deserted. Liz pulled over to the right and parked the car.

Wordlessly they got out and began to pick their way across the field to the north, then entered the woods. The tracks Darrell's van had left there six weeks before were still faintly visible, and it was that trail they followed until they lost it and turned left toward the sound of lapping water.

A short while later they came out of the sheltering pines and onto a mossy bank overlooking a thin strip of natural beach. Before them was the lake. To the left, almost hidden by a hump of forested peninsula, was Bloody Bald. The naked rocks at its mortal summit gleamed vaguely pink above a zigzag of trees.

"Too bad we couldn't have come at sunset," David said, pointing at it. "Then I could have given you the Sight, and you could have seen the palace that's really there. Even with the Sight you can see it only at sunset and sunrise. That was the first thing I ever saw that gave me any idea about the Faeries."

Liz did not answer, and David suddenly wondered if she was doing the same thing he was: recalling the last time they'd both been there.

It had been at the end of the previous summer, right after their journey to Faerie. Right before school had started. Right when David was beginning to think their years-old friendship might turn into something more. But he had been too scared, too confused to pursue it, so they had picked blackberries instead and complained about the heat. She had told him that her parents' divorce had been finalized and that she was going to spend the next year in Gainesville with her father. The schools were better there, she had said. They'd almost had a fight, and he'd practically had to bite his tongue to keep from smarting off. He had always wondered if she'd noticed.

"I didn't dare try for Lookout," Liz whispered. "Couldn't get all the way in the car, and didn't want to risk your folks seeing us, anyway. No way we could have gone up that road unnoticed." Her voice quivered ever so slightly.

"Right," David mumbled awkwardly. "Sure."

They sat down on a layer of smooth pine straw atop a carpet of moss. Thirty feet beyond them water lapped gently against the rocky shore. The moss felt cool beneath them, and they kicked off their shoes.

David flopped back against a fallen tree trunk, and Liz lay down beside him. They looked up at a medallion of starlit sky that was brighter by far than the trees that framed it in three directions.

Liz took a deep breath. "I've missed you, David."

David's breath was even deeper, and tinged with a trace of nervousness. "I've missed you too, Liz. I— Why was it so hard for me to say that?"

Liz rolled onto her side and plucked a dandelion that grew between them, then looked up at David as she rolled the stem between her fingers.

"I can't answer that, David—but I think you ought to listen to what your heart's saying once in a while. You might get some interesting answers."

David regarded her seriously. "Do you do that, Liz? Do you listen to your heart?"

"Always; even when my head seems to be ruling, it's my heart that's giving it the choices."

David folded his arms behind his head. "You were pretty good about that during the Trial of Heroes. Do you really think I was that way then? The selfless hero? Funny, I can never think of myself as a hero—even though I've gone through the ritual to prove it. It doesn't make any difference in the real world."

"You're a hero, David," Liz said slowly, "because what you did wasn't for yourself. It was for other people."

"Yeah, I guess." David cleared his throat and swallowed. "But that's getting off the subject. I've . . . I've said one thing that was hard to say and shouldn't have been, and now I'm gonna say another. I . . . Oh, I don't know."

Liz laid a finger against his lips. "Don't rush, David. Heart over head. Just turn off your brain and let your tongue go."

David grinned nervously and folded the hand in his own, lowered it to his chest. "Easy for you to say."

"What are you afraid of?" Liz asked quietly. "Surely it can't be of me."

"Liz, I thought about you all summer," David blurted out. "I mean I met a lot of girls at Governor's Honors. Lots of bright girls, nice-looking girls. Kind of girls I ought to be attracted to. Kind of girls my body told me I *was* attracted to. Some of 'em liked me, too. But there was no sparkle, Liz, no magic—not the kind I get from you."

"That's good to hear."

The corners of David's mouth quirked upward in a foolish smile. "Yeah, well, I hoped it would be."

Liz's tone turned serious. "The same thing happened to me, David, down in Gainesville, but I didn't dare do anything. Because there was always you in the back of my mind, doing crazy things, with your brain running ten times as fast as your mouth, and your imagination ten times faster than that."

"Liz . . . Do you want to know something really scary?"

"How scary?"

"Pretty scary."

Liz raised an eyebrow. "Tell me, and I'll let you know."

"I think I love you."

"I love you, too, Davy, and there's no 'think' about it—but you know, I'm not sure I could have said it until just now."

David grinned and levered himself up on his elbow. Moonlight cast a silver-blue veil across Liz's features.

"You want to know something *really* awful?"

"Awful as that was scary?"

"Worse: I've never kissed a girl. Seventeen years old and never kissed a girl."

"That I don't believe."

"Well," David amended, "never kissed a girl like I meant it."

Liz's eyes twinkled. "That's more likely. Now, *you* want to know something?"

"Sure."

"I've never kissed a boy!"

"That can be easily remedied."

Liz's breath was a touch of sweetness on David's cheek. He moved toward her, slid his left hand over her waist, and pulled her to him.

It was awkward and funny—clumsy and quite simply the most wonderful feeling he had ever known: her soft lips, her wonderfully firm and supple body next to his. They broke apart, smiled foolishly, then drew together again, this time with more authority.

And something awoke within David—something that had never been far from the surface but which he had ruthlessly denied.

"Shirt's a little hot for close contact," he mumbled. He pulled away and skinned off his CommArts jersey.

The third kiss lasted a very long time. But finally they separated, giggling like idiots for no apparent reason.

David rolled onto his back, facing the stars. Liz flopped over on her belly and began to run her fingertips lightly over his smooth, hairless chest. "I've always envied you this," she said.

"Huh? Surely you don't want to be flat-chested!"

"No, foolish boy, being able to go shirtless whenever you want to. Being free about your body . . . Going skinny-dipping with Alec."

David's eyes flicked sideways and caught her own. "You've envied Alec a lot, haven't you?"

"Yeah . . . I mean, I know he's your best friend, and all. But he's been so close to you so long—he knows so much more about you. He's seen so much more of you—both figuratively and literally—than I have."

David took her hand and kissed it. "I can't help that, Liz, and I wouldn't want to. But you want to know something funny? He's been pushing me toward you, too, just like everybody else. He could see what I couldn't—or wouldn't."

Liz's finger began to trace the curved outline of David's pectoral muscles, occasionally venturing up to mid chest, more rarely and more enticingly slipping down the valley of his stomach to draw circles around his navel.

"Know something?" she whispered.

"Hmmm?"

"I like you better when you don't talk so much."

"Do something about it then."

She did.

Eventually David slipped his hand under her T-shirt. She wasn't wearing a bra, he'd known that. And she did not resist, though he heard her breath catch. Her breasts were small, no more than a palmed handful. But they were firm and smooth, and they responded to his touch.

Liz's hands too began to wander, becoming ever more venturesome. Even as David's hands slid down to probe at the waist band of her jeans, her hands found the top of his.

He reached down and popped the snap, unzipped his fly.

"What the heck," he muttered, and sat up to slide them the rest of the way off.

He looked inquiringly at Liz, reached down to tug shyly at the tail of her T-shirt.

"Your move."

"I . . . I don't know, David." She looked suddenly very unhappy.

David fought the urge to snap at her. Romantic that he was, he could not have contrived better circumstances than these—and he'd never been so intimate with a girl. But Liz was frightened, and, he admitted, so was he. There'd be other times. Just once he'd do the right thing when it came to Liz. But still . . . maybe . . .

"Yeah, all right," he said at last, looking away. "But since you've got me all hot and bothered, you've got to help me cool off."

A faint frown furrowed her brow. "What do you mean?"

David pointed at the lake and wagged a mischievous eyebrow. "Skinny-dipping. Then you won't have any reason to be jealous of Alec anymore; you'll know as much about the bod as he does. More in fact, since you already know what most of it feels like."

Abruptly, he stood up, stepped into the moonlight, then glanced around. Liz was still hesitating. He stretched a hand toward her. She took it and he pulled her to her feet.

He raised her hand to his lips and kissed it once with extravagant chivalry, then grinned and sprinted to the shore.

With one decisive move, he skinned his skivvies off. The night breeze was cool against his bare skin, and he shivered slightly.

"You've got a cute fanny, you know that, David Sullivan?" Liz giggled nervously as she joined him.

David felt himself blushing. "I guess I do now."

"Well, seeing you in one of those little Speedo bathing suits kinda woke my suspicions—but I think I like the real thing even better."

"I think this is gonna be fun." David grinned. "Alec never tells me things like this."

"I hope not!"

He paused, staring at her, hoping the eagerness he felt stirring within him would not show in the moonlight. "It's kinda your turn now . . . I mean if you don't want to take it all off, you don't have to, just 'cause I did. Course, you'll have wet clothes to explain otherwise. *Because I'll throw you in!*"

He made a grab for her, but she sideslipped him and turned away. Her back to him, she stripped in a series of efficient movements.

David could not help the smile that broke out on his face when she turned back around. "You've got a cute—a cute everything, Liz."

She stepped closer.

He thought of something then, reached back and unhooked the chain that held the ring. He cupped it in his palm for a moment, staring at it, then took Liz's hand and slipped the silver circle onto her finger.

She looked up at him uncertainly.

David stopped the unspoken protest with a finger against her lips. "Just until I can get another. It's the most precious thing I own—or maybe the second most precious, now. But it's not really mine to give—not yet. I don't know how I know that, but I do. But for now . . ."

"You know—"

"You know, I think kissing you naked in the moonlight's more of a fantasy of mine than anything in Faerie."

Liz's eyes twinkled. *"Anything?"*

David smiled awkwardly. "Well, almost."

They kissed again, standing on the beach with sun-warmed lake water nipping at their toes. Liz began to giggle, and David found himself tickling her ribs. She pulled away. He reached for her, lost his footing. They fell into the shallows, came up laughing.

"We did come to cool off," Liz gasped between fits of mirth.

"We?"

"Of course," Liz snorted indignantly. "You're not the only one with hormones, David Sullivan."

They waded a bit farther out, until they felt the lake floor falling away. Eventually they were swimming. David hadn't realized how hot he'd been, until he felt the water swallow him. He dived; surfaced; dived again. Felt Liz near him in the water and broke surface with her. Ventured a kiss—and felt the fire reawaken. He pulled away, suddenly embarrassed.

Again he dove, and felt the water's sensuous caress upon his body, now less sensuous than his memory of Liz's touch.

His hand brushed fingers: soft and delicate.

He grasped the hand eagerly, began to pull it toward him, toward the surface. He was getting low on air, though the notion of an underwater kiss was certainly intriguing. Perhaps a little later...

But that hand was pulling him *downward!* Downward into the dark with a greater strength than he'd ever expected from Liz. His chest began to throb; red lights swam behind his eyes. His head hurt. And still he felt that tugging. He tried to focus the Sight, but could not. Why was she doing this? And who was *she?* His thoughts were slow, dull. Like he was going to sleep.

Why?

Bubbles trickled from his mouth.

Why?

Asleep.

Asl...

Somewhere above him, closer to shore, a silver ring woke upon Liz's finger, sending pulses of heat up her arms. Bright as day the ring glared into her startled eyes.

"David!" she whispered as the awful truth struck her. "No! Not now! Not now!"

PART III

FLAMES

Chapter XV: Water, Fog, and Fire

(Sullivan Cove, Georgia— Sunday, August 4)

"Not now!" Liz gasped aloud as she surfaced, desperate for air. "Oh God, Davy, *no!*"

Light flashed into her eyes so brightly that it hurt. She looked down, saw David's ring glowing white-hot like a magnesium flare. It burned against her skin too, becoming hotter with each passing second. *So this is what it feels like*, she realized. *The mystery of the ring.*

Davy!

She dove then, farther and farther down, until the water became as cold and dark as the knot of fear in her stomach. Her chest grew tight. Her fingers brushed a tangle of slimy weeds, then muddy sand.

Davy?

And distant as a dream, words filled her mind, like a brush of cold air behind her eyes: *He lives, girl. Now begone. This realm is mine.*

Davy...

Silence.

Davy...?

And then silence gave way to despair.

Help: she had to get help, had to find someone to help her—to comb the bottom till they found him, maybe. If necessary drain the lake—

No! She gave herself a mental slap—she was being irrational. She had to help David, but panic would do no good.

She broke surface again, took blessed mouthfuls of air. The moon beat down upon her, cold and distant. Water glittered blue and silver about her. And the ring no longer glowed, no longer warmed her hand. She wondered what that meant. It had to have some sort of limit of detection, she supposed, so David must truly be gone. But whose thought was it that had sounded in her mind? Somehow it had seemed female. Yet David didn't know any women of the Sidhe— did he? *He'd better not!*

Her toes touched bottom, and she dragged herself to shore, toweled herself vaguely dry with David's discarded jersey, and dressed hurriedly. After a moment's indecision, she picked up the rest of his clothes and made a clumsy bundle of them. A brief search for his glasses proved unsuccessful, and then she remembered that he hadn't worn them since some time in the spring. The Sight had done that much for him, at least. But it hadn't kept him from being captured—if that was what had happened.

Suddenly it was a long way to the car. As suddenly she was running. Branches tore at her, fallen limbs tripped her as she fought her way through the intervening wood. Her breath quickened, became a series of short, painful gasps, each a greater torment to her lungs. Eventually she developed a stitch in her side that made her cry out. She careened to a stop, panting heavily, fingers digging into the sticky bark of a pine tree. Finally the pain faded, and she was off again. Briars ripped her flesh, and then there was open space about her and broom sedge flogging her legs.

She reached the car, threw David's clothes in the back, but then hesitated. It wouldn't do for someone to find them there and ask questions. Resentful of the time it took, she stowed them in the cubby where the spare tire went.

Now where to go, she wondered. Not to David's parents; they'd only go to pieces. And besides, David had left home under a cloud of anger, and she'd sort of been an accomplice. And she was wet—they'd wonder what the two of them had been up to, and while she wasn't exactly ashamed, it wasn't the sort of added complication she wanted to deal with just then. The absurd image of a shotgun wedding with JoAnne Sullivan wielding the gun appeared from nowhere in her mind.

God, how stupid! Panic was making her silly.

She cranked the car, slipped it into first, then paused. *Alec, maybe?* No, wait, better Nuada first. This was a Faery problem, let them provide the answers.

She mashed the gas, sending the little car skittering over the rough gravel as it tore back up the road.

Far ahead and to the right she could see a corner of Davy's house silhouetted against the night. No lights burned there except the single mercury vapor in the yard.

But there *were* lights closer by: at Uncle Dale's cozy cabin. Now, that was an idea! He had always seemed more sensitive to what was going on with her and Davy than anyone else in David's family. And he had always been open-minded. After all, he had sensed the presence of the banshee that had almost taken him last summer. And maybe he knew about the Tracks as well, and the Sidhe. He'd said some things . . .

Almost without thinking she found herself turning up his narrow, rocky driveway.

She dared not stop to compose her story. If she did, she might simply quit—might just drive on and on till she ran out of gas, and then press on afoot. But she knew she could not do that.

Hurry, girl, hurry, she told herself. Park the car . . . up the long flight of wooden steps . . . onto the porch, not caring how loud her staccato tread sounded on the ancient boards.

A knock on the screen door. Another. And then, as fear finally took her, a pounding. Her knuckles hurt.

A naked light bulb came on among the exposed beams of the sloped porch roof above her. The inside door cracked open, then swung wide, as Uncle Dale unhooked the screen. He was dressed in a pair of rumpled khaki work pants and a worn white undershirt. Without his glasses, his deep-set eyes were nests of squinting darkness.

"Why, Liz, girl, what in the world are you doin' here this time of night? What's happened?" His gaze darted over her—missing nothing, she was certain—at last coming to rest on the ring. An eyebrow lifted ever so slightly, and a ghost of a smile twitched across his lips, before his mouth hardened. "It's Davy, ain't it? Somethin's happened to Davy? And I just bet you it's somethin' . . . unusual."

Liz nodded breathlessly, suddenly unable to speak. She made no move to go into the house. "Yeah," she panted. "Davy and I were swimming, and . . . and he dove down deep and disappeared."

Uncle Dale grasped her by her shoulders. "Swimming? You mean he's drowned?"

Liz shook her head. "No. No—I don't know. I don't think so. No," she finished decisively. "It was—" Her voice froze. "I heard a—"

Her eyes widened in horror. "Oh, God! I can't tell you. I *can't* tell you! But believe me, oh please, Uncle Dale, believe me! We've got to get to the Traders, they're our only hope. They're from Ireland and this is an . . . an Irish matter."

Uncle Dale fixed her with an appraising stare, then steered her through the doorway. "Come on in, girl. Let me get you some coffee. Get you a towel."

"You believe me?"

The old man paused in midstep. "I believe you're scared to death, and I know you well enough to know you don't scare easy. But you're not actin' like you think Davy's dead, so you must think he's still alive. Must be somethin' like what happened to Little Billy, maybe? Somethin' to do with them funny-lookin' folks he kept talkin' about? Like that boy I saw when I had that stroke that time."

Liz's eyes widened incredulously. "You saw that?"

"Saw somethin'. Teenage-lookin' boy in funny clothes. Thought he was an angel, only he didn't act like one. Finally told myself it was a dream so I could sleep with some peace of mind; you may have noticed I been goin' to church more lately. Now let me get that coffee. Maybe hot cider? Yeah, that'd be better," he muttered as he shuffled into the kitchen.

Liz flopped back on the sofa and closed her eyes. She had a headache, she realized. She stared at the fireplace on the opposite wall, at the stuffed deer head above it. And that reminded her of what David had said about the Crazy Deer. But that had been male, hadn't it—she thought that was what David had told her. And the mind that had touched hers had been a woman's, she was almost sure of that. She shook her head. It made no sense.

Uncle Dale returned a moment later with a steaming mug. "Might be a touch hot. Did it in the microwave. There's a little 'shine in there with the cider—help you calm your nerves."

Liz took it with shaking hands.

"Now, what was that you was tryin' to say?"

Liz set her mouth, forcing herself to remain calm. "It was the Shh— The Irish F-f-f— Uncle Dale, what has David told you about last year? About—about when you were sick? About all that run of bad luck, when Little Billy was catatonic, and all that?"

The old man scratched his beard thoughtfully. "Hmmm. Never told me nothin'—not directly—and I didn't ask. But I figured out a lot. Took a look or two at some of them books of his. Always liked books, I did—boy takes after me there. Figured David was actin' strange for a good reason, recalled what my daddy used to say about that old Indian trail. Put two and two together. Don't know what the answer was though."

"I do," Liz began: "A little over a year ago Davy heard music one night and followed it into the woods behind his house. He met some p-p-p—" Her tongue froze in her mouth. *Shit! The blessed Ban of Lugh again. What a time for* that *to rear its ugly head.* She started over: "It was the—" Her tongue locked tight.

"Tell me!"

"I *can't!*" she almost sobbed.

"Sure you can."

"No, I can't. My tongue won't work. It's mmmmm—"

Uncle Dale chewed on his upper lip for a moment. "You really can't? Like somethin's *keepin'* you from talkin'?"

Liz nodded vigorously.

"Like magic, maybe?"

Liz nodded again.

"Well, that clinches it, then. You say some of them Irish fellers might be able to help? Well, I guess we'd better be gettin' over there, then." He stood up abruptly and stalked toward his bedroom.

"You mean you'll help me? You'll come along?"

He nodded. "Just let me get my shirt—gun too, I guess."

A disturbing thought struck Liz. "What about his folks?"

"Bill and JoAnne?" Uncle Dale called from his room. "No time for them. They'd just cause trouble if this is the kind of thing I think it might be. If everythin' works out, maybe they won't find out. We'll give it a try. But if we don't learn somethin' in a hurry, I don't see as how we've any choice but to tell them and then get ahold of the sheriff."

"Yeah, I guess you're right."

They made it to Enotah in a time that David would have been proud of, and then pressed on to MacTyrie. Uncle Dale drove Liz's car, roughly at first, but later with surprising finesse and authority. Liz allowed herself ten minutes of tears, grateful for the silence that had fallen. She was beginning to consider the implications now, each more dire than the last. She had feared the old man might ask her to explain what she and David had been doing, but he had asked no questions. All he'd inquired about had been the ring.

"Davy gave you that?" he'd asked.

She'd nodded.

"Tonight?"

"Yeah."

"'Bout time" had been his only comment.

"Want to stop and get Alec?" Uncle Dale asked, as they sailed across the long curve of the MacTyrie bridge.

Liz shook her head. "Not now. Maybe later, if this doesn't work out. For now just hurry. Something tells me we need to hurry."

"You're the boss," the old man replied, and turned north toward the ball field.

Two minutes later they lurched to a halt outside the Traders' encampment.

Liz threw open the car door and hit the ground running, but Uncle Dale called her back.

"Hold on there, girl! Folks as old as me can't run much fast. You may be the guide, but a guide with nobody to follow ain't worth a lot."

In spite of her panic Liz found herself smiling. She stopped and waited for him.

A glare of headlights cut the night then, making her blink as they flashed across the side of the concession stand and the wire-wall of kudzu.

A car horn sounded as a flaming red Chrysler Laser scrunched to a halt behind them. A throb of too-loud Smithereens quieted. Voices called her name—and David's, she thought: young male voices. A head of short, dark hair stuck itself up above the driver's side of the car's T-bar roof.

"It's Gary!" Liz told Uncle Dale, "Gary Hudson—one of David's friends. Wonder what *he's* doing here?"

And then another boy was clambering over the door on the far side and into the ghastly blue glare of the single streetlight.

It was Alec, running on ahead while an apparently unconcerned Gary sauntered over to look at Liz's car.

"Liz!" Alec sighed when he reached her, looking very relieved. "Thank the Lord we've found you!" He noticed Uncle Dale then, and his cheeks puffed in consternation. *"You're* not Davy!" he exclaimed.

"David's gone, boy," Uncle Dale said solemnly. "Tell him, Liz."

"It was the Fff—" Liz began, and found her tongue once again locked tight.

Alec bent close and whispered in her ear too quietly for the old man to hear, "Faeries?"

She nodded vigorously, then saw him looking at the ring. "He gave it to me before— We were over at B.A. swimming. I think one of them . . . caught him."

She dragged Alec far enough away from Uncle Dale to be able to speak freely. In a few short phrases, she sketched out the story of David's disappearance.

"Christ!" he groaned when she had finished. "Good thing we came along when we did."

Liz frowned at him uncertainly. "Yeah, but what are you *doing* here?"

"Good question, girl," Alec responded quickly. "Your mom called my house about ten minutes ago wanting to know if you were there. Said she'd called up at Davy's, and you weren't back yet, so she hoped you were at mine."

Liz rolled her eyes in dismay. "What'd you tell her?"

"What'd you think? I told her you'd said something about going back to see the Traders; finally had to promise her we'd go check and send you home if we found you. Figured that was safest for both of you. Darrell went to check out the Tastee Freeze; he may be by a little later."

Gary trotted up to join the group, a gray shadow in nondescript sweatpants and jacket.

"Nice car, Liz!" he panted. "How 'bout a ride sometime?" Then he too noticed Uncle Dale. "Hey, where's Sullivan?"

"Gone," Alec hedged carefully.

"What d'you mean, gone?"

"I mean gone, like in 'not here.' Not *anywhere,* possibly."

Gary frowned.

Alec laid an arm across his shoulder and drew him aside. "Look, G-man, Liz and I kind of need to talk privately, so could you, like, boogie off a ways. I'll fill you in later."

"Oh, come on, man . . ."

Liz eyed Gary nervously. "Please, Gary," she said. "I— We have some business inside. So could you sort of wait out here?"

"No way," Gary replied, shaking his head emphatically. "No goddamn way. Hell, girl, all I have to do is look at your face to figure out one thing: you're scared as shit. Something weird's going on, and I aim to find out what."

"It's none of your business, Gary."

"None of my business! Well, maybe not, but it's sure as hell somebody's business, and I think it concerns Davy, who's my friend, which *makes* it my business. I mean, what is this crap about him being gone, anyway? Sure sounds weird to me. And that business just then—that stuff about not being able to talk; you think I didn't see that? And you wanta know something? It was just like something I saw old Mad Dave do right before him and McLean left for Valdosta. I saw that note you wrote him, too: the one about the book and the otherworld. And I've heard a bunch of other stuff."

Liz sighed and folded her arms in exasperation. "Oh, all right. I don't have time to argue."

She led the way through the turnstile, followed closely by Uncle Dale, Alec, and Gary. Something made a clinking noise behind her, and she looked back, noticing for the first time that Alec wore shiny links of metal chain threaded through his belt loops, with a heavy combination lock for a buckle. It had struck against the iron post.

Alec noticed her looking. "It's a MacTyrie Gang affectation," he told her, "nothing more."

She shrugged and pressed on ahead, passing quickly under the sagging roof and into the Traders' camp.

Once again the vague sense of otherness folded itself about them, seeming at once to rise from the short, damp grass beneath their feet and to trickle down from the clear heavens above them. The sky shone midnight blue, the wagons and tents were cutout shapes of blackness

except where torches flared in the center of their circle, mixing fire gold
with the gilded reds and greens and purples of the wagons, and the more
sullen green of the tents. A sparse ground fog had begun to ease up from
the river, and dark-clad shapes stalked here and there within it, flickering silently among the wisps like distant memories.

One of those shapes stopped, looked around, then turned toward
them. As it approached it clarified into a tall, blond man with a
single arm.

As the rest of the group held back, Alec and Liz rushed forward
to meet him. A horse whickered somewhere, as if alarmed.

"I thought I was finished with you," Nuada cried loudly with
unexpected (and unjustified, Liz thought) anger. "Can we get no rest
from you? Disturbance and more disturbance, and still the horses
need tending." He reached over and grasped Liz's shoulder roughly,
his mouth a hard, fierce line.

Her mouth gaped in horror. But the words began to shape themselves in her mind.

*Ignore my voice, girl. There is fear here. I can hear it as if it
were screamed aloud. Quick, take the boy's hand. He should hear
this as well.*

Liz reached down surreptitiously and enfolded Alec's fingers.
Somewhere above her she heard the voice of the Faery lord still
berating her, but this was a public show; the real conversation was on
another level, at a point of finely compressed time.

*No need to talk. Nothing is clear to me of what has happened, but
with what you told me before, I have no good feeling about it.*

But I haven't told you yet!

Images speak faster than words and with more eloquence.

Can you help us?

*I do not know. I should notify Lugh. Our role here is not to
interfere. You know what that may bring.*

But David's gone!

But alive! You showed me that! You believe that!

Nuada—

I will do what I can. But these others . . .?

Our friends: David's Uncle Dale; his friend, Gary Hudson.

Very well, then, come along.

"It's okay," Liz said aloud, when she and Alec rejoined the group
a moment later. "We can all come."

A thought echoed in Liz's mind, then; not Nuada, but another
heard from farther away. Calming. A woman's thought, but not one
she had touched before. *He lives, girl. Your heart tells you that.*

There is nothing to fear. But you must keep your head clear, keep yourself in control.

They gathered in Nuada's tent, a motley crew. The three Sidhe: Cormac and Regan and Nuada; Lin the Trader and a gray-haired woman they had not met before but who introduced herself as Katie. She and Lin kept well to the background, saying little but missing nothing.

Gary smiled uncertainly, as if he sensed some vague wrongness about the circumstances that he couldn't quite put a finger on. Uncle Dale seemed blessed with infinite patience, though he took the pipe Nuada offered. Alec looked as edgy as Liz felt.

Nuada stared at the assembled company, then spoke: "Some of you know, though perhaps not all"—he fixed Gary with his gaze—"that David Sullivan has disappeared." He cleared his throat and continued. "And believe me, I would not reveal what I am about to reveal to the ignorant among you, were I not convinced of the need for haste. I will mince no words: what we must speak of—what we must use in order to find him—is Power. Mortals would call it magic."

"Magic," Gary whispered. "I don't believe in magic."

"You better learn, then," Alec gritted. "Look, Davy's in trouble. These folks can help him. They're the—" He looked imploringly at Nuada.

Nuada smiled briefly then. "Ah, yes, Lugh's ban. Well, I can be of some help there, for I am his warlord and charged with enforcing his laws. And if I choose *not* to enforce the law, then the accounting is on my head."

"—the Sidhe," Alec finished suddenly. "The Irish fairies. Like in those books David was always reading."

"I think I believe you," Gary said with simple acceptance.

Liz nodded, wide-eyed. "Believe him."

Nuada sighed with some exasperation. "Good folk, I do not choose to reveal myself or my companions—or the Power we command—lightly, but I fear I must. David Sullivan has vanished under mysterious circumstances. I think we may yet be able to find him, if we hurry. If Liz is willing."

Liz nodded. "Anything. Just get him back."

"Very well. We will need a focus. And we will need to put away the substance of this World."

"What's he talking about?" Gary whispered in Alec's ear.

"What they're made out of," Alec grunted back from between his teeth.

Cormac rose. His fellows joined him, three points of triangle.

"We could perhaps do it in man's substance," Nuada said, "but the substance of Faerie works far better. Liz, if you would come stand between us?"

Liz nodded and moved to the center.

"You do not have anything in your possession that belongs to David, do you?"

Liz shook her head, then remembered the ring. "This?"

Nuada's eyes widened slightly, but he shook his head. "No, that is too powerful a focus. It has had too many owners."

Alec riffled his pockets, and pulled out the bloodstained handkerchief he had given David when he had cut his finger on the mountain. "What about this?" he offered. "I'd forgotten I had it; it's even got some of his blood on it."

Nuada took the square of brown-stained fabric. "Oh, aye! That will do very well indeed!" He handed it to Liz. "Lady, if you will . . .?"

Liz took it solemnly and wadded it into her fist as the Sidhe joined hands, with Cormac resting his left one on Nuada's shoulder.

Light filled the room: a white glow that seemed to emanate from the tall forms themselves. It was a cold light, and it brought with it a sound of music: a soft tinkling like harp strings and bells.

Then as quickly as it had come, the light was gone. The Sidhe released their grip on one another's hands. They looked no different, except that there was now a sort of glow upon them. Or glory, Liz thought.

"Like angels," Uncle Dale breathed. "Oh, Hattie, I wish you could see this!"

Nuada closed his eyes for a moment, then reopened them and rested his single hand on Liz's right shoulder. She found herself returning his stare. Her eyelids grew heavy, and she felt her body released from the tension that had filled it for what seemed like hours.

"Water," Nuada whispered after a moment, then: "Cold. And a place of fire—that I do not understand, for it is not of Tir-Nan-Og, nor of the Lands of Men either. A desire for vengeance, too, that is hotter than Fire. And fear: the fear of a mortal boy alone in an unknown place."

"Where?" Alec cried urgently. "Where, Silverhand? Liz?"

Nuada shook his head. "Water. And a not-place and . . . Aiiiiieeeeeeeeee!!!"

The Faery lord's scream cut the thick silence of the tent. The Sidhe seemed to collapse upon themselves. Their glory faded as they became human once again. One by one they sank to the floor.

Katie's brogue floated thick upon the air: "Mother of God!"

"Nuada!" Alec gasped as he rushed forward. "Liz!"

Liz swayed, but remained standing as Alec caught her. "Liz, what happened?"

Within the circle of Alec's arms, Liz found herself shaking. "It was awful, Alec. We could see David—alive. Feel his fear. But then it was like a knife cut through our thoughts."

Nuada began to stir. "It is Tir-Nan-Og," he said heavily. "We are cut off, Powerless, forced to put on the flesh of mortal men to save our minds."

"What do you mean?" Liz cried frantically. "What about Davy? Can't you reach him?"

Nuada wiped a long-fingered hand across his eyes and shook his head. "Not without more Power than we can now muster: the substance of Faerie was the source of our Power, and now we may not reach it. It is possible that a little may remain trapped within us, but it will quickly fade and cannot be renewed, nor will these bodies allow us to use more than a trickle of *that* at a time."

Liz looked hopelessly confused.

Regan laid a hand upon her shoulder. "It is what Nuada spoke of earlier as something that could never happen, yet now it has: something has snapped the thread that binds us to our homeland, the thread down which our Power flows. We had to return to the substance of this world, or face the Call that denied leads on to madness. We have a problem of our own now. But that does not mean we will not help you."

Liz looked up at her. "But—"

Shouts from outside interrupted her. "I *will* go in," a male voice snapped clearly. From his place by the door Lin jumped to his feet, but almost fell backward again as the curtained front was thrust open. A Faery youth stood there, looking more than a little dazed and angry. His hair was black and he wore a black silk cloak above a loose velvet tunic, from the heavy linked belt of which depended a sword hilted in gold and ivory.

"Froech!" Nuada cried, rising unsteadily to his feet. "What in the name of Dana brings you here?"

"I am too late, Lord. And I beg your forgiveness."

"That may very well be true," Nuada replied dryly. "But if I am to forgive you I must know your crime."

"It is Ailill, Lord. He has escaped. His sister aided him, and it is believed he fled onto the Tracks, or else into this World. Lugh sent me to tell you this, and then, as I see you have discovered, he sealed the borders. One word only he had for you. And that was to seek Ailill in the Lands of Men, or if need be, through all the Worlds."

Nuada's face went suddenly pale. "*Not Fionna!*" he cried. "And me with no more strength than a mortal. She is among the strongest of her folk; I would think twice about matching Power with her even were I in my own flesh!"

"But what does it mean that Lugh has sealed the borders?" Alec burst out. "How could anyone do that? I know he's powerful, but—"

"The King is the Land," Nuada replied tersely. "The Land is the King. He has built a wall, you see, a wall of arcane fire fueled by his own blood that surrounds Tir-Nan-Og, not only where it touches other lands, but where it touches other Worlds as well. We cannot go back now, for though we might follow the Tracks there, we could not get off them. The Walls between the Worlds, once clear, are now opaque and faced with fire."

Froech interrupted. "Pardon, Lord, but Lugh's command was for action, not talk."

Nuada frowned. "I have known Lugh somewhat longer than you, boy."

Chastened, Froech inclined his head slightly. "Aye, Lord."

Uncle Dale levered himself up. "Now, what's this? Somethin' goin' on we ought to know about?"

Froech's gaze fell on the old man. *"More* mortals, Silverhand? What is wrong with that one? Is it *age?"*

"It would seem we are all mortals here, Froech, except yourself, though it will not be long before the Call comes upon you. You would have served yourself better to have put on the stuff of this World."

"It did not occur to me, Lord, while I was within Lugh's realm, for I do not often visit other Worlds, and then but briefly. And by the time I was on the Tracks and did think of it, it was too late: the thread was severed. Lugh should have warned me of the sealing, at least. I—"

Nuada held up a quieting hand. "Enough, Froech. Perhaps it is fortunate that you kept Faery flesh, for that makes you the mightiest of us all, and we may need your Power later. We now have two problems to consider, though they are not necessarily things apart from one another: to seek David Sullivan, who has been stolen by someone evidently of Faery blood, and to seek Ailill Windmaster."

"You are correct, Lord," Regan said. "But I think it quite likely that the two might be bound together. Recall what young David told us only this afternoon about what he called the Crazy Deer."

"Right!" Alec cried almost eagerly. "And if the Crazy Deer was Ailill, then we know where to find him, or where to start, anyway."

Nuada looked at him thoughtfully. "I have been wrong, Alec McLean, for not listening to you before; I thought in my folly that Ailill was beyond reach. But he too numbers some few friends, and his sister first among them. I have met Fionna nic Bobh, and she is not someone with whom I would choose to spend much time. Can you take us to where you saw this deer?"

"But you're forgetting about David," Liz almost screamed, as her control slipped away.

Katie tottered forward, setting her feet carefully among the scattered cushions and guttering candles. She took Liz in her arms. "No, child, they ain't forgettin'. But it seems to Katie that if they find the one, there's a good chance they'll be findin' the other."

Liz nodded slowly, but buried her head in the old woman's shoulder.

"So," said Nuada, "here is what we should do: Froech, you and Cormac—"

Sirens split the night, pouring chills down the necks of the mortals and setting all eyes to darting furtively about.

"Christ, it's the cops!" Gary shouted.

"Cops?"

"Huh?"

Liz looked up in consternation. "What would the cops be doing here?"

Alec stuck his head outside the tent. "Cops, all right," he called softly. "Out by the gate." He suppressed a giggle. "Looks like they've caught Darrell—can't hardly tell for the kudzu."

"He *was* coming by if the Tastee Freeze didn't pan out," Gary noted, as he joined his smaller friend at the front slit. "I've warned him about that blessed muffler of his."

"Right," Alec replied, "but if they find your cars, they might start to get other ideas. I know they don't like having the Traders around, and this might just give 'em the excuse they're looking for: corrupting minors, or something." He looked around, embarrassed. "Sorry, Lin; but not everyone knows the truth. Folks up here can be mighty suspicious of outsiders."

"Hey, Alec, I think a couple of 'em *are* coming this way."

"Better do something quick," Uncle Dale urged from behind them. "Won't do us no good to get caught here."

"Nor for them to find these folks—'specially Mr. Froech and them fancy clothes of his," Lin added. "Don't want anybody askin' questions about *Them*."

"Aye, yer right there," Katie affirmed.

"We need a diversion," said Nuada. "Froech, since the three of us are Powerless, could you cast a glamour?"

"What kind? In this land I am unaccustomed—"

"Never mind that stuff," Lin said decisively, as he shouldered his way through the door slit. "You folks be gettin' outta here. I'll take care of the law—had years o' practice at it. Come on, Katie, you wake the wagons; tell 'em it's the burnin' plan."

As the others made their way outside, Liz saw the Trader chief run into the circle of tents and grab a smoking brand from the smoldering camp fire in the center.

"Fire! Fire!" he yelled, as he swung it thrice around his head to fan the flames, then tossed it atop one of the canvas roofs.

"Empty," he confided to the startled Alec, who dogged his heels. "We make our numbers look greater by using lots o' empty tents. Fire! Fire!" he cried again, almost gaily, as he torched another tent, then crammed a fist into his pocket and flung something toward the startled boy that jingled as it arched through the air. "Here's the keys, boy. Open the gates; take the horses! Now! Take 'em and ride! We'll hold here. Fire and fog be a fugitive's friends, as my ol' da used to say."

The first two tents had already begun to send sparks shimmering into the sky as Lin fired a third. In the circle of wagons beyond them Katie was pounding on wooden half-doors with her cane, crying, "Get up! Get up!" at the top of her lungs.

The bitter smell of smoke began to thicken the air.

"Quick!" Nuada cried, waving an encompassing arm at all four mortals. "Better all of you are with us."

More sirens then, and flashing blue lights out by the gate. Fire and smoke everywhere. Half-dressed men and women scrambled out of wagons, stared around in confusion, then joined the fray as realization dawned on them, and they began running hither and thither in contrived confusion, some heaving buckets of water on burning canvas even as others set more fires.

Liz could see figures moving around beyond the fence, too: blue-clad men pushing through the turnstile and sprinting across the grass toward them. And a boy who looked like Darrell. He fell; another helped him up. Something bumped her shoulder, and she glanced around, saw Froech beside her, already mounted on the horse he had posted beside Nuada's tent.

And then, to her horror, the Faery youth leveled an outstretched arm at the blazing tents, then arced it around the whole campsite as though cracking an invisible whip. Flames followed that unseen wake, leaping from those already burning to embrace the remaining tents—and the deliberately untouched wagons beyond as well. Even the grass came alight as a wall of flame reared itself across half the enclosure, cutting off the approaching policemen.

"No, not our wagons!" somebody screamed.

"Fool of a boy," Nuada cried furiously, as Froech's horse brushed by him. "You have ruined these people's lives!"

"They are only mortals, Lord—"

"And so am I—for now!" And with that he reached up and ripped an ornately jeweled boss from the edge of the boy's saddle, which he tossed to the startled Lin.

"Ill guests have we been," he said. "Maybe this will atone for the moment. I will settle the rest with you later."

Lin bit the metal experimentally. "Ten times the damage it will pay," the Trader said, grinning, "if this be what I think it is. Now will you folks *get?* Take the horses and go!"

"But what about Darrell?" Gary cried.

"We'll look out for him—now move it, boy!"

"But you don't even know him!"

"Get goin', boy! All of you get goin'."

A moment's hard jog later they reached the paddock, which was on the northeast side of the enclosure and fairly well screened by the body of the camp. The fog was thicker there, as well: more concealing. Alec fumbled with the keys at the gate.

"No time for that," Nuada called. Froech vaulted the low barrier, and the others followed as best they could.

Suddenly they were among horses, and the odor of straw and dung and horseflesh was strong in their noses. White eyes flashed wide, and ruddy nostrils flared like caverns. There was little time for choosing, no time for saddling or bridling.

An explosion split the night; sparks of red and orange burned the stars.

"Quick, now!" Nuada cried, as he claimed a splendid black, even as Cormac climbed atop a long-limbed roan. "Get dark ones if you can, but look for the ones with the silver shoes, they come from Tir-Nan-Og; there is no time for other choice. You all can ride, can you not?"

"You're asking the right feller the right question now." Uncle Dale grinned. "Come on, Liz. You're with me."

The old man climbed with unexpected agility onto the back of a black mare nearly as large as the stallion Nuada had chosen, then bent down to give Liz an arm up behind.

Nuada raised startled eyebrows. "You ride bareback, Mortal?"

"Since I 'uz a boy!"

"Hurry, then."

Another explosion, more fire. Red lights flashed down the hill from the direction of MacTyrie.

"Somebody must have called the fire department already" came Alec's nervous giggle. "Bet Pa's pissed."

"Mine too." Gary grinned. "Teach them to volunteer."

"Yeah—" Alec's words were cut off as Cormac grabbed him by the collar and physically set him on a horse behind the Faery lady, Regan. He twisted his fingers into her belt and held on grimly as the horse began to shift uneasily.

"Hey, wait for me!" cried the still-earthbound Gary.

"I'll take him!" Cormac's voice carried clear into the night.

Froech spun around in place, grabbed Gary under the armpit, and half flung the boy up behind the dark-haired Faerie.

Gary's eyes caught Alec's. "Here's to adventure!"

Alec did not reply.

"*Now!*" cried Silverhand. "Froech, whatever Power you still command, use it!"

Froech's teeth flashed in a wild smile. He stretched a hand backward, fist clenched, then released it.

A ball of brilliant light took form among the already nervous horses. One spooked (one that wore iron shoes). And then they all were running—away from that arcane light, and through the gate someone had finally got open, heading through smoke and fog in the direction of the Traders' camp. The ground seemed to shake beneath them.

And as the mass of horses poured into that chaos of flame and shouting, five other horses bearing eight riders gathered themselves and followed, but turned eastward into the night.

Liz, who rode behind Dale Sullivan, thought only of David. And of the image she had seen shadowed in Nuada's mind before the pain began.

One final explosion sounded. Liz twisted around to look back, saw a bloom of fire take root in the sky, shooting tongues of red into the darkness: flames the exact shade of red as the vision-woman's hair.

Chapter XVI: Pursuit

(Tir-Nan-Og)

Fionna was mostly the fox now, for the fox knew the business of survival far better than the woman ever could. And survival was what it had finally come down to—that and running, which were very much the same at the moment.

How much farther to a border? she wondered. Lugh's enfields were getting closer now—too close. Fionna had never failed to underestimate how quickly they could move, in spite of the taloned front legs made more for grasping or tight infighting than for speed. Their catlike haunches did it, launching them over the ground in long, flat bounds, with their front limbs used mostly for stability and balance.

For herself, she trotted quick as a fox could go, which was almost not fast enough. She was tired, her mind still clouded from her labor, and she doubted she had Power for more than one more shape-change without a rest. That she would save until there was no other choice. Tir-Nan-Og had come alive after she had fled the stables, and men and beasts were everywhere—searching, she was certain, for a fox that was also a sorceress.

Even worse was the hot wind blowing behind her, approaching faster than even the enfields.

Another half league covered, and the beasts were nearer yet. She could hear their breathing now, the click of their talons against the occasional stone. Sometimes she could hear them whistling to each other in their odd, musical language.

The wind was closer too, and hotter—*much* hotter.

Suddenly she recognized it.

He would not dare! Not even Lugh would seal his borders. Does he truly fear my brother so?

A Track glittered in the distance and she turned toward it.

The wind ruffled her fur.

Faster, then, Fionna!

Behind her the doom-wind was gaining, rippling the waves of

grass about her; and, as if fanned by that blast, the enfields too pressed forward.

Not two lengths behind her, they were of a sudden. And then, in the middle of a flying leap, a talon grazed a footpad.

Startled, she jerked reflexively, twisting sideways to land awkwardly, her stride broken.

The other one was beside her then. Its claws flashed out to slash across her flank. The pain dazed her, and she crumpled, panting. For a moment she thought she was dying—or would be as soon as the creatures found her throat. But the expected did not happen, for these were trained hunting beasts. They did not kill their quarry.

A wet nose nuzzled her haunch; another matched it opposite. That tiny touch of coolness was like a balm against air that was hotter than any she had felt in all the realms of Faerie.

The sealing comes!

She closed her inky eyes, felt deep within herself to see if any Power remained there.

There was—a tiny shard. She touched it, fanned it, brought it to life, spread its essence throughout her body. And called upon it.

Suddenly she was a sparrow.

The enfields sprang back, startled.

She flew, though her wounds ached. Grass tips brushed her feet, then fell below her as she gained altitude, barely out of her pursuers' reach. She dared not falter.

But she could see the Track, thirty wing-beats distant.

Hot air crackled at her tail. She heard the enfields' high-pitched howls of dismay as it caught them, passed them by, and laid a barrier before them that was an impassable wall of flame.

Gold on the ground, gold in the grasses: the Track was before her.

She collapsed gratefully to its surface, felt its Power tingling beneath her heart.

The last thing she saw before she closed her eyes was flame racing toward the Track, lapping over it, around it, enfolding it, but—blessedly—not passing through to devour her.

Fionna lay exhausted within a tunnel of fire and thought about Lugh's Power.

She thought about survival too, and eventually she thought about vengeance.

But before she was done, she was sleeping.

Chapter XVII: The Room Made of Fire

(The Burning Lands)

The room was made of Fire frozen in Time and carved by a Powersmith in Annwyn. The arts involved in its shaping were subtle —too subtle for even the crafty Sidhe to understand, much less the gloom-dulled Tylwyth-Teg. Morwyn herself barely commanded their intricacy, and she had been trained in that tradition of artist-mages to whom such wonders were in no wise the most remarkable.

It was an impressive piece of workmanship.

The arching ribs of the high-domed ceiling met four man-heights above the floor, and spanned curved walls ten times that measure wide. Yet by a certain application of the Fireshaper's art, the room could be made to fit into the palm of a woman's hand.

And it was beautiful, a marvel of design as much as engineering.

Both walls and ceiling—and what little floor gleamed forth beneath the fine-wrought carpets—bore the ever-changing tinctures of coals within a furnace: now copper green, now amber; sometimes a blue that shaded close to violet. But red predominated, the fickle, bloody crimson that lay at the heart of fire.

And red, in its many shades, was everywhere.

The heavy-folded hangings on the walls were scarlet silk couched with golden thread in shapes of salamanders and other beasts evocative of fire. The thick-piled rugs were wrought of wine-dark wool and strewn with the crimson pelts of manticores and cushions of carmine satin.

Panels carved in high relief enhanced the ruddy walls between the hangings. Scenes they showed of Ailill's people, the Tuatha de Danaan of Erenn, and depicted that race's history from their coming out of the High Air until the Second Battle of Mag Tuired.

Lower down, encircling the room at waist level, were smaller panels that concealed drawers and cupboards, shelves and small receptacles. These bore interlaced designs of birds and beasts, men and monsters, all wrought in silver and copper, bronze and golden wire.

A few were shaped of rare, hard-to-work aluminum stolen from the Lands of Men.

Floor-to-ceiling screens of wood and fire-pierced stone split the chamber into sections, one of which included a shallow pool for bathing. In another an eternal hearth provided cooking flame. What furniture there was hinged forth from walls or floor upon demand.

Except, in the precise center of the room, the bed—in which David Sullivan was fast awakening.

His fingers gripped fine sheets of vermilion silk. His eyes, when he dared crack them, beheld a dome of brilliant red brocade.

The world whirled.

No! He snapped his lids shut again, squeezing them desperately, first against the pervasive color, and then, with greater force, against the fierce ache that was exploding in his head.

He had almost drowned.

Sleep, he decided. That was what he needed: more sleep.

Not wine. Not the heady, aromatic liquid that someone had set against his mouth, the same someone who was holding him half-upright, he noted, though he could not recall when that had been accomplished.

"Sleep," he muttered. "Dream. Liz."

"I fear not, my pretty boy." A woman's voice thrummed against his ears.

Somehow David swallowed. Wine burned into his throat, cool and tart, setting sparks to shimmering through his blood. His nose twitched as tortured sinuses were soothed. The pain in his chest receded. The throbbing behind his eyes became more distant. He began to feel a tiny bit more human.

He lifted a hesitant eyelid. It was as he'd feared: the red room was no dream. Which meant the rest was no dream: the capture, the motionless journey through cold, wet darkness . . .

The woman before him was certainly no dream—though perhaps she deserved to be:

She was beautiful, with hair the color of spun copper wire laced with gold which fell past her shoulders. Her high-boned face was pale as porcelain, her lips red as the wine he had just been offered—from a massive two-handled chalice, he discovered, held in a slender hand. He blinked a refocus, looked higher, into eyes the green of bottle glass raised before a candle.

Her dress was ruby velvet sewn with tawny gold. Long sleeves trailed off the side of the bed; the neckline plunged in a deep vee, showing more than a little of the full swell of her breasts. David's gaze lingered there until he realized she was watching him, then he looked hastily away, blushing furiously.

The woman's eyes caught his and held them in a stare that was both frank and sensual. One part of him became alarmed, even as another part assessed the situation rationally: This wasn't right. He shouldn't be here. *Couldn't* be here. He'd been swimming, hadn't he? With Liz. They'd been naked. He'd given her something . . . but what? He couldn't remember.

Damn! Where memory should have been was only darkness. His past was a haze, a cloud. A cold murkiness through which he could not pass. He tried, but the pain returned.

"The present is master of the past, boy—and a thousand times more pleasant," the cat-voice purred again. "It could be very pleasant indeed, if you were to ply your talents properly."

A hand touched his forehead. Two rings sparkled there, one with interlaced dragons of silver and gold, their heads side by side. The sharp-pointed nails were lacquered the color of garnets.

The finger continued downward, tracing a fine line along the slightly concave ridge of his nose, across the soft fuzz on his upper lip, tickling the lower one, dropping then beneath the outthrust angle of his chin to pause at the hollow of his throat. Then down again, across his bare breastbone—

Jesus! David realized, in his first truly lucid moment. *I'm naked!*

"And very nicely so." The woman smiled.

"Stop that!" David cried, aghast.

The finger poised at his solar plexus, inscribing small circles there. "Don't you like it?"

"I . . . *No!* Not *that!* Stay out of my mind! Who are you anyway?"

The woman's mouth tensed ever so slightly as she drew herself away, but the finger never wavered. "As to *who* I am, or what I am, that is long in telling. I know *your* name, however. All in Faerie know your name, *David Kevin Sullivan*. Windmaster's Bane, they call you. But I have another word for you, pretty boy, and the word I have is . . . *murderer.*"

The woman's eyes blazed then, the fingernail stabbed down into his flesh.

David gasped; his hand shot out in reflex to imprison the fragile wrist.

"No, lady. It wasn't murder" came his desperate reply, "if you're talking about Fionchadd. I *spared* him the Death of Iron. Ailill killed him!"

"With iron! With a common iron kitchen knife lashed to an ash

wood staff—which would not have been within his reach had you not brought it into Faerie!"

David released the arm and sat up, scrambling backward until his shoulders thumped hard against a padded headboard. He glanced down, snatched a strip of ruby velvet coverlet across his lower body.

The woman smiled, her anger fading quick as a summer shower. She laid a hand on David's upper thigh, stroked the tanned flesh absently.

David tensed, but did not move. *Dared* not move.

Abruptly, the woman withdrew the hand and reached toward a low, cast-metal table that stood beside the bed. A golden wine ewer gleamed there, from which she filled two of the double-handled chalices. One she offered to David, which he accepted with some reluctance.

"I would drink a toast to you, boy."

"A . . . a toast?" David replied uncertainly as he took the proffered wine.

The woman paused with her lips upon the rim. Beads of condensation had formed on the metal surface.

"A toast," she repeated, "to murder."

David felt his breath catch; he swallowed hard. "To murder," he managed to croak, as he raised his drink in turn.

The woman took a sip, her eyes never leaving his. "No, *not* to murder," she amended. "Let us rather say to *death*."

"To death," David whispered hopelessly.

Her brows lifted ever so slightly.

"The death of Ailill!"

David's throat locked and he nearly spit out his wine, but clamped his jaws, curling his lips inward even as his cheeks puffed out. A thin stream of crimson nevertheless trickled from the corner of his mouth and slithered down his chin.

The woman intercepted its flow with a corner of her sleeve.

"Ailill! Christ, who *are* you?" David choked out in a strangled voice, then coughed in truth as a bit of wine burned into his lungs.

The woman's face hardened abruptly, became cold and dispassionate. "My name is Morwyn, boy, since you seem determined to know it: Morwyn verch Morgan ap Gwyddion."

David frowned. "Sounds Welsh, not Irish. I thought—"

The woman's brow wrinkled. "Wales—yes, that is what men call Bran's Country now. Annwyn is my home—most lately. That place where I was born, the place my father came from. But my mother's land has no true name in any tongue you have heard of."

David stared incredulously. "You mean you're not from Faerie?"

"Oh, aye. Or at least in part I am. My father was from that realm, but not my mother. *She* is a—*Powersmith* is perhaps the best term for it."

"Then you're not Sidhe?"

The woman shrugged. "Nor wholly Tylwyth-Teg. But do not change the subject. There are other names I would speak of: Ailill mac Bobh, for one, King's brother to Finvarra of Erenn. Once That One's Ambassador to Annwyn. Of late his Voice in Tir-Nan-Og. Stormshaper, Windmaster—all these names they call him. But to those I would add another: Kinslayer. And that an abomination!"

"Kinslayer," David whispered, recalling how that word had rustled through the host of the Sidhe nearly a year before when he had stood before their assembled Riding after the Trial of Heroes, while a makeshift spear protruded from the chest of a fair-haired Faery boy who might someday have become his friend. The boy's father had wielded that spear, but it had nevertheless been of David's making. And then the accusing Faery chorus had begun: *"Kinslayer."*

"Kinslayer," Morwyn said again, her voice cold as bitter ice. "And among my mother's kind such deeds demand accounting."

David sat up straighter and rearranged the cover, wishing the woman would go away at least long enough for him to get his act together. "Why are you telling me this?" he asked slowly. "What's it got to do with me?"

The woman leapt to her feet, spun about to glare at him. "Because, fool of a mortal, Fionchadd was my son! Because Ailill was my . . . husband, you would say, though *he* would not. Because I loved him once and he betrayed me, then betrayed Fionchadd perhaps beyond any Power to recall, and for that I must have my vengeance!"

David was suddenly wary. "Wait a minute—what do you *mean* 'Beyond any Power to recall'? Does that mean Fionchadd's *not* dead?"

Morwyn shrugged again and began to pace back and forth beside the bed. "Who can say? What is death? Death is the breaking of that which links Earth and Air: matter and spirit. With your fragile kind, there is no mending. With the Sidhe, the link can ofttimes be rejoined, but by strength of will alone. Yet with the Death of Iron, it is not so simple. Iron blasts the body past repair. Sometimes it can even shatter the spirit, so that it remains forever lost, forever fearing a return of the agony that marked the breaking."

David nodded thoughtfully. "I suppose there would be pain."

"What do you know of it?" Morwyn shot back fiercely, stopping dead in her tracks. "Imagine, boy, that you cut yourself. A mere scratch. Then imagine that the scratch takes fire. Imagine each tiny part of your body aflame. Burning outward from that point, slowly, oh so slowly, but without quenching or hope of solace. Were the flesh in truth consumed, the pain would be no greater!"

"But you still haven't told me whether or not Fionchadd's really dead," David ventured at last.

Morwyn shook her head emphatically. "Oh, he is dead—in that body. Whether his spirit may find or build another, I cannot say. Such a thing requires Power. It requires will. I do not know how much of either Fionchadd had. I tried to teach him well, but he had been long from my keeping when he died."

"But he was your son—"

"I have seldom seen him since he was a child. He was fostered with Finvarra."

David couldn't take much more. His head was clearing rapidly. The wine was helping a lot. Memories were returning; the cobwebs of muddle were nearly gone.

"Okay, look," he said carefully. "What do you want? You wouldn't have snagged me from . . . while I was . . . while I was swimming, if you hadn't wanted something. So what is it? I presume it has something to do with Ailill, but what? And can I have my clothes, if you don't mind? I'm a little sick of sitting around here naked!"

Morwyn raised an eyebrow. "As to what I want, that I will tell you shortly. As to your clothes," she added airily, "I suppose they are where you left them."

"Well, that's just great!" David snarled bitterly.

"I rather like you the way you are."

"Humph" came David's derisive snort, as he tried to adjust to another of Morwyn's abrupt mood swings. "Do you no good."

"And how do you know that it has not already?"

David felt his cheeks burning. "You didn't!"

"Maybe." The woman's smile was cryptic. "It is best when both desire it, when spirits link as well as bodies, when—"

"Okay, okay, I get the message," David snapped, his voice rising on every word. "And I know I'm probably stupid to do this, probably stupid to get pissed off and holler at a sorceress who's got me naked and helpless and half-drunk and God knows where—but if I'm *not* dressed and out of here and on my way back home by the time I count fifteen, I'll—"

Morwyn laughed aloud, the sound oddly light and crystalline, yet filled with biting mockery. "What? In one of my dresses? At the bottom of a lake? For that is where this World touches yours. Would you *like* to drown? You almost did, you know. Of a certain it would be no problem to arrange."

"What do you *mean?*" David asked with forced civility. "Isn't this Tir-Nan-Og?"

Morwyn laughed again. "Oh no, young sir. Lugh's realm is closed, its borders lately sealed. *We* are in quite another place, a place a Powersmith alone might venture."

"Not Tir-Nan-Og?"

"Oh no. A bubble into another World, perhaps. The fires under your land, as Tir-Nan-Og is the sky above it."

Damn! David raged, in large part at himself. *More Faery metaphysics!* Distracting him from the matters at hand. Like escape, first of all. Like figuring out Morwyn's intentions for him, which seemed to be the only way to accomplish the former.

Morwyn's voice became suddenly earnest. "I need a hero, David. More to the point, I need a thief."

David's mouth popped open in amazement. *"Me?* You stole me from my world and now you want me to steal for *you?* You've *got* to be kidding. And steal what? The friggin' crown from Lugh's head? That'd be a trick, wouldn't it? Or maybe a pile of shit from Ailill's stable? Bet you could grow some fine taters with that stuff! Give me a break, woman. I've never stolen a thing in my life—and even if I could, why would I do it for you?"

Morwyn fixed him with an appraising stare. "To save your life, perhaps? To save your family?"

"Bullshit. I'm protected!" He felt automatically for the ring, first at throat, then at finger. A cold fist gripped his heart.

"By Oisin's ring?" Morwyn suggested coolly.

"Yeah, by the ring," David flung back recklessly. "I gave it to my girl friend, but it should—" His voice faltered as a shadow of doubt clouded his conviction. "It should protect whoever *she* loves now. And I think she loves me, at least she *said* she did."

Morwyn's lips curved wickedly. "But about this ring . . . Tell me, does it have Power?"

David folded his arms and looked away sullenly. "I expect you know that. You know everything else."

"It protects you and everyone you love against the Sidhe? Against physical intervention by the Sidhe?"

"No comment."

Have you asked yourself, then, how, if your lady's love protects you, I could capture you?"

David's breath hissed a sharp intake as horrible realization dawned on him. An edge of fear stabbed into his gut and twisted there like a dagger.

"Half of my blood is not of the Sidhe, David Sullivan, and that half is enough."

"But Fionchadd? The ring worked against Fionchadd, and he's your son!"

"Fionchadd's blood was quartered, mine is half."

"Oh," David said in a small voice, suddenly feeling very foolish.

Morwyn smiled her triumph. "So you see, you have no choice. No real choice, except to aid me."

David shook his head. "No, I don't guess I do."

"Good. So we can talk now. We have plans to make."

"I'd be more willing to talk if I had something to wear."

The woman's eyes filled with sudden merriment, making her look almost girlish. She pointed absently toward the wall opposite the foot of the bed. "I forget, sometimes, how tiresomely modest you mortals are. You may find some clothes behind that panel with the golden dragon on it."

David sighed and heaved himself out of bed, wrapping the velvet coverlet about his hips with an angry flourish. It dragged behind him as he found the panel indicated. A gold-worked dragon indeed coiled there, devouring its own tail, its legs an intricacy of knotwork.

"Press the eye," Morwyn called.

David did. The panel popped open; inside were piles of velvet and silk—red, of course. He pulled them out and stared at them doubtfully.

On top was something that looked like a pair of tights, but with a series of laces at the waist and a flap tied on in front. David knew what that was for, what it was called. But even thinking of it made his cheeks burn. He glanced around at Morwyn, made vertical, spinning motions with his fingers.

"Could you?"

"Indeed not!"

He sighed again and sat down on the floor with his back to the woman. With some difficulty he began to tug on the hose. It was damned awkward. Halfway through he had to stand up. Inevitably the wrap slipped off. He shrugged, and pulled them the rest of the way up. At least they weren't too uncomfortable.

A glance at a nearby mirror showed Morwyn's face. She looked amused.

David completed the ensemble as fast as he could: a long shirt of crimson silk (why hadn't he found that first?); a tight red jacket that the hose laced to; a short, pleated tunic of burgundy velvet with absurd flowing sleeves that fell almost to his calves. Thigh-high boots of scarlet suede.

"I feel like an idiot," he choked when he had finished, certain his face was redder than the fabric. He tried to fold his arms and look disgusted, but the unwieldy sleeves got in the way.

"You *look* magnificent," Morwyn countered pleasantly. "Quite the Elven prince. Rather short, perhaps, but one can't have everything. And the color sets off your cheeks to perfection."

David rolled his eyes. "Tell me about it."

"Your anger seems to be subsiding," Morwyn noted.

"Anger won't get me out of this," David gritted. "Common sense might. If I didn't have *some* of that, Ailill would've got me the first time I met him." Seeing no obvious chair nearby, he helped himself to a seat on the floor.

Morwyn's eyes sparkled as she tossed him a cushion and sank down beside him. "Ailill is that way, isn't he? But still too devious for his own good."

"This *is* about him, then? This business about stealing?"

"Oh, aye," Morwyn replied instantly, handing David a goblet of wine in lieu of the earlier chalice he had not finished. "Ailill has escaped."

David paused, his hand frozen above the offering. *"Escaped?* But Nuada said there were locks on him, locks and spells!"

"Four metal and four magic," Morwyn quoted. "Not counting the binding spells—according to his sister."

"His sister?" David's face contorted in a mask of horrified dismay. "Oh, Jesus, no!"

"Oh, yes! Ailill has a sister—Fionna nic Bobh, by name. Worse even than him, I suspect, from our two or three encounters. Or at least less scrupulous. She it was released him. I sought to capture him, but he escaped. I tried to scry him out, but he eluded me. My summoning did not find him."

It was *him,* David thought. *Ailill* was *the Crazy Deer.* "Maybe he *couldn't* come," he said slowly. "I think he may have been in deershape—elk-shape, actually. And he may have been wounded; a car hit what I suspect was him, anyway—you know what a car is?"

"I am not ignorant, boy—and what you have told me seems very likely, for deer are Fionna's favorite animals. But tell me of this wounding. Was there blood? Does Ailill's essence color the Lands of Men? If so—"

It was David's turn to smile. "What's it worth to you?"

"What is your sanity worth to you?" Morwyn shot back. "If you do not tell me, I will rip your mind apart and search the fragments until I find that memory!"

Watch it, Sullivan! David warned himself. *Play it close: Draw her out. Let her do the talking. Give nothing away without something in return.*

"So you can't find out yourself?" he said at last. "Well now, *that's* interesting. Are there, like, maybe, limits to your Power, then?" He raised an inquiring eyebrow.

"Something limits it right now," Morwyn snapped angrily. "A wall of arcane fire through which I cannot pass—and curse Lugh to the Cold for that. That is why I need you."

David took a sip of wine and tried to look wise and crafty. "Ah! A wall of flame that even a sorceress can't get through. And something to be stolen, something to do with Ailill, I bet. Well, that's right up my alley! I just took *Locks-and-Keys 101* in school last year."

Morwyn took a sip of wine. "Your tongue leads you onto dangerous ground, my boy," she said sweetly. "And if you are not careful, you may find no ground beneath you at all. But come, I will tell you my tale straight out. And then you will tell me about Ailill's wounding. Is that fair?"

David tasted the wine. "If you say so."

Morwyn ignored his sarcasm. "My intention in bringing you here was twofold. To use you to bait a trap for Ailill was one part; yet that portion of my plan has been rendered unworkable if what you have just told me is true, which I am almost certain it is. With the borders sealed, Ailill would be trapped in elk-shape and would not know you. That is unfortunate, too, for were he in his own form and thus cut off, his Power would be greatly reduced, and I could summon him easily."

"So why keep me here, then?"

"Are you deaf, boy? I said I had *two* uses for you. And my second use is this: there is one thing I need, one instrument that would make Ailill's doom exquisitely painful, whatever shape he wears—and exquisitely final as well. The problem, as you may have surmised, is that I do not have this instrument. It lies in Tir-Nan-Og: beyond my grasp, but not, I think, beyond yours."

"Ho now, wait just a minute!"

"I aim to capture Ailill, David; it is simply the means of capture that has altered. Now that I know what form he wears, I will set a summoning upon him, using his blood as focus. But to work his doom, I also need a certain Horn Lugh has in his keeping. While I seek out Ailill, you will seek the Horn of Annwyn. With that I will destroy him."

"Ohhh nooo!" David cried, shaking his head emphatically. "Stealing's one thing. Being an accomplice to murder's something else again. And I haven't even said there *is* blood yet."

Morwyn's eyes glittered with a dangerous light. "Have you forgotten your peril already? That and your family's as well?"

David shot her a sullen glare. "I'd rather hoped you had."

"You hope in vain!"

"But you'll release me when I fulfill this quest? *If* I fulfill this quest?"

Morwyn nodded gravely. "You have my word on it."

"And whose word is that? The thief's? Or the murderer's?"

The sorceress's face became dead serious. She reached down and drew one of her nails across her wrist so that a thin line of blood welled forth. "I swear by my blood and the Fire that burns within it that I bear you no ill will. Fulfill my quest and I will set you free."

David scowled. "That's as good as I can hope for, I guess—for the time being, anyway. Now, how am I supposed to pull off this robbery of yours—and I want it understood right here and now that I'm having nothing to do with the rest of your little plan, got it? If the borders of Tir-Nan-Og are sealed and you can't get through, what makes you think I can? *I'm* just a snot-nosed mortal, remember?"

"Let us just say that I think I may have ways of getting around Lugh's barrier."

"I don't suppose you'd mind telling me what they are? If I'm going to do this thing, I'll obviously need to know as much as possible."

"Now is not the time."

David's lips drew back in a snarl of suppressed rage. *"Not the time?* When the hell *is* the friggin' time? And what's this about some magic horn? Could you at least bring yourself to tell me about *that?"*

Morwyn's eyebrows arched delicately. "I take it we have a bargain, then?"

David heaved a weary sigh. "Looks like I have no choice—but I sure as hell don't like it. I just want you to know that." *And I'll find a way around it if I can,* he added to himself.

"No choice at all," Morwyn affirmed as she rose to her feet. "And as for the Horn of Annwyn, we will discuss that and the plans for its retrieval when we have finished eating."

"Eating?" came David's shocked reply, as he recalled the dangers incumbent upon consumption of Faery food—like being trapped forever in that land.

"I'm . . . not hungry," he stammered.

Morwyn smiled her amusement. "No need to fear, my pretty boy, but a feast must seal the bargain. Venison, I think, would be the thing—I trust you like yours bloody?"

Chapter XVIII: Running

(The Straight Tracks)

Running. That was what the world had narrowed to: running and pain and fear. And spiraling ever closer like the twisting black shadow of a carrion bird: madness.

Blood like dark wine oozed from a gash deep in the Faery-flesh of the stag's hind leg. Gray-haired hide flapped around it in ugly, festering tatters.

It had been running for hours, the stag had, fleeing the pain it could never escape, which was a part of it, bound to it as surely as the tortured nerve and sinew that was its source.

The pain of iron it was, that ate at the substance of Faerie, that chewed away slowly, oh so slowly—not in a mortal spot, but rendered more painful thereby, for that gnawing could never end. Flesh burned and flesh renewed in a cycle only death could sunder.

And another pain there was, one which was far more subtle, for it crept into the mind and nagged there like an insidious goad. *That* pain was a memory or a wishing or a longing; the substance of Faerie calling to its fugitive own.

Running: a strip of golden light between . . .

. . . trees flashing by, elm and ash and maple, and bushes with leaves like waxy paper. Conifers hung with finger-long needles filling the air with a smell of freshness . . .

Pain: a strip of golden light upon . . .

. . . a beach of gray sand where twelve-legged crabs contrived geometric courtship dances between a circle of standing stones carved with the faces of weeping women. Purple clouds slashed across a green sky . . .

Running: a strip of golden light between . . .

. . . endlessly billowing curtains of shifting metallic whiteness that drift from an infinite height to lose themselves in unfathomed depths.

Pain.

A flash of gold beneath the feet and then more running.

Chapter XIX: Flight

(Enotah County, Georgia)

. . . a pounding of hooves, and trees flashing by in pencil shadows of dark and light . . .

A broken pine twig sneaked around Uncle Dale's shoulder and snagged Liz's cheek. She swore silently, but did not cry out. Another brush of outthrust needles loomed ahead, but this time the black horse beneath her veered neatly around it, sending her slipping sideways—almost too far. She did not ride often enough to be really good at it, and galloping bareback through the scanty fringe of woods north of MacTyrie was not the way she would have chosen to improve her skills.

Maybe a half mile behind them, sirens droned like angry bagpipes, contriving a sort of insistent, keening dirge with the shrill hiss of wind in her ears and the muffled, bodhran pounding of silver horseshoes against hard earth.

The black shifted again and slowed. Liz felt Uncle Dale's back muscles tense, and she wrapped her arms tighter about his wiry waist as they bent forward to half jump, half slide down a short, steep slope laced with bracken that fronted along a shallow, curling stream. Water splashed high from among the moon-rimmed rocks, drenching her shoes and the cuffs of her jeans.

Trees arched in closer overhead, and laurel became a screen to left and right. Liz did not know where she was, only that they were moving along the stream bed with far more speed and silence than any normal steeds could achieve.

But these were *not* normal steeds. Their coats were too glossy; their legs and trunks too slender to encompass the sort of strength and endurance they had already shown that night. And their elegant heads were a touch too narrow, even as the jaws of the Sidhe tended to be narrower than those of mortal men.

As if it mattered.

All that mattered was Davy.

Branches reached out to caress her with glossy leaves, and then suddenly there was clear air around her, and water glittering ahead. Horseshoes cracked against the rocks of the lake shore as Nuada urged his stallion to a gallop and the others followed.

Faster now—for pursuit might appear at any time, might erupt from the woods and end their flight with more questions than any of them could answer. Liz's car was still at the camp, David's clothes still in it. Two questions right there that would be a long time answering. And what about Uncle Dale's gun? What about the fire? What about *Gary's* car?

What about Davy?

Her concern for him had become the pervasive blankness across which all other questions were scrawled like bits of dark graffiti.

What *about* Davy?

He was alive, and that was all she knew. Alive and captured by the Sidhe.

And she had to get him back, she knew that of a grim certainty, though how that was to be accomplished, she had no idea.

Abruptly the horse swerved to follow Nuada's lead closer to the shore, and Liz was forced once more to focus on retaining her seat.

Beach flew fast below them; long-legged shadows leapt among the layered shelves. The lake shimmered on the left, a shard of blue-black mirror laid before a scowl of mountains.

More trees ahead: a looming darkness like black feathers; and then they were in the forest again. Pine needles slipped and scurried, and Nuada brought his stallion to a halt. Light sparked from the Faery lord's eyes, as his single hand sought for purchase in the long strands of silky mane.

"Hold!" he called clearly, though a hush enclosed his voice. "Easy there, Blackwind, halt we here a moment."

The black stopped still beneath him, bowed its head. The heavy hiss of equine breathing filled the air.

"'Bout time, too," Liz heard Alec mutter, saw him grimace painfully as he availed himself of a welcome opportunity to shift to a more secure seat behind Regan, who in turn scooted slightly forward to accommodate him.

"A moment only," Cormac muttered, "for unless I miss my guess, these humans will not be slow in pursuing us."

"I figger we've got about a ten-minute lead on 'em," Uncle Dale volunteered.

Nuada's lips curled thin in pensive agreement. "The form of our escape may have purchased us some time, for the mortals are bound to their chariot roads, or else their legs, and it will take them a while to discover that we have gone at all—and longer still to find out our direction. Yet it is clear to me as well that we will soon need a place to stop and plan."

"What about my house?" Uncle Dale suggested. "I figger it's about halfway between the last place David was seen and the place Alec and him saw that Crazy Deer."

"Won't it be watched, though?" asked Alec. "Won't the law eventually go to David's house, and wouldn't David's folks try to notify you? May have already."

Uncle Dale tugged thoughtfully at his whiskers. "Got a point there; I—"

"Where is this place?" Nuada interrupted.

The old man gestured southeast toward the lake. "Bunch of miles by road, not far a'tall if you can make it overland. Nothin' between here and there but woods and that little arm of lake. Lake's the biggest problem."

"How so, sir?" Gary asked. "Bridge is just around the bend."

"Good chance it'll be watched, too," Alec pointed out.

"But couldn't we swim across or something?"

"That might work for us, but what about the horses?"

"Swim them too, I guess" came Gary's somewhat chagrined reply. "That's what they'd do in the movies."

Uncle Dale's voice cackled softly into the night. "You ever swim a horse, boy? As like to drown you as to save you. Nothin' *I'd* do, less'n I had to."

Froech suddenly wrenched his mount around. "Enough of this. If there is a bridge, then we should use it. *I* have no fear of mortals."

With that he jabbed his spurs into his horse's flanks and bent low across the high pommel of its saddle as the silver stallion hurled itself forward.

"Froech! No!" Nuada cried, even as he whirled Blackwind around and charged after.

The others followed, too, not much of their own free will; for the Faery horses were fey, and both more intelligent and more capricious than the steeds of men. Liz saw Froech's horse burst through the trees ahead of her and pelt down the lake side, its hooves sending fist-sized dollops of clay flying into the air behind it.

They all followed, faster and faster, with Uncle Dale and Liz third in line. The world became a blur of wind and streaking stars, and the relentless roll of the horse between her legs. Liz's thighs were getting sore already. And what of poor Alec and Gary, who didn't ride even as often as she did? She was surprised one or the other of them had not fallen off by now.

Maybe it's the horses, Liz thought. *Or maybe the craft of the Sidhe.*

They pelted around an outthrust arm of land, and suddenly the MacTyrie bridge slashed the horizon before them, its white pylons glimmering in the moonlight, carrying its span thirty feet above water that was far deeper.

Froech had dwindled to a dim spot against the steep, raw slope that loomed to their right.

Closer now, and Uncle Dale urged the black onward. "Get 'er, Bessie, come on, you can do it. Horse like you can do anything."

Liz grinned in spite of herself. Bessie was about the last name in the world she ever expected to hear applied to a Faery steed.

Ahead of them, Nuada had almost caught the fleeing youth. A bare ten yards separated them.

But beyond, half a mile across the lake to the left, where the road from Enotah swung down the mountain and burst upon the bridge, lights showed a car fast approaching.

"Froech!" Nuada's shout cut the night.

But Froech ignored him, and spurred his mount up the steep slope at the bridge's nearer end.

He turned left onto the span, and the company followed close.

"Gotta catch that boy," Uncle Dale gritted, as he urged Bessie up the bank, with the rest at his back in a tide of black and gray and silver.

Lights bounced across the railing an eighth of a mile away, as the company surged onto the bridge. Liz saw the Faery youth shudder as he passed near the iron railing.

But then he was riding again, spurs digging into the silver haunches, as fear rose red in his horse's eyes.

Headlights glared onto the bridge.

Froech froze—in the exact center of the left-hand lane.

The lights burned closer, setting the boy's handsome face into a one-dimensional cutout of shock and horror. Slanted Faery eyes slitted in the light of General Electric halogens. The youth raised a screening arm across his face.

High beams dipped, flashed, dipped again. A horn blew.

Froech grimaced. The heat of iron born of the World's first making was rushing down upon him, even as it surrounded him to either side. He spurred the horse, and jerked it in an awkward sidestep onto the walkway beside the railing. Water sparkled below.

A longer blast on the horn.

Froech jerked the reins, dug his knees in.

Another set of lights swung onto the bridge. Heavy motors rumbled.

Froech's horse revolted then, and flung itself across the wide roadway directly in front of the oncoming vehicle . . . and calmly arched itself across the low railing on the opposite side.

Suddenly the whole company was galloping after, the four remaining horses inspired by their fellow's recklessness. And facing them was a gold Camaro, its brakes squealing a cacophonous counterpoint to its horn.

There followed a moment of frozen time when it seemed to Liz the world was lost in a chaos of movement in which the only anchor was Uncle Dale's khakied back.

And then *their* mounts were leaping in pursuit of their fellow, as much from high-hearted joy as from fear or their riders' urging.

Lights blazed to Liz's left and the railing loomed ahead of her. Silver shoes rang loud on pavement, and then she felt the horse's hip muscles tense beneath her.

"Hold on, girl!" Uncle Dale cried as she buried her face desperately between his shoulders.

There was sidewalk beneath her, and then a gray glimmer of railing, and then air and darkness.

"Shiiiiiit!" a voice cried, and Liz glanced sideways to see Gary's mouth and eyes round to astonished circles as Cormac launched his mount into the air.

The horn dopplered into silence as the Camaro sped past behind them—

Above them.

Raw, sick fear bloomed in Liz's stomach as she realized that Uncle Dale had kicked free, and they were simply falling . . .

Water, cold and hard, slapped her diaphragm against her lungs, hammered the air from her chest. A sour burning flooded into her nose, her eyes, her gaping mouth.

Arms flailing automatically, Liz sought the surface.

Other heads broke water around her, and she saw Nuada to her left, ponytail slicked thin across his shoulders, as he grasped Blackwind's mane with his single hand and sent him paddling into the bridge's shadow.

She began tallying those dark blots: herself, and Silverhand, and Gary, who was already swimming strongly, and there was Regan dragging Alec with one hand and clutching her horse's tail with the other. A splash beside her as Uncle Dale's head broke surface— minus his hat, which was floating somewhere out of reach. And further to the left there was a sullen Cormac swimming behind his former mount. Finally, already almost within arm's distance of the nearest pylon, there was Froech. The Faery youth was still seated, though only his head and upper torso showed above the inky surface, even as his stallion's head and arching neck alone were visible, riding low within the water. He was leaning far over the pommel, eyes closed, his body absolutely motionless except for his lips, which seemed to be chanting some unvoiced litany.

Nuada paddled up beside him, just as the youth's lids quivered open. "Present wisdom a trade for previous folly?" the fair-haired man asked. "Or was that not a glamour I felt you casting?"

Froech nodded groggily. "Aye. The minds of men are easy things to cloud when they do not wish to trust their senses. The chariot drivers will but think themselves too much enthralled by wine. That much at least I could do—that, and break the force of our fall somewhat."

"Perhaps the first well-considered thing any of us have done lately," Nuada replied, as Blackwind pulled him past.

Liz concentrated on swimming, which she did well in spite of the increasing drag of her soggy clothing, all the while keeping a close eye on Uncle Dale. That old man was a continuing source of surprises, she thought, having seen him in the last few minutes ride a strange horse bareback with complete authority, jump that same horse over a bridge railing, and now seeing him swimming beside her. Granted the style he was using was not Olympic standard, but it seemed to serve him well enough.

They were under the bridge now, and its pale ribs arched above them. She caught at one of the pylons and rested a moment, her hand wedged into a concrete joint. There were two more ahead, maybe a hundred feet apart, the farthest, she knew, in water that was not deep at all. She pushed onward, crossed the intervening distance, and then the next hundred feet, conscious more and more of the weight of her clothing.

A horse splashed beside her and she thought she recognized Bessie, though in the darkness it was hard to tell. Her feet brushed bottom then, and she wrapped a hand in the dripping mane and allowed the mare to tow her the rest of the way to the steeper northern shore.

Trees grew closer to the water's edge there, and Liz released her hold on Bessie's mane to fall gratefully against the rough bark of a pine. Around her, other shapes, some two-legged, some four, were emerging from the lake, and she found herself again taking mental inventory: Regan, Alec, and their horse; Froech and his own mount . . .

They were all there. All conscious and none the worse for wear.
The four Sidhe were seeing to the wild-eyed horses, breathing words
of calm and comfort in their ears. One at a time Froech laid a hand
between their eyes and with that touch they quieted.

Liz looked around for Uncle Dale, saw him quietly tending to
their shared mount, then busied herself with trying to wring as much
water from her clothes and hair as she could. Alec, Gary, and Cormac had stripped off their shirts, and were twisting them between
their hands as thin sheets of brownish water squirted from between
the spiraled bundles.

Nuada was also scanning the group, counting silently to himself.
He frowned when he saw Froech, and Liz noticed that the Faery boy
appeared to be quite dry.

Gary approached Froech, grinning, his sodden gray sweat pants
slapping together noisily. "Way to go, man. You sure got things
moving—but next time give me some warning, huh? I'll bring my
bathing suit." He clapped a friendly arm on the Faery youth's
shoulder. "Hey—why ain't you wet?"

Froech thrust him roughly back. "Keep away from me, human!"
he snarled. "Don't touch me!"

"Now, wait a minute, man, I—"

Froech's hand shot to his left hip, and grasped the hilt of the
sword that hung there. He had the blade halfway out before another
hand closed over his and thrust it back into the scabbard with a click.

Nuada stepped from behind him. (How had he moved so fast? Liz
wondered. He'd been behind her an instant ago.)

"This is an interesting sword, Froech," Nuada said smoothly. "Is
it yours?" His voice was silky calm, but Liz could sense a deadly
anger just behind his eyes as he continued:

"It is perhaps not appropriate to sheathe this sword in any wrapper
but its own, boy, at least not at a time like this. I doubt human blood
would improve the temper of the blade, do you? In fact, might there
not be enough iron in this boy's blood to ruin this weapon entirely?
Neither Lugh nor I would find that amusing."

Froech's face appeared to darken in the moonlight.

"I—I am sorry, Lord. I am unaccustomed to dealing with humans.
And truly, in our haste I forgot the sword. Lugh gave it to me to relay
to you, before he sealed the borders. I pass it into your keeping
now." He unhooked the scabbard from his link-belt and handed the
whole thing to Nuada.

Nuada fixed him with a glare as he clipped the sword onto his belt
one-handed. "Peace," he said at last. "There is too much at stake
here for contention."

Froech inclined his head slightly, though his eyes still blazed.

Gary offered him his hand. Under Nuada's frozen stare the Faery youth took it briefly, but obviously with little relish.

"I will do what I can," Froech muttered.

"Right. No hard feelings, huh?"

"There is strength to that boy he is not aware of himself," Regan said softly from the silent shadows nearby.

Liz turned toward the woman's voice, saw her already remounted on her horse and giving Alec a hand up behind her. "How do you know?" Liz whispered.

Regan smiled enigmatically. "Perhaps I am a seeress. Or perhaps I am simply a weaver, and can follow threads from one end of a pattern to another."

"But one never knows when someone else will cut the cloth," Cormac added as he too swung up on his steed. He had not put his shirt back on and in the moonlight his bare white torso looked to Liz like some idealized Greek sculpture, so perfect were the Faery lord's proportions, so clean the long, strong lines of his muscles. Except for Fionchadd at the Trial of Heroes, it was the first time she had seen the bare bodies of any of the Sidhe, and she was frankly curious. But then she remembered the last time she had seen David, seen *his* bare torso shimmering slick and pale in the moonlight, and she felt tears welling in her eyes. Suddenly she was a mass of nerves.

"Can we get going now?" she heard herself cry, more desperately than she'd intended.

"We can indeed," replied Nuada. "And let us do so now." The Faery lord glanced at Uncle Dale. "How far is this place you suggest we seek?"

"'Bout six miles, but it's mostly easy travelin'. We can follow the beach some, and most of the rest is pine woods, so they won't be hard to get through. Once we get there, we can pick up whatever supplies we might need and head out. I 'spect we all could do with a bite."

"We could use some weapons too," Alec suggested. "Knives and stuff, if you've got any."

"But what about the cops?" Gary insisted.

"Do not forget on what you ride," Nuada answered, as he exchanged an enigmatic glance with Froech. "Perhaps that journey will not take as long as you expect."

"Long enough in wet clothes," Alec muttered.

Nuada raised an eyebrow. "Aye. Froech, do you suppose you could dispose of some of this . . . dampness?"

Froech frowned. "Of course I could. But do you forget that I am cut off from Faerie now, the same as you? I must rely solely on the Power that remains within me, and that is not great. Do you think it well to spend it so frivolously when we may be in greater need of it later?"

Nuada's eyes narrowed. "I think it best that you do what I ask you."

The younger Faery's nose twitched irritably, but he closed his eyes. A warm wind seemed to thread its way among the trees, brushing against Liz's face like a breath of high noon in the desert. She discovered that she was almost dry.

"And now," said Nuada Airgetlam, "let us ride. And"—he eyed Froech again—"let us hope our riding passes quickly."

For most of the company, the ensuing journey through the bright, moon-shrouded silence of the Enotah National Forest seemed, indeed, to take almost no time at all. They maintained a brisk, steady pace through open forest, briefly uphill at first, but eventually turning right onto a narrow, rutted trail—probably an abandoned logging road—that traced a clear path along a gently rolling ridgeline. A range of small mountains stretched away before them in an almost straight line from north to south.

But for Liz, that journey seemed to take forever. *Her* world had narrowed to the closeness of Uncle Dale's back, and the physical effort involved in retaining both her seat and her hold.

And, of course, to worrying about David.

Her head was clearer, and one part of her knew that there *was* nothing to worry about—in the sense that she knew David was alive, albeit in Faery captivity. But she had no certainty she'd ever see him again, and *that* she couldn't bring herself to face, especially in the light of what had so recently passed between them. It had taken a lot out of her: getting up the nerve to take the initiative in their relationship, then going along with David's sudden burst of amorousness (though she had to admit she'd enjoyed it as well). But she hadn't expected things to go so far so quickly, from total restraint to almost no restraint all in a matter of minutes.

And now, it looked like it had all been in vain; and, she realized as well, she felt guilty—because, if not for her, David would have kept the ring and presumably have been protected against whatever had made away with him. *That* was what filled her with the sense of desperate urgency she was trying hard to keep distanced, but which threatened to overwhelm her.

"Well, that didn't take near as long as I'd figgered," Uncle Dale exclaimed, shaking Liz abruptly from her dreamy reverie. She looked up just in time to see the forest open abruptly before them.

And indeed, at the bottom of a grassy slope directly ahead lay the Sullivan Cove road. Beyond it was Uncle Dale's house, nestled dark in its comfortable hollow among the pastured hillsides. And a couple of miles beyond *that* lay Franks Gap: the true beginning of their journey.

Chapter XX: Tracking

(A Straight Track)

There were odors everywhere: the tickly mustiness of overdry moss; the staleness of close, still air; the metallic bitterness of empty beetle shells; and strongest, most pervasive of all, the sickly, corrupt sweetness of oozing briar sap and the cold sterility of the Track.

Fionna, who was a fox again, wrinkled her nose as she sorted the thousand scents that drifted round her, but did not diminish the forthright pace of her trotting.

The Track flowed beneath her, now thick as heavy satin, now thin as golden gauze, but her sensitive footpads knew it only as a tingling, an unheard sound of Power to which her slender bones sang back in a counterpoint of their own. Power called to Power, magic to magic. Every quick-bounced step brought a surge of strength. Soon she would be back to normal, even without the trickle of Power that reached to her from Erenn.

The Track continued on, an infinite tunnel tight-twined with briars that shut out all light but the yellow glow of its own surface, which was enough for vulpine eyes.

A breeze twitched Fionna's whiskers, a lost wanderer from Outside whispering in her large, attentive ears of fresher air and wider skies, and land that held its own self-born Power. A faint tinge of brine rode that wind, and the part of the fox that was yet Fionna knew which sea in which World had sent its breath upon the Track.

But another odor laced in and out of that hint of ocean: a hot smell that told of life and movement, a sourness that spoke of fear, a sweet saltiness that grew to overwhelm the scent of that unseen sea. That new odor Fionna recognized, for it was what she sought: Ailill.

She trotted faster and faster, at last broke into a run.

It is merely blood, her fox-mind told her without much interest.

His blood?

Faery blood.

Another Track blazed in from the right, and the odor intensified. Down that way now, a brief two body lengths, and then she saw it: a red splatter upon dry oak leaves that smelled hotter than they should. The tiniest acrid hint of burning in the air.

The fox nosed the blood, looked up, sought wider, saw the prints: cloven hooves wide apart as if some great stag had run mad upon the Straight Tracks.

A deeper sniff told the story.

So they have wounded you, my brother.

The fox dabbed a tongue absently upon the bloody smear.

I have been a fox too long, Fionna thought. *Would that I might wear my own shape again, but if I would make the haste I need, I must need put on yet another.*

And with that Fionna set one part of her mind to the summoning of Power, and another to spiraling it through her body, stretching this bone, compressing that, enlarging this muscle, twisting that nerve. Longer legs and shorter gray-red hair and a splayed branching of backswept antlers.

And Fionna became a deer.

With a joyful leap forward, she set off on her brother's trail.

Chapter XXI: Hard Talking

(The Burning Lands)

I have just committed myself to murder, David reminded himself gloomily as he stared at the half-empty goblet in his right hand. The thick red wine reminded him unpleasantly of blood, and that did nothing to improve his mood, which was darkening by the instant.

He took a final reckless swallow and slammed the goblet down beside his heavy golden plate. A smear of grease and a fan of suspicious orange fungus were all that remained of what had truly been the finest feast he had ever eaten—if only he'd had the stomach for it. Or the nerve. The food was safe—so an amused Morwyn had told him, but he wasn't sure he believed her.

That lady was rustling about somewhere behind one of her screens—the same one from which she had somehow produced the sumptuous meal on ridiculously little notice, probably by a method that would not stand close scrutiny by any rational mind. Not that he had time for such considerations just now.

Or a particularly rational mind.

Not with his head awhirl with what Morwyn had told him about the Horn of Annwyn. (And there were things she *hadn't* revealed, of that he was equally certain, though her description of the Horn itself had been excruciatingly precise, and she'd made him repeat it a score of times to make certain he had it exact.)

And not with her equally obscure and evasive directions on how the theft was to be accomplished, though the film of grease on her plate displayed an intricate series of maps and diagrams of portions of Tir-Nan-Og, Lugh's palace, even the treasure chamber itself. She had promised more information upon her return. Like how he was supposed to get in once he got there, and then where the Horn was, once he got in.

David skewered the final shrimp from one of the small cloisonné bowls that surrounded his plate, and munched the sweet morsel absently. (At least, the finger-long curls of white and pink *looked* like

shrimp, except that they had two tails—and that was another thing
he didn't want to think about too much.)

When he got down to it, in fact, there was very little he *did* want
to think about.

It had all been very remote, his conversation with Morwyn—
partly, he suspected, because of the wine—and he'd agreed to her
terms without giving them the full and careful analysis they deserved.

But now he *was* thinking about it, thinking hard. The business
about Ailill bothered him most—not that he'd been given a choice.
It was either deal with Morwyn or see his family endangered.

Perhaps he could find a way to fulfill the letter of his obligation
and still not be an accessory to murder. If Morwyn wanted Ailill
dead, that was her concern, but the responsibility should be hers as
well.

David's perplexed frown was still wrinkling his forehead when
Morwyn returned with yet another ewer, this one in the shape of a
slim-necked bird—a stork or heron, maybe.

*More wine? Hell, I'll be high as a kite in no time, and then
what'll happen?* The lady did not seem to be in any particular hurry
to set him on his way, and David very much feared that her idea of
dessert might include him. Not that that would be *bad*, necessarily;
his body probably wouldn't complain. But his conscience certainly
would. He'd been so close to Liz, and so recently. It had been marvelous to be that close to someone else without guilt or fear. Very,
very special. Anything else would seem very much like betrayal.

David found himself blushing as Morwyn bent close and tilted the
contents of the ewer into tiny, delicate goblets of smooth white jade,
goblets thin as eggshells and more transparent. The liquid was thick
and creamy green, yet it sparkled in his nostrils like champagne; its
bouquet held a distant suggestion of mint.

He took a tentative sip—it was delicious, of course—and all the
while Morwyn's eyes watched his every movement with that languid
expression of distant amusement that he found so damned discon-
certing. All at once he recalled that she could read thoughts, and
then, to his horror, exactly what his thoughts had been scant seconds
before. His ears commenced to burning.

"So . . . you were going to tell me how I'm supposed to do this,"
he ventured at last. "Assuming I can find the palace, how do I get
into the vault—how do I even *find* it?"

"Why so hasty, boy?" Morwyn replied with elaborate indifference. "Finish your drink, then we will talk."

"No," David said firmly, setting the fragile goblet down hard. "We'll talk now!"

Morwyn's face stiffened as she eased down opposite him. "Very well," she whispered icily. "We *will* talk, and you had better listen, because your life may depend upon what I tell you. Is that clear?" She smiled primly and folded her arms.

David nodded slowly.

"Good. Now, as to where the Horn is, it is in plain sight, in the center of his treasure chamber, or so I have it on good authority; Lugh makes no secret of it."

"But?" David interjected. "I can just tell there's going to be a *but* right about now."

Morwyn smiled disarmingly. "Very perceptive, boy. *But* what is *not* known is the exact location of this treasure chamber, except that it is somewhere beneath Lugh's palace."

"And?"

"And that it is accessible only by an iron stair leading to it from Lugh's private rooms. The stair, at least, is common knowledge, though few have actually seen it. But what is not nearly so well known is that there is another way—a secret way, known only to those who built the chamber, a way that leads outside: an iron road with walls of glass."

David raised suspicious eyebrows. "I thought the Sidhe couldn't touch iron."

Morwyn's nostrils flared with impatience. "And so they cannot. But the *Sidhe* did not build the vault, the Powersmiths did—my grandfather, to be precise, which is how I know of its workings. He told me all about it, as much as he knew, anyway, for Lugh was careful not to allow any one person to see the master plan. Thus, those who built the road did not construct the chamber or the stair. This, however, *is* certain: the walls of glass are in reality Walls Between Worlds; the World of the iron road is not the World of the stone to either side.

Realization began to brighten David's face. "Oh, I see. Lugh never thought a mere *human* might try to rob him. But what about the Sidhe or the Powersmiths? Couldn't one of *you* folks make yourselves human and steal it?"

Morwyn shook her head. "It is one of the Rules of Power: neither the Sidhe nor the Powersmiths may put on the substance of your World while in Faerie, any more than you could put on the substance of Faerie in your own."

"But still, if the Powersmiths built the road, and they can touch iron, then one of them should be able to break in whenever they pleased, assuming they knew about the road. Or is there something you're *not* telling me? You're not trying to trick me, are you?"

"Oh, never that, never that." The lady's eyes sparkled in amusement. "But not once have I said that Powersmiths can touch iron—and indeed they cannot. They have other ways of dealing with that metal, however, methods that do not require touch. Unfortunately, I do not know them."

"But what about Lugh? If the only way to the treasure is over iron, how can he get at his own stuff?"

"It is as I have said: the iron road and the iron stair are not truly in Tir-Nan-Og. There is a method known only to Lugh whereby the iron may be banished to its own realm for a space of time. He contrived the rune of banishing in consultation with two druids of the Powersmiths, neither of whom knew the other's part, then took it from their minds with their approval, so that he alone now recalls it."

David took a long breath. "But I'll be going into this blind. So how am I even going to find the iron road? Your maps aren't exactly what you'd call clear. And what about the treasure room? You've told me about some of the safeguards, but aren't there bound to be others?"

Morwyn shrugged. "I will tell you how to find the road in all good time. As to the matter of safeguards— You underestimate our fear of iron. A small amount we may abide; you have seen what a blade's worth can accomplish. An iron road two arm spans wide is enough to consume us completely."

"I don't know. I think I can deal with the road, but I *really* doubt that this treasure chamber is as unguarded as you say."

Morwyn flicked a haughty glance at him. "Then you will simply have to trust me. Now finish your drink, for we must be on our way."

David quaffed the liquor uneasily, stood up, and began stalking restlessly around the room as he waited for the woman to rise. Eventually he became aware of her frank, appraising stare following his every movement. He spun around, folded his arms as belligerently as he could, given the awkward sleeves, and glared at her. "What is it *this* time? I thought you were in a hurry!"

The lady's eyes twinkled. "Those clothes are hardly appropriate."

David rolled his eyes. "Well, I kinda thought as much, since I can barely move in this silly tight jacket. But if you think I'm taking everything *off* again, you're crazy."

"Do you intend to wear such fine array into Tir-Nan-Og, then? You would be a beacon to the blind!"

"Of whom I doubt there *are* any, except perhaps Oisin," David retorted sullenly.

"It is *your* safety with which I am concerned."

"Oh, all right." David sighed. "What've you got in mind?"

Morwyn smiled her cat smile. "Armor."

Chapter XXII: Ashes

(MacTyrie, Georgia)

Smoke filled the Trader camp, rising in arrogant spirals from the charred and twisted ruins of tents and wagons. A few of each remained, but the loss had been terrible.

Katie blinked once, twice; raised a rag of spangled silk to dab her tears: smoke and sadness. Gnarled old fingers crushed the bright, soft fabric. It was all that was left of her boy's things: the brilliant gold and sea-green wagon whose complex panels had taken young Pat McNally two years to design and three years more to execute.

And not a fragment left—not a bolt or nail but was melted, not a board that was not turned to ashes. The color was one with the wind and the air now. One with the fog and the night.

The fog: which wrapped all about the quiet camp like a waiting thing; wrapped the police cars and the fire trucks, wrapped their still-flashing lights, wrapped the uniformed men and the loud-voiced circle of Traders who faced them, gave them challenge for challenge, and charge for charge, and lie for lie.

But here amid the wreckage, where Katie sat forgotten, was only emptiness and cold—too cold for Georgia in August, but then, she was always cold now. Katie reached for her cane and groaned with pain as arthritic fingers closed around it. With great care she used it to stand, then draped the scrap of bright silk around her head and shoulders like a scarf. It was not sufficient. Too thin to keep out the cold, and not nearly long enough.

Another tear rolled down her cheek. *All this trouble to please Them Ones,* she thought. *All this trouble to help Those!* But the local girl had been nice enough—like her own lost Ellen, she'd been. Hair the same red and everything. Too little a thing, too pretty a thing to get mixed up with the Perilous Folk. Maybe all this burning wasn't so bad, if it had helped the young folks escape. Besides, it had been Lin's orders she'd followed, and Lin was her chief, head man of all the Traders in this part of the world. Lin's people had fought beside hers for five hundred years. Friends close as brothers of both her folk and his lay together 'neath the green fields of France—and of England—and of home.

A knot of breeze snatched away the smoke, eased aside the fog, showing Katie other cause for grief.

There was Lin now, up there with those policemen. Trying to explain things. Trying to talk about horses and fires, about two brand-new cars with no drivers, with that blond-haired boy not making things any easier.

But he'd fail, Lin would, in spite of his efforts, because he was too honest. He'd lie, but they'd see through him. Tomorrow, sure as sunrise, it'd be the road for them again, or the lockup.

Katie hoped it wasn't prison. She was too old for that.

She started forward, then shook her head. "I'd do them no good," she muttered. A lock of gray hair escaped her makeshift shawl and tickled her nose. She let it.

She was so tired. Maybe she'd go over there by that stack of horse blankets piled by the empty corral and grab a wink or two. Maybe—

No, Katie McNally. The words had drifted in from the swirling mist behind her. Or were they words? Had she truly heard them?

She whirled around, quick for an old woman, raised her cane—but saw nothing except a thick place in the white, a congealing of fog that might have been man-high.

"Who's there!"

A friend.

"Come where I can see you."

That would not be a good thing for me to do.

"Ah, it's another one of Them you are, then? More playing of pranks with the folk of God's green world, I'll wager. But I'll be havin' none of ye!"

She turned her back on the fog.

Not one of Them, no. One of you—flesh and blood as you are flesh and blood. Old as you never thought of being old.

"Who are ye, then?" Katie muttered over her shoulder.

My name is not important, though you have heard it spoken, I think, and read those words I never thought to write that Macpherson gave to me. Think of me as the one who watches without seeing, who hears with more than ears.

"Riddle me no such riddles!"

Very well, come with me and I will tell you my name.

"I'll not!"

"But you must!" And Katie realized suddenly that those were the first words she had *actually* heard her unseen temptor speak.

"The devil hides behind words like yours!"

"But I am not the devil. I am *with* Them, but not *of* Them. I stayed outside, hidden by the command of he who rules Them. I felt the fire, heard the screams, the sirens, but I also felt five horses run away, and on those five horses eight riders. And I knew where they rode and why, for such things are sometimes given the blind to know, when those who see—even Themselves—can only guess."

"And what did you see, old man?"

"I saw a road of gold, and you and me walking on it."

Katie sighed. "I am too old to walk on golden roads."

"Not if I am there beside you," said the voice. "Now come, for we must pass through darkness for a way."

Katie closed her eyes and held her breath; a coldness gripped her heart. All at once a hand gripped hers, warm as the air was chill. She looked down, saw flesh old as her own, but firmer, saw fingers curved around her own—saw rings upon those fingers, and every one of them solid silver.

She glanced up into fog that had somehow become more man-shaped and looked upon eyes as gray-white as that swirling.

"Come, Katie McNally," the man said, gently twisting one of his rings in a certain manner and thus wrapping darkness about them. "The golden road is waiting."

Chapter XXIII: From Trail to Track

(Franks Gap, Georgia)

Thank God for moonlight, Alec thought as he scanned the graveled shoulder of the highway on the south side of Franks Gap. *Now if we could just find what we're looking for.*

The pavement to his right was a uniform pale gray, showing clearly the dark swirls the Mustang's tires had left that afternoon. The sky was more blue than black: the apocryphal midnight shade seen far past its proper hour, with the moon blazing gold-white within a pale corona. The mountain *was* black: a looming, fractured wall of raw rock shadow-drowned beneath tier upon inky tier of oaks and maples just like the ones they'd ridden through on their way overland from Uncle Dale's farm.

He straightened for a moment and shrugged to relieve the stiffness in his shoulders, wishing he could do something about the more painful stiffness in his thighs that an hour's impromptu riding had given him; wishing too that he'd had time to grab a nap during their brief stop at the farm. The old man had plied them with coffee laced with moonshine (which the Sidhe had appeared to enjoy), but it didn't seem to be doing much good just then.

Together with Uncle Dale, Nuada, and Froech, he was scouring the side of the road for the telltale cloven prints that would mark the beginning of Ailill's trail. So far they'd found nothing except gum wrappers, a couple of beer cans, and a page from a paperback romance novel. Twice they'd been forced to scramble back downslope when they caught the flash of approaching headlights around the whiplash curves. Froech had always been the first to leap, too; and he avoided the metal guardrails as if they'd been set afire. It would have been hysterically funny—if only the surrounding circumstances hadn't been so grim.

The rest of the company was either seeing to the horses they had tethered in a clearing fifty yards or so below the highway, or else trying to explain as much of the current situation to Gary as they could. Liz was helping there—deliberately keeping herself busy, Alec decided, and that was a good thing.

She'd helped with the weapons too, ransacking Uncle Dale's house to unearth the collection of hunting knives they all wore clipped to their belts or thrust into their boot tops. And she'd made the company's four spears as well, by lashing some of the old man's kitchen cutlery to broom handles and such-like. He hoped he wouldn't have to try out the one he'd been using for a paper sticker.

He yawned, twisted his neck, felt it pop, and stooped to renew his search. More rocks, more paper, a half-full can of Classic Coke that he sent clattering down the mountainside with a flick of his spear.

And then Nuada's joyful exclamation cut the night: "Here it is!"

Alec whistled his relief and jogged the ten yards downhill to where the Faery lord was squatting by the side of the road.

"'Bout time," Uncle Dale muttered, as he joined them from beyond the guardrail. He stared at the ground intently, then pointed a knotty, horn-nailed finger. "And ain't that blood on that rock there?" He hunkered down beside Nuada, and Alec heard his knees crack.

Nuada touched a finger to the brownish stain that had splattered across a flat, plate-sized chunk of garnet-encrusted schist. "This is better than I dared hope; for it is possible a scrying might be done from this, if Froech is willing." He glanced up at the younger Faery, who did not look as if the suggestion pleased him much.

"It is for such things as this I wished to conserve my strength earlier," Froech replied a little sharply. "But still, I have renewed myself somewhat since then. I will make the attempt—but I can promise nothing. I—"

The soft, quick rattle of frantic climbing on loose stone interrupted him, giving way to grunted profanity as a breathless Gary vaulted over the railing. He poked Alec with the tip of his make-do spear. "Any luck?"

"Yeah." Alec nodded. "We've found the trail, and what's better, some bloodstains. And now your friend's gonna do a scrying to see if he can locate Ailill from them."

Gary flipped the weapon onto his shoulder and sucked his upper lip thoughtfully. "Uh, Alec, I hate to sound stupid . . . but what's scrying?"

"It's like what Nuada was trying to do back in the tent: using something that's been part of something else to try to locate that thing's current whereabouts. Apparently blood's about the best focus you can have—and we've got some of Ailill's blood right here."

Nuada carefully picked up the suspect rock and rose to his feet with more grace than Alec had thought a one-armed man could possibly muster. "Best we do this somewhere else," he explained, with a trace of irony in his voice. "It is not good to be interrupted suddenly."

He cast a final, wary glance along the deserted strip of highway, stepped neatly across the rail, and started down the bank.

In a moment they had rejoined their three companions, and a moment after that Froech began the ritual.

It was really not very complicated, Alec discovered, certainly not as complex as the one he had witnessed earlier in Nuada's tent, though why that was he couldn't say.

The young Faery simply sat down in the middle of a circle comprised of the linked hands of the rest of the company, cupped the stone in his two hands, and closed his eyes. His breath stilled.

Suddenly the only sound was the quick whisper of a night breeze among the trees; then that too was gone and Alec fancied he could almost hear the tinkle of the moonlight itself as it fell glittering upon the oak leaves.

No one moved.

And then Froech opened his eyes again and shook his head as if to clear it.

"What'd you see?" Liz asked eagerly.

Froech turned distant dark eyes toward her. "Nothing useful, I fear," he whispered slowly. "It was all unclear: running, and more running, and a confusion of fright and pain . . . Oh, there was landscape, but nothing to remember: trees and grass, trees and grass, and yet more trees and grass. And I could not tell what was now and what was memory. I think," he added slowly, "I think Ailill is close to madness. And for that reason, I doubt he has anything to do with the missing boy."

"But that can't be!" Liz almost shouted, leaping up, fists clenched hard at her sides. "It's all wrong! There's water involved, and a woman—I'm sure of it. We're on the wrong track; we're bound to be! This is turning into a wild-goose chase!"

Alec stood up beside her, took her arms firmly in his hands. "No, Liz, there may not be any direct connection," he told her softly, wishing he believed his own words more fervently. "But there's no way all this stuff could be going on in Faerie and none of it be related. I mean, think for a minute: none of us can breathe underwater except maybe Froech, so it doesn't make sense for us to look for David there, anyway. On the other hand, we've already located the Crazy Deer's trail. And I still think if we find Ailill, we'll find Davy."

"The boy is right," Nuada said decisively. "And now, I think, we have no choice but to follow Windmaster's trail and see where it may lead us. We know where he was half a mortal day ago. There is only so much farther he could have gone in the intervening time. Froech, if Firearrow tracks as well as I have heard, I think you must ride vanguard."

Froech nodded as he rose to his feet and started for the silver stallion that nosed unconcernedly among the weeds at the edge of the clearing. "My horse can track as well as any hound, in this World, or another. Wind or rain or water, none will keep him from his goal once I have set it."

"I hope your boast is not in vain," replied Nuada. "Let us travel, then."

For several minutes the night resounded with the clatter of spears being gathered (Liz held hers white-knuckled, grim as a Valkyrie, Alec thought), of daggers and knives being adjusted; and finally with the muffled grunts and groans of sore bodies once more resuming their mounts.

Throughout it all Gary said nothing. Nor did he say anything when Cormac once more gave him a hand-up behind him. But Alec, who was watching him closely from his place behind Regan, noticed that his eyes sparkled with a strange, fierce joy, as if he were finding this new worldview not a threat but a revelation.

"Would that I shared your delight in this adventure," Cormac sighed, as he urged their mount in line behind Nuada's. "But alas, I have no good feeling about it."

Froech was already on his way out of the clearing, his horse keeping its nose close to the ground in what seemed to Alec an appallingly unhorselike posture.

"He has found it," Nuada called, and as Regan's Snowwhisper followed Bessie downslope, the forest closed around them.

If I never see another laurel bush, it'll be too soon, Liz thought sleepily to herself, as Bessie thrust through yet another thicket of the thick, shiny leaves. *And if I never ride another horse again, that'll be too soon as well.* For what felt like the millionth time she peered around Uncle Dale's back to see, beyond the mare's narrow skull, the dark shapes of Cormac and Gary riding in front of them. Gary's shoulders were wider than the dark-haired Faery's, she noted idly. Froech and Nuada were somewhere out of sight at the front of the line.

The trail bent steeply downhill then, forcing her to grab Uncle Dale's belt to keep her balance. Simultaneously the laurel began to diminish, giving way at last to the rough trunks of a stand of ash and poplar through which moonlight filtered like gold-tinged fog. Liz held her breath for a moment, caught up in the beauty of the night. It was peaceful, so relaxing . . .

Her eyes closed. Her head tilted forward . . .

The horse stumbled, shaking her. She started, jerked her eyes wide open; blinked, looked around. Felt once more the heavy, insidious drag on her eyelids. Drifted off again, and was only vaguely aware when the land flattened at the bottom of a valley.

"Halt!" Froech called suddenly, wrenching her to squinting, muddled wakefulness, just in time to see him dismount and kneel in the leafy mould beside a trickle of small stream. A brace of ferns feathered about the hem of his dark gray tunic.

"He drank here," the Faery boy said. "The prints are close together. And this leaf shows blood drops spattered atop each other, as if he paused here for a long time."

Nuada stared at the water with a twisted smile upon his lips. "So even the mighty Ailill stoops to consume the substance of the World of Men," he chuckled. "That is a thing I never imagined I would see."

"How so, sir?" Gary asked innocently.

Nuada shrugged, suddenly distant once more. "It is the way he is. As you would not eat rottenness, so Ailill refuses the food of this World. It is a function of his overweening pride."

"Sounds like a real son of a bitch."

Nuada raised an amused eyebrow. "Not an unlikely comparison, I think."

Uncle Dale had crossed the stream and was pacing Bessie a few yards farther down to their left, following a scrap of weed-grown sand that clearly showed Ailill's footprints. All at once he brought the mare to a halt and commenced staring at the ground intently.

"Well, I'll be a . . . ! Damn tracks just ends!"

Dismay grabbed Liz's heart with a gauntleted hand. "What? What?" she cried, leaping off to scan the ground by the mare's silver-shod feet. "Oh no! They do—but they *can't!*"

Froech stood up abruptly, leapt easily across the creek and joined them, staring not at the cutoff line of footprints, but at a certain piece of ground a yard or so beyond it. He frowned and sketched an intricate series of curves in the air, frowned again and sketched another, then nodded decisively.

A sparkle of golden light sprang into being along the forest floor, as a Straight Track woke to life. Liz glanced expectantly at Nuada as the rest of the company joined them, but the Faery lord's eyes seemed blank and distant.

"It is as I feared," he said at last. "Ailill's presence has awakened a Track and he has taken himself upon it. And though we can certainly follow his way there as clearly as anywhere else, I am not certain that we should with so large and inexperienced a company."

"What do you mean?" Alec protested. "We've come this far, we're not going to stop now. Not when we're finally on to something!"

Nuada grimaced. "Perhaps, but I think you mortals should wait here. The Tracks can be dangerous, more dangerous than you dare suspect. And what of these others? Do you think they are strong enough to see every belief they have ever held called suddenly into question?"

"What *is* a Straight Track, anyway?" Gary asked.

"They are roads between the Worlds," Nuada answered. "Both the Worlds as you know them: spheres in space, and other Worlds as well. Worlds that lie against each other like the pages in a book, Worlds that lie inside each other like the layers of an onion, that follow each other in time like beads on a string. Do you begin to see?"

Gary hesitated. "I think so."

"The Tracks connect them all. They can stretch distance, or compress it—as Froech did when we were fortunate enough to come upon one on our way from the lake to the farm, though I did not tell you then for fear of arousing such questions as this."

"But why are they so dangerous—and why haven't we heard about them before?"

"As to the latter, humans cannot usually see them, unless they have the Second Sight, and only then if they are activated. And as for their danger—why, it is because of their very nature. You might step off a Track at one place and enter one World, and step off it again a few paces farther on and enter a different World entirely. And if a person should then attempt to reenter at the wrong point, he stands a chance of becoming irretrievably lost. Do not forget that the Sidhe have had thousands of your years to study the Tracks, and yet we understand only that they are mostly made of Power and a little of how to travel upon them. They are tools to be used, but not to be trusted. *That* is a concept you should understand very well, considering some of the forces you folk would turn to *your* service!"

"Well, I'm not scared," Gary replied. "Davy's my friend, and I'm going."

"Right," Alec affirmed, nodding vigorously.

"Absolutely," Liz agreed, though the idea of once more traveling that hazy golden ribbon almost made her sick with fear. She fought it down. "Right, Uncle Dale?"

"Ain't got no choice, way I see it. Always did like to see new places, anyhow."

"I think it is decided, Nuada," Regan said softly. "I think we are all bound to ride the Road."

Nuada bit his lip. "So it seems. Let us hope then, that this Road finds an ending soon."

"I think we all wish that," Liz said, trying to sound braver than she felt. She glanced at Alec, tried to smile. "So let's to it."

Froech nodded to no one in particular, and led Firearrow onto the Straight Track.

Things seemed normal at first, as Alec recalled they also had on that August evening when he and David and Liz had set forth on the Trial of Heroes. There was simply a straight path among the trunks, not obvious, even; it simply happened that no trees grew where the Track lay. And the Track itself was faint, a mere glimmer upon the ground—though he suspected that some eyes saw it differently.

But gradually the forest changed. There were more briars at first, then blackberry brambles, and then a wilder, thicker kind of briar he didn't recognize. Soon even the trees grew taller and more widely spaced, fading from oak and ash and maple first to pines, then to vast, tall spruces; a little later to thick-trunked conifers with hairy red bark; and finally to dark-leaved trees whose first limbs sprang out two hundred feet above the ground. Alec had never seen their like before. Right in front of him Uncle Dale was craning his head in appreciative, silent awe, and farther ahead he could see Gary rubbernecking as well. His friend's joyful "All right!" suggested that he too was enjoying this part of the trek.

Eventually the briars closed in again, first rising scarcely knee-high, then to waist level, finally piling on top of each other until they towered far above the riders' heads where they collapsed together to shroud the Track in a tunnel of living green. And as the briars rose in height, they increased in girth, becoming thick-stemmed monsters big as Gary's biceps, red as blood, and with thorns that made his sturdy hunting knife look cheap and flimsy.

"What *is* it with these blessed bushes?" Gary said irritably as one of them snagged his pant leg, leaving a clean rent in the gray fabric. "Good thing it wasn't my friggin' leg!"

"There is nothing beyond them but chaos," Nuada answered

calmly. "Perhaps a bubble of air, or an island of grass, but beyond that only the not-stuff of which everything else is made."

"Awesome, just awesome" was Gary's only reply.

The briars closed in more, twining so closely together that there was scarcely space between them for leaves. Here and there they curled so tightly that their thorns gouged one another's stems, sending a disturbing red liquid trickling across their smooth surfaces.

Time ceased to have much meaning. And then Alec became aware of a slowing of the file.

Another Track had intersected their own, almost like the intersection of two large-diameter pipes at right angles to one another except that there was a small, round clearing at that juncture, maybe a hundred yards across. Grass and moss grew there, and a few flowering shrubs mingled belligerently with the briars, but that was all. Alec did not dare consider the chaos Nuada had mentioned. The nothingness that yawned just beyond those thorny walls, that perhaps lay scant feet—or inches—below his feet. Suddenly he began to sympathize with David's fear of heights as his own sporadic claustrophobia threatened to reawaken.

Froech's horse started into the right-hand Track, then hesitated and turned toward the left; then it paused at the Track in the center.

Apparently frustrated, the Faery youth vaulted from his saddle, and fell to examining each in turn.

"Got a problem, boy?" Uncle Dale called as he joined Froech on the ground by the central tunnel, then examined the other two in turn. "Yep, I see," he mused. "They's a whole bunch of prints goin' every which way in and out of all three of these here things. Well, that's a fine howdy-do; can't tell which ones is freshest! That'un was here, all right, but which way he went when, no way I can figger. How 'bout you, Mr. Froech? Looks like that fancy horse of yorn's met his match!"

Froech glared at the old man and started to say something, but then bit his lip and nodded sullenly.

"Perhaps if we explored a bit farther down the Tracks," Nuada suggested. "It is possible we might find clearer prints somewhere farther on."

"Oh, lord," Gary groaned. "Not more riding."

Nuada looked at him. "Perhaps you are right. You young folks rest here with Regan and Cormac. Those of us who know something of tracking will each take a trail and ride half a thousand paces down it, then return. If we have no clearer answer then, I think we must try another scrying. Maybe here on the Track we will be more successful."

"Now wait a minute," Alec noted, as he slipped off from behind Regan. "I thought you guys were cut off from Tir-Nan-Og."

"And so we are," Regan answered, joining him on the ground. "But the Tracks have a Power of their own, and we can draw on that a little. It is much, much easier if one wears the stuff of Faerie, though, as Froech does."

"Well, if we're goin', let's be gettin' at her," Uncle Dale called, holding Liz's spear while she slid off from behind him.

Alec watched them go: three riders on Faery steeds down three very disturbing passages. A startled grunt drew his attention to the right just in time to see Gary fall on his butt beside his former mount while a grinning Cormac looked on beside him. Even the reserved Regan stifled a giggle.

Gary hauled himself to his feet indignantly and stalked over to join his two friends by the left-hand tunnel. He stabbed his spear firmly into the ground beside theirs, threw himself down on the grass next to Alec, and began massaging his thigh muscles thoughtfully, grimacing all the time.

"Feel like I'm rubbed raw," he confided to Alec. "It'll start rubbing my balls off next, I guess."

Liz sat down beside them. "I'm sore too, and *I* know what I'm doing."

"I sure could use a nap," Gary sighed, as he flopped back in the grass.

"Gary, how could you—at a time like this!" Liz flared.

"Simple. I'm sleepy."

"Sleepy! With David gone how can you—" Her eyes misted, and she swallowed awkwardly, unable to continue.

Alec heaved himself up and laid his right arm across her shoulders, gave her a brotherly squeeze. "Easy, girl. G-man's not your enemy. Know what I think?" he continued, finding his eyes suddenly misting. "I think you and me both need a real good cry."

Liz laid her head on his shoulder. "Maybe so . . . Maybe— Damn!"

Alec glanced down at her finger, saw David's ring suddenly pulse with a blue-white light that hurt his eyes.

He glanced around fearfully, a sick feeling in his stomach; started to say something, but Liz's voice rang out ahead of him.

"Cormac!" she yelled. "Come quick, it's the ring. It's—"

The dark-haired Faery sprang to his feet, ran toward them. "What?" he demanded. "Where . . . ?"

"There, I think!" Liz cried, pointing to the Track by which they had entered the clearing.

The rough hiss of labored breathing and the clatter of running hooves assaulted the air.

"Cormac—behind you!" Regan shouted from across the glade.

Abruptly an enormous reddish gray deer bounded into the open almost at Cormac's back. He leapt aside barely in time, as the deer whirled around, lowered its antlers, and prepared to charge.

Cormac crouched warily, hand flashing to his side to draw the bronze-bladed dagger that was his closest weapon. He angled his body, the blade carving careful circles in the air before him.

The deer checked itself, its eyes red flame.

"That's not Ailill!" Alec shouted, leaping to his feet. "The Crazy Deer was bigger."

"Fuckin' big enough!"

Alec reached for the knife at his belt, his other hand grabbing behind him for his spear. Liz and Gary did the same. Regan had hers, too, and was running toward them from the other side, screaming like a banshee.

The deer's ears flicked that way; it paused in midstep.

Cormac flung his dagger with unbelievable speed and force straight at the deer's exposed chest.

But fast as Cormac's cast was, the deer's reaction was faster yet; it flicked its head sideways and down, caught the dagger on a point of antler and flipped it casually away, sending it pinwheeling into the pulpy mass of thorns yards beyond the creature's shoulder.

The beast spun around again, to face Cormac head-on. Fire burned brighter in its eyes, an evil fire fueled by fear and hate and anger. Cormac drew back, fumbling for his other knife.

And the deer charged.

Cormac had no time to turn, no time to flee, for he stood midway between the entrances to two Tracks. Behind him were only briars, and beyond *them* only chaos.

He dodged left, away from the humans—too late.

The deer's antlers struck him full in the belly, lifted him, shook him, flung him free to sprawl motionless and bloody against the barrier of thorns which impaled him and held him fast. His mouth fell open, but only a trickle of blood oozed forth. His eyes rolled backward, then closed as his head lolled sideways across his shoulder.

"Dead," Regan cried bitterly. "Dead, for this time and place."

The deer whirled again, then commenced leaping here and there in a frenzied half-dance that was almost more rapid than eye could follow. But always it kept its antlers lowered, and always there was fire burning in its eyes.

"Yiiii!" Gary screeched, as he ran forward and cast his homemade spear. The throw was awkward, though, the weapon poorly balanced, and the deer dodged it with appalling ease.

He stared at his empty hands, then looked up—and screamed.

He was alone in the middle of the clearing. And the deer was facing him.

Its head swung down.

The boy's eyes widened.

"Quick, Liz," Alec shrieked, as he raced forward to impose himself between his friend and the deer, his spear lowered purposefully at the tangle of antlers. Liz joined him. A bare instant later Regan too was there, her face grim. Together they wove a pitifully inadequate web of steel-tipped wood before them.

"How 'bout it?" Alec sneered, feeling a sudden anger burn into his heart. *"Iron,* deer. We all have iron!"

The deer paused, though volcanic fire still glowed within its eyes.

Hooves sounded again, from behind them: horses at a gallop. Blackwind flung himself out of the center tunnel, skidded to a halt.

The deer jumped back.

Nuada's eyes flashed fire, widening when they glimpsed Cormac's lifeless body. He drew his sword.

And then Froech was there, barreling out of the far tunnel, and Uncle Dale to their left.

Regan raised her spear, took a step forward.

Alec and Liz did the same.

Nuada paced his horse in, then Froech and Uncle Dale.

Another pace, and the circle of deadly iron closed a notch.

The deer backed up another step, but Froech slid into place there, cutting off retreat, a dagger in each hand.

"You can surrender now, Fionna," Nuada said.

Slowly, deliberately, the deer turned to stare at him. Its mouth jerked open in a horribly distorted articulation, and one word cracked forth.

"Fools," the deer said.

And its shape began to shimmer.

Chapter XXIV: On the Porch

(Sullivan Cove, Georgia)

"I hope to God they find somethin'," JoAnne Sullivan muttered into the cool, still darkness of the front porch as the last set of tail-lights flashed out of sight up the Sullivan Cove road to the left. Moonlight regained the night, casting a pale, sparkling veil across the short grass of the lawn. She took a sip of bitter hot coffee and stood up, pausing one last time to look westward toward the lake.

They had found David's clothes in Liz's car, the sheriff had told her during the time he and his deputy had spent asking her and Big Billy questions. His jersey had been wet and smelling of lake water. And they'd found Dale's .22 in the car as well, and the old man hadn't answered his phone when they'd tried to call over there, which was very strange indeed. So they had gone to his farm to investigate further, and Big Billy had gone with them.

The screen door squeaked open behind her. A head of bed-rumpled blond hair insinuated itself through the crack; a small hand rubbed sleepy blue eyes as Little Billy paused half inside and half out. The sound of tentative breathing whispered into the night. "What time is it?" the little boy yawned, his forehead contorted in a frown. "When's Davy comin' home?"

"Oh, Billy, you're s'posed to be in bed, baby." His mother sighed her distressed surprise as she squatted down beside him.

"Yeah, but when's Davy comin' home?"

"I don't know, honey," his mother said softly, as her younger son trotted over to stand beside her. She ruffled his hair absently and took another sip of coffee. "Truly I don't know."

"He's in some kinda trouble, ain't he?" Little Billy insisted, his eyes searching hers trustingly, but a little fearful as well. "I know he is, 'cause I sneaked out an' peeked while the sheriff was talkin' to you an' Pa. They think him an' Liz has run off with the gippies, an' maybe Uncle Dale's helpin' 'em or somethin', don't they?" He paused thoughtfully, but then his face brightened again. "Reckon maybe they're gonna get *married*, or somethin'?"

JoAnne frowned. "I wish it was somethin' that simple, baby. Right now I wish they *was* gettin' married. That I could understand."

The momentary joy faded from Little Billy's face. "But they wouldn't be doin' that at night, would they? And they'd have told us an' all, and the sheriff wouldn't of been askin' questions about that fight Pa and Davy had, would they?"

"Smart, ain't you, to figger all that out?" His mother smiled.

"Davy says I am," Little Billy replied proudly.

"Well, your brother's right there, I guess. I just wish he was as smart sometimes—leastwise, smart enough to hold his tongue once in a while." She drained the last grainy contents of her coffee cup and set it down on the rough gray boards beside her.

"Yeah . . . but if they was gonna git married, Liz wouldn't've left her car, would she?"

"Oh, I don't know," JoAnne cried, tears starting involuntarily into her eyes for the fourth time that evening.

"Yeah, but you don't believe it, do you?"

His mother shook her head sadly, and slipped an arm around him, drawing him close. "No, honey, I don't."

"Sheriff'll find 'em. Sheriffs always find 'em."

"This ain't TV, baby."

"Know what I think?" Little Billy said, as he pulled away and started back inside.

His mother turned around and watched him go, feeling the solitude already closing in on her again. "No, what?"

"I think the boogers got 'em."

Chapter XXV: The Ship of Flames

(The Lands of Fire)

David stepped out from behind the enameled copper screen he had commandeered for privacy and aimed a soulful glare at Morwyn before turning his full attention to the image he saw reflected in the sheet of mirror-polished silver set in the flickering wall beside her.

Not bad, actually, he told himself, upon closer inspection. At least *this* outfit wasn't that absurd red. There were still hose, unfortunately; but these were a subtle grayish green, the more embarrassing parts mostly covered by the lower flaps of a padded gambeson that fit snug about his torso. There were thigh-high boots of silvery leather, too—wyvern skin, Morwyn had said, the single substance in Faerie to which iron was not inimical. Any other material would have been consumed by the Iron Road.

And then the good part: the suit of fine mail that rested close across his shoulders and hung shimmering to elbow and knee. The stuff had looked heavy, but had in fact been as surprisingly light as it was proving comfortable to wear—once he got it on right. It had looked easy: you simply raised the whole thing over your head and let it slither down your arms and over your body like a flood of silver water.

But then he had discovered that he'd put it on backward, and getting it off again had proved both more complicated and far less dignified than putting it on had been. You had to pull up the bottom, then bend over and sort of half thrash, half wiggle from side to side until gravity got into the game and gave the stuff enough momentum to carry it the rest of the way off. And the tiny links had gotten tangled in his hair on the way, which hadn't made things any better.

It'd really been a shame to cover it, he thought, when he finally got it right; but Morwyn apparently considered it necessary, so he'd reluctantly added the sleeveless, calf-length, gray velvet surcoat she'd tossed over the screen to him. A belt of scarlet leather went with it, looping twice around his waist and hanging down in front.

And finally, there was the best thing: the sword Morwyn had fastened upon him herself when he'd been forced to ask her how. The gray leather scabbard (wyvern skin, too, it looked like) hung low on his left hip. He fingered it experimentally, began to loosen the scarlet peace-ties as he turned once more toward the lady.

Morwyn gripped his wrist with a warning hand before he had scarce begun. "No, do not draw it here. The blade is of iron—iron of a particular sort and origin. To draw it here would not be good for this chamber."

David stared around in confusion, not at all certain what she had meant. "Lot of good it'd do anyway," he muttered. "Don't know how to use it."

"Perhaps it will find a way to use *you*, then."

David raised a dubious eyebrow. "Oh yeah?"

Morwyn shrugged noncommitally and handed him one final object: a medium-sized pouch embroidered with salamanders and closed by a drawstring at the top. He opened it, reached inside, felt something cool and softly slick, and pulled out a bundle of some light, semitransparent material that looked a little like spun glass. A quick unfolding showed it to be a hooded, ankle-length cloak.

"Wear that as you enter the Iron Road—or beforehand, if you have need," Morwyn said. "It will make you all but invisible."

"Invisible?" David's nose twitched doubtfully.

Morwyn took it from him, refolded it in what looked to him like a very particular manner, and returned it to the pouch.

"The stuff of which it is made is cousin to that which comprises the glass walls of the Iron Road. When warmed by the touch of a living body, it bends the Walls Between the Worlds enough to confound the eye of the unwary. But beware, for it may confuse your own perceptions as well, and if you wear it for very long it will almost certainly make you ill. Human bodies are not meant to walk in two Worlds at once. Finally, do not let it be damaged, for its strength rests in the sum of the parts, which any flaw diminishes."

David glanced around the room. "No helmet?" he said with a trace of disappointment.

Morwyn shook her head. "I do not have one here to fit you, and were I to provide you one that did not, it would cause you more trouble than good. In any case your role is not that of warrior; what I have given you is to protect your body from—"

"My head *is* part of my body," David interrupted. "Or it was last time I looked."

"From such beasts as may attack you unlooked for, I was about to say. Few there are and cowardly, at least in the country you will travel. What you now wear should be enough to make them avoid you."

"That's *real* comforting."

Morwyn ignored his sarcasm. She folded her arms and regarded him thoughtfully. "Well, you are as ready as I can reasonably make you," she said at last, "and we have no more time to squander."

Without another word she turned and strode to a section of wall where matching life-sized carvings of mustached warriors in full armor flanked what appeared to be an archway. Each statue held a silver sword upright before it. Morwyn nudged the right-hand blade the barest distance to one side.

At once a bright-lit crack showed in the wall between the figures. Morwyn stepped aside for David to go through before her.

But even before the door came fully open, a wave of heat blasted against David's face, and he became at once bitterly aware of the remarkable, pleasant coolness he was leaving behind in Morwyn's quarters. He held back uncertainly.

And then the door had opened completely, and almost against his will he found himself stepping outside to gaze upon a plain of featureless whiteness that stretched as far as he could see in all directions. Heat blazed up from that whiteness like invisible fire, and the glazed glare of the pale sky was so bright that he dared not raise his eyes much above the horizon.

The air was clear and still, but the heat throbbed from the ground with such ferocity that it seemed possessed of some subtle, watchful life that devoured without moving, sucking out strength and will until only despair remained. David could feel his skin growing tight across his cheekbones. He blinked and stared at the ground, eyes watering; saw then the tiny pattern of cracks that fractured the whiteness like fragments of a jigsaw puzzle slowly being dragged apart.

"Damn!" he whispered to himself as he discovered that he had already begun to perspire, though he had done nothing more exerting than take a dozen paces. Hot air rushed into his lungs, and he gasped. It was like breathing fire. He took another step, found himself panting. His throat felt dry as the desert around him.

No! This wouldn't do. He couldn't stand this kind of heat; nothing human could. If Morwyn expected him to go traipsing around in some absurd getup while the sun (*was* there a sun?) boiled him alive in his shell like a lobster, well, by golly she was mistaken.

All at once he swung around to face the sorceress. "I thought you said your house was underwater, lady," he shouted, his voice cracking as the greedy air sucked his tongue dry. "But if that's so . . . well, looks like the friggin' tide's been out a couple of thousand years! Find yourself another bloody fool to do your dirty work!"

"Fool indeed!" Morwyn shouted back, raising her arms. "If it is water you want, boy, then water you shall certainly have!" She clapped her hands once and closed her eyes.

And David found himself unable to breathe. He was underwater, he knew that at once, from the cold darkness around him—a cold so insidious and pervasive he felt his bones would shatter. And there was a pressure on his chest, a darkness clamped close against his eyes and nose denying him sight or breath. He made feeble attempts to swim . . .

But he could not rise. His waterlogged accoutrements weighed half as much as he did, and he could not push himself more than a foot or two above the bottom. His fingers ripped at the fixtures of the sword belt, but he couldn't work the buckle. He kicked at his boots but they would not come off. The rising tails of the surcoat floated up to encumber his arms. And in his eyes and his sinuses and the back of his head a red pounding had begun, the significance of which was only too familiar.

I'm going to drown, he thought grimly. *I'm going to—*

Die? came Morwyn's thought. *You might. Perhaps I will simply discard you now. After all, you are not the only human who might suit my purposes. Perhaps your friend Alec McLean would like to try my quest. Do you think so? Shall I send for him, and leave you here to ponder?*

"Or shall I fetch you back, *now?*" Morwyn's voice rang harsh in his eardrums as David found himself again on the blasted plain. He choked out his relief, then looked down, expecting to see the surcoat ruined, his feet in a puddle. But he was quite dry.

Morwyn stood in front of him; behind her was a vast sphere of flame half as tall as the sky, which, he surmised, was the outside of the room she had first brought him to.

"What did you just *do?*" he gasped.

Morwyn smiled placidly. "Sent you through the Walls Between the Worlds. I take it you did not find that pleasant?"

"Not hardly," he muttered sulkily, as he deliberately turned his back on her and began to stalk away. His defiance was pure sham, though, and he feared at any moment to find himself cast back again into darkness—until something occurred to him.

"Wait a minute." He skidded to a halt and spun around. "If it's that easy to pass between the Worlds, why even bother with the Tracks?"

"Because, " Morwyn responded patiently, "only where realms actually touch each other can such things be effected."

"But don't the Worlds overlap all over?"

"Indeed not. Think of two sheets of parchment on which maps are drawn, which are the Worlds. Both maps are crumpled and then laid flat again. Yet they no longer lie so close together as heretofore; some parts touch, some do not. Now imagine that there are golden lines drawn on both maps: those represent the Tracks, curved or bent from *your* point of view, but not from theirs. Then thrust golden needles through those sheets, joining them one to another, and you begin to gain a notion of how the Straight Tracks function. And of course there are *many* more layers of Worlds than I have spoken of—nor do they all lie in layers."

She took a deep breath. "Now—if you have finished pouting, and are willing to walk a very short distance—we will soon be at our voyaging." She stepped past him and strode toward the horizon.

David followed with some reluctance as Morwyn led the way across the plain. They had covered three hundred paces (David had been counting, to distract himself from the heat) when a rift suddenly opened in the land at their feet: a rift with walls so clean and sheer that it had been invisible within the masking heat-haze until they were almost upon it.

David found himself standing on the brink. Perhaps ten feet below, at the bottom of the narrow canyon, a wide, shallow river glided languorously, its water clear as glass, with more of the white sand visible on the bottom. The river ran arrow-straight from horizon to horizon. And almost at its further shore a strip of golden glimmer showed where a Straight Track lazed upon it.

Morwyn led the way down a flight of wide steps cut into the bank to their left, and a moment later they stood upon the square lower landing.

"This Track leads to Lugh's realm," she said, pointing to the right, "but from a seldom-used direction. I do not think Lugh will have set a watch at the place it enters, for this land is most times empty, and Lugh has no interest in it. Perhaps he has even forgotten it. Indeed, were I not what I am I would not know of it myself. But a Fireshaper does well to know all of the Lands of Fire."

David stuck his hands on his hips in exasperation. "But I thought the borders were sealed, even against the Tracks."

"And so they are: one may not step from the Tracks into Lugh's kingdom, for the fires of his sealing prevent it. Yet if one were to find the right place of entry, then find a way through the sealing . . ."

"Which you, of course, know how to do."

"Of course: the sealing makes use of Fire in its elemental form, and since the sealing is a thing of Fire, a ship made of Fire may make that passage safely."

Morwyn smiled, and reached into a red velvet pouch that hung at her left hip.

David could not help but gasp when he saw what she held out before him an instant later.

It was a tiny model ship, perfect in each detail, from the needle-spear of the single mast to the delicate webbing of furled sail and rigging, to the high, curling stern and even more impressive prow which was marked by a gleaming dragon's head no bigger than the end of his finger. A low, flat cabin lay behind the mast, and the dramatic swooping sides were scalloped with what appeared to be tiny shields. It reminded David of a Viking ship, though there were no oars, and he didn't think the cabin was typical.

"Very pretty," he said with forced indifference. He liked models and intricate craftsmanship and suddenly wanted very much to hold the object. "Small, though. Mighty close quarters for two people."

"Is it?" Morwyn challenged. "Perhaps it only *seems* so."

Before David could reply she set the boat gently into the still water beyond the landing, then brushed a long nail across the head of one of the tiny dragons on her ring. Its mouth popped open obediently, and a tiny flame shot out. She turned it toward the model, the flame continuing to spark on her knuckle, and set it against the miniature prow.

David held his breath in dismay as the toy ship caught fire.

Yet in spite of the flames that enwrapped it, it did not seem to be consumed. In fact, as the fire took hold, the ship began to grow, to swell, second by second, seeming to draw substance from the flames that lapped about it, so that in two breaths it was a yard long, and in four the size of a small canoe. Ten breaths later it had reached the size he imagined by rights it should be. And all the while fire leaped and curled around it.

Eventually the flames began to subside, as though they were absorbed into the wood and metal and fabric of the ship itself. The air cooled, and the last persistent flicker of green about a copper shield boss winked out. A breeze from the west set the water to rippling, and the rigging to swelling gently in its wake.

"Neat!" David cried in spite of himself.

"It is the Power of the Fireshapers," Morwyn responded flatly. "A simple thing, in truth. Indeed, mortal men do much the same."

David stared at her. "You're kidding!"

Morwyn shook her head. "It is common with your kind, is it not, to draw the water from a thing, so that little remains but a dry shell, and then renew it at need by returning that water to it?"

David nodded slowly. "Freeze-drying, dehydration, whatever."

"So it is with this ship, except that instead of adding water I used fire. I could do the same with my dwelling."

"God," David whispered. "I sure haven't seen the *Sidhe* do anything like that."

"Nor will you," Morwyn replied archly. "The Powersmiths could rule the Worlds, if we wished to," she added, her voice at once very still and solemn, her eyes taking on a distant glaze. "We suffer them to reign: the Sidhe and the Alfar and the Tylwyth-Teg all."

David discovered he had no reply, so set himself into uneasy contemplation as Morwyn gestured the ship toward them. A moment later its sides scraped gently against the steps. She motioned David on board, then followed him into the bow.

"Your sword, now: draw it."

David commenced fumbling with the peace-ties and a moment later had freed the weapon.

It gleamed in the hot air, sun-fired lightning: a simple silver blade and plain golden cross hilt bound with pale gray leather. But the balance suited him perfectly, as he found by making feints and lunges across the deck.

Morwyn frowned. "Such frivolity becomes neither you nor the sword. Now give it to me, for it will be our guide."

David rather reluctantly handed the sword to Morwyn—hilt-first, as he had heard was the proper manner.

She took it, tested its weight, then grasped its quillons firmly in her two hands—and plunged it into the deck within the narrow vee behind the high, curving neck of the dragon figurehead.

It entered the wood like a blade thrust into water. A subtle shudder rolled across the planks beneath them. David reached impulsively toward the blade.

"No!" Morwyn cried. "Leave it. Neither boat nor weapon are damaged. The sword is made of the same metal as the Iron Road; as long as it stands there, the Road will draw it onward. Once you have come to land again, withdraw it; it will be your guide as well. You have only to heed its tugging."

"I was wondering about that," David muttered.

The sorceress did not reply, as she made her way to the stern and took up the tiller with her right hand. A flip of a finger set the great sail unfurling, almost catching David unaware as it billowed out behind him a little above his head.

He swung around, ready to protest, but then awe filled him. A magnificent rampant dragon was embroidered in gold on the shimmering scarlet fabric of the sail. Turning again, he moved back to the prow, to stop finally beside the sword. He rested a cautious hand on its pommel, felt it thrum beneath his fingers, oddly comforting.

As wind filled its sail, the ship began to glide across the water. Morwyn pointed the prow toward the glitter of Track by the left-hand wall of the canyon— And then they were there, darting on the slightest of breezes, while Track and sword kept them locked on their path and the slim prow cut the water with knifelike ease.

A guilty eagerness woke within David. He was enjoying himself, and he felt certain he shouldn't: he was racing headlong into danger, with one set of lives threatened if he failed, and another life threatened if he didn't.

But as the dragon ship raced forward, and the sail rose red and glorious behind him; as a cool breeze slid around it to caress his hot cheeks, bringing with it the sweet sound of Morwyn singing in the stern; he decided, for the nonce, to give over. He'd relax, take it easy. Let Morwyn call the shots.

And hope that none of them hit him.

Chapter XXVI: Waiting

(Tir-Nan-Og)

In the morning stillness of Tir-Nan-Og, Lugh's throne room was cold and lonely. Fog had crept inside and now floated in furtive, anxious tendrils about the floor. Beams of sunlight slanted through the windows to the left, touching the walls and pillars with the pale tints of dawn.

His hand ached where the dagger joined it to throne and map and land. No one would ever know the agony it cost him. And another thing that no one would ever know: the dagger talked to him, told him about the borders of his kingdom, and who went there. And told him other things as well, which a certain matching sword relayed to it: what that sword saw, the dagger saw; what its master knew, he knew. That Ailill's trail had been found, for instance; that Fionna was all but captured, which was certainly a relief.

David Sullivan was missing, too—another problem there, to which the resolution might be interesting, if it led in the direction Lugh was beginning to suspect. *Someone* had interfered with Fionna's plan, after all, for she would never have set Ailill to run the Tracks in beast shape. So there was at least one more person involved: someone with no love for Fionna or Ailill. And there was something else of note going on at the well that had recently appeared by the ford: something had awakened there which had long been sleeping. Perhaps he should investigate that, maybe exert a little divine intervention. It might prove very useful if certain things went as he more and more expected.

No sound disturbed his ensuing reverie except his breathing and the dry rustle of the enfields' talons as they paced on the marble floor beyond the dais. Their padded hind paws made no noise at all.

The larger of the two, Ceilleigh, broke formation and came forward to have his fox ears scratched. Angharad, his mate, followed more tentatively. Lugh smiled and stretched his free hand toward her, grimacing as the movement caused the bones of his other hand to grate against the blade. A thin line of new blood trickled between his second and third fingers.

With a faint creak the great doors at the far end of the hall cracked open. A fluttering of wings disturbed the fog; a swirling of red-black mist occluded the spears of sunlight—and the Morrigu stood before him, her face cold and pale against the red and black of her elaborately dagged gown. A formation of crows swooped in behind her to array themselves in fan-shaped patterns at her feet.

"So, Lady, it is early you are about," Lugh said pleasantly. "Are you preparing to renew your search? Or are you only now returning?"

The Morrigu's face clouded. "The latter, Lord Ard Rhi. I have searched, and all the men and women of your kingdom search even now. They search on foot, who may, and on beast back; and they search with Power, who are well versed in its use. Some comb the past or the future; some the seas or the air. One inspects the tiny Worlds that lie inside our own. Had you not sealed the borders, we might search outside as well."

"And what of the Tracks?" Lugh demanded. "Are *they* being watched?"

"Most certainly they are, Lord," the Morrigu replied, indignantly. "Many have I set on lookout there, though I think it an effort in vain. One could not pass from them into Tir-Nan-Og—or from Tir-Nan-Og to them."

"Only a flame could pass that barrier," Lugh noted cryptically. "A flame hotter than my wrath."

The Morrigu eyed him narrowly. "Aye, Lord," she whispered, "but no such flames exist."

"It is to be hoped," Lugh replied with a smile. "But what have you learned from this watching, Lady? Is there any sign of those we seek?"

The Morrigu shook her head. "No, Lord. Neither Ailill nor Fionna are like to be found in Tir-Nan-Og. Other Powers we have felt probing about your borders, yet we have not been able to find the source of those Powers, for, as I have said, your binding likewise binds us."

She took a breath and stared hard at the High King, who returned that stare mildly. "And I must say it now, Lord, that surely another way might have been found to achieve your ends. For this waiting game you are playing is dangerous in the extreme. Surely, at least, you could have sent a force seeking Ailill and Fionna upon the Tracks, for that is certainly where they have gone. It would have been better than putting every one of your subjects on watch!"

"No," Lugh replied. "That would have been folly. First of all, there was a dire need for haste, for I did not dare give Ailill a chance to flee my realm entirely. Had I waited it is possible he could have returned to Erenn and thus have escaped my justice. With the borders sealed, he cannot now reach that land, for the few Tracks that lead there from Outside will not support him in this season.

"And second, Morrigu, there is an excellent chance that Ailill may have fled into the Lands of Men, since that realm lies closest to our own. A large force of our folk suddenly appearing there would truly have upset the balance between the Worlds. Almost certainly it would have provoked too much curiosity on the part of humankind —and we have already seen the trouble one human's knowledge has cost us. To send more could quite possibly prompt the very war Ailill has long desired: between Faerie and the Lands of Men. That, I dare not risk."

"That choice may be taken from you," the Morrigu observed.

Lugh nodded grimly. "Aye, but I do not think that time is come, though I am not so optimistic as once I was. Yet that is another debate for another time."

"Have you other commands for me, then?"

"Call off the search—and trust me."

The Morrigu stared at him. "That is becoming a hard thing to do, Lord, unless you trust me in turn. You know more than you tell; this much is clear to me."

Lugh smiled cryptically. "I am not called Samildinach without reason. Besides," he added, "a king should test his Warlord now and then, it seems to me. And his Mistress of Battles as well." *And,* he continued to himself, *I suspect I may soon get to test David Sullivan. I will know, as soon as I have checked on the well.*

Chapter XXVII: Boogers in the Woods

(The Straight Tracks)

"Fools," the deer repeated, staring at the company that encircled her. "Poor fools!"

Somehow, as Liz looked on aghast, the creature's body quadrupled in size.

And then the change began in earnest: The gray-red hair changed to stiff scarlet fur that massed upon its shoulders in a heavy mane; the dainty hooves became wicked black claws. Its legs thickened, chest expanded, shoulders became more massive as the body assumed the muscular, low-slung contours of a vast feline. Even its short tail altered, grew long and naked and hard-jointed as a scorpion's, with that creature's dreadful barbed stinger at its tip.

And the head that now looked out from a thick ruff of mane had become a horrible, fanged travesty of a woman's.

"A manticore!" Regan gasped, as the monster crouched.

Fionna growled, black lips curling away from teeth like ivory daggers. No trace of the deer remained except the eyes: the same red, hate-filled orbs that scant seconds before had glared at them from above a narrow muzzle. Now they cast their baleful stare from a snarling woman's face eight feet above the ground.

Liz felt her nerve desert her, saw her spear point waver in hands that were suddenly clammy. She found herself drawing back in horror. Beside her, Alec did the same.

"Shit!" Gary gasped.

"You said it, man," Alec muttered. "I think I'm gonna!"

A horse screamed, and Liz saw Snowwhisper running wild and panicked around the farther side of the clearing. Cormac's horse was there too: poor Cormac. Regan whistled a single pure note, and the horses calmed, though they continued to pace nervously.

"Surrender, Fionna," Nuada thundered for the second time in as many minutes. He leveled his sword at the sorceress, his eyes blazing like small suns.

"To what?" she sneered. "A handful of children, old men, and crippled Sidhe?"

"Maybe not so crippled," Nuada cried. He set his mouth, focused his gaze straight at his adversary. His body shifted, expanded, strained against clothing that was suddenly too tight. His skin darkened, became hard and slick. An extravagance of scaly horns bristled around his face.

Beneath him Blackwind snorted, shook his mane, but held his ground.

The manticore took a clumsy step toward him.

Nuada swept his arm out and up, the sword a glitter of fire; and his arm stretched impossibly far beyond his sleeve in a quick snap that sent the blade slashing close to Fionna's face.

But the blow did not connect. At the limit of extension, the Faery lord's grip seemed to lose its strength. He managed a pair of wobbly thrusts, and then his arm was drawing back, regaining its proper proportions. His face returned to normal, pale with disappointment. He shook his head, wiped his arm across his face and cast an apologetic glance at Regan. "I cannot; this body will not let me, not even with the Track."

"Oh, so the mighty Airgetlam wears the stuff of the Lands of Men, does he?" came the manticore's sarcastic growl. "Well, it seems you do not find that substance of much service, when you ask it to change shape for you and it refuses. You are—"

"Froech, now!" Regan shouted, lunging with her spear at the monster's unprotected side—once, twice—and drew back as its jointed tail lashed at her.

She flung herself flat on the ground. "Knives! Throw the knives!"

Faery daggers flew then, and human kitchen knives—and two more broom-handle spears: a sparkling, hissing rain of steel and Faery alloys thumping into leonine flesh. Froech threw, and Alec; Uncle Dale, then Liz; Froech again, and then Gary.

Fionna bowed her head, presenting only her mat of mane to their attack, shrugging the weapons aside though her flesh and hair smoked at the touch of iron. Regan cast her last weapon at the creature's eye, but Fionna batted the stiletto casually away. And Froech's lone remaining dagger was a mere trinket meant for show and flimsily made, useless against so vast an adversary.

"Pick away," Fionna roared. "These iron toys are like bees to me, for my fur is thick. No weapon I have seen so far could kill me before I ripped its master asunder. And I *feel* like killing just now—"

The manticore whipped around to face the terrified group of humans at its left, took a heavy step forward. "Perhaps one of the mortals first?"

"No, Fionna! In the name of Lugh I command you!"

"Enough, Silverhand," Fionna snarled, twisting around again. Her right arm whipped up and over in a horribly casual slash of claws.

Nuada paled and tried to move Blackwind back with knee pressure alone.

He was too late. One claw, one single black claw ripped across the stallion's side, bare inches behind his thigh. It continued across Blackwind's rump in a terrible wound that deepened as it went, flaying muscle and nerve amid a dark gush of blood.

The horse screamed horribly, even as Nuada threw himself forward across its neck.

Another flash of claws, and the stallion crashed to the ground.

Nuada too hit the earth, rolled, then rose in a bent-knee crouch.

Paws tore the air before him. He leapt backward, and the deadly claws swung by his head, missing by mere inches. His sword ripped through fur but missed flesh.

And then he was on his feet, lunging forward, the sword raised high before him as he entered the monster's shadow. His blade cut: an upper front leg; whipped across the chest. Snicked out at the throat, even as the beast drew back.

"Froech, Regan—do something!" Liz screamed, glancing aside to see Regan's face straining as she too attempted a shape-shifting without apparent success. Beyond the manticore, Froech was fully involved with a panicking Firearrow.

Nuada pressed the attack, stabbing, feinting, drawing lines of blood from paws and forelegs, but never able to get close enough to finish her.

Fionna responded savagely with raking paws and occasional stabs of tail; but kept her face and chest well away from that sliver of metal. And then—

A quick left–right, too fast for him to parry, sent claws scraping across his single arm and into his hand.

"*No!*" Liz screamed, as she saw the Sword of Lugh fly from Nuada's nerveless grasp.

Froech stretched desperate fingers toward the blade as it whirled past—missed—leapt off his horse and after it. But there was another body in his way of a sudden, knocking him sideways as the manticore hurled itself forward to imprison Nuada's chest and shoulders beneath its vast forepaws. Its scorpion tail swung around, arched above his stomach, and with savage delicacy stabbed home right beneath the ribs. Nuada's scream was muffled by the mass of scarlet fur. He shuddered, then lay still.

The manticore raised its head, roared triumphantly.

"Quick—Alec, Liz," Gary muttered, nodding to his right. "The Track. It's too low for that thing, I think. Maybe our only choice. I'll run up there and grab one of those spears, poke ole Fionna real good while you guys run for cover."

"Gary, no!" Alec shouted.

"Go! Dammit!"

Gary gave him a shove in the direction he had indicated, ran forward and recovered his spear, then drew back and stabbed at the creature's side. The spear struck home, hanging for a moment amid a smoking mass of fur until Gary jerked it out and prepared to stab again.

The tail snapped toward him.

Gary ran.

"Here, Fionna! Look here!" Froech yelled. He took a deep breath and paused, tense and motionless as his shape too began to shimmer. Seams ripped in his tunic, in the shirt and hose beneath, fell away in tatters to reveal a mat of thick black hair on arms and legs and torso. His pointed shoes frayed from feet that had sprouted claws. The link-belt strained across a thickening middle, then snapped, to pin-wheel crazily into the grass behind him.

Fionna saw what he was about and a strange sort of smile contorted her mouth. She heaved herself off Nuada, and turned to face the Faery boy.

"Oh, Froech, is it? Froech my would-be lover . . . *as if I would stoop to embrace such a miserable thing as you!"*

Froech solidified into a he-bear even larger than Fionna. He took a shambling step toward her, but she did not move.

"Froech the gullible, I should say," Fionna taunted, though the bear was almost upon her. "Or Froech the fool! Froech who could have given me no pleasure even had I allowed him to touch me!"

Froech snarled, enraged, and he raised his arms and flung himself at the sorceress, who reared up to embrace him like the lover he had never been.

The clearing resounded with their impact; the company drew back as the two beasts locked together and began to sway back and forth across the clearing. It was not an elegant encounter, for both combatants were too large, too clumsy, too unfamiliar with their unwieldy bodies to engage in niceties. It was a battle of grunts and pushes, of raking claws, of snapping teeth. Blood flowed through red fur like a thousand muddy rivulets.

The Sword of Lugh lay between them, now in serious danger of being broken.

Liz had joined Alec at the mouth of the central tunnel, holding him tight across the shoulders. As the battle took Froech and Fionna farther away, Regan and Gary rushed out to drag Nuada's body into the shelter of the tunnel.

"Wonder if this stuff'll burn?" Uncle Dale mused, looking at the briars around him. "Maybe we could cut her off that way."

Regan shook her head. "No fire is hot enough to set these plants alight. And even so—"

"Oh, Jesus Christ!" Liz screamed all at once, as the ring erupted into more extravagant life upon her finger. It had been glowing because of Fionna's threat, but now it blazed so brightly that Liz had no choice but to rip it off and stuff it into her pocket—

—Just as an immense stag rushed into the clearing. It was the same strange color and configuration that Fionna had previously worn, but even larger—and with a bloody gash visible across the lower part of its left thigh.

"Jesus *H.* Christ," Gary echoed.

The stag paused, its pain-reddened gaze darting wildly about. Madness showed in its eyes, a madness that was more horrible, more terrifying, than Fionna's raw, acid hatred.

Then the stag leapt, twisting around the combat, and arching across the remaining distance in half a bound, heading straight for the central tunnel.

"It's Ailill!" Alec yelled. "It's gotta be him!"

"Snowwhisper!" Regan shouted frantically. "To me! Quickly!"

Somehow the mare was there, blocking the stag, with Firearrow right behind her.

The stag turned, started toward the left-hand tunnel.

Regan ran forward, found her mount, leapt onto her back. Uncle Dale stuck his heels in Bessie's flanks and followed, cutting off Ailill on the other side.

The stag bounced uncertainly between them.

Regan reached toward his neck, only to draw back quickly as antlers slashed in her direction.

Gary rushed up, spear in hand.

"No, you fool!" Regan yelled. "Get back!"

Gary dodged flailing hooves and jumped aside—straight into Alec and Liz.

The way before him suddenly clear, Ailill broke free of the press of horses and charged into the left-hand track, leaping neatly over Nuada's body as he entered the green tangle of that tunnel.

Regan pounded after him.

Liz claimed Cormac's mount and started to follow, but the lady was already a distant spot against the green-gold haze of the Track.

"Hold, girl," Uncle Dale called before she had gone twenty feet. "We've gotta put an end to this business. You see to Firearrow."

Liz reined her mount hard, jerked her head around to see the two boys trying helplessly to mount one or the other on Froech's fractious stallion. But Uncle Dale's shout interrupted them. "Quick, Alec, give me your belt!"

Gary looked puzzled, but Alec began to spin the combination lock that bound the twenty-eight inches of chrome steel chain about his waist. "Oh, yeah, I see," he acknowledged. The lock clicked open, and he jerked the chain free and handed the whole apparatus to Uncle Dale.

"Froech! Now!" Uncle Dale's thin cry rang into the clearing.

Froech heard him. He drew upon all his strength, called upon his last dregs of Power, and willed himself larger still, though he felt his very substance begin to fray as muscle and bone and skin stretched too thin.

Fionna's grip faltered, and Froech sensed her weakness and put his full strength into one final blow that sent the manticore staggering backward into the wall of briars.

Claws raked both his sides as Fionna released her hold and let out a roar of agony. The manticore wriggled and twisted in a moment of outraged futility, but succeeded only in digging the thorns more viciously into her body.

Froech released his hold on the Power that had sustained him and dived toward his companions, even as his shape collapsed upon itself. By the time he reached the entrance to the Track, he again wore human form, though now that shape was naked.

Light burned into his eyes, as he saw before him the old man to the right and mounted, and whistling round and round in his hand the source of that light: a blazing wheel of iron flame that arced across the Track above his head. He ducked under and joined the two human boys beyond, turning quickly. "Look!" he shouted.

For back in the clearing the enraged Fionna had ripped herself free from the wall of briars, though vast bloody patches of ruddy fur remained there. She had dropped onto all fours, casting her eyes about—red pig-eyes that glowed above a snarling, slavering mouth.

Then she charged.

"Come on, kitty!" Uncle Dale yelled, twirling the chain faster and faster.

The manticore reached the tunnel's mouth, hesitated . . .

Uncle Dale released his hold, sent the chain spinning straight at the hulking shape scant yards before him.

But as the length of chromium-plated iron spun through the air, one end snagged on a protruding thorn and hooked itself there, sending the other end flying pendulum-fashion straight into Fionna's face. The manticore seized it, though her great paws smoked at its touch; snapped it apart, and flung it to the ground before her, where the two parts fell atop each other in the shape of an equal-armed cross.

"And now who is a fool, Fionna?" came Froech's gleeful cry from his point of safety.

Fionna gathered herself for a leap across the wall of heat already welling from the chain. But then a sheet of actual flame blazed up from the Track, startling her—a flame hotter than any iron-born fire she had ever encountered, and centered on that gleaming metal cross.

The Track itself began to shudder. A patch of darkness showed in its substance where the chain touched it—a darkness Fionna could not cross—and that blackness grew wider as she watched.

And as the flames spread farther, reached into the thorns to spread their contagion higher in a ring of fire, a cross-shaped rift expanded as the golden shimmer crisped back into nothingness, withdrawing from the power of the metal. Back and back it curled, until a dark gap maybe ten feet across had burned into the Track. Then its very substance began to fall away, revealing patches of nothingess: a total absence of light or color that was blacker than black, whiter than white, and into which the pieces of chain fell at last as they burned through the final layer of the Track and entered chaos, burned through that, and burst at last into the skies high above the Lands of Men.

On one side of that gap stood the snarling manticore that was Fionna, and on the other a frightened company of mortals and Sidhe gaping in appalled wonder.

"What've you done?" Alec shouted.

Uncle Dale shrugged helplessly and tugged his whiskers. "Didn't mean to do nothin' like *that*, that's for darned sure! I knowed iron's dangerous to have around Faery things, so I figgered it wouldn't do that there animal no good if I could get a good clear shot at her face. That there chrome platin' must be even worse."

A pounding of hooves sounded from farther down the Track, and a moment later Regan rode up. There was no sign of Ailill. The lady's gaze took in the smoldering end of the trail, the furious sorceress who stood beyond it—face contorting in what was obviously speech, though no sound crossed the space between them.

"Where is the sword?" a weak voice asked from the ground.

"Huh?" Gary and Alec said at once.

"Nuada! You're okay?" Suddenly Liz was kneeling by the Faery lord's side.

He shook his head. "No, I am wounded—Fionna's sting carries a slow poison that saves heart and brain and mouth for last. Now tell me of the sword!"

"The sword is lost, Lord," the lady said. "It is somewhere in the clearing."

"No!"

"I fear so, my Lord."

Nuada fixed his gaze on Uncle Dale. "I don't know whether to laud you or to curse you. By sealing the Track behind us you have saved our lives. Fionna must now find another way to pursue us—if indeed that is still her goal, with her brother now close by. But the Sword of Lugh was left behind and is now beyond our reach. If Fionna finds it and realizes its power, no one will be safe!"

"What *is* its power?" Alec asked carefully.

Nuada's face was cold as ice. "That I may not say. In that matter Lugh has laid a ban on me, and I could not tell you even if I tried."

Regan dismounted and knelt beside Nuada. "Can you ride, Lord?"

Nuada nodded, tried to rise, grimacing. Regan laid a hand across his stomach, drew it away bloody.

"You should not . . ."

"I have no other choice. If I stay here, I will surely die."

"You may anyway, Lord."

"Regan!" Liz cried. "What a thing to say!"

The Faery lady looked at her. "I meant him no discourtesy. Death is a thing that happens." Then, to Nuada, "Lord, will you ride with me?"

"Aye, Lady—though I caution you, I may require some holding." He tried to laugh, but pain caught him.

"Well, there's no point in waitin' around, I don't reckon," Uncle Dale said. "Best we be on our way. Leastwise we know the right road now. Better do a little re-sortin' of riders, though. Let's see: we got three folks that can't ride, and four that can. Liz, you better ride by

yourself, I 'spect. I'll take Alec; Regan, you said you'd carry Silverhand."

The lady nodded. "You have my thought exactly. I have some
healing skills, and perhaps I might be able to apply what little Power
I yet possess in strengthening my master."

"Okay, so that leaves Froech with Gary—everybody got it?"

Gary stared for a moment at Froech's nakedness, then stepped out
of his sweatpants, leaving himself in his inevitable black gym shorts.
He tapped Froech on the shoulder and handed the garment to him.

Froech smiled sheepishly and took it.

As Alec gave Liz a boost onto Cormac's horse, their gazes locked
for a moment, and he saw a glaze of despair in her eyes. "Want to
talk?" he whispered.

Liz shook her head emphatically. "Can't. No time. No time for
anything but haste and hurry now. Hurry to catch Ailill . . . But can't
they see, Alec? Can't they see that since the deer was Ailill, and he's
obviously crazy, and since Fionna's little better off, we're no closer
to finding David than we were before. I don't think the manticore's
the woman I saw in my vision; she just doesn't feel right. I can't
explain it any better than that, but I think there must be another
woman involved in this. We're off chasing Ailill while David's getting farther and farther away."

"Can't be helped, though," came Uncle Dale's gentle voice, as he
helped Alec up behind him. "Can't go back now, gotta keep on
ahead. You by yourself won't do nobody no good. And you sure
won't do nobody any good if you don't worry about the trouble at
hand. We don't survive this hunt, won't be nobody left to hunt for
Davy. Think about *that*. You've done well enough so far—now try
lookin' away from your fear. Might see some hope if you look hard
enough."

A wan smile crossed Liz's face. "Yeah, right . . . and thanks,
Uncle Dale, thanks a lot."

A sudden chill shook her and she glanced back down the tunnel.
Beyond the uncrossable gulf behind them, Fionna the manticore had
vanished from sight.

But somehow Liz was not comforted.

Chapter XXVIII: Visions

(In a Place Between)

Katie had never felt so good in her life. There was energy everywhere: in the gold of the Track below her, in the shimmer of the air around her. When she breathed, it was like breathing youth. When she moved it was like walking away from time. She had to look down constantly to see that her wrinkled bag of a body was not that of the young woman who had wedded Liam McNally sixty years ago and more.

And there was the man beside her. He held her hand—necessary, he had said, to save her mind from madness. He wore a long robe the color of moonlight, and that was strange. But no stranger than other things she'd seen young folks wear, all leather and spikes and paint and pointy things. And he was handsome as only old men can be, handsome as an heirloom, smoothed and polished with age, as decades of absent touches can smooth a chair or table, softening the contours, changing them, but never hiding what they once had been.

He still had not told his name, but he had told her many things instead: things about Those Ones, whom now he called the Sidhe, things about Nuada she had never dared to guess, about Cormac and Regan and that wild young hellion they'd called Froech who'd brought disaster riding on his back with his fool's talk about High Kings and swords and the sealing of borders with fire.

Only it had not been wild talk. It had been the truth, of that she was now convinced; and the one beside her had told her, when she had asked, how he alone now had Power in the Lands of Men, for he alone was *of* that land, soul and flesh, and he alone knew how to command the Powers of that world as even the Sidhe did not. It was his Power that had taken her from the camp to the Track, though it had tired him, he'd admitted. And it was his Power that now bore them along.

It would be her own Power she must soon find and discover how to use; that was something else he had told her, and it puzzled her.

But her questions brought only: "I know only that you are to follow the cross in the sky."

"What cross?" she'd said, thinking perhaps he meant Cygnus the Swan, that some called the Northern Cross.

But no answer had he given.

They had walked onward then, in silence.

Eventually the man spoke again. "We are nearly there, Katie McNally, and beyond here I cannot go. You must walk your own roads now."

Katie squeezed the warm hand in her own.

It squeezed back, sending warmth and love and comfort into her. But then it was slipping away, releasing her hold though she sought to drag it back. Going . . .

My name is Oisin . . .

Gone.

Katie was alone at the edge of a forest, gazing down at a slope of field. Ahead was a house old and wrinkled as one of her hands. There were several cars there, and the buzz of conversation came to her even where she stood, a quarter mile away across the valley. Closer in was a dirt road, and far left on this side was the silver steeple of a tiny church. Almost across the road from it was another house. Lights glared there too, from the top of the rounded hill where that house sat, and she squinted her good eye (now *very* good, she was surprised to note), and saw that though similar to many of the older houses she'd seen in north Georgia, it had a sprawl of new additions tacked onto the back.

"Bright for moonlight," she muttered, then gazed skyward, checking.

And saw the cross in the sky.

Truly there *was* a cross in the sky, an equal-armed rent in the heavens, maybe an outstretched hand's breadth wide, shining like Sunday above the black mass of mountain that dwarfed the tiny homes before her. It was as if the night itself had been ripped open and a glimpse of God's True Light allowed to peek through.

It was a sign of Our Lord if ever there was one, and it proved to Katie once and for all that Oisin had told the truth——for surely the devil could not lie about such wondrous things.

She continued staring, as wonder crept within her veins and set her soul to joyful blazing.

"God be praised," she whispered.

And saw a spot appear at the center of that cross: there and then gone, a spot so quick and tiny she thought her eyes must be playing tricks.

But no, there was something there, not in the cross now, but falling out of the dark.

She blinked, knew an instant of fear . . . and something whistled past her cheek and smote the ground before her. She felt the land tremble beneath her feet as she had never felt it before.

She opened her eyes again, saw lying in the broom sedge before her two fourteen-inch lengths of chrome steel chain that lay atop each other in the shape of a cross.

"God *be* praised!" she repeated. Then she frowned, for the wind once more had found her, bringing a return of the cold.

But no, that wind was now her friend; chill it might be, but with it came scents that spoke to her: of horses that were more than horses and men that were more than men, and of men who were *only* men as well, young ones and an old one. Of the subtle perfume the red-haired girl had worn, of the smell of coffee and moonshine on their breaths. And those smells came from the road ahead, and the mountain beyond, and the sky above as well.

And a sound rode that wind with the odors, a sound from out of the east where the little house was: the sound of a woman weeping.

Chapter XXIX: The Burning Road

(The Lands of Fire)

David jerked himself awake with a start. He'd fallen asleep somehow, wedged into the tight angle of the dragon ship's bow, his head pillowed on the arm he'd stretched along the railing. His tongue felt swollen. A distant ache pounded against the back of his eyes—a result, no doubt, of his earlier drinking; the same indulgence, he suspected, that was responsible for his drowsiness in the first place. His body felt strangely heavy too—and damp; he became aware of a steady prickle of spray against his face. The air pulsed in time to the slap of wavelets against the hull, as loose-fastened timbers creaked a counterpoint. He glanced down, saw sunlight strike painful sparks from the glitter of mail exposed on arm and leg, and scratched his cheek distractedly, certain it now bore the imprint of those circular links. A trace of roughness along his jawline told him he would soon need to shave again. That would be twice a week now—as if it mattered. It might never matter again.

He shaded his eyes with his hand and squinted into the hot air, careful not to let his gaze shift too high—the blazing sun would surely blind him. Before him lay the slope of pinewood deck, with the arrogant sweep of mast and gaudy sail erupting amidships, and standing in the stern, proud as an ocean goddess, Morwyn. Her hands rested lightly on the tiller, her face shone rapt and distant as if her thoughts were a thousand years away. She was beautiful; any man would gaze on that beauty and despair.

But not David, because he knew her for what she was. Almost he was sorry for her, because a part of him truly wanted to like her, in spite of what she had done to him. God knew she'd had plenty of justification for her actions—his own encounter with Ailill had proven that one's callousness. But in spite of Morwyn's beauty, in spite of her lavish generosity, he dared not drop his guard, dared not trust her. For he was certain that, given the need, she'd suck him dry in an instant: use him for everything he was worth and then discard him, and immorality be damned. He was mortal, she was Faery; and for her—for all her kind—there *was* no immorality, as far as the World of Men was concerned.

He twisted around to gaze down at the river swishing by the hull, then across to the nearside bank, where the surrounding escarpments had grown lower, so that the plain itself was sometimes visible in dips and hollows.

It was cooler there in the river-rift; for that, at least, he was grateful. What did Morwyn mean, anyway, to dress him in such heavy and confining attire, when—to judge by the glare of the sun on the deck and the heat devils that now swept along the cliff tops almost at eye level—it must be well over a hundred degrees in the surrounding desert. Only the steady breeze along the river's surface and the boxed-in sides of the canyon relieved that pervasive oppression.

He hoped it would not abandon them.

A good while longer he watched, then found himself nodding again.

The banks had lowered considerably when David roused himself once more, to discover to his dismay that the breeze was losing its battle with the sun. Sweat had sprung out on his forehead, and a trickle had begun to ooze down the hollow of his spine. He reached back to scratch it, but found his movements confined by the mail so that he finally had to stand and rub against one of the spines of the figurehead.

A dreamy lethargy fell upon him, and he gave himself up to watching the featureless white landscape passing by, grateful for any random touch of wind that might stray from the channel to brush his face. Once or twice he twisted around farther to watch the sparkle of Track streaming by, its golden motes blending with the clear water and white sand.

"Pay close attention," Morwyn called from the stern. "You may see a thing that surprises you."

David squinted into the blazing glare of light and water, trying to observe the Track both with his natural vision and with the Sight. He succeeded in part, saw the glow increase an order of magnitude as the Sight kicked in, then realized he was seeing *two* Tracks. One lay atop the other, as if the golden ribbon had split horizontally and they now sailed the upper arm of an infinitely long vee laid on its side, while the other arm fell farther and farther away below them. He looked up. The landscape to either side was as bleached and desolate as ever, except now it was not so flat. Hills stretched in the distance, and terrible golden lights speared the sky at points here and there like bolts of frozen lightning.

The banks grew narrower, and strange excrescences rose from the whiteness, becoming twisted shapes of tortured, fluted stone that here resembled bones, there crystals, and in other places the complex siliceous skeletons of ancient corals. Mostly, though, they resembled thorns, for they curved away from the wind, slanted at identical angles, with concave curves on the leeward side, sharpening to needle-points where the two sides tapered together at the top.

And then David noticed dark shapes moving among those curious, hooked pillars like shadows without substance. Once, one came almost to the edge of the bank, and he saw that its naked body wore a man's shape, but nothing showed in its black eyes except a feral blankness that marked it either idiot or mad.

The striated stone spires became more frequent, too, growing taller and taller and ever closer together, so that their buttresses overlapped and their points sometimes touched each other. It was like the lacy calcined pierced work of a piece of human bone sliced crossways; or like a frost-chilled forest wrought of silicon strands and salt. And always there was the hot white glitter, like a sprinkling of powdered diamonds cast upon the air and burning there.

Here and there serpents slithered among the strange stone growths, and some of them were titanic. An emerald green one stretched a barrel-sized head far across the river, long black tongue flickering curiously, as though it sought to converse with the figure-head.

David drew back instinctively. Snakes, *per se* did not bother him —but when their heads were as big as his entire body . . . He found himself reaching for the sword, but Morwyn shouted something, and the creature drew back, hissing.

And spat: a spray of oily black liquid. And where those drops fell upon the deck, thin tendrils of smoke trickled into the air from tiny pits eaten in the woodwork.

A larger drop splashed the back of David's left hand and he screamed as the venom seared his skin. He jerked it toward his mouth, stopping himself only just in time as he stared in curiously removed incredulity at the blistering redness that was spreading across his flesh. Already he could see the skin peeling back as the poison ate its way inward.

"Goddamn! Oh, goddamn, goddamn!" he shrieked, trying to wipe the pain away upon his surcoat, only to discover as he did, that contact with the velvet merely increased his agony.

"Morwyn! Oh God, Morwyn!" He wrenched himself awkwardly

to his feet and staggered toward the stern, his injured hand smoking before him. His balance deserted him amidships and he clutched vainly at the mast as he tottered past.

Pain became the focus of his universe.

Suddenly Morwyn was beside him, a whisper of fabric, a sweetness upon the air. Words thrummed in his ears. Something touched his wrist.

The pain was gone. David stared first at his own hand, and then at the smaller, smoother one that held it tightly while its mate described careful patterns in the air above.

"Is that better?" Morwyn asked, her voice soft as he had ever heard it.

David nodded slowly. "Yeah, much better." He hesitated. "Thanks," he said finally, looking up.

To his surprise, she smiled. "You are healed? There is no pain?"

David flexed his fingers experimentally. "I think so. That's a real neat trick you've got there."

"It is a thing I do," Morwyn replied quietly. "Would that I could restore my son so easily." She rose gracefully and returned to her place by the tiller.

David watched her, and for the first time he saw the sadness that lay at the heart of her every thought and word and action.

Suddenly he was sorry for her.

Very slowly he climbed to his feet, steadying himself against the mast until he found his legs again. It was cooler here in the aft section; he wished he'd thought of that earlier. The sail cut off most of the breeze that might otherwise have reached him. But, he supposed, when he'd taken up his position in the bow his single motivation had been to get as far away from Morwyn as possible.

Somehow that didn't matter so much now. Her single gesture of concern for him, the look of sadness on her face as she spoke ever so briefly of her fallen son, had given him a glimpse of the woman behind the image. Morwyn verch Morgan ap Gwyddion—Powersmith, Fireshaper, Sorceress of the Tylwyth-Teg, whatever she was —was far from happy.

Bracing himself against the rail with his newly healed hand, David slowly worked his way to Morwyn's side.

Her eyes had regained that strange unfocused quality that earlier had so unnerved him. Her lips moved in the words of a slow, plaintive song. She did not look at him.

David stared at the gleaming deck, at the soft draping of Morwyn's red velvet gown across the toe of one of her slippers, at the pointed tips of his own silvery boots. Thoughts warred in his mind.

He cleared his throat. "He was . . . my friend," he said quietly. "Fionchadd was my friend. Or he would have been, I think, if we'd ever had the chance to get to know each other."

"You are much like him," Morwyn whispered, though she continued to stare into the air. "Brave and foolish, rash and thoughtful, arrogant and naive."

David found himself grinning at the accuracy of the lady's assessment. "Snakes and snails and puppy dog tails."

"What?" She looked at him curiously.

"It's what little boys are made of. A . . . a nonsense rhyme of my people."

"Not far off, either." Morwyn smiled back.

"Maybe not," David replied, then took a deep breath. "Do you really think it's possible? Not the thing with Ailill—I don't want to think about that right now—but Fionchadd. Do you think he may really be able to rise from the dead some way?"

Morwyn laid a hand on David's, and for the first time he sensed no threat in that gesture. "Truly I do not know. I can only hope. That is where Power lies: in desire—whether for good or ill does not matter. If Fionchadd wishes life enough, if his spirit itself was not wounded, he may find a way to return. Love may fuel that desire. Love for a person, love for life itself. Or maybe its dark shadow, hatred."

David stared at her.

Her voice went suddenly cold. "Hate and love are much alike, for when unrestrained they consume. I know it, for I have felt them both. Hate prods me to vengeance against Ailill—but do not forget that once I loved him. And that love was a wonder and a glory."

"I think I know, or I'm beginning to," David said. "About the last part, I mean." An image of Liz's face took form in his mind's eye. He felt his throat tighten.

Morwyn smiled. "I hope for your sake it is true," she said.

David felt his face coloring as he gently withdrew his hand from under hers.

"Yeah, right," he mumbled. "Well, I guess I'd better be gettin' back up front—wouldn't want that old dragon head up there to get lonesome."

"David?" Morwyn called, when he had reached the mast.

He turned curiously. Her voice sounded different.

"Thank you," she whispered.

"Yeah, sure," David replied, nodding, as he ducked beneath the sail and returned to his accustomed place.

The landscape had not changed, was still a lacy canopy of intersecting white and crystal like the fan-vaulted ceiling of some vast Gothic cathedral frozen in rime. Somehow, though, it did not seem so threatening. Somehow, too, it was cooler.

Eventually they passed from beneath the last of the interlaced crystals and entered clear air again. At once it was hotter, but the glare was less a torment, and the air was fresher, so that he could breathe more freely. A second wind was blowing now: a wind from the east which warred with the westward one that directed their sailing. And *that* wind was not merely warm—it was hot.

And getting hotter by the moment.

One final brittle formation slid away to the side, and for the first time David had a clear view of the source of that heat. A pillar of fire had appeared on the horizon: a narrow strip of light that hurt to look at, though it was still many miles away.

David closed his eyes. All at once it had become too hot to move—almost too hot to breathe. Through slitted lids he could see the crimson sail, not as certain in its purpose now, its full curve sometimes collapsing in upon itself to flap uneasily before it billowed forth again. Beyond it, Morwyn remained as distant and implacable as before.

The banks had lowered again, and the landscape had resumed its featureless flatness. And then, so abruptly that David almost gasped, a gap broke the sheer slope of the bank to the left, matched by a twin on the right. Another band of golden light lanced across the Track on which they rode: another Straight Track. Closer and closer they came to it, and then they were there, the figurehead casting red shadows upon the golden cross that lay in the water before them. Morwyn twitched her fingers in a subtle movement, and the ship slid to a dead halt at the exact point of their juncture.

Morwyn strode forward to stand beside David, giving him a hand-up as he rose unsteadily to his feet. She took a wineskin from her hip and squirted a long arc of red wine into her mouth, then smiled and handed it to him. He took it uncertainly and aimed the nozzle carefully. He missed the first time, wetting his cheek, but got it right the second, and sent a stream shooting far back on his tongue. It was sweet and cold and as refreshing as anything he had ever tasted. Energy surged into him. He felt ready to face anything.

"That was great," he gasped. "Thanks, it was . . . it was just what I needed. So why are we stopping here?" he added, wiping his mouth. "This doesn't look like any part of Tir-Nan-Og I've seen."

"Nor is it," Morwyn replied. "But it is as far as I may go. The rest of the journey is up to you."

"Oh, come on!" David was horrified. "I can't run this thing!"

"The ship will sail itself. But in order to summon Ailill I must disembark. When you return with the Horn of Annwyn I want him ready to receive what justice you will provide for him."

"But—"

"We have no time for talk, David. Your quest is upon you. When you come to the pillar of fire, take shelter in the cabin amidships. If you are still on deck at that time, I cannot vouch for your safety."

"What about the ship?" David protested. "It's pretty big. Won't people notice it? Suppose somebody finds it and I can't get back?"

"I do not think that will be a problem. I doubt the route you will take will be watched." She paused, gazing intently at David's uncertain expression. "No, perhaps I should take additional precautions," she said finally. She muttered a word, slipped something off her finger, and extended it to him.

"Can't seem to stay away from these magic rings, can I?" David grinned as he took the sparkling band from her. Interlaced dragons coiled there, one silver, one gold; their heads lay side by side though facing opposite directions.

Morwyn's face was serious. "Once the ship has touched land and you have disembarked, stroke the gold head three times. When you are ready to return, stroke the silver one a like number."

David nodded solemnly.

"And now truly I must be on my way. But before I go—a kiss for luck." She bent her head and placed her lips against his. They were soft and sweet, but not as sweet as Liz's.

"Farewell!" And with that Morwyn stepped off the railing, to stand supported by nothing more than a ribbon of golden light that radiated upward from the Track. With her own nail she pricked her finger so that a single bead of blood welled forth, then she traced an elaborate figure in the air.

With a groaning and snapping as of some ancient timber moving in protest, the dragon head bent down so that the huge carved face hung inches away from hers. She reached up and set the bloody fingertip against the figurehead's flaring nostrils, a drop for either side. "By this it will know the way to return," she said, then turned to run quickly across the strip of glamour.

"Farewell, my pretty thief," she cried from shore. "Serve me well—for, friend or foe, you know how I will serve you if you fail."

David waved his own uncertain farewell and assumed Morwyn's place by the tiller. A narrow bench was set there, curving along the railing. He slumped down on it and drank another long draught of the wine she had left with him.

A shoreward glance showed her still looking at him. He grinned and brandished the skin; and she, for her part, clapped her hands twice. The sail billowed again, and the ship began to slide forward once more.

A moment later David was alone. Alone on his very own personal quasi-Viking ship following a strip of golden light through a bone-white landscape, heading for a rendezvous with a pillar of fire through which he must pass to steal a jeweled horn. It made his head hurt.

All at once he was wishing desperately for company, not only because he feared for his own life, but because he didn't want to face whatever might happen alone. Always before he'd had Alec or Liz along to keep him straight, to prevent him from doing something capricious or stupid or wrongheaded. They were the practical ones, he the dreamer. But going into Tir-nan-Og without them almost broke his heart, not the least because he still feared—when he allowed himself to think on such things—that he might never see them again. The unknown was bad enough in company. Alone, it was frankly terrifying.

He surveyed the landscape. It was too flat, too dead. Too hot. It lulled one into a sense of false complacency which he feared could become fatal with little encouragement.

For the first time since he'd awakened in Morwyn's chamber, he allowed himself to think about Liz, about the last time he had seen her. What would she have done when he turned up missing? Roused the whole county, no doubt. Enotah County was probably crawling with people looking for him; maybe they were even dragging the lake for his body.

He took a long swallow of the wine. How did he keep on getting in these situations?

The light grew brighter, and David closed his eyes against the torture of the glare, wishing he had a pair of sunglasses. He'd need to take shelter soon—before the ship reached the pillar of fire. It was still a little ways off, though; he'd just rest his eyes a couple of minutes longer . . .

The heavy sound of fabric flapping jolted him from his reverie, and he jerked his head up, saw the red sail go slack as its own wind failed. His heart leapt to his throat.

He dashed to the bow—and blanched in fear, for the pillar of fire was almost upon him. It filled three-quarters of the forward horizon, straddling the Track from side to side, a scant hundred yards in front of him—its heat scoured his face. But the pillar was drawing them on now, faster and faster, like a rising tornado of fire.

He froze, transfixed by awe.

Closer and closer it came:

Four-fifths of the sky eclipsed . . . five-sixths . . .

David felt the whole fabric of the boat shudder, so that he had to grab the railing to keep his footing.

What was he doing still standing there?

Desperately he released his hold and started toward the shallow cabin that lay amidships just behind the mast. But the boat lurched suddenly, flinging him flat on his face so that he had to half crawl, half slide the rest of the way as the deck began to tilt beneath him.

A glance over his shoulder showed the dragon head entering that flaming wall. The boat heaved up at an angle, steeper and steeper. Heat lashed across David's back.

But he had his hands on the hatch then, and an instant later had it open. Just as he thrust himself inside, the ship trembled, slamming him against the far end of the enclosure. Above him the hatch banged shut as he lay panting upon the floor. His senses whirled: one moment he was certain he was upside down, in the next that down was the end against which he lay.

David was inside the pillar now, rising upward in a kind of spiral around the flaming inner wall, as the golden line of the Track bent to follow more subtle paths between the Worlds. Always ahead, if he looked ahead, the Track seemed straight, but he could see it curving away on the other side. Or were those other Tracks? He had no real sense of direction.

David closed his eyes and held on, ignoring the dreadful vertigo that had claimed him when he had realized where he was: a fly on the wall of a pillar of fire that ran from Heaven to Hell. But closing his eyes didn't help, for his stomach still spun, his semicircular canals whirled like drunken gyroscopes. And the most extravagant images had begun to flicker behind his eyelids: creatures from nightmares or his most outrageous fantasies.

Another glance out the window showed him the Track spinning by, but it was spinning faster and faster now. He took a long swallow of wine from the skin he had slung across his shoulder, and immediately regretted it. The stuff made him dizzier, made his head hurt. Almost made him sick to his stomach. He felt his grip on reality slipping away.

In the end, he was forced to lie down and clasp his hands over his ears to keep out the droning of the flames, the creaking of the timbers. The floor heaved and shuddered once more. Fear filled him. His stomach was a knot of queasiness threatening to rebel. "Liz—Alec," he whispered hopelessly. "Oh, God, I need you now." And with that, tears burned in his eyes, bringing with them a strange calming peace that carried him into oblivion.

Chapter XXX: Searching

(The Lands of Fire)

The tail of the dragon ship slipped into the pillar of fire in a spiral flourish of carved golden wood that merged quickly with the red/yellow/white flicker that wrapped the base of that immense construction: briefly seen, then gone: a leaf within a conflagration.

From the riverbank nearby an arm-long serpent watched, the tiny brain within its angular blue skull crammed almost to madness with the pulsing, watchful thought of Morwyn verch Morgan ap Gwyddion.

"Fare you well, David Sullivan." Morwyn's low voice curled into the heavy heat of the flat, white plain on which she stood a half-day's riding distant. "May your journey be safe and your quest a successful one," she added.

Abruptly the sorceress withdrew the thread of awareness that had stretched thin across the leagues between her body and the serpent. It was out of her hands now: the boy was on his own.

The snake blinked its slitted eyes in sudden, vague relief. A dainty scrape of claws hinted at a mouse nearby; a thrust of tongue confirmed it. Hungry, it turned its attention there, its tenure as a vessel of Power ended.

Morwyn, however, had a great deal more trafficking with Power in mind. She frowned and addressed herself to the task she had set: the summoning of Ailill Windmaster.

His blood stained the Mortal World, she knew: leaking from a wound sustained in that land and shadowing him into the maze of the Tracks where it would be well-nigh impossible to find him. This would be a difficult searching. But at least she had a point from which to begin.

She closed her eyes and called upon her Power, grateful that she, at least, was not cut off from its source as Ailill surely was from his by the sealing of the borders. The Land of the Powersmiths was still open, she knew—as open as it ever was, anyway—and she could sense it feeding her strength across the intervening distance: as sure and unobtrusive as gravity or sunlight.

At first nothing marked the ruddy darkness behind her lids as she sent her Power questing, but then she fixed four things in her mind and made those things her focus: a splatter of blood upon the earth; the grim, dark-eyed face of a black-haired Faery lord; the antlered head of a red-gray deer; and a moonlit mountain in the Mortal World down which a man-road twisted.

One by one she reached out and caught the threads of force that bound her to the land; severed them; allowed herself to float free a handspan above the ground.

She began to turn in place then, very slowly, and as she did the images she had conjured shifted in relation to one another, now to the left, now to the right, drawing ever closer together and sometimes touching. And the more she turned, the more they touched, one now overlapping the other, nearly merging.

Too far a rotation—the images drifted apart again. She must back up.

Man, rock, deer: three of them lay atop one another.

Man, rock, deer . . .

And road.

She found her beginning place.

And then she began her Calling.

Chapter XXXI: Wanderings

(The Straight Tracks)

The company rode onward for a time uncounted: a time that attenuated or compacted—time that scarcely felt like time. And all the while the cloven prints of Ailill's feet, the occasional thin spatter of his blood, were a marker and a guide for Froech's silver stallion.

No one spoke for a long while.

Eventually, though, Nuada's shoulders began to sag, his head to droop farther and farther forward. Regan, who sat behind him, found herself bearing an ever-increasing share of the work of holding the Faery lord upright. Finally she had to contrive bindings from pieces of torn fabric and guide Snowwhisper by the strength of her mind alone, though that effort, coupled with the Power she was already expending at her healing, made her dizzy, and ate up Power faster than the Track renewed it. Nuada groaned often and coughed more than that, though he was still occasionally lucid.

And then a series of violent spasms wracked him, and Regan felt something warm and wet drip onto the arm she had snaked around his chest. She drew it back fearfully and stared at it: a glob of glistening saliva veined with telltale red. Then she noticed the spreading crimson stain on the Faery lord's plaid shirt.

"Halt! We must halt," she cried. "Help me get him down, if you will, Froech."

"Wha? Huh?" came Gary's sleepy mumble, as Froech slid off his mount and ran back to where Regan was already untying the knots that bound Nuada upright.

Gary stretched and yawned. "What's goin' on?"

"If you'd stay awake, you'd know," Liz hissed at him. "Nuada's getting worse."

"Crap!" Alec muttered. "All we need. If anything happens to him, we're sunk!"

"That's no way of thinkin'," Uncle Dale told him sharply. "Hey, you folks need a hand? Hang on a minute."

Froech held Nuada's opposite leg as Uncle Dale slipped up behind him and helped the dark-haired lady ease the Faery lord from the horse's back. By the time they had laid him on the ground Nuada was unconscious.

The Track flowed around him, turned his fair hair to true gold, washed his white Levis with light. But nothing could disguise the horrible yellow pallor that colored his skin, or the sickly ochre that tinged his eyeballs when Regan raised his lids. The tips of his fingers showed bluish purple.

Regan bent close to examine him, gently pulling aside his shirt. The place where the manticore's stinger had struck was bad enough, for that ugly red gash right below the heart had become surrounded by great, festering blisters ripe with blood and fluid. But even worse was what she found when she drew his shirt farther to the side. Wide parallel bruises disfigured the smooth flesh along Nuada's ribs and chest, and in those ugly, swollen blotches cracks had formed, from which blood and a foul-smelling yellow ichor had begun to ooze. The stench made Regan's stomach heave. What it would do to the mortals she did not dare imagine.

"His battle with Fionna gave him more serious wounds than he led us to believe," she observed with more dispassion than she felt. "The poison does its work. It takes all my strength to turn that evil aside from his heart and his brain, yet that strength is not enough, for he has other wounds inside, and the venom feeds there now. I fear our friend may die."

"That didn't seem to bother you before," Liz muttered.

"I spoke the truth then; I speak it now. Dying is never a thing to do capriciously."

"Is there, like, any choice?" Gary asked with heavy irony.

"But Nuada's Faery," Alec interjected. "Aren't you folks supposed to be immortal? I mean, I know about iron and all, but what about sickness and stuff?"

Regan did not look up. "We *are* immortal—in our proper flesh; yet pain is still pain regardless. Were the barriers not sealed and Nuada able to reach into the substance of Tir-Nan-Og, why, then he might heal himself, and think no more of these wounds. But since the link to Tir-Nan-Og is severed, Nuada has been unable to renew his strength."

"What will happen if he doesn't?" Liz asked, fear shadowing her face.

"He will simply fade; in time his spirit will flee the body. Only when Lugh's sealing ends—and let us hope that is soon—may he commence his own healing. If it is not too late."

"And in the meantime, we've still got a deer to catch and a boy to find," Uncle Dale reminded them. "You think he can travel? Or you think we ought to leave him and somebody stay here with him? I can, if you need me to."

"Here or there, it makes no difference," Regan sighed, as Froech lifted Nuada and carried him once more toward Snowwhisper.

"It will be *there*, if I have any say" came Nuada's unexpected whisper. His eyelids fluttered open, and he managed a ghost of a smile.

"If it is your will, Lord—but I am fearful."

"So am I," said Nuada. "But there are worse things to fear than dying."

It was a grim-faced company that hastened on.

Sometime later Liz rode up beside Regan. The Faery lady raised an inquiring eyebrow. "Something concerns you, child?" she asked.

Liz nodded slowly. "I hate to bother you with questions, while Nuada's . . . like he is. But, well, I'm still confused over some stuff."

"What would you like to know? I am far from the wisest of my people."

"Well, uh, I'm puzzled about Fionna and all. I mean she's Faery just like you and Nuada and Froech are, yet she seems to have a lot more Power, or at least she did back at the clearing. Why is that?"

Regan sighed. "Oh, child, what a question to ask when a thousand years are not enough for its proper answering; yet I suppose I must try. Part you know already: that Nuada and I now wear the substance of the Lands of Men. We put it on when we entered your World, for we intended to remain there for some time, and if we had not, Faerie would have begun to draw on us, and that draw would have become greater the longer we were away. Eventually we would have had to heed it, and perhaps not at a time of our own choosing. And there is the matter of iron and its wielding, as well; we knew we would have to handle it in your World, thus another reason for wearing your flesh—but of that Nuada has told you already.

"You know, too, what he said of your kind's small tolerance for Power: that great magic will consume your very flesh, so that in order to *work* any great magic in your world, we had to once more put on the substance of Faerie—as we did when we performed our first scrying."

"But what about Froech? And the Tracks—and Fionna?"

"When Lugh sealed the border Nuada and Cormac and I were already engaged in a working of Power. The sealing cut us off—so abruptly that we had no choice but to return to man's flesh while we could, for we had no idea how long that sealing might last, and to continue as we were would not only have risked our minds, but made us too vulnerable to iron—and now we cannot change back.

"Froech, however, does not much like the Mortal World and does not often travel there, thus it simply did not occur to him in time to change his substance to suit your World. Or perhaps he had no idea how long his visit would last. But whatever his reasons, the fact that he alone among us now wears Faery flesh makes him more Powerful than either Nuada or I, for he yet has recourse to that portion of his own Power he brought with him out of Tir-Nan-Og. Unfortunately for us all, that is a finite amount, and with the linkage severed, grows ever smaller the more he uses it. He can—we all can—draw some Power from the Tracks, but compared to the strength we derive from our own land, it is very little. Froech can draw more, because the stuff of Faerie more easily accepts such things. Such Power as Froech spent on his shape-shifting would have destroyed Nuada utterly."

"And the deal with Fionna and Ailill's the same as with Froech, I suppose?"

Regan looked thoughtful. "Somewhat—at least in Fionna's case. She too wears the stuff of Faerie, and almost certainly she was on the Tracks when the sealing rose, so that it probably caught her unaware, as it almost surely did Ailill. But Fionna is stronger than Froech. She is stronger than I; as strong as Nuada, so he says, for Fionna is of the royal house of Erenn, and they are very Powerful indeed. Thus, she had more of her own strength to start with, as well as having the Tracks to renew herself from later.

"There is another factor as well, though you may find it confusing, and that is that Lugh's sealing applies only to his own realm, not to all of Faerie. Fionna, being but lately come from Erenn, still has recourse to the Power of that land, as would Ailill, were he to return to his proper mind, had he not offered his blood to Tir-Nan-Og in the Rite of Allegiance—but of that it is best not to speak to outsiders. Erenn is very far away, however; indeed, it does not exist in this Time of your World at all. And it may not be reached except from Tir-Nan-Og, for the Tracks that lead there from outside Lugh's realm cannot support a body in this season. Some of them *will* admit the Silver Cord, though, so even with the borders sealed Fionna yet has some contact with her homeland, and can thus draw on its Power. Fortunately, the Cord is very thin, and it feeds her strength but slowly."

"What you're saying, then, is that Fionna's both more Powerful to start with, and has better access to means to recharge herself?"

Regan's brow furrowed. "That is much too simple for so complex a subject, but yes, you are correct."

Liz frowned. "So Fionna's more Powerful now than you, or even Froech?"

"Much more so. She is probably the most Powerful being on this side of the ocean, except for Lugh himself, or perhaps the Morrigu."

"So why doesn't Lugh do something?"

"I think he has his own plans, child. He is very patient, and very, very subtle. But his Power cannot reach here, at least not directly, any more than our Power can reach back to Tir-Nan-Og."

Liz sighed. "Looks bad for the home team, then."

Regan looked at her curiously. "If that means what I think, you are correct. And now I must see to Nuada."

Eventually the briars began to shrink, to regain more comfortable proportions. Tree trunks at last showed between them: gray shadows behind the green spirals; and to Alec's great relief they were a familiar species: willows. The briar patch thinned to nothing, and the company rode in solemn file through a half-lit drapery of trailing, sweet-smelling strands which dabbled their tips in a series of narrow puddles.

The air was thick with moisture. Drops slid down the leaves, smearing their clothes with damp, making Alec's nose prickle, dewing Uncle Dale's whiskers with drops that took on a sudden rainbow sparkle as unexpected beams of brilliant light broke upon them.

Alec glanced up hopefully, saw a ragged flag of possible sky beyond the froth of treetops. But when the willows opened a moment later onto a wide meadow of short orange and yellow grass, he saw that the radiance came not from the expected sun, but from the glare of twin moons that hung impossibly close together within a pink-gold haze of sky. He squinted and thought he could make out the familiar lunar markings on the larger one. But he had trouble focusing on the other, and the markings there were a strange, random cross-hatching of narrow lines etched upon a surface that was otherwise smooth as an egg.

Beyond the meadow was another forest, which did even more to lift Alec's spirits, for it marked the first true taste of otherness they'd experienced on their trek, not counting the manticore, the omnipresent briars, and various bits of shape shifting, which he *didn't* count, because they were either old hat, or else not very pleasant. If you were going to go wandering around in Faerie, you ought to at least get your sense of wonder stimulated once in a while. And this new forest certainly provided that, for it was truly no forest of the Mortal World, nor ever would be. It was the trees that did it—the trees that might have been oaks, except that their leaves were blue and gold, and their acorns rang like silver bells when he flipped an idle finger against some in passing. He reached up, stripped a handful off a twig, and handed a couple across to Liz, who answered his tentative smile with a puzzled frown.

Their passage through the fabulous oak wood did not last long, though, and a moment later there was again clear air above them. But now the light had faded to a softer gleam, like twilight; and a single moon—the strange one—showed pale against a sky of dusky purple. Lilies appeared along the Track, beautiful white lilies that smelled like cinnamon and tarragon and cloves, and whose waxy, spiral trumpets were half as long as Alec's forearm.

The land slowly fell away into a shallow, open valley, filled almost to overflowing with those same pale blossoms. But commanding the heights, a brooding forest lingered, grim and dark and threatening.

They pushed through a final screen of shrubbery, and the way steepened abruptly. The forest drew in closer on the left, and at the heart of the vale, where that wood crept nearest to the sparkling line of Track, lay a liquid shimmer like a sheet of water.

"Oh, no!" Liz moaned.

Alec turned to stare at her. "What's wrong?"

"We've seen that lake before, Alec—just look at the color. And see that Track bearing in to the left, from out of the woods? There's another one, too: straight across from this one!"

Alec squinted into the sudden gloom. "Christ!" he gasped. "It's —it's the lake of blood, isn't it? One place *I* never expected to see again!"

Liz nodded her resignation. "Yeah, this is the lilied way we saw when we were here before, the path we didn't take."

"Does this mean Lugh's raised the barrier?" Alec asked. "This is part of Tir-Nan-Og, isn't it?"

"Alas, no" came Nuada's slow reply. "This realm but lies close by it."

"Close enough for the Watchers to have an interest?" Liz inquired far too casually. She pointed to a half dozen low-slung creatures that had begun to amble out of the forest and amble toward the left-hand shore. Each one bore a dome-shaped lacquered shell taller than a man. Each one had glowing red eyes fixed straight at them.

And even as the company looked on, more Watchers wandered from the forest.

Chapter XXXII: Curses and Vows

(The Straight Tracks)

Halt!

The command stabbed into the ferret's mind, a momentary dazzle of images adding to the confusion it already felt. Its size was wrong, for one thing, and that made perception strange and awkward. The ground was so very far away—four feet at least, and that alone almost made it panic, for it felt always as if it were toppling forward.

And what a world had appeared around it! A strange, tingly golden thing beneath its feet, a rush of smells that made it giddy. A looping tangle of briars to every side that it could not escape, though it had tried several times, to its sorrow. More than one tuft of creamy fur hung upon bloody thorns as token of such futile efforts.

And the weight on its back which was the source of those hateful commands.

The ferret skidded to a halt, its back arching a bit, as if its length of spine made its hind legs a fraction slow responding.

Beast! The mind-daggers carved into its brain, though this time the ferret did not understand the images that burst upon it. It closed its eyes, blinked, and waited.

On its back Fionna nic Bobh was tired of waiting.

Ensorcelling the ferret so that it was a suitable size to ride had taken a great deal out of her, though not as much as walking would have. And the endless series of shape shiftings that had ended with the resumption of her own human form had done little either to improve her mood or increase her strength. Especially as she was beginning to feel the Call.

That was far worse than the deep wounds she had cloaked in a filmy gown magicked from spiderwebs and oak leaves, and which even now were on the way to healing. The make-do clothing gave her a vague sense of security, but did nothing to shut out the tugging of Faerie upon her substance, a tugging that passed even through Lugh's sealing and was made far, far worse because of it, even with the slow increase of Power that reached her from the Tracks, and the trickle that followed the Silver Cord from Erenn. She could not return home now, unless Lugh unsealed the borders, so the Call would persist moment by moment, day by day, until it drove her at last to madness, as it surely had her brother.

"Curse you, Lugh Samildinach," she gritted.

She closed her eyes, tried to compose herself, but a dark thought circled among the ways of her consciousness: failure. It could happen, she knew: almost completely cut off from Faerie, growing madder and weaker until she was but a ghost of discontent lost forever among the Tracks between the Worlds: her splendid brother no better.

"No." She rested her hand on the gold and ivory hilt of the sword that now hung by her side, almost by accident let a trickle of Power wander there—and found it answered tenfold! The scales had shifted, of a sudden. Suddenly hope had been reborn.

There is Power here, she exulted, as her despair gave way to a joy she could scarce contain. *Power such as I never suspected, Power which may yet see me to victory. Poor Silverhand, whose mortal flesh could not control it, though he must have known! How our battle must have cost him!*

Very casually, she dropped her hand to stroke Cormac's roughly severed head, which was tied by its hair to her belt, its glazed eyes staring at nothing.

"You *will* die, Silverhand," she whispered fiercely. "The means are surely within my grasp, now. And my brother will watch it happen!"

Chapter XXXIII: The Well of the Bloody Strand

(Tir-Nan-Og)

Cliffs marched across the horizon: cloud-high; orange-pink where morning sunlight shattered against vertical rock faces. A blur of green crowned those crags; a sky of pearl-blue hovered above them; a slow-motion splatter of silver plumed from their heights into white mist. It took David a moment to realize they were waterfalls.

Only Tir-Nan-Og could look like that, he knew; only that land held colors so wonderfully bright, light so incredibly clear.

He had made it, then; Morwyn's ship had brought him through Lugh's sealing.

For a long while David stared at the distant spectacle, watching it grow slowly larger and more distinct. The ship was still moving forward, he knew, though he could discern that motion only by the steady curling of pale wisps of low-lying sea fog around the dragon prow. No wind enlivened the air, yet odors came and went as if at will: salt spray and evergreens and the thick, rich scent of flowers.

David glanced over his shoulder, past the flaccid weight of sail to the distant flame of the pillar of fire. Looking forward again, he half expected to see the glimmer of Track before the prow—but that familiar companion was gone. They had left it, he supposed, when they had passed from pillar to ocean. He shuddered involuntarily when he recalled how narrowly he had escaped being caught on deck. Man! Just *thinking* of that made his balls crawl right up next to his liver.

As if in sympathy, his stomach growled, which only served to remind him he was hungry.

And why.

He'd regained consciousness abruptly, gratefully aware that the howling outside had ended, more grateful that the giddy motion, the constant reversals of perception, of up and down, of dark and light, had ceased. But his stomach had not been as forgiving as his head and had demanded its own accounting, which he had given—over the rail of the ship.

He felt better now, but only slightly. He had found no water on board, so he'd slaked his thirst with Morwyn's wine—not such a good idea. He *had* managed to snag a bucketful of water from the sea, only to discover that it was bitterly salty, so he'd used it to wash up with—which hadn't been so smart either. Finally he had resumed his place in the bow and begun trying to get his act together.

He still hadn't succeeded.

Eventually the ship arched across a skim of waves before a wide, black beach and entered a cleft in the rock face where a small stream issued from the land beyond.

And stopped, its bottom grating across sand, the great outstretched spars that braced the sail barely clearing the dark, wet rock to either side.

"This is it, then." David struck a theatrical pose with his legs braced wide apart and drew the sword from the deck. He started to sheathe it, but it twitched in his hand as if it were possessed of some life of its own. David raised an eyebrow and drew it out again, holding it at arm's length, balanced on his palm.

To his amazement, the blade twisted about, the point angling at least ten degrees to the left of where he had originally pointed it. He shrugged and took a firmer grip as he vaulted over the railing.

A stronger wave dashed against the shore, sending a low crest billowing up the narrow estuary in which the boat had come to rest. The sturdy timbers creaked and groaned as they rode the swell.

David looked at the ring Morwyn had given him. He thrust the sword into its scabbard and, with both hands free, scratched the head of the golden serpent three times.

A prickle of heat traced itself up his finger, and the tiny serpent swelled almost imperceptibly, as though its metal body sought to breathe. David felt a little foolish standing there with a fancy ring pointed at an absurdly beautiful ship, but then, he recollected, there was no one to watch him anyway. And then the metal beast *was* breathing, minute sides pumping furiously in and out.

He caught his breath, for a breeze had sprung up, a mere tickle of the air at first, and then stronger, skipping and cavorting around the boat in curious puffs. It gained in strength as the tiny serpent's sides pumped harder, and very soon loose sand was stirring on the beach and ripples upon the water.

A small whirlwind engulfed the ship, and as it spun, the boat dwindled, until perhaps a minute later the same immaculate model David had seen earlier floated placidly among the wavelets.

He reached over to snag the vessel, then looked around for a place to hide it. There was a narrow shelf just above eye level in the cliff to his left, with a distinctive zigzag pattern in its dark granite. That would do, he decided, and set the tiny ship safely in the hollow.

And now to it. He sighed as he drew the sword, feeling its insistent tug to his left even before he had it fully free. *I've no choice but to follow the stream till the cliffs lower, I guess, otherwise I might lose my landmark. No way I'm gonna climb anything that high*, he added as he examined the dark rocks to either side. An idea struck him, and he piled three small stones in what he hoped would be an unobtrusive heap directly beneath the ledge on which he had stowed the ship.

And set forth into Tir-Nan-Og.

Lugh's realm was empty.

That was what David told himself as the land unfolded around him. Nothing moved out there, though he could feel eyes everywhere. Once he had seen the dark silhouettes of mounted riders flashing across a distant plain. One had stopped, stared toward David, shading his eyes with a hand—and had moved on, raising no cry that David could discern. *Maybe there's a glamour on me*, he thought, only half believing it. *Or maybe mortal matter can't be seen in this World, as the Tracks can't be seen in mine . . . or maybe they're only waiting.*

Through delicate bushes to either side of the stream he followed, rolling meadows were visible; and once or twice he had seen tall towers or low-slung halls of stone and heavy wood. But there were no people. The land seemed to be holding its breath—like the monster in a horror movie, waiting for exactly the right moment to dart out and— He didn't want to think about it.

But for now the land was empty and peaceful, its lush greens made even richer by contrast with the stark whiteness of the Lands of Fire.

A little way ahead the stream entered a dark wall of forest. David paused, checked the sword, and felt with some relief its pull in that direction: he'd be less exposed there, he hoped, though there'd be more places for watching eyes to hide.

Moments later he was in the shelter of ancient branches. At his side, lily pads made a blue-green mosaic on the water.

It didn't take him long to reach the end of the wood. Beyond a last screen of maidenhair ferns lay a broad, undulating meadow, sunlit and artfully dotted with boulders on whose sides primitive faces were carved in low relief. Beyond a clump of trees to his right, he could see the peak that in his own land was called Bloody Bald, and atop it the cascade of terraces and gardens, walls and faceted towers that was the High King's palace.

He checked the sword. As he expected, the blade pointed toward the castle, but a little to one side. Probably the secret entrance opened outside the immediate precincts.

He began to jog again, setting a springy pace across the meadow, his mail jingling softly as he moved, spongy turf giving his every step an added bounce. The wyvern-hide boots were fabulously comfortable. Either there were no stones at all in the earth of Tir-Nan-Og, or else the boots, though thin-soled, filtered out the shock of such encounters.

Something nagged at him, though, as he came to a smaller stream that blocked the way before him. *Go right*, the sword's pull told him, and he obeyed, following the stream bed as the nagging became stronger and stronger.

All at once he realized that he'd been here before. In this very field his previous journey to Tir-Nan-Og had ended—here he had met the Sidhe to complete the Trial of Heroes . . . and Fionchadd had been killed, and Ailill Windmaster brought low.

But there was nothing here to mark that episode now, only a well-beaten path in the grass, and farther to the left a glimmer of Track.

Something *was* different, however: close by the stream, though not connected to it, lay a small, deep pool, barely a yard across, almost like a well. Its clear waters looked very cold and *very* inviting.

And he was thirsty. Throwing caution to the winds, he knelt and scooped a handful of water into his mouth.

It was the best he had ever tasted—cold and vaguely sweet, with the barest hint of carbonation. He paused, and took another, longer drink, then unslung his empty wine flask and refilled it.

He splashed a final handful on his face and stood up, looking again toward the palace. A sudden dizziness caught him, giddy and invigorating. His blood seemed to dance to a faster tempo. He ran through a quick series of stretching exercises, and was surprised at the supple ease with which his body moved, in spite of its various encumbrances.

David started toward the castle, but had taken barely three steps before a flash of color to his right focused his attention once more on the ground.

At the far edge of the pool a small green lizard was watching him, narrow head upraised at a perky, interested angle. Its iridescent scales shone bright as faceted emeralds. It was the first animate thing he had seen in what seemed like hours, and he was frankly grateful. David knelt and extended a tentative finger toward it. The lizard backed away, skittering on wide-splayed legs, then crept forward again. Its tiny black tongue darted out and neatly flicked a drop of water from his finger.

David extended his hand farther, ran a finger along the flat skull, and at last, emboldened, picked the lizard up and placed it on his shoulder, where it remained by his ear, clinging tightly with tiny serrated footpads that felt like velcro.

And then he began the trek to Lugh's palace.

Chapter XXXIV: Awakening

(Sullivan Cove, Georgia)

Little Billy Sullivan couldn't sleep.

He was worried about Davy, mostly. It was past four-thirty in the morning by the bright green numbers on his new digital wristwatch (the one that turned into a car if you did one thing to it, and into a robot if you did something else). Four-thirty and Davy wasn't back yet, and his mama and daddy weren't saying much, though his daddy had come back an hour or so before, looking like he'd looked the day Uncle Dale got sick that time, and his mama hadn't said a word but had cried a lot. They were sleeping now—or pretending to, Little Billy suspected. But he knew that they were worried.

And so was he.

He wanted to get up and look for Davy, but he had no idea where to start. His brother had last been seen at the gippy camp—the Gypsy camp, he corrected himself—so that might be the place to go first. But he couldn't get there 'cause it was too far to walk (and dark besides, and he suspected there were things in the woods that sometimes had designs on little boys), and he couldn't drive (though David had let him sit in his lap and steer the Mustang once, while he worked the pedals and shifter), and it would take *forever* on his little bicycle. So he didn't know what to do.

He scratched his head, sat up in bed, and stretched. Flipping the curtains aside, he gazed idly out the window toward the dark wall of mountain that sheltered the house by day (and threatened it at night, he always thought). It was light out there. Funny, 'cause it really shouldn't be, or at least not light like he saw. This demanded investigation.

He slipped out of bed and dressed quietly: jeans and T-shirt and new Reeboks, just like Davy's.

Out the door, onto the porch, into the yard.

He looked up—

Saw the cross burning in the sky.

"Davy," he said.

*   *   *

JoAnne Sullivan wondered how Big Billy could snore like that while all the current mess was going on. She wondered how he could even sleep at all. But he was, and that was a fact; she ought to know that by now, ought to know that Big Billy Sullivan could sleep through anything. He'd do what he could, and if that wasn't enough, well then, it was out of his hands. If they'd started a search, he'd have been there in a minute. If the sheriff had suggested dragging the lake or riding in a helicopter, or inspecting the back forty with a magnifying glass, he'd have been first to say, "I'll do 'er." But as far as acting on his own volition was concerned, well, he was a little lacking there. He loved David, she knew that, though they fought a lot, as boys will who were trying to become men, and men will who were trying to stay boys. And he loved Uncle Dale as well. Loved her and Little Billy, too. But sometimes he took a peculiar way of showing it—like trusting those very people to look after themselves. "Davy's a smart boy," Bill had said. "And Dale's been his own boss longer'n I been alive. If they ain't back by suppertime tomorrow, *then* I'll start to worry."

But that didn't help her any.

She wondered about Little Billy too—how he would take it if anything really had happened to his beloved brother.

And she was still wondering when she heard the little boy's door squeak open, heard his footsteps padding down the hall, heard the back door swing open and then thump shut again, exactly as if the little varmint had tried to shut it quietly and not quite been successful.

Better check on him, she thought. *Things been a little strange 'round here the last year or so.*

She climbed out of bed, spared an almost contemptuous glance at Big Billy's naked, snoring figure. No housecoat, just her thin blue nightie—it was warm, and who'd see anyway?

She paused in the kitchen, her finger on the light switch, then decided against it. It was awfully light out there already; a blue-white light was streaming into the kitchen. She crossed to the back door (open, except for the screen, to let the night breezes cool the house), and breathed a sigh of relief.

He was there, all right. Standing in the yard.

"Billy, honey, come back in," she called softly, as she came down the steps.

And then *she* saw the cross in the sky.

"Pretty sight, ain't it," an old woman cackled from the shadows by the barn.

Chapter XXXV: Toro! Toro!

(The Straight Tracks)

"So what do we do?" Alec asked, casting a dubious eye toward the sanguine surface of the lake of blood. "I don't want to have to deal with *this* again."

Uncle Dale pointed to the left of the body of noxious liquid. "You may not have to, boy. This here Track leads into the lake, all right; but looks like ole Ailill's trail kinda curves around to the left-hand side—right in front of where them funny-lookin' animals is, I'd be willin' to bet. Can't quite make it out for sure, but *somethin's* shore got them things interested over there. Gotta be that ole Crazy Deer's trail. And if I'm not mistaken, that's another Track over on t'other side, straight across from this'un. Prob'ly picked it up again over there."

Alec frowned, his cheeks puffed out thoughtfully. "Maybe, maybe not," he said. "It's not always that simple with the Tracks. And there's still that closer one that comes out of the woods right where the Watchers are. He could have gone that way. Hell, he *could* have been eaten by now—those things are carnivores. But there's no way we can find out unless we check, and somehow I don't think the Watchers'll just stand by and let us prowl around between 'em. We're still a fair ways off and I don't think they've scented us yet, but if they do—look out!"

"Ailill is bleeding more," Froech broke in from the ground beside them. He had been examining a line of blood that stretched along the sand in front of them. The droplets had fallen so close together that there was scarcely space between them.

"God, how *can* he be?" asked Alec. "He's been going on like that for twelve hours or more, our time. He can't have that much blood *in* him."

"Oh yes he can," Nuada replied hoarsely from where he sat in front of Regan, still beneath the eaves of the forest. "Do not forget that our bodies are not alike. Human blood clots faster than Faery blood, yet also flows more freely. But still, the Dark One must surely be weakening." He broke off as a coughing fit wracked him.

"He is not the only one weakening," Regan said. "If we do not find rest soon, it will not—"

Nuada interrupted her. "Ailill is not far in front of us now, and if we hurry, I think we may soon catch him. I would like to see that."

"Except that there's a couple of small problems," Alec noted.

"Yeah, like the Watchers, for one thing," Liz said. "And like the lake, for another."

"But we don't have to go into the lake," Gary pointed out. "If the trail goes around it."

"Do you *want* to face the Watchers, Gary?" Liz shot back. "They may seem slow and ponderous, but they can move a lot faster than you think, and they're meat eaters. Just 'cause they *look* sort of like glyptodonts, doesn't mean they are."

"So you're saying we should cross the lake and try to pick up the trail on the other side?"

Liz nodded. "It's shallow. We can wade."

"Yeah," Alec agreed. "We could do like we did before and use our iron-tipped staffs to keep the worst of the blood off." He paused, looked around. "That is, if anybody's still got theirs."

"I have," Gary volunteered, handing his spear to Alec.

"I've still got a knife," Liz added, patting the sheath at her hip meaningfully.

Regan's face was grim. "We lost many a weapon in the confusion of Fionna's attack."

"Well, maybe one'll do it." Alec sighed. "So let's be off, before those things change their minds."

Nuada opened his eyes, his face a mask of pain and weariness. "It is not as simple as that, I fear. I am wounded; and if you were to bother to took at Froech, you would see that his sides, too, bear some tokens of his encounter with Fionna."

Alec spared a glance at Froech, and noted that the Faery boy did, indeed, show deep gashes along his bare ribs, though they seemed to be well on their way to healing. Still, there was more than a little fresh blood to blend with that which was already crusted there.

"So what's the deal, then?"

"It is the quality of the lake of blood that if a wounded man enter it, and his blood once mingle with the substance of the lake, then the lake will suck him dry. I would prefer not to risk such a thing—nor, I think, would Froech."

Froech shook his head. "That is more than I am willing to dare."

"What about using the Track?" Gary suggested. "Use it to get around the lake by passing through a World where it doesn't exist, or something."

Regan's brow furrowed. "It might be possible, if any of us commanded more Power than would spin a wheel, and we could thus bend the Track to our will. But even were we to do that, it might take us long and long to return to the trail on the other side."

"Huh?"

"The way might seem clear to you, but the distance could be deceptive."

"But we've *got* to do something, and soon," Liz observed, a hard edge to her voice. "That closest Watcher keeps glancing this way."

"Yeah," Alec added, "and if we *don't* act soon, there's a good chance that not only will we be attacked, but that the trail may be obliterated. I mean there's always a chance it *doesn't* rejoin the Track again."

Liz cast a hopeful look at Froech. "Isn't there anything you can do, Froech? Surely this is all familiar to you. And you have more Power than anybody else."

The Faery boy shook his head. "I used nearly all the strength I had in my battle with Fionna, and what little the Track has added in sealing up my wounds. And as for the Watchers, Lugh alone commands the talisman that masters them. He showed it to me, once, when I first came into his service."

Alec took Liz by the arm. "Hey! Remember last time?" he said urgently. "Remember how the beasts didn't follow us into the lake? They'd nose the stuff, but wouldn't come in."

Liz's face brightened. "You're right, Alec!" She glanced at Nuada. "What about it, Nuada? Why is that?"

"The Watchers partake only of fresh meat and hot blood. The blood in the lake is . . . dead blood, I suppose you would say."

Alec sucked his lips thoughtfully, his eyes shifting from side to side as an idea began to form in his mind. "Aha!" he cried after a moment. "I may just have a solution. It's a little gross, to be sure. But it might just save our skins."

"So spill it, McLean."

"Easy. I think these things track mostly by smell, so we dip ourselves and the horses in the lake, so that we're covered with 'dead' blood, or at least enough so that we smell like it, and then we simply follow Ailill's trail along the shore, keeping to the shallows if we can. That way we can keep an eye on the trail and on the Watchers at the same time, and hopefully they won't come near us."

"But what if we can't follow the trail from the lake?"

"Then we'll just have to come back here and wait for the Watchers to leave."

"We cannot wait that long," Nuada said. "Or at least, I cannot. We are close to success, I believe that. We have no choice but to chance it."

Regan cocked her head thoughtfully. "Well, the boy is correct about the Watchers—and I think, in the absence of any better suggestions, we had better give his a try."

"But what about Nuada and Froech?" Liz asked. "They can't go in the lake."

"No," Gary observed. "But if we were to leave Nuada's shirt with all the blood on it here, and we kinda clumped up around him while we passed the Watchers, maybe they wouldn't notice him. Maybe it'd even draw them away!"

"Likely this solution will displease both our horses and our noses," Nuada said slowly. "Yet it seems the best plan."

"Yep, shore does," Uncle Dale agreed. "Can't say I'm too keen on takin' a bath in a lake o' blood, but I reckon it won't be the worst thing I've ever done."

"Firearrow will certainly not like it," said Froech. "He hates the smell of blood, and he hates the Watchers more."

"Snowwhisper does not like them either," Regan replied, "and the other two are likely to be worse, for they were bred for duty in the Lands of Men."

"Couldn't you blindfold them, or something?" Gary suggested.

Alec shook his head in disgust. "You can't blindfold their noses, dummy; even I know that."

"But if we were to lead them," Regan continued, "and maintain strict control . . ."

"And somebody'll have to stay on shore with Nuada, in case they decide to attack then."

"Why can't he just stay on Snowwhisper, and somebody lead her in just a foot or so?"

"But that still leaves Froech!"

The Faery boy slapped Snowwhisper's sleek gray hip. "I will sit behind Nuada, and hold him. It would be an ill thing were he to fall off."

Regan shook her head. "Not a pleasant possibility."

"Looks like it's the only one we've got, though."

The decision made, they rode toward the lake, following Ailill's trail as far as they could until it deserted the Track and arched away to the left. Fortunately, their earlier speculations appeared correct: the shell-beasts *did* seem more interested in Ailill's trail.

Though it had been his idea, Alec found himself suddenly reluctant to enter the lake of blood. Instead, he stood at its margin, staring dubiously at the wet copper sand. The stuff was inches from the toes of his Nikes, moving with a fearful sluggishness. The odor of corruption was almost overpowering.

Liz did not pause. She simply set her mouth in a hard line and strode into the stuff until she was a little more than knee-deep in it, then sat down so that only her head showed above the surface. When she rose an instant later, her white jeans showed dull red. She wrinkled her nose in disgust, and slogged back to shore.

The precedent set, the others followed her example, with Uncle Dale, Regan, and Liz leading the skittish horses, all except Snowwhisper, whom they left on shore with Nuada.

Alec watched them return, their clothes dyed red in all its myriad shades from pink to deepest burgundy. Even the horses showed dark stains almost halfway up their barrels.

Gary was the last to emerge. "Well, how do we look?" he cried jauntily as he dashed up to stand before Nuada. The Faery lord opened crusted eyes, managed a half-smile. "Red is how you look— red and wet, and smelling of death." He glanced at Regan. "May I presume we are ready?"

Regan nodded from the ground beside Snowwhisper's head, and took up the makeshift reins as Froech climbed up behind Nuada, pausing to help the Faery lord out of his bloody shirt, which he tossed to the sand distastefully. The rest of the company closed in tight formation around the mare, with Liz and Uncle Dale and the reluctant Gary leading the remaining horses.

"Now!" the Faery lady whispered. "And may Dana's luck go with us."

Slowly, carefully, they began to move toward the line of footprints they could dimly see ahead. Alec found his breath coming slow and shallow, at odds with his pounding heart.

Closer. . .

One of the Watchers looked up, its nostrils dilated uncertainly, its horn-ringed head snaking in slow arcs from side to side. One of its fellows did the same, and then another, as agitation spread among the shell-beasts.

"Damn!" Liz gritted.

"And shit too," Gary added, pointing toward the nearest Watcher.

The creature had commenced waddling toward them, its horn-shod claws gouging into the copper sand. The pearlescent interlaced swirls lacquered on its shell reflected the moonlight in a way that was almost hypnotic.

Alec found himself tracing one of those patterns with his eyes until they began to water. When he blinked and looked again, the beast had come twice its body length closer. It was now scarcely fifty yards away.

Another beast took a tentative step forward. A clawed foot smashed down on one of Ailill's delicate footprints, obliterating it.

The leader looked up, nostrils flaring wide as it sifted higher breezes.

"It has noticed us," Regan whispered.

Firearrow screamed, nipped viciously at Uncle Dale's restraining hand.

Bessie started, reared, eyes flashing.

Cormac's horse did likewise, jerking free of Gary's grip.

"Shit!"

"Hold 'er, boy!"

"Can't."

"Ohh!"

All at once the three riderless horses were rearing and stamping, white-eyed as the scent of shell-beasts and blood drove them wild with fear.

"Damn things are getting closer, boys!"

"Dammit, do something!"

"It's this friggin' horse!"

"Let them go!" Froech's voice rang out. "Perhaps the beasts will follow them."

"But what about us?"

"We can run."

"What about Nuada?"

"He's okay. Regan's still got control—"

"Can't hold on—"

"Damn!"

"Shit, there they go!"

Faced with more than they could reasonably stand, the horses broke loose and galloped wildly back down the beach.

Snowwhisper alone did not run. Regan had closed her eyes, and laid one hand firmly against the mare's forehead, and though the frightened horse's eyes were red and wild, she remained steadfast.

One or two of the shell-beasts shambled after the frightened horses, but the bulk of their number remained where they were, continuing their slow approach toward the horrified knot of people.

"Dammit!" Gary shouted suddenly. He grabbed his spear out of Alec's startled hands, and began to run after the horses.

Alec was beside him in an instant, caught him by the arm. "What the hell do you think you're doing, fool?"

Gary pointed to his feet where the tatters of Nuada's bloody shirt lay upon the sand. He swept up the discarded garment and wrapped it around his hand. "Gonna be a decoy." He grinned and inclined his head toward the beasts, which seemed to have slowed in confusion as they began to notice him.

"God, no!" Alec cried. "You're crazy, G-man, maybe Darrell could, but you're—"

"Not crazy, just fast—faster than anybody else here, I bet. I'm pretty sure I'm quick enough to avoid them on foot. Anyway, we're not talking about the Peachtree Road Race, it's just a quarter mile or so."

Gary grinned and took off, loping at first in long, easy, effortless strides toward the nearest Watcher. At the last possible moment he veered off to pass between it and the one closest to its left.

He was behind them, then, and running faster, as the beasts whirled around, some tripping over each other as he flashed along at their backs. Sometimes he leapt over their long, club-ended tails, sometimes *stepped* on those tails, and once—to Alec's dismay—he ran up onto one beast's shell and vaulted from it to the next and the next before returning to the ground.

"Christ, what's he trying to do, kill himself?" Liz moaned, as Alec rejoined them and the company began to jog along the lake's edge.

"No," Alec panted beside her. "Look. He's swatting them with Nuada's shirt—leaving a trail of blood. See? They're attacking each other."

And indeed they were. One shell-beast had reared onto its hind legs and was trying to gnaw a hole in the blood-spattered shell of its neighbor, while that beast in turn snapped its turtle beak helplessly, unable to twist far enough around to nip its attacker's leg.

And more were joining the fray.

The company pounded breathlessly along the shore, keeping one eye on the trail, one on the beasts, and one on Snowwhisper, who was trotting along with the rest of them. Froech was doing his best to keep Nuada upright. Nuada himself seemed to be hanging on, though his face was almost white.

Three-quarters of the way now, and Gary was waiting for them.

No—he had turned and was running back toward the nearest beast. And as he did, he wadded up the shirt, and—when he dared come no nearer, for the beast had lowered its snout to meet him head-on—threw the bloody fabric at it so that it slapped across the Watcher's eyes, effectively blinding it.

The beast shook its head, but a sleeve snagged on one of the short horns near its eye and would not come off.

"Toro! Toro!" Gary cried happily, and with that he raised his spear and thrust it into the gap between head and shell—exactly, had he known, as David had done during his own first desperate encounter with the creatures.

Smoke welled forth, a foulness in the air, and blood came streaming out to hiss on the copper sand.

One of its fellows saw it then, or smelled it, and bellowed loudly before it began a mad clamber across the wounded creature's shell to clamp its jaws firmly in the loose, naked skin at the base of the neck. The others quickly joined it.

"Gah!" Liz cried. "Gross!"

"But he's bought us the time we need," Froech panted. "Hurry now. We have but a short way to go."

And so they ran, as they had never run before, their leaders pattering beside Ailill's prints, the followers simply doing their best to keep up, with Froech holding the now unconscious Nuada upright before him.

Gary joined them a moment later, a gloss of sweat sticking his hair to his forehead. He grinned, and raised hooked fingers to Alec. "You owe me one, kiddo."

Alec clasped the hand in the MacTyrie Gang grip. "Right on, bro!"

"But did you have to throw away the spear like that?" Liz groaned.

Gary looked suddenly contrite. "Oh, well, I kinda got carried away."

"Indeed you did," came Regan's voice, sounding unexpectedly decisive. "You lost one of our few remaining weapons, for one thing. Leaving the shirt was no bad notion, but casting your spear away thereafter was."

"Too late to cry over *that* spilt milk, though," Uncle Dale interjected. "Best we be hightailin' it, since we don't have but one horse now! That'll set us back, some."

"Aye," Regan agreed. "Froech, since we have lost Firearrow, you must be our Tracker now."

"As you will, Lady," he replied, "if someone will see to Nuada."

Uncle Dale and Alec braced the wounded Faery while Froech slid off Snowwhisper's back and Regan resumed her accustomed seat. "The trail leads away from the lake, I think," Froech said after a moment spent examining Ailill's spoor.

"And let us hope nothing chooses to follow us," Regan added, "for Nuada is beyond my help now. Only his own will sustains him."

And Alec, who heard this, could only shudder.

Chapter XXXVI: Off the Track

(The Straight Tracks)

Pain was all the world, and all the world was pain.

And Ailill-who-was-a-deer could not escape it.

He had tried, had run till he could run no farther; walked until that effort, too, became too great; now staggered on, though all he wanted was to rest, to sleep the dreamless sleep of tired beasts.

But he must keep on, for Faerie had laid a call on him, which he could neither answer nor ignore. And now a newer, more compelling summons dragged at him as well, to which he *could* respond.

Morwyn's spell had found him, had he but known. And it drew him like a salmon on a line.

He fell, tried to rise, fell again, felt muscles rip along his wounded haunch, felt his skin tear as rough rocks grabbed it. Cracked an antler. The sun beat against him: too hot, and the air too wet.

Finally he rose, followed the Track, followed the Call. The gold was before him and that was enough.

He was fading quickly now. Ailill was almost gone, a pale shadow traced upon a well-drawn map of bestial instinct: dreaming and walking—running sometimes—all in a fog of pain.

A wall of rock rose up before him, shocked him almost awake. A cleft broke the brightness of the sun's glare on a thousand flecks of mica. The Track led there: a promise of coolness at the heart of the mountain.

He entered, passing under a veil of water that he scarcely felt. Darkness enfolded him; his antlers scraped against damp stone. The Track was the only light.

The way narrowed; the Track carried him forward. Air rushed in around him as the ground dropped away, leaving him suspended on a narrow span of Rock almost too slender for even his own narrow body.

But the Track was ahead, drawing him on, comforting him, filling him with strength of a kind, if only he could remember its purpose.

He paused, one foot raised, flicked an ear. There was that other Call again.

But he liked the Track better. He'd go that way.

Or would he?

A step; a *misstep*—and then he was falling . . .

The Track whirled away, and with it his sparse security; all in a spin of Worlds and images and flashes of dark and light as two things called out to him: a woman, and a place he could never reach—

Falling . . .

Farther than the ground had any right to be. Farther than it *could* have been. The man-part jerked awake, felt panic, expected pain—but there was none.

The world spun; the darkness was swept away.

Pines loomed around him; hard red earth pressed up against feet that were suddenly upright. Smells floated upon the air: the odors of a forest late at night when morning starts its final dreaming.

Where was the Track? Nowhere, it seemed; at least, he did not sense it. *You . . . we fell off,* Ailill told himself.

Deer instincts drowned him, asserting their own desire. There was a road, and it lead downhill. He'd follow that; perhaps there would be a Track beyond it. He smelled water. That would be nice, too.

Trees closed in, a looming tunnel of black and midnight green. He entered it, enjoying the feel of soft moss under hooves worn tender from running.

A clearing opened before him; light sprang into his eyes—moonlight. A persistent tinkle to his left became a waterfall sliding down rocks into a shallow pool. A shadow to his back sharpened to a wall of trees arcing from mountain to the top of a precipice beyond which more distant mountains slept under summer stars, under Cygnus the swan.

Under a cross that burned in the sky almost straight overhead.

It was a beautiful place. A place to rest, to ignore the Calls for a while and sleep. He'd have a look at that pointed mountain there, and then he'd sleep.

That pointed mountain. He'd seen it before!

Half his consciousness shattered. The older part, the stronger part gleamed forth, banished the deer-mind utterly.

Ailill Windmaster came full awake.

I know this place, the dark Faery thought. *Lookout Rock, men call it: David Sullivan's private Place of Power.*

"And ours too," Fionna said, as she stepped from behind him, smiling.

Chapter XXXVII: To the Vault

(Tir-Nan-Og)

David gazed back down the way he had come and shuddered in disbelief. Lugh's palace had looked close by, but it had taken him excruciating hours to reach: hours of stalking along paths, or scrambling over walls, or skulking through gardens, or trudging up endless steep flights of stairs. His legs were sore from the constant climbing and the extra weight he carried. And his shoulders were beginning to protest as well, for exactly those same reasons. He was starting to get worried, too: there had been trees of every kind, and flowers—even, to his shock, a stand of Cherokee roses. But no animals. And no Sidhe.

But surely I must be almost there, he thought, as he paused for breath among a stand of redwoods. *Surely soon*, as he struck off uphill once more. He negotiated a switchback in the gravel path he'd been following among the stringy red trunks—and gasped a sigh of relief. Three hundred yards to his right the huge outer gates to Lugh's palace gaped wide open in ominous invitation.

But there was still no sign of the Iron Road, though the sword yet led him on, its insistent tugging bringing him ever closer to the heart of Lugh's kingdom.

Where is everybody?

Silence reigned, and emptiness. David found himself wondering just how many Sidhe there were. Millions? Thousands? Maybe only hundreds? Were they stretched so thin and tenuous across Tir-Nan-Og that even in their own country they were seldom seen? Or was something else afoot? He was nearing the center of the web now, and the spider still hadn't shown.

He couldn't stand it any longer. It was time to begin, time to put on the cloak.

Morwyn had warned him about it once again, aboard ship. It

might make him sick, she had said; the material was so insubstantial that once unrolled it would last but a little while.

Sticking the sword firmly into the ground, he withdrew the folded fabric from its pouch, shook it out, and settled it across his shoulders; felt rather than saw the intricate clasp click shut at his throat. A chirp of protest by his cheek told him the lizard was not happy with that arrangement, and a scurrying by his ear indicated that it was seeking higher sanctuary by the protruding collar of his padded gambeson. He grinned and felt for it with his finger, to be rewarded with another chirp and a flick of tongue across his knuckle.

And then the cloak began to take effect, as it suited itself to the rhythms of his body. David did not actually disappear—from his own point of view—but he began to feel vaguely stretched, wrenched a little sideways or inside out. As if his skin and muscle and organs and bones were each a quarter-turn out of synch with one another.

His head spun, and he staggered a step. Squinting back the brief spell of dizziness, he retrieved the sword and balanced the blade once more on his palm. The point swung hard left toward a stand of red-woods a little way off the path. He let it lead him, moving as quietly as he could. A quick glance down showed him his own body, clear and solid as ever—but he seemed to have no shadow.

The cloak was working.

The point of the sword began to tip downward.

He followed it quickly, and then more quickly as its tug became stronger. David knew that he must be drawing very near the entrance.

So intent was he in following the pull, in fact, that he was caught unaware when the sword suddenly thumped home against the side of a huge gray boulder set artfully in the steep hillside between two of the larger trees.

He looked up, incredulous, and with more than a little irritation. The boulder towered three times his own height above his head, its sides covered with a heavy encrustation of lichen. He thought he could make out some half-obscured carving there, paused and scratched his chin, then reached for the sword to scrape off some of the thick, gray impediment.

A sharp tug at the hilt succeeded in bringing the blade free of the stone. But as soon as he relaxed his grip, the sword shot forward again—to embed itself to the quillons in the rock. He jerked at it, but it would not come out. Tugged it from side to side; no luck. Twisted—

The rock moved.

Twisted more.

Abruptly the sword slid free, sending David skidding onto his backside. He stood up and dusted himself off, then returned to the rock. His efforts had ripped loose a section of lichen taller than he was.

No, not loose, he discovered when he examined it more closely. The rock behind was hinged, displaying a crack of opening barely wide enough to admit him.

The sword fought his grip like a fistful of angry fish, tore itself free and went skittering along the carpet of redwood needles directly into that opening.

A clink. A whiff of stale air.

David had found the Iron Road.

He entered cautiously, suddenly aware as he bent to retrieve the sword that he had brought no light.

But light did not seem to be necessary, for the walls around him glowed of their own accord, a weak, fitful glimmer that slipped across slick, curved surfaces: the glass walls of the Iron Road.

David crept back to the doorway, pulled it as nearly shut as he could without an inside handle, and set off.

The way was wide enough for two men to walk abreast with their arms outspread, the arching glass ceiling at least that distance above him. The floor was smooth and patinaed the brownish-black of old metal. It sloped gradually downward in a line that was as straight as one of the Tracks. David's footfalls sounded strangely dull against its surface.

He did not have to walk long before the Iron Road ended abruptly in a plain semicircular archway. Beyond it, he could make out the topmost treads of a narrow, spiral staircase. He sighed, glanced back one final time, and entered.

The stairs went down in a tight twist of iron and dark glass, and he was reminded unpleasantly of the swirling motion of the pillar of fire. But at least he was less queasy now. In fact, he realized, he was feeling stronger by the moment, almost exactly like that peculiar jolt of vigor he had experienced after drinking from the well. He paused, took another long swig of that same water, and pressed on.

He felt better immediately, more energetic at each step, his senses clearer, his nerves infinitely more calm. It was not what he had expected at all.

Down and down and down.

One final turn, and David found himself facing another sheet of opaque black glass. He touched that smooth surface, pushed harder, to no avail.

"Well, *shit!*" he muttered. "This was bound to be more complicated than Morwyn let on. So here I stand at the bottom of a friggin' staircase with a blank wall in front of me and no bloody way to get through."

Irritably he sank down on the small landing at the foot of the stairs, and as he did, the tip of the sword slipped from his casual grip and tapped against the bottom of the glass wall.

Something clicked.

David found himself gazing through a low archway into the place he'd been seeking.

He leapt to his feet, then peered warily out.

—And caught his breath:

Lugh's treasure chamber was a circular, high-vaulted room, big as the domed space of a cathedral. It rather reminded David of a picture he'd seen of the interior of Hagia Sophia—except that here the walls were broken up by a soaring ribwork of pillars, with the spaces between ablaze with mosaicked interlaces in blue and gold and emerald.

In the center of the room—perhaps a hundred feet away—a smaller openwork dome like a small pavilion rose atop eight slender columns of ivory, the sides between wrought of pierced stonework set with jewels. Through the lattice, David could make out a dazzling array of colors and textures.

An unsourced light filled the place, and now that he examined the room more closely, there was a vague distortion surrounding the smaller structure. By squinting slightly, he could see the shimmer of glass walls that rose from a pattern of concentric circles on the floor. Half of those circles were pale, dull-toned stone (the better not to distract from the hoard, David supposed), the others of the same brownish-black metal as the Iron Road. Indeed, the single odor that he noticed was the sour smell of hot metal, like a foundry or a forge. No Faery could cross that floor, he knew. Not even Lugh, unless he used his rune, and from what Morwyn had intimated about the nature of the sealed borders, he doubted the High King could even do that at the moment.

Taking a deep breath, David stepped onto the outermost circle of floor—a pale one—and found to his surprise that the smooth stone pulsed gently beneath his feet.

He almost bumped into the first wall of glass before he saw it, but a sharp chirp from the lizard served to warn him, and he found himself compelled to slide his fingers along the transparent surface until he found an opening.

Through it, and he was on iron. The sensation of heat and the throbbing of the floor became instantly stronger. He crossed to the inner wall, began feeling along it, and had to make almost a full circuit before he found the next doorway. Along the way he discovered that both the iron circles and the walls were rotating slowly—and not all in the same direction—so that what was the straightest path going in would not necessarily be the straightest one coming out.

Then he was on stone again, and then on iron once more and feeling the wall for the last opening in the final wall of glass.

An instant later he was standing on the rough-textured limestone that encircled the Vault of Lugh Samildinach.

It had been too easy, David knew. No way could he have sailed a huge, gaudy ship along the coast of Tir-Nan-Og, crossed overland several miles through open country, then walked brazenly into a place he had never seen before to find its most precious artifacts unguarded by anyone or anything—and all the while passing its most potent wards and protections without a hitch.

Unless something was very wrong.

Yet he had no idea what it was, though he was more certain than ever that he was a particularly gullible fly. Whether Lugh was the spider, or Morwyn, or someone he had never met, he didn't know. Perhaps this was all part of a scheme to destroy him. Perhaps Ailill was not Morwyn's former lover at all, but her brother, or some other close kin, and this was an elaborate plan for revenge. Perhaps Morwyn and Ailill were even now watching his progress by some arcane means. Perhaps he was meant to disappear for well and good, thereby providing added impetus for Ailill's long-sought war with humanity.

Yeah, that made sense: send a human to steal a valuable Faery artifact, and the human naturally gets killed, but he also gets the blame, and maybe Lugh gets really pissed at the human race in general and decides to have it out with them once and for all.

Why else would the High King not have acted, if the Horn of Annwyn was the most precious thing in his kingdom?

Unless David was being set up. Unless Lugh *wanted* him to take the Horn, had some plan of his own of which David was unwitting executor.

But that didn't make sense either, because if Lugh and Morwyn had been working together to contrive Ailill's downfall, he saw no reason why the Ard Rhi would not simply have given her the Horn, or used it himself. What *was* the Horn, for that matter? What did it do? He didn't really know.

No, it was simply too easy.

Still, he knew, he had no choice but to fulfill the quest as best he could. That in mind, he squared his shoulders and turned toward the lacy metal gateway of the pavilion.

And then something moved among the tangled vaults overhead, wrenching him abruptly from his reverie. A shadow fled across the floor before him. He jerked his head up in horror, found he had raised the sword by pure instinct, then hesitated, staring at the blade foolishly. He didn't want to kill unless he had to, wasn't even certain he knew how, but—

Something was falling toward him, falling fast. Something he had mistaken for a carved decoration upon the ceiling: a shape of silver-gray that seemed all talons and wings and scales and teeth.

And that would be upon him in a bare instant.

Sword up again, higher—too late.

But whatever it was did not smash him to the floor. At the last possible moment, it swooped toward the opening of the pavilion where it landed neatly, its feather-eared head towering twice his height in the air. Tiny silver scales glittered across its body.

It's a wyvern! David almost gasped aloud; it looked just like the pictures he had seen in heraldry books. All at once he felt very guilty about the material from which his boots and scabbard and pouch were made.

The wyvern advanced a step. Its neck snaked down to eye level.

David backed away, assuming a defensive stance he had never consciously learned—*The sword's influence?* he wondered. What had Morwyn said? *Perhaps the sword will find a way to use you, then?*

The wyvern squinted in his direction, its tongue flicking, barbed tail thrashing across the floor. Its red eyes narrowed, and its nostrils flared. The fanlike ears twitched at his every breath.

It knows I'm here.

The creature folded in upon itself, squatting on hind legs like those of an immense ostrich; coiled its neck even lower.

—And struck: launching itself abruptly toward him by force of legs and massive tail.

David leapt back—too late.

The creature was upon him, *above* him; he was lying on his back with one three-clawed foot pinning his chest and right arm to the floor, a single talon inches from his unprotected throat; while the other foot poised above his stomach for what he very much feared was to be a quick disemboweling stroke. The sound of his own heartbeat echoed back at him through the stone floor, even as he scrabbled vainly for the sword he had dropped a few feet away.

The claw flexed; raised. Opened.

He closed his eyes and prayed.

The lizard made frantic chirping sounds by his ear.

—But the claw did not fall.

Through slitted eyes David looked up—and saw a puzzled expression widen the wyvern's eyes. The grip on his body relaxed a fraction.

Incomprehensible thoughts buzzed in his mind, seeming more curious and confused than threatening.

He risked a movement, tried to slide out from beneath the creature.

Its grip relaxed, but a tug at his throat told David it had tangled its claws in the fabric of the cloak. Another tug, though, and it freed itself, leaving a visible rent in the material.

Carefully he stood up, and to his surprise the wyvern bounced away to stand by the open entrance to the domed chamber. It bowed its head slightly. David was reminded almost exactly of the doorman in one of those fancy Atlanta hotels.

David took a deep breath. *Heeeere we gooooo! All or nothing— before it changes its mind.*

He ducked inside—and caught his breath in wonder. Gold was everywhere, in bars or coins or armor or weapons, or vast, jeweled chalices and massive flagons and bowls. And there was silver as well, and every surface was carved or jeweled or inlaid or wound with wire in an infinity of shapes and patterns. He could have spent a lifetime there—*two* lifetimes—and never seen it all. A thousand pieces called out for examination. Ignoring them was the hardest thing he had ever done.

And in the exact center of the chamber, on a plain pedestal of black stone, stood the ornate ivory curve of the Horn of Annwyn, its jeweled bands flashing even in the subdued light. Almost without conscious volition, David found himself reaching toward it.

Still too easy—far too easy.

He had it then, and slung the plain leather strap across his shoulder under the cloak.

The sudden effusion of elation and relief that filled him was almost more than he could contain. He had completed the first part of his quest, even if he could not trust the means of that completion. He was almost high, high as only certain books had ever made him, books like *The Lord of the Rings* or *Gods and Fighting Men*. He was Frodo and Aragorn and Angus Og and Finn MacCumhail all in one.

He made himself slow down, though; for he still had to escape and the wyvern had damaged his cloak. He didn't know how much longer it would be useful.

As he reached the entrance, he paused, peering outside to see if the wyvern was still there. And as he did, something caught his eye in a rack immediately to his right, something that sent an unexpected thrill racing through his body—or was it simply the lizard's sudden excited trilling in his ears? He frowned and turned to take a closer look.

It was a bow of plain white wood, bound with gold about the tips. There were others with it of far finer apparent workmanship, yet he found himself drawn to that one in particular. It looked vaguely familiar. Completely by reflex he found himself reaching toward it, then hesitated, puzzled at his own action; for an instant it had seemed as if some other will had controlled his body. *That bow is so damned familiar . . .*

Sudden realization dawned as he gave in to the compulsion and lifted the weapon from its place. It was *Fionchadd's* bow! Goibniu the Smith of the Tuatha de Danaan had made it, the boy had told him. It was the most precious thing he owned. A piece of master weaponwork worthy of the High King of the Sidhe in Tir-Nan-Og—especially when its original owner conveniently seemed to have left no heirs.

Perhaps Morwyn would like it as a reminder of her son, David decided, as he took the smooth wood into his hand. She had more right to it than Lugh, after all.

The decision made, he sheathed his sword and slung the bow over his shoulder, adding a moment later the quiver of white-fletched arrows that lay beside it. And thus encumbered with sword and Horn, pouch and water flask, quiver and bow—and a cloak of invisibility bunching in and out of the multitude of straps—David began thread his way out of the vault.

Something whirred in his ears, and he realized finally that it was the lizard humming happily inside his cowl. Well, if the lizard was happy, so was he.

The wyvern had resumed its place amid the carvings on the dome. David shrugged and hastened on his way, finding a path out of the maze of shifting floors and walls and doorways more quickly than he had earlier by the simple expedient of walking against the rotation of the walls, so that the openings came up more quickly.

Up the stairs now, and onto the Iron Road, suddenly acutely

aware of the thump of his tread, of the dry hiss of his panting as he struggled to maintain a quick pace up the slope.

The slit of doorway lay before him; freedom beyond—and he was through!

Sunlight hit him; his shadow flickered before him as he ran down the hillside.

His shadow! Not full dark, as it should be in so intense a glare, but his shadow nonetheless. The cloak was beginning to fail.

Down the slope at a sliding run, the quiver bouncing on his back, the sword pounding against his thigh, one hand firmly fixed on the hard curve of the Horn of Annwyn.

It was all downhill now. He would go overland, he knew the way. A fringe of lower trees reared ahead. In a moment he would be among them, free from casual observation. In a moment he would be safe. In a moment—

"Thief!" a clear voice sounded behind him. "Thief! Thief! Thief!"

David spun around just in time to see a file of armed warriors issuing from a door concealed in the marble wall above him and to the left.

And as his last shred of invisibility faded, those warriors lowered their swords one by one.

Chapter XXXVIII: A Debate in the Night

(Sullivan Cove, Georgia)

JoAnne O'Brian Sullivan eyed Katie McNally dubiously. "I can't go with you, I gotta stay here an' wait for my boy."

Cold dew sparkled on the grass at her feet. She curled one set of toes across the other absently.

"I can't go alone."

The younger woman bit at her upper lip and stared at the ground. The arcane light in the sky gave her an unearthly shadow and imparted a greenish sheen to Little Billy's blue eyes. She clutched his wrist firmly.

"Then don't go. Stay here. I got at least one extra bed, God knows."

Katie reached out shy, knotted fingers and touched JoAnne's hand. "Why won't you believe me?"

"Believe *what?* I seen the cross in the sky, same as you. But I don't take it as no sign. It scares me, if you want to know the truth about it."

"You ever know a woman my age t' lie?"

JoAnne heaved a weary sigh and rubbed a bare wrist across her forehead. She shook her head.

The Trader looked up at her: so tall, so pretty—so closed to the wonder of living. "I've seen some things, girl. Eighty years an' two countries. I've seen things most folks say can't *be* seen, 'cause they ain't there to see. But they are: I've seen the Fair Ones—once as a girl, and once as you see me now—an' they scared me to death both times, but I'm still here. An' I heard the banshee cry when my grannie died, an' that scared me worse than I ever been. But lightnin' I've seen crashin', too; an' storms at sea; an' heard the thunder, and they're frightenin' things as well, 'cause they come when God wants 'em to, and leave by His will, and there ain't nothin' none of us can do but wait 'em out. But I rode in a airplane to get to this land, an' that wasn't no pleasure, let me tell you. An' I been ninety miles an hour in a box o' flimsy tin an' rubber, with my drunken son a'drivin'.''

"But what makes you think that thing in the sky's got anything to do with Davy?"

The old woman's brow wrinkled further. "I told you. I saw him this evenin', saw his friends again a little later, an' them scared to death 'cause he'd vanished. Saw a pretty red-haired girl so eaten up with love an' fear for him she'd risk everything to find him, an' a brown-haired boy near as bad. I ain't got time to make things like that up. An' I sure don't go a'botherin' honest folks in the middle of the night."

"That ain't no proof."

"Well, I seen the ones who went with 'em, too. I seen the old man with the whiskers. *He* believed." She glanced down at Little Billy. "This boy believes old Katie."

JoAnne found tears welling up in her eyes as worry and confusion warred within her.

Katie reached into her heavy canvas bag—too shapeless to be called a purse—and felt for a hanky. Her nails clinked against metal.

The chains. She'd forgotten about them; her mind wasn't what it once was, even with a mission from God at hand. Or *was* it God? Or Those Ones—or both? Or were they all the same in the end? The stars shone on them all.

Katie handed David's mother the square of soft linen, then set the bag on the ground, and drew out one of the lengths of chain. "Ever see this?"

"That's Alec's!" Little Billy squealed. "Or Gary's or Runnerman's one! I seen 'em all wearin' 'em!"

His mother's eyes widened and she snatched it up.

"Where'd you get this?"

A trace of self-righteous arrogance ghosted Katie's face. "Fell out of the sky. Out of that cross in the sky."

"Well, it belongs to one of my boy's friends. I've seen them usin' chains just like this for belts."

"It fell out of the sky," Katie repeated. "As the Lord is my Witness."

JoAnne eyed the old woman suspiciously. "How do I know you didn't steal it? Or find it? Hell, how do I know you didn't kill them for it, an' it just cheap chrome steel?"

Katie reached in her pocket, pulled out her cross and her rosary. Held them straight before JoAnne Sullivan's startled eyes.

"Because Katie McNally does not lie!"

Little Billy tugged free, started to run toward the logging road that snaked into the mountain behind the farm, then paused, bouncing from foot to eager foot.

"Let's go, Ma!"

His mother had snagged him in an instant. "Go where, honey?"

"Lookout Rock, Ma!" Little Billy cried, pointing. "It's Davy an' Alec's special place. An' that cross is right over it!"

"You're mighty sure, ain't you?"

"Come *on*, Ma!"

Very, very slowly JoAnne Sullivan nodded. "Well, it'll just take a little while to find out one way or the other, won't it? An' twenty years from now I'll never miss the time. Maybe a walk up the mountain'll help take my mind off things." She glanced back at the old Trader woman. "I'll put Little Billy to bed, an' go tell Bill, an'—"

Katie shook her head. "*You* was hard enough to convince."

"Okay, then," said JoAnne Sullivan, as she squared her shoulders and stared first at the chain, then at her fractious son, and finally at a fading cross in the sky. "I've got a pair of britches a'hangin' on the line."

Chapter XXXIX: Between a Rock and a Hard Place

(The Land Beyond the Lake)

A fluff of damp ferns brushed Liz's face. She stopped in mid-stride to wipe a hand across her brow, looked for a dry place to rub it on her pants; found none, then dashed forward again. A little way ahead she could barely make out the hunched shape of Regan supporting the unconscious Nuada on Snowwhisper's back. Closer in, Gary was pushing through another mass of shoulder-high fronds. One of them flipped back toward her. She slapped at it. "God, it's sticky here," she muttered irritably.

"Yeah," Alec agreed, as he trudged along behind her at the tag end of the weary company, "but at least all these leaves've managed to wipe off most of the blood Froech couldn't magic away. We look *almost* human."

"*You* may think so."

Alec didn't answer; he had slowed and was gazing around at the surrounding verdure.

"You know," he mused after a moment, "you could almost forget you were in another World sometimes. Places like this, for instance; it's like the Pacific Northwest, or something. The Olympic Rainforest and all that. You know: moss all over everything, and these confounded ferns and bushes, and all this mist, and—"

"*I* don't forget, McLean," Liz snapped, spinning around to glare at him. "I remember why we're doing this, even if you don't!"

"I remember too, girl," Alec flung back, startled at the unexpected vehemence of Liz's remark. "He *was* my best friend, in case you've forgotten!"

"*Was?* That makes him sound like he's dead, Alec!"

"*Is* my best friend, then. Satisfied?"

"Stuff it!"

"The hell I will! You think I don't care? I've known him longer than *you* have!"

Liz's eyes narrowed dangerously. "Shut up, Alec. Just shut up!"

My pleasure, lady. My absolute pleasure!"

Alec paused, blinking rapidly; then: "Dammit, Liz, all I was trying to do was to take your mind off things." A tear oozed down his
cheek. He brushed it aside and looked up doubtfully, smiling an
embarrassed smile.

Liz sighed heavily, reached over to take his hand. "It's okay,
Alec. We both know what we really mean, and why. But we're tired
—tired as convicts, as Granny used to say. God knows what time it
is, how long we've been traveling, where we are, when we'll get
food or rest."

"And God don't seem to be saying," Alec replied as they rejoined
the company. "Ho! What's that?"

A noise reached them: muffled by vegetation at first, but becoming a louder roar as they continued forward. The earth began trembling beneath their feet. Then the thick screen of overreaching leaves
and branches that obscured both the sky and the view ahead fell
back.

"Oh my God!" Liz gasped.

It was a waterfall: plunging freely a thousand feet or more from
atop a ragged rampart of glowering gray stone that erupted from the
earth maybe a hundred yards ahead. A wide black pool lapped about
the bottom.

Liz found her eyes tracing the Track toward that water, hoping
that some trick of perspective would deny what she now feared: that
the golden road led straight beneath the torrent. "Crap," she muttered
in Alec's general direction. "We can't go under that!"

"It may be we have no choice," Regan said. "For that way lies
Ailill's trail, and it is fresher than it has ever been."

"Lady, look!" Froech cried from the trail ahead. "I think he fell
here."

Keeping her arms wrapped firmly around Nuada's waist, the
Faery lady bent over to stare at a patch of matted grass.

"How long, Froech?"

"Not long ago at all, I think; maybe a tenth of the sun's arc."

"Hear that, Liz?" Alec whispered. "Just a little way ahead of us.
And then we can look for David."

"If he's not dead."

"Don't even think that!"

"Sorry."

They said no more as Froech followed the Track to the edge of the
pool, then skirted around it to the fall itself. Mist veiled him for an
instant. A moment later he was back.

"Both trail and Track lead beneath the falls," Froech said. "But the Track has Power enough to turn aside most of the water's force. There is a cleft in the stone behind the fall, and at its entrance I found more footprints."

"Any clue as to what might lie within?" Regan asked. "I do not like the notion of traveling underground with Nuada as he is."

Froech shook his head. "Alas, I cannot say. But Ailill's antler marks show clear against the rocks to either side. He passed that way; we must therefore follow. And as for your other concern, I think it might be best if you remained here with Nuada while the rest of us go on ahead. You are, after all, our best healer; perhaps if you do not have to worry about keeping Silverhand in his seat you can help him more."

"Not a bad idea," Uncle Dale observed. "I 'spect me or you could do the trackin' now, anyway. If that there cave's like most I've seen, why, ain't but so many places a deer could get to in there. You folks get me some light, I'll follow that trail for you. This here mountain don't look too thick. Oughn't to take us long to figger out whether to go on or turn back. If we go on, we can send somebody back to tell Miz Regan."

Liz's eyes widened in horror. She gazed up at Nuada's closed eyes, his slack limbs, the poison-ravaged body still encircled in Regan's arms. "You mean you're just going to let them *stay* here? With the shell-beasts somewhere back there!"

"There is little need to worry," Froech replied. "This is not the World that was; the Watchers do not come into this one. Our friends will doubtless be safer here than we, if we are as close to Ailill as I think. But Nuada should not go on, that much is certain."

"But—" Liz began.

"Enough," the Faery youth said. "His fate is no concern for mortals."

Liz stared at him, teeth gritted as she sought to control her anger.

Froech looked away deliberately, glanced toward a stand of rushes that grew by the edge of the pool. "I think I can make torches from those."

"Torches? Can't you magic us some light?" Gary asked.

"I am nearly out of Power," Froech replied. "I used much to dispose of the blood, since you mortals insisted on it; what little was left I have been directing toward my tracking—or to Nuada."

He set himself to breaking off bundles of reeds.

Regan was eyeing the margin of the pond where a variety of small weeds and bushes twined. "Katie has taught me of the healing arts of men," she said. "Some of those plants may have some virtue, if I can just recall . . . Gary, if you will help me with our friend?"

A short while later the remaining companions faced the fall, with one of Froech's bundled torches for each of them. Uncle Dale was the first to step upon the Track, first to cross the pool—not wading, but walking *on* the water itself—then go beneath the rumbling cataract.

Liz looked up as her turn came to pass beneath the wall of water. She could see it before her, feel its electric coolness in the air. But then she stepped into it and the force diminished. The roar dulled and receded. And though she could see the water falling above her, feel it around her, it was as if it fell at a slower rate, as if she walked in the most delicate of spring rains. And then she was through and looking upon a dark wall of smooth and shiny rock, against which a vertical fissure showed darker yet, illuminated to perhaps knee height by the yellowish glow of the Track.

Alec's heels were already disappearing through that slit, and Liz followed as quickly as she could, at once disturbingly aware of the mountain's mass as an almost palpable oppression upon her spirit.

It took her eyes a moment to adjust to the flickering torchlight that one instant splashed a uniform glare of red across the walls, and the next highlighted every knob and plane with its own capricious black shadow. She found herself blinking too, as smoke burned into her eyes. The way was fairly narrow at first, but after fifty or so paces, the tunnel began to widen. The echoes of Alec's footsteps called back to her. And then the walls swept away, as the tunnel opened into a vast, almost spherical cavern, maybe two hundred feet in diameter. She gasped: only the shallow ledge on which the company now crowded stood between them and the gulf. A narrow, rail-less arc of natural stone bridge bisected that emptiness, carrying both trail and Track into a darkness that was broken only by the stark glimmer of a vertical slit in the opposite wall.

Uncle Dale stooped and scraped his index finger along the floor, then raised it to his nostrils. "Deer passed this way not long ago," he grunted confidently, rubbing the red stain with his thumb. "Blood's so fresh it's still got some warm to it."

"Want to go back and get Regan and Nuada?" Gary ventured.

"Let's see what's other side of that there crack, first."

And with that the old man stepped onto the span, the others following, Liz again bringing up the rear.

She very nearly lost her balance at the halfway point, very nearly tumbled headlong into the darkness that yawned beneath her. More

than once she had to stop, to stand swaying as she regained her
nerve. Three times she had to steady herself with a hand on Alec's
arm. And then she could see the walls again, curving in to meet her
at the sliver of light.

That light was straight in front of her now, the Track humming
beneath her feet. But underlying its vibration was another: a trembling of the rock of the mountains.

Alec's body blocked most of the view ahead, though a breath of
dampness crept by him to kiss her cheek.

And then he was gone and she was following.

All at once she stepped into light.

A veil of falling water lay before her, and she thought for a moment that the Track had played some trick on them, that they were
back where they had started.

But as Alec's head disappeared beneath the curtain ahead, Liz
heard his joyful cry: "Good God, I know where we are, Liz, it's—"

The sound was cut off, for Liz had followed him under the veil of
mist.

And emerged in the rich pink glow of sunrise in the Lands of
Men. She looked down for an instant, saw the Track paling into
vapor as it arched away above the small, placid pool at her feet.
Beyond that pool was a clearing circled with pines and strewn with
boulders and fallen logs that broke off suddenly into a sheer precipice. Beyond the precipice were mountains, like a pile of nubby,
red-purple blankets spread loosely on the bones of the land. A shimmer of water flattened the low places between the nearer peaks, one
of which was particularly pointed.

"That's Bloody Bald!" she gasped, as she followed Alec off the
Track. "We're on Lookout Rock!"

But as her foot left the strip of gold, a pain stabbed into her hip
from where she yet carried David's ring. She started to cry out, but a
dull paralysis suddenly clogged her throat. Her tongue felt thick; her
limbs abruptly weak and distant. Her brain filled with a buzzing that
drove away her own will and left her helpless. Dully she followed
Alec's stooping shoulders into full light. From somewhere derisive
laughter sounded in her ears: two voices, one high and clear, one
lower but no less melodious.

Her awareness rapidly fading into lethargy, Liz nevertheless
strained her vision, seeking among the black-shadowed rocks for the
source of that unnerving laughter.

And found it—for stepping from beneath the boughs at the edge
of the lookout were the shapes of a tall, black-haired man, and beside
him a beautiful, black-haired woman who looked to be his close kin.

The man held a naked sword at arm's length before him, point-up, its S-curved quillons at near eye level. He stared at it with a vague, unfocused intensity even as he continued to walk forward.

The weapon's fine taper seemed distressingly familiar to Liz, but she couldn't place it; couldn't concentrate at all. She tried, but the effort brought only a flash of pain stabbing and twisting behind her eyes. A scream rose in her throat, but her mouth would not respond: her vocal cords seemed frozen; her lips would not open.

The woman threw back her head and laughed again, her black hair rippling about her hips and across her shoulders like a shawl. She stepped forward.

Something bobbed against her thigh; something white and red, tied to the woman's waist with strips of thick black cord.

Liz stared at it, felt her gorge twitch, as the thing swung around.

It was Cormac's head.

A stray tendril of hair caught on a pointed canine in the slack-jawed mouth as the woman continued forward. She jerked at it nonchalantly.

The man inverted the sword, lowered it, blinked his eyes as if he had just awakened, then allowed his gaze to drift idly across the motionless company before returning it to the woman. He raised an elegant eyebrow.

"This is not quite what I expected, sister, yet I see fortune has found us already. It seems that this sword has virtues beyond the restoration of shapes and the healing of minds. If only it could restore our own Power as easily as it controls that of another." He stared at the hilt curiously. "There is something familiar about it, though; maybe when I have lived in my own shape longer I will remember—"

The woman's curt nod cut him off. "You must keep up the Calling a short while longer, my brother, and be sure it stays wound with the Binding; it would be a pity for our quarry to escape us now—though we have already caught more than we summoned!"

Chapter XL: A Sudden Change of Fortune

(The Straight Tracks)

Morwyn was caught.

Her summoning had touched Ailill at last: briefly, then more firmly, but so subtly he had not felt it until he was beyond escape. He had been injured, so it had not been possible to bring him to her as quickly as she desired—though she had used Power as a goad with a certain degree of satisfaction, driving him harder and harder.

But just when she thought she had him wholly in her grip, she had lost him. On the Track one moment, off it the next—then nowhere.

She had searched for him, looked in all the Worlds that layered near the place she last had sensed him.

But instead he had found *her*, he and one other; had ripped her Power from her and turned it to their own use.

And now *Morwyn* was being summoned, being dragged as fast as she could go through a fog of varied Worlds: the salt plain, then a not-place; through forests and groves, and then the Realms of Chaos where briars alone kept out the nothingness.

Only the Track was the same.

And ever the Call grew stronger, and her efforts to resist it weaker.

But all was not lost, she knew, rubbing the finger she had pricked when she had left David.

You may summon me, Ailill Windmaster, she thought. *But I, too, leave a trail. And there exists a certain thing that is bound to follow me!*

Chapter XLI: Battle

(Tir-Nan-Og)

There were at least twelve of them, quickly spreading out shoulder-to-shoulder to span a quarter circle behind him: crack wall-wardens of Lugh Samildinach. The white marble walls of Lugh's palace gleamed at their back; massive trunks of red-barked trees provided sporadic cover as they advanced down the slope. Their feet made no sound at all on the carpet of tiny needles.

They were tall, and every one had jet black hair hanging past his shoulders. Beneath black velvet surcoats, dark-toned mail shimmered from head to foot. Each of those Faery warriors had drawn his sword—and every sword was leveled at David's heart.

David's mouth dropped open; nerveless fingers stretched wide and weaponless. Almost, he turned and ran; almost, he threw himself upon his knees and begged for mercy.

But something woke within him—a fire he had not felt in far too long. Anger and fear fueled it: this new found determination to be lord of his own fate. No, he would *not* run; he would stand and fight. Die, maybe, but not as a coward. No Faery blade would nail *him* to the ground, if he had any say. And with that hard-won thinking came an acknowledgment from some unsuspected shadow-self that he *was* doing the proper thing; a secret voice that claimed the right for that time and place to set his course on the road of battle.

David found himself dodging to the left, to claim the scanty shelter of the uppermost of a grove of twisted oaks that sprawled below the last of the redwoods.

Above him the warriors began at once to spread out and advance, taking their time, flicking sunlight from blade to blade as entertainment.

David tensed warily; gnarled branch-wood brushed harsh against his forehead as conflicting choices warred within him. But even as his mind laid out alternatives, his hands had unslung the bow and begun a quick restringing. And then he was reaching into the quiver, nocking an arrow. An instant more, and he had taken aim and fired his first shaft, the bowstring releasing with a gentle, satisfying *twang* that resonated in the hollow of his back as the arrow whistled clear.

A stare of blank surprise flashed across the face of the closest warden as the triangular head ripped mail asunder and buried itself in his body. He flung down his sword and fell, both hands clutching at the soft flesh between left-side ribs and hipbone from which a white fletching protruded. Two other warriors stepped sideways to take his place, as their fellows slowed their advance and dropped to wary crouches, dark eyes darting from side to side as they found their cover fading.

One of those guards let his glance linger a breath too long on a possible place of concealment to David's right, and that distraction proved his downfall as another arrow buried itself below the outer angle of his collar bone.

David couldn't believe it.

He knew a little about archery; it had been one of the many skills to which David-the-elder had exposed him. But he hadn't practiced in a couple of years—not since he'd gotten too big for the small bow he'd used as a boy. Yet here he was, shooting with absolute precision, almost without thinking about it. Almost, in fact, without aiming. A part of him felt very satisfied, but another, better part twisted a dagger of conscience in his stomach as he realized what he had actually done: sent a shaft of wood thumping into the living flesh of another thinking being. At least neither shot had struck a vital spot.

But he shouldn't be able to do it at all.

Pay attention!—his thought, or another?

The surviving wardens were spreading out now, arcing forward to surround him.

Panic tasted sour in his mouth; he started to run. But then his body took control again, and he had sent two more shafts smacking into warriors before he could consciously choose one target.

And then the warriors were charging, racing straight toward him by an unspoken command that he too felt—as a vague metallic buzzing in his brain. The first two got arrows in thigh and elbow respectively before they had gone four paces.

Another approached, only to take a shaft in the shoulder, and then the remaining five were falling back, crying out for their wounded fellows to follow as best they could, while David loosed arrow after arrow, piercing sword arms and knees with uncanny accuracy.

The lizard had become extremely agitated, David realized suddenly; he could feel its frantic scurrying about the inside of his hood, hear its excited chirpings. Small explosions of excitement burst within his brain; half words, half emotions: *good, good, good, good.*

Beyond him the remaining wardens had taken cover behind a

convenient log; he could see them scurrying about, regrouping, some of the less-wounded jerking arrows free of bloody flesh, or breaking off shafts in wounds that stopped bleeding far too quickly.

Of course, David thought. *They're immortal. A simple arrow wound wouldn't hurt them, once the shaft itself is removed.*

He checked his own arrow supply, frowned. Three left: by no means enough for every one who remained—and now the soldiers he had first wounded had crawled back to join their comrades.

No, not nearly enough. But maybe they didn't know that.

David skirted right, toward an immense tree that grew close to the woods—

Then the guards too were moving again, and he had to loose two more shots; and yet one elbowed closer. He reached for another arrow, and felt the cold brush of terror against his heart, for the quiver was empty.

And then something snapped within him. He felt himself explode from cover and launch into a mad, headlong sprint toward the startled warriors. He ripped his sword from its scabbard and waved it in furious circles above his head, all the while yelling at the top of his lungs in a language he could in nowise understand.

The warriors paused, astonished. One or two almost grinned, but their faces clouded again as dreadful realization filtered through.

"Iron," one screamed, as David's blade whistled through the air.

Several of them fell back, but three nevertheless rushed in to encircle him.

Though David had never drawn a sword in anger in his life, his body slipped automatically into a defensive crouch that seemed completely natural: knees bent, right leg leading, sword arm angled before him, blade tip poised above his shoulder. More bursts of excitement sparked in his brain. *Right. Right. Right.*

Who's there? he had time to wonder.

—And then a lightning flash of silver metal whistled toward his face.

At once his arm was up, the blade suddenly horizontal above his head, the Faerie sword crashing against his own, driving it back toward his startled eyes as sparks splattered into the air.

And then another blow sliced toward his legs; and his sword flashed down to meet it—and another to his left, and his blade was there too; and again; and then to the right in a feint. Metal clanged and belled in harsh cacophony, as—beyond all hope—Mad David Sullivan held off three Faery warriors with a single iron sword.

But the rest were circling now, darting in, then rushing out. David began to despair.

A stab of pain across his left arm (the one he had snagged in his belt behind him lest he find himself tempted to use it as a shield) showed the worth of Morwyn's mail, but showed also that he was *not* invincible. He cried out in anguish, almost releasing the sword. And in that brief, distracted moment, another edge caught him from the front, parting surcoat and mail above his knees, sending blood coursing down his calves.

"Die, mortal!" one of the guards called scornfully.

—And then they were upon him: all of them.

David did his best, and one or two of his blows found targets. He slashed across a velvet surcoat—alarming plumes of flame shot up it, until its owner quenched them against the ground. A clever flick of his wrist left a long gash across a smooth, flushed cheek, sending the owner screaming away as the skin drew back in quick, dark crisps.

But there were too many of them, and more blows flying than David's skill could counter.

And he was getting tired.

More swords pricked him. None did any lasting damage, but each added its accent of pain to his rapidly increasing fatigue.

An edge flashed straight toward his face, and David thrust up his trembling blade to block it, but his hands had lost their strength. He felt his wrist go numb with that impact, and saw, with strange detachment, the sword fly from his helpless fingers.

The wall-warden grinned and grabbed David's shoulder roughly with a slender black-gloved hand.

But even as David stared at him, the man's mouth gaped wide open, his eyes growing wider by the instant. A shadow flowed around them both, and a familiar, musty odor tickled David's nostrils.

The Faery released his grip, thrust himself away in horror. Shouts echoed among the trees. The wardens were falling back, dropping their swords and running.

David stood as if frozen, his eyes shifting frantically from side to side.

All the guards were running now, turning black-clad backs toward him. David too was terrified—whatever could send Lugh's soldiers flying was too awful to think about. But he had to know. He risked a glance across his shoulder—and saw, looming behind him, the towering form of the wyvern he had so lately seen inside Lugh's treasure chamber.

Now how did that *get here?* he asked himself stupidly.

The lizard resumed its scampering inside his hood; buzzing filled his brain. *Good, good, good!*

David still did not dare move.

Yet he felt no fear, he realized, as the wyvern swept past him and continued in pursuit of the guards, now running on its ostrichlike hind legs, now flapping clumsily for several yards before rising into a steady distance-eating glide above the ground. Once David saw it grab a helpless warden in its claws and carry him into the air, only to drop him again among his comrades.

David shrugged and retrieved his sword, the bow, and as many undamaged arrows as he could salvage—not as many as he would have liked. Then he set off at a jog downhill straight toward the dark smudge of forest he could see across the plain below him. A towering golden filament emerged from the lands beyond that line of trees: the tower-Track, he suspected, by which he had entered Tir-Nan-Og.

David let his body carry him into the oak wood, through the gardens, over the walls, down the stairs.

The spider had shown—perhaps:

But the land was still too empty.

And his escape had been too easy.

Chapter XLII: Impatience

(The Enotah National Forest)

"Slow down, Little Billy!" JoAnne Sullivan called. "Don't run off and leave us!"

But Little Billy did not slow down. Partly because it was fun to run, even uphill, even on a dirt road, even with his mother panting along behind him.

And partly because if he stopped he might start to look around at the surrounding dark woods, might start to see things hiding there between the trees. The sky was lighter now: almost morning. But there were still things that could catch a little boy during that perilous hour. He knew: the memories had come trickling back one by one over the past year. He'd been caught before. And David had saved him. Now he owed him one.

"Slow down, or I'll take me a switch to you!"

That did it: a greater fear replaced a lesser one.

The little boy skipped to a standstill, twisted around to see his mother and Katie trudging up the road behind him. Mama could go faster if she didn't have that old lady with her, Billy knew. But the old lady was too nice to leave behind. And besides, she was a friend of Davy's.

He hopped from foot to foot until the two women were a little closer, but then he couldn't stand it any longer, and threat or no threat, fear or no fear, started to run again.

It was nearly dawn, Davy was in trouble. Davy needed him. And his mother was too slow.

"Come back here!" JoAnne Sullivan called.

But this time he chose not to listen.

Chapter XLIII: A Message

(Tir-Nan-Og)

"Speak, Mistress of Battles," the Ard Rhi said. "Your face betrays some trouble."

The Morrigu folded her arms and took a deep breath to compose herself. On her right shoulder a crow ruffled its feathers nervously and pecked inquiringly at a pale cheek.

"I bear ill tidings," the war queen said heavily. "I fear you have no choice but to rise to action."

A dark brow lifted. "Oh?"

"The Horn of Annwyn has been stolen, Lord," the Morrigu replied, her voice desolate as the emptiness between the stars.

A ghost of a smile twitched the roots of Lugh's mustache. "I am very glad to hear that, Mistress of Battles," he said. "Very glad indeed."

Chapter XLIV: The Empty Shore

(Tir-Nan-Og)

Step, breathe, feel the pain; step, breathe, feel the pain. The pain: a stitch in David's side like a dagger thrust and twisted, a tightening in thighs and calves and ankles, a gall across his shoulders as mail rubbed through along a sword cut. And there were *many* of those cuts, though none so deep as to pose much hazard beyond discomfort. Which was more than enough just then.

David was tired beyond caring; too tired, almost, to think. But he staggered onward, aware only of the constant pounding of his legs, the driving of his blood. Behind him dark shapes cut out above the grass showed the vanguard of Lugh's foot soldiers pressing forward. A single blast of trumpet split the air, and he risked a glance over his shoulder—and saw mounted figures issuing from the palace gates.

I knew it was too good to last, he told himself. *Only a matter of time before one or the other of them got word to the king and he called out the heavy artillery.*

A quick glance aloft showed the wyvern still pacing him in an easy glide, its dark shadow flickering among the tall grass a little way behind. *Thank God for him, anyway; maybe he'll buy me the time I need.*

More running, not daring to stop to tend his wounds, not daring to strip himself of the heavy mail and padding that were now more an encumbrance than an asset.

Harsh cries crackled aloft, and immense bird-shapes began winging skyward from field and castle alike. David realized to his horror that many of the Sidhe—perhaps all of them—were shape shifters. And that there was nothing to keep them from adopting forms that could easily outpace him. Indeed, one of his pursuers had already stopped and begun stripping off his clothes. A moment later an eagle rose into the clear, still air above the plain.

The wyvern saw it, arrowed down toward it, and, with a casual sideways snap of its whiplike tail, sent the eagle-man spiraling back to earth, his neck at a ghastly angle.

A *whoosh* of wings, a raptor cry harsh in David's ears, and another eagle deftly eluded the wyvern's jaws and dove to tangle its talons in the hood of his cloak, setting the lizard to screeching in alarm. Feathers flogged David's face, and then the eagle was gone again, as reptile jaws snapped closed.

Another brush of wings; a reckless flailing of the iron sword he had almost forgotten; the dry acrid scent of burning feathers. A shriek, another blow; but the forest was ahead now, scarcely a quarter mile away. Beyond it lay the river.

Mud squished beneath a silver leather boot. Through a gray-green screen of bracken a liquid glimmer showed. David threw himself down the bank and plunged first his hands, then his face, and finally his entire head into its coolness. He drank mouthful after heaven-sent mouthful, finally abandoning himself to instinct and flinging his whole body briefly into the stream.

Reluctantly he heaved himself up again and set off down the narrow trail that crested the bank, the heavy folds of his sodden velvet surcoat slapping against his calves, his boots squirting water with every step.

The forest lay behind him; beside him ran the river.

A quarter mile away was the cleft in the sea cliffs where the ship of flames was hidden.

An eighth of a mile—and David's feet felt like lead encased in concrete, his thighs like long-rusted iron cables that could snap at any moment, his lungs like bellows that had fanned one too many fires and that for far too long.

A sixteenth . . .

The riders were closer, though the eagles had drawn away, too many of their number smashed or broken, some even flapping headless and ludicrous across the plain.

But the knights came on, and arrows whispered through the air.

An ear-shattering scream sounded right above him. David whirled around . . .

The wyvern had been hit. Even as he watched, it crashed to the ground behind him, one pearly wing bristling with no less than three arrows which the beast was trying to worry free one at a time with its horny beak.

Images slashed into David's brain, images, thoughts, shadows, words: *Runrunrunrunrun!*

And run he did, into the shelter of the cliffs.

The boat was not far now: the rock with the zigzag pattern lay just up ahead.

David lurched to a swaying halt, stretched a trembling hand into the crevice to lift the model from its hiding place. Quickly he placed it on the water and began to stroke the golden serpent's head.

"C'mon, fire, *burn!* Get me outta here!"

—Nothing.

He rubbed the ring again.

Still nothing.

Maybe he was doing something wrong. He stared at the ring. Which head had he scratched? And how many times? It was gold to return, wasn't it? *No,* dammit, it was *silver!*

"Shit!" he groaned.

But now he could hear thrashings in the high bushes along the stream to his right as the pursuit drew nearer.

A mounted knight appeared at the top of the bank and leapt down, grinning. David spitted him on the sword almost without thinking. The Faery began hacking at the wound with his dagger, as his flesh sloughed away in smoking globs of black and red.

Perhaps he could salvage that body.

David wished him luck—

—And then emptied his stomach on the sand, even as he tried the ring again.

"C'mon." Faster this time: the silver, no, maybe it *was* the gold. Both— "Dammit, ring, c'mon!"

Suddenly both tiny serpents were awake, their metal sides heaving and pumping. But as fast as a spark emerged from one mouth, a breath of wind from the other blew it out. He was getting nowhere.

Another thrashing, and then a silver-skinned form shoved through those bushes, a filigree of blood lacing the tattered wing it held above itself like a flag.

David's eyes met the wyvern's. Thoughts buzzed. And then, to his complete surprise, a spurt of real fire leapt from the creature's nostrils to wrap a nearby bundle of reeds with flame.

All at once David realized what it was doing. He sheathed the sword and reached into that blazing thicket, snapped a brittle stem, and rushed back down the strip of sand to set the flame against the stern of the toy vessel.

Fire shrouded the ship as the wyvern fought against a second knight who had appeared on the bank. Arrows whizzed through the air. One struck David in the calf, sending him stumbling as he tried not to scream.

Pain washed over him, then heat as well, as the ship drank in the flames that gave it substance.

Abruptly they were gone. The heat fell from the air, and David flung himself across the low bulwark, giving vent to a stifled cry as the arrow impaling his leg caught on one of the ornamental shields. He flipped over onto his back, saw the blue sky beyond the loom of cliff tops, then saw those cliffs begin to move as current and Morwyn's magic set the ship adrift. A final arrow thumped to the deck at his feet, and David moaned as he dragged himself upright. He reached down, grasped the shaft that protruded from his calf, snapped it, and drew it out, then felt around behind and yanked out the other end. A gush of blood followed, and he jerked off his belt and wrapped it around his leg above the knee. He gave the tourniquet a quick twist and held it there until the flow of blood began to diminish, then slipped his boot off and contrived a makeshift pad and bandage from strips torn from his cloak. That final task completed, he gave himself to sleep, too tired to care any longer whether or not he lived or died, much less whether or not his quest succeeded.

David slept, awakened, slept again. His eyes cracked open once to see pink clouds above him, and again somewhat later to a wash of heat upon his face and a glare of harsher light. He levered himself up, saw the pillar of fire before him, and had just strength and sense enough to drag himself into the tiny cabin where unconsciousness again overwhelmed him. He did not see the dragon prow reenter that burning tower-Track; did not feel the appalling giddiness. Time passed in a blur that, had he known it, warped back upon itself. But David was aware of nothing as he slept in the cabin of the dragon ship, his left leg bound with the makeshift bandage, his right hand cradling the curve of a gold-and-ivory horn.

Heat aroused him finally, a return of the thick, pulsing air of the Lands of Fire. He rolled over groggily, felt the knobby roughness of the Horn hard against his hand, then fumbled at his hip until he found the water flask. He had drained more than half of it before he realized that perhaps he should ration himself.

He started to stand, then remembered his wounded leg. It didn't seem to be hurting much, a fact he found both curious and disturbing. Cautiously, he felt along his calf until he found the bandage, then probed beneath it to explore the wound itself: no pain. *Is that good or bad?* he wondered. *Maybe it means infection.*

He untied the bandage carefully. *Good, not too much blood.*

Finally, he held his breath and removed one of the bloodstained pads—and found a small, neat wound that was already scabbing over.

A soft scratching along his right cheek drew his attention, and he raised a hand in some annoyance before the gentlest of chirps reminded him of the lizard in his hood. Miraculously it had survived his afternoon's adventures and was still with him. He reached carefully into the mass of sweat-stained fabric until he touched dry scales, then removed the lizard, feeling a slight itch as the tiny claws released their hold on the skin beside his ear.

He brought the creature to eye level and looked at it. Suddenly curious, he squirted a bead of water onto his left forefinger and raised it to the creature's mouth. A tiny tongue flicked out; once, twice, then the lizard chirped again and wriggled free to skitter to a spot on David's shoulder.

David ventured a look outside, was not surprised to see dead white plains stretching in all directions. Mercifully, he had survived his second passage through the pillar of fire without noticing it. He wondered idly what time it was—or whether time was even a factor within this complex of Tracks and layered Worlds. Wearily, he hauled himself on deck.

The open air brought no further clues to his location; there was simply the plain and the billowing sail and the line of the Track before him.

His neck began to itch, and he scratched it awkwardly, until he realized that there was no longer any reason to go about with so much clothing on. He unclasped his cloak, let it fall, then pried the lizard from his shoulder long enough to strip off the soiled and tattered remnants of his surcoat. The mail was harder, but he managed, and finally the sweat-stained gambeson and remaining muddy boot joined his other accoutrements on the deck.

Now clad only in shirt and hose, David felt forty pounds lighter and immensely cooler. He reached down to pick up the lizard, but the creature had scampered up his leg and was nosing about the arrow wound in his calf. Its tongue flicked out, touched a drop of blood that had trickled from the opening.

Then, to David's surprise, the lizard was licking around the wound, and as it licked, the wound shrank, until a minute later a tiny red slit was all that remained. David rolled over to give the creature easier access to the other side of the injury, and almost before he knew it, that too was closed, and his lizard friend was scrambling up to lick his knee wound. He grinned wryly and let it choose its seat, reaching down to relocate the tiny claws ever so slightly when they tickled.

So intent was David on his scaled physician, in fact, that he scarcely noticed when the ship began to slow. But a flap of sail behind him caused him to raise his head, and he saw the billow falter, go limp for a moment. He jumped to his feet—*No pain. Thanks, lizard!*—and scanned the shore anxiously. The formations were becoming familiar again—he remembered the peculiar double point of those salt thorns over to the right.

But where was Morwyn? He stretched farther, straining onto tip-toes, eyes shaded by his hands.

No Morwyn.

But there was the Track, a line of pale yellow across the whiteness of the plain.

"Where *is* she?"

The lizard clambered up the front of his shirt and trilled in his ear.

The intersecting Track drew nearer; he could see where it lay above the water just ahead.

The boat slowed, stopped.

Still no Morwyn.

A timber creaked.

David risked a glance at the carved dragon, thought he saw the wooden nostrils flare almost imperceptibly, the neck shift slightly to the right.

A shudder ran through the hull, and the sails billowed fitfully.

Suddenly the deck lurched beneath his feet—*tilted!*

The ship was slewing around—turning over?

David cried out as he lost his footing, and slid toward the mast. The prow rose above the surrounding banks, then leveled again.

They were floating in the air, describing a shallow climb above the level of the river.

Over the bank now, and there was no longer doubt about it: they were flying!

David felt his stomach flip-flop as the ship rose into the heat-charged skies, the sail now straining at its ropes behind him.

Carefully he crawled to the railing and looked down, saw the world speeding by perhaps a hundred feet below, saw the narrow shadow of the ship as it fled across the empty plains, sometimes distorting fantastically over one of the salty excrescences.

He swallowed hard and crawled back to the cabin, where he found a flask of red wine. He drank a long draught.

A trickle spilled to his chin, and a flicker of tiny tongue was there to taste it. He laughed, and reached up to once again find the lizard. He set it carefully on his crossed knees and offered it drops of wine on one finger as he stroked it gently with the other.

So green! Such a beautiful, beautiful color . . .

Something tickled David's mind: an itching in his brain that made him want to scratch inside his head. Images spun there, mingling with sounds, sounds-becoming-words, then words in truth, and then the words acquired a strangely familiar voice.

You have fulfilled your quest very well, mortal lad, said Fion-chadd.

PART IV

EMBERS

Chapter XLV: The Secret of the Sword

(Lookout Rock, Georgia)

Ailill stared at the jeweled hilt of the sword he held point down before him. His eyes widened very slightly; his mouth curled in a wicked grin.

"The Horn of Annwyn," he whispered suddenly, "is hidden in the hilt!"

Fionna's head snapped around. "*What* did you just say?"

"Hidden *as* the hilt, I should have said," Ailill continued. "I am surprised I did not notice it sooner, yet ages have passed since the Horn and I were last acquainted, and my memory has dimmed a little. You have not really looked at it, have you? Would you like to? Now that you know what it is?"

He extended the blade hilt-first toward his sister.

Fionna virtually snatched the weapon from his hand, her face lit with triumph.

"You are certain?"

"Very."

"And to think we drew on its Power for our summoning! Perhaps that is why it went so well—I *thought* we reversed Morwyn's spell too easily, what with our wounds and Lugh's accursed sealing."

Ailill yawned. "But now that we have it, it will take little Power at all to maintain the binding, especially since most of them are mortals. Tell me, do you have plans for our unexpected visitors? Or shall we simply turn them loose and watch them panic?"

"I am certain I can think of something, brother. They might do as appetizers, for instance, until the other one gets here."

"You intend to use the Horn, then?"

"Oh, aye. It is only a matter of ordering my victims. Silverhand is not here, for instance, nor is Lugh—though the Hounds can surely find them."

"It is dangerous, Fionna. I have seen it work. Lugh does well to fear it."

"It is a fool who fears Power, Ailill."

"As you will, sister." Ailill sighed. "I myself am far too weary to be much of a host just now. The Call has become quite persistent—though if you were to set the Hounds on Lugh first, that would cease to be a problem." He sank down upon a boulder and resumed staring at the assembled company. The merest ghost of stiffness marred his movement.

Liz felt her heart skip a beat as the implications of the dark Faery's words sank in. *That's why Silverhand was so secretive about the blessed sword we had to leave behind! Lugh tried to smuggle something valuable to him disguised as the hilt.*

The same hilt Fionna was now unscrewing.

Liz watched in helpless fascination as the woman's fingers twirled, wishing desperately that she could move to stop her and knowing full well that there was nothing she could do with her muscles frozen. The Horn of Annwyn, was it? She wondered what that was. Even across the intervening several yards she could tell it was a thing of immense Power. But what sort of Power? Jewels sparkled there in bands. And between those bands were carvings of ivory, interlaced with gold and copper wire. At the small end was an opal the size of a quail's egg.

"Je . . . sus" came Alec's sluggish whisper beside her, the words stretched and muddied like a record played too slowly. His sentiment was matched by an attenuated "Oh . . . my . . . God" from Gary.

Liz dragged her gaze sideways to survey her comrades. Alec was apparently all right. Gary's breath was coming in slow, shuddering gasps. Uncle Dale looked stoic, but his mouth was set in a grim frown, and the muscles of his face twitched and quivered against the binding-spell. As for Froech, neither his face nor his carriage betrayed anything at all, though his eyes were slowly filling with hopeless dread. *At least the Sidhe have some options,* Liz thought. *This could be it for us.*

She tried to scream. "Nnnnnnnnnnnn—"

"Silence!" Fionna snapped, gesturing idly with her left hand.

Liz felt her tongue cleave to the floor of her mouth. She tried to swallow—failed. She shifted her eyes—all she could move now—back toward Fionna.

The sorceress looked extremely pleased with herself, striding purposefully among the boulders and fallen trees of Lookout Rock as if they were marble tables and oaken thrones. She reached the edge and

stared briefly into space, a perilous step from the precipitous ledge
that gave the place its name; then spun around and strode back to
survey the semicircle of captives, pausing at last before Froech. She
raised the Horn to her lips, poised it there a moment, mocking him
with her gaze. Then she lowered it and flipped the opal closed as she
saw the boy's eyes widen with what Liz very much suspected was
genuine fear. And if Froech was afraid, there was no hope for the rest
of them.

Liz's heart skipped another beat.

"You know what this is, don't you, boy?" Fionna purred. "It *is*
the Horn of Annwyn, isn't it?—that the Powersmiths made and
Arawn gave into Lugh's keeping. But Lugh has not kept it very well,
has he? Nor, it seems, has Nuada. Poor Nuada—does he still live?
He will not for much longer, now that I have this Horn!"

Froech could not reply, but a glint of hatred appeared in his eyes.

What an absolute loonie, Liz thought. In spite of the binding, she
found herself shuddering: cold and then warm, cold and warm
again . . .

Warm!—a warmth that stayed!

A pulse of warmth against her hip where the ring was yet concealed: a momentary distraction from this hopelessly one-sided confrontation.

"Our last guest should be here soon," Fionna continued, raising
the Horn again to gently stroke the opal along the angle of Froech's
jaw, then following it with a lacquered fingernail so that a fine line of
blood showed against the smooth, fair skin. "I doubt you know her,
boy. She sought to trap my brother, but we trapped her instead. Even
now she answers the summoning we two have laid upon her. It will
be she, I think, whose flesh will be the first to tempt the Hounds of
Annwyn. Her body . . . and then her soul. And then *you,* Froech"—
she carved a matching cut along Froech's other jaw—"and then . . .
we shall see. Perhaps Silverhand and Lugh. And when I have
finished"—she turned toward Liz—"I will seek out David Sullivan.
But *his* pain will last much longer."

Liz felt anger start to simmer, burning away the fear. She *had* to
escape, for herself and her companions—and for David. There had
to be something she could do—but what? Fionna's spell had trapped
her as surely as it had the others. *So much for the protection of
David's ring,* she thought.

As if in answer the ring pulsed again, almost painful this time, a
vain reminder that the Sidhe were somewhere nearby—and threatening.

Or was it?

Fionna stepped sideways to stand directly in front of Liz, her eyes level with the top of Liz's head.

Liz fought to raise her gaze to meet Fionna's. It took all the determination she could muster, but she managed to lower her brows as well, matching her adversary glare for glare, hate for hate. And as she did, she felt the ring's pulse grow hotter.

Fionna continued to stare hard at Liz, and Liz continued to meet that stare. Fionna's face receded from Liz's sight except for the sparkling black pits of her eyes—which expanded to fill the world.

No sound for five heartbeats . . . ten . . .

"Sister," came Ailill's careful whisper, "I think the last one comes."

The air beyond the precipice brightened. Fionna whirled around eagerly. "Ah yes," she said. "Are you ready to expand the binding? This one will be harder to hold than these puny folk, you know, for her Power is far greater than theirs. Once she is bound, you will not be able to relax for even an instant; if you do, all will be for naught. Are you certain you are strong enough?"

Ailill nodded. "With the Horn to draw on, I will be ready."

Liz blinked—slowly, yet not perhaps as slowly as before—as the brightness grew in splendor. For a moment it seemed as though the sun itself had been summoned and now hovered in the morning mist just beyond Lookout Rock. A shape slowly took form within that haze of light: a woman-tall darkness stippled against the glare. And then a fire-haired figure stepped onto the ledge to Ailill's right.

The Sidhe lord rose stiffly and strode with extravagant gallantry to extend a slow, mocking bow toward the mother of his child. A subtle movement of his hands preserved the binding spell; another expanded it to include the new arrival.

Fionna stared first at the Horn, then at the woman before her. Her eyes narrowed. A flick of her wrist set the woman walking.

Morwyn verch Morgan was in a fine rage: her eyes blazed, her bright hair crackled wildly about her head. Her movements were stiff and jerky, as though she sought with every forced pace to batter down that clutching fist of Power which dragged her step by step toward Fionna.

"Welcome to my gathering, Lady Morwyn." Fionna smiled, then nodded toward Ailill. "You will remember my brother, of course."

Ailill inclined his head slightly in mocking response and returned to his seat. His eyes again unfocused.

Must take a lot to hold up his end of the spell, Liz thought. *He must not be able to leave it for more than a minute or two, or we'd have been free by now. In fact, I think I felt it slip a little just then,*

*when he was talking to Fionna. I wonder what would happen if he
were distracted for more than a moment.*

Morwyn's mouth twitched, but all that issued forth was a slow,
dry crackling.

Fionna's nostrils flared. "You have something to say, Fireshaper?
Well, say it then!" She moved a finger.

"He once had a son name Fionchadd!" Morwyn spat. "He—"

A glare; a click of nail on nail; and Morwyn once again fell silent.

"You will be the first," Fionna continued. "I thought it only fair to
tell you that." And with that she thumbed down the opal and once
more raised the Horn of Annwyn—then hesitated, the instrument a
finger's width from her mouth, her eyes never leaving Morwyn's.

Damn her! Liz thought, as Fionna continued to toy with her vic-
tim.

She *had* to do something. If she did not, and soon, she very much
feared she would burst apart from sheer frustrated rage long before
the Fionna got around to whatever she had planned.

Godfuckingdamn her!

The warmth flared suddenly against Liz's hip, as if in response to
that anger. It had become truly hot, and was getting hotter by the
second. And as she focused her attention directly on that pain for the
first time, Liz felt the slightest relaxation of the force that numbed
her limbs.

She blinked.

Power! That was what David had called it: Power—the force of
belief manifested in reality; the active principle of the spirit world,
bearing the same relationship to spirit as energy bore to matter. And
this was her world, she realized; her magic—if she had any—was
strongest here. She turned her thought inside herself, oblivious to the
burning on her hip, seeking those secret places where her own Power
lay.

"I wonder what it is like to die?" Fionna was saying as she paced
a small circle around the stationary Morwyn. "I would ask you to
send word, but I doubt you will be able—not with the tatters of your
soul writhing in the guts of the Hounds of Annwyn."

Once more she smiled her cruel-sweet smile.

Liz had taken shelter deep inside herself, hoping to find there
some hidden place of calm where Power was and pain was not. The
ring had long since transcended mere discomfort and was a raw
burning agony, a devouring, gnawing torture that drove away fear,
anger—all emotion but the desire for escape.

And she was winning, finding relief in the blessed silent coolness
of her soul.

She reveled in it, let it wash over her, filling her. All the world became her soul and her soul was all the world—the pain of the ring was as the stirring of a breeze against a single pale hair on her arm.

Cooler and stiller, stiller and cooler, further and further in, so that she collapsed in upon herself . . .

. . . and expanded again to fill the universe.

Liz opened her eyes. She was free.

But could she act? What could she alone do against a sorceress?

Fionna's lips brushed the ivory.

Morwyn's eyes grew large.

It's on my head, now, Liz thought. *Got to do it soon. But what will I do? And the timing must be perfect, must be exactly right.* She glanced at Ailill and was relieved to see that he was still intent on maintaining the binding. If she *was* going to do something, she must do it before he could interfere.

"Gotta find Davy, gotta find Davy, gotta find Davy . . ." Little Billy's gasps had become a chant as he thumped along the tunnel beneath the trees. He didn't dare look anywhere but straight ahead, because the dark woods scared him. He leapt across a fallen limb (he *hoped* it was a limb, and not a boa constrictor, or an—an *arm,* or something), and resumed his alternate litany: "Slowpoke Mama, slowpoke Mama . . ."

He twisted around, danced backward for a step or two. Boy, Mama *was* slow. He didn't know where she was—back there somewhere, just trudging along with Katie like there wasn't any hurry.

But there was.

Back around, and running again.

"Gotta find Davy, gotta find Davy . . ."

There was light up ahead, there where the trees thinned out. Daylight, almost. And he could hear funny voices, like he'd heard once or twice before. Those voices scared him, too, but at least it wasn't dark where they were.

He slowed, began to creep forward.

Something made a clicking noise at his waist. He gritted his teeth and reached down, undid the chain he had got from the old lady and threaded partway round there so he would look like Davy. *Gotta be quiet.*

He backed into the shadows and began to edge sideways, peered cautiously around a tree.

Somebody was sitting on a rock right up there ahead of him: somebody with his back to him—a man with long black hair and a funny-looking robe.

And there was a woman there, who looked just like the man, and another woman who didn't and Liz and Alec and Gary—and Uncle Dale; and a good-looking boy with no shirt on. None of the ones he knew were moving; they looked like those plastic people you saw in department stores. He frowned. That redheaded woman wasn't moving either. What was the matter with 'em all?

He'd better take a look.

Closer.

The black-haired woman was doing something with some kind of horn he didn't much like, dragging it along that strange boy's jaw— *cutting* him! His lips puckered. *Yecch!*

The closer man shifted his head a little sideways, and Little Billy could see more of his face.

His heart flip-flopped. Memories he'd tried to forget leapt out at him: awful memories. That man had kidnapped him, changed him into a horse, whipped him and hurt him.

He was a booger.

And he didn't like iron, Little Billy remembered, as he fingered the chain.

"I'll kill you!" he screamed, as he launched himself forward.

"I'll kill you!"

Liz 's eyes widened, darted sideways.

"I'll kill you, bad man!" a childish voice shrieked as a small, blond form erupted from the trees behind Ailill and threw itself atop the Faery's unguarded back. Something glittered hard-bright in its hands, arcing sideways to wrap around Ailill's neck like a striking serpent.

"No!" Liz's scream cut the air so suddenly she hardly recognized it as her own.

"You hurt me! Hurt my brother! You die!" Little Billy squealed, as he tangled one small hand with the dark Faery's hair and tugged the chain free, then sent it whipping around again, this time into Ailill's face. Steaming red welts erupted across the fair skin where the shining metal struck Faery flesh. Blood streamed from the Faery lord's nose.

Not Little Billy! Oh God, no!

Fionna spun around.

Now or never . . .

Liz lurched forward, her body unexpectedly numb and awkward. She grabbed for the Horn—missed—lost her balance and staggered into Fionna. Her arms flailed, brushed Cormac's head, and closed on something hard and knobby. It jerked, she jerked back—and pushed.

Fionna stumbled backward onto the ground, her mouth agape in out-raged astonishment.

Liz looked down, found herself holding the Horn, and paused in midstride, staring at it foolishly. Maybe she should—

"Liiiiizz!" Little Billy screamed from Ailill's back as the Faery lord leapt up, fingers scrabbling behind him for the child's throat.

She snapped her head up, saw Little Billy swing the chain again, right around Ailill's neck. Saw him catch the other end, let go and slide down the Faery's back, hanging on for dear life, the chain a garrote around his enemy's throat.

Ailill gasped, raised both hands toward the smoking metal as Liz continued to stare.

"Liz, help!"

She started forward, but a hand like steel enfolded hers, dragging her back—a hand with a red velvet sleeve attached. Something jolted her wrist, numbing her hand, calmly prying the Horn from her grasp.

Morwyn! Ailill had relaxed his vigilance and the spell had failed, freeing the Fireshaper—which meant Liz's friends should be free shortly if it worked like she thought it did—

"Curse you girl, let go!" Morwyn was shrieking in her ears.

"Liiiiiizzzz!"

That did it. Let her have the bloody Horn; Little Billy was more important. If Ailill hurt him, she'd kill the bastard.

Liz flung herself away from the Fireshaper, felt at her waist for her dagger. Two quick strides and she had reached Ailill. A jerk at the hilt freed the weapon; a turn of her wrist jabbed it clumsily to-ward Ailill's unprotected belly.

The Faery lord shouted his surprise, but one hand flashed down to stop her, grabbing her wrist and twisting. Agony coursed through her arm.

She dropped the dagger.

"Don't you hurt my baby!" JoAnne Sullivan suddenly appeared at the edge of the clearing, her blonde hair wild as her face was fierce.

"Mama!" Little Billy shrieked.

"Don't move! Nobody move," JoAnne hollered. She halted then, looking puzzled as she tried to assess a situation that was far beyond her.

"And what will *you* do, mortal?" Ailill shot back.

"Miz Sullivan, help!" Liz kicked at the knife, saw it go sailing in JoAnne's direction.

JoAnne scrambled after it.

Ailill yanked Liz completely off the ground and pushed her toward the startled woman.

JoAnne tried to intercept Liz as she stumbled forward, but both women went down in a tangle. The breath thumped from Liz's lungs; her eyes spun wildly. She saw Fionna, still on the ground beside Morwyn. The sorceress was trying to rise, but Morwyn was making motions in the air above her. To her left she could see her comrades' bodies straining against their unseen bindings. *Maybe if we can delay a little longer, they'll be free.*

Little Billy lost his grip and slid to the ground behind Ailill. The dark Faery was on him in an instant. The fingers of one hand locked around the boy's throat, even as he sought with his other hand to reinforce the failing binding spell.

"You goddam bastard, leave my boy along!" JoAnne shrieked as she found the dagger and dived toward Ailill.

"No! He is mine, mortal!" Morwyn shouted, holding the Horn of Annwyn aloft while a newly frozen Fionna glared in silent fury beside her. Already the Fireshaper's free fingers were expanding their spell toward Ailill.

JoAnne skidded to a confused halt.

"Put the boy down, Ailill," Morwyn snapped, as her fingers continued to work automatically. "I have the Horn."

"Do you indeed?" Ailill cried—and with one smooth movement he ripped the dagger from JoAnne's startled fingers and hurled it straight toward the Fireshaper.

Morwyn's spell was at a critical juncture, her fingers moving just so . . .

The dagger struck her upraised wrist.

The Horn went flying.

She grabbed at it, screaming, even as her spell collapsed. She wrenched the weapon from her wrist, flung it smoking to the ground—

—As another hand curled about the Horn of Annwyn.

A second only it took Fionna to raise the Horn to her lips. A second for breath to set wind to it.

Around her—behind her—all movement ceased on Lookout Rock.

A deadly silence fell upon the mountain. The waterfall's hiss was stilled. The ragged breaths of the assembled host issued into air that was suddenly too thin to sustain their volume. Little Billy slipped out of Ailill's grasp and came to stand beside his mother. Liz too stood, moved sideways into JoAnne's dubious comfort.

Liz found herself gazing toward the Lookout again, at the pearl-blue sky of morning, the curls of fog among the mountains, the green of the leaves, the brownish gray of the rocks, the red of Morwyn's gown.

And the gut-wrenching, alien awfulness of the *not*-color that marked a rift in the air at the edge of the precipice.

Suddenly they were there: the Hounds of Annwyn: tall, slender dogs, their feathery coats the white of snow in a place that had never been warm; the cold color of death and fear and ultimate futility. And their ears were as red as blood.

One by one those Hounds leapt from the rift: ten, eleven, twelve of them. Thirteen, and the rift was closed.

Sound returned to the world; the falls resumed its roar.

But all upon the rock were frozen, not by magic, but by fear. The Master Hound had drawn back his lips the merest fraction, showing the tiniest gleam of fangs. But that sight alone was enough to send Liz's mind reeling. It was as if that one glistening point embodied every image of devouring that had ever haunted her dreams. The shark's maw from *Jaws* was as nothing beside it. She shivered uncontrollably.

The pack approached Fionna soundlessly. One by one they encircled her, the Master standing aside as the others arrayed themselves around her, then sank as one to icy haunches.

The circle completed, the Master came to stand directly before the sorceress, front legs braced wide, his elbow fringes brushing the ground beneath him. He raised expectant green eyes.

Liz felt JoAnne's grip tighten on her arm.

Fionna smiled, her gaze skipping quickly across the crowd.

"Hear me, o Hounds," she whispered. "Once a mortal matched wits against my brother, and by cheating, thought to make a fool of him. Once a mortal caused the death of my brother's son. Once a mortal dared lay hands on *me*. It is therefore my duty to redress my wrongs, and thus do I offer you a feasting. I had thought to offer you Morwyn first, but I think instead it will be . . . a human." Her eyes searched the crowd as she held the moment, drinking in the smell of fear as though it were the bouquet of fine wine.

"I hereby set you upon Liz Hughes!"

Chapter XLVI: Cause and Effect

(Tir-Nan-Og)

A tower of light ten times her height silhouetted the Morrigu, then she was gone.

Massive bronze doors boomed shut behind her, deep-carved faces thundering home with a sound like an ancient gong. The walls trembled with that sound.

Lugh listened to it reverberate down the length of the hall, felt the vibrations touch the far end and return, setting a pattern of harmonics dancing about his throne. Beside him Angharad awoke, raised an inquiring head, then fell again to doze.

"I think it is time, little eagle-claw," the Ard Rhi whispered, "for I have heard the Horn of Annwyn."

He took a breath, clenched his jaw—and very carefully wrapped his right hand around the hilt of the dagger that bound his left to map and throne and land.

There was a hush in the air, as if all Tir-Nan-Og waited

One smooth motion, and it was over. The red slit closed painlessly and left no scar.

Power returned to Lugh Samildinach, as the sealing faded from field and forest, sea and stream, from the air above and the land beneath. That which had been dispersed as flame, refocused and returned as Power. The Land gave up to its master that which its master had lent it for a space of time.

Lugh stood, stretched, flexed his fingers, felt his muscles slide in long-neglected patterns. His robe flowed from his shoulders like a waterfall.

He smiled and sat back down, took the dagger in his left hand and with his right began to unscrew the ivory hilt.

Katie had no choice but to stop and rest. She dropped down on a log, set her purse on her lap, and tried to still her breathing. She didn't have far to go now, if she read her feelings right. She was sorry she'd been so slow, sorry the little boy had run off, and sorrier when his mother had gone after him. JoAnne had apologized when she'd left her, but it just wasn't right to leave an old woman alone in the woods in the dark—especially with the Fair Folk about. At home, with the Traders, she was safe, even with Them around. Nuada was nice, Regan listened to her tell old stories and talk of healing. Cormac had helped her paint her wagon. But she wasn't safe here, she could feel it. There were others involved now, so she'd heard, and They might not be as pleasant.

She sighed, reached for her cane, rose.

A sound reached her ears—a horn? No, she wasn't sure, wasn't sure she'd even heard it. It was more like her bones had suddenly been shocked, like she had stepped on something electric. But it had still sounded like a horn—a hunting horn. And where the hunt was, she'd best be going. The cross had faded now, so she'd have to follow Gabriel.

She started back up the mountain.

Regan was losing him. Moment by moment Nuada of the Silverhand, once High King of the Sidhe in Erenn, was slipping from her grasp. And what a death: his body rotted by poison. Not like it should be, if it had to be at all. Not a glorious defeat on the field of battle, a more glorious resurrection a short while later on. No, he was in man's flesh, and man's flesh would not support him. He would die, and being unable to reach back to Faerie, might have to spend long years finding himself a new body. Or perhaps he would not return. She wondered what happened to men's spirits when they died. She'd have to ask Katie about that—if she ever saw Katie again.

Nuada moaned, stirred; she wiped his face with her sleeve.

Something nagged at her ears—a sound?

Yes—a sound, yet not a sound! She held her breath. Nuada had described it once, and she knew it from that description. Someone had winded the Horn of Annwyn.

Fear gripped her. She stretched her little remaining Power, not toward Nuada, to ease his soul, but toward Tir-Nan-Og for comfort.

The sealing had weakened, was weakening more as she touched it. She could almost get through.

"Just a little longer, Lord," she whispered to Nuada. "Lugh has unsealed the borders."

Nuada opened his eyes and smiled.

Chapter XLVII: The Hounds of the Overworld

(Lookout Rock, Georgia)

"Upon Liz Hughes!" The words echoed in the air.

Liz nearly passed out. She couldn't move. Only JoAnne Sullivan's hand around her waist supported her. But even so she could feel the older woman's grip go slack as her own fear began to rule her mind. Somewhere behind her she could hear Little Billy whimpering.

She glanced around frantically, desperate for help. But her comrades were still immobile, though she thought their bindings might be loosening more, now that Ailill evidently wasn't minding them. Morwyn too was motionless, caught up in the terror of the moment. Liz could almost see the Fireshaper's mind working, but she somehow knew the Hounds were beyond even that one's Power. And Ailill . . .

"Look at me, girl!" Fionna cried. "I want to watch your terror."

Liz found herself obeying.

The sorceress very calmly raised her hand and pointed it at her.

Without a sound the Master Hound turned and began to stalk toward her. One step. Two . . .

Liz crammed her hand into her pocket, found what she sought, put it on. "I have the Ring!" she cried desperately, holding her hand aloft. The silver band was now a circle of blazing fire. "The Ring of David Sullivan. These beasts may not harm me!"

She lowered her hand, interspersing it between herself and the approaching pack. Maybe it would protect her. *Maybe* it would protect her friends.

The Master Hound took another nonchalant pace forward; its fellows rose, began to fall in behind it. One of them stretched its mouth in a bored half-yawn.

Liz ripped her eyes away frantically, focusing only on the silver circle on her finger.

The Hound looked at the Ring curiously, cocking its head

sideways in an all-too-canine gesture, so that Liz for an instant felt that perhaps they were not, in fact, as threatening as she had feared.

But the Hound simply stared at the Ring.

And the Ring stopped glowing, became a lifeless band of metal on a clammy finger.

The Hound took another step, surveyed the company. Sniffed at Alec's immobile leg, prodded Gary's foot.

Fionna looked surprised. "Ah, I see it now," she said. "Oisin's Ring shielded you from the full power of our binding—but these beasts are *beyond* the power of the Ring. They are not creatures of the Sidhe at all! They are beyond any power in Tir-Nan-Og, or in Annwyn or Erenn either. Even the dark Realm of the Powersmiths contains nothing that can stand before them. I alone command them now!"

The Master Hound was close, scarcely a foot in front of Liz. It was looking at her, as if considering which portions of her might be most succulent. Its eyes sought hers, but she avoided that gaze.

Its nose brushed her knee.

She shuddered violently. She was vaguely aware of JoAnne's choked gasp, of her supportive hand falling away, of Little Billy starting to cry.

She was alone.

With a movement too quick to follow, the Hound rose onto its hind legs, dropping vast white forepaws on her shoulders as its head rose above her own.

Liz closed her eyes, certain her throat would be ripped out at any instant.

—But the weight lifted suddenly from her shoulders.

The Hound had fallen onto all fours, a brighter hatred burning in its eyes, as it whipped around.

Fionna's mouth dropped open—too late. The Master Hound was upon her, its fellows following in a wind-smooth curve as they redirected their headlong rush. The first one leaped head-high; a second followed. A scream cut the air and Ailill's sister went down amid a mass of snowy bodies. A single slim white arm rose above that confusion of seething fur: an arm grasping a curving cone of bright-gemmed ivory— And then it was gone.

One last scream: then silence.

A dog raised its head, its muzzle red as its ears. Another did likewise. One opened its mouth in a silent baying, and the rift reappeared in the sky. They hurled themselves toward it.

Abruptly they were gone.

No blood remained upon the stony ground. No scrap of fabric, no grisly reminders of what had just transpired. Only the Horn of Annwyn lay sparkling among the pebbles.

A long-fingered hand reached down to lift it. "This has failed in its purpose," Morwyn said, her voice strangely tremulous as she clipped the Horn to her belt.

Liz took a long shuddering breath, feeling JoAnne's renewed grip upon her shoulders. She turned, embraced the older woman, let her tears flow. "It's okay, girl," JoAnne whispered. "It's all done and over."

A choked cry reached her ears, and she found herself looking up again, toward Ailill.

Beneath the sheen of his own blood, the Faery lord's ruin of a face was deathly pale and calm, his eyes glazed, as if they surveyed some distant vista. And even as she watched Liz saw that face grow paler yet, and a look of blank and hopeless despair cross those once-fair features.

"Her soul too," Ailill said quietly. "I felt her soul devoured."

"Her *soul* was rotted long ago" came Morwyn's quick reply. "If indeed she ever had one. She was your *twin,* Ailill: two bodies with but one soul between them, and that not enough, for it turned the thought ever more inward, so that her own desires became the center of the world."

Ailill's gaze fell heavily on Morwyn's face, as the lady began a slow walk toward her former lover. There was an emptiness about Morwyn's expression too, Liz realized—as though some fire had been extinguished.

A yard now separated Ailill and Morwyn, and they stared at each other eye to eye, their faces nearly on a level. Liz felt a stirring of Power, like a wind of strangeness whipping around the mountain.

But Ailill sank to his knees before the Fireshaper. "My soul grieves for my loss, Lady. Surely you understand."

"I understand that I have lost my *son,* Ailill. Your son, too—in spite of all you said afterward so that you could break the binding upon us. Do you think I could forgive you for that? You knew the truth, though you did not say it. But I say that truth now."

Ailill bowed his head, black hair swinging forward to mask his face. "I cannot resist you, Lady. My pride is broken, and I am a hollow man. Is it possible you could forgive me?"

Morwyn raised her chin imperiously, though Liz thought her lips trembled the merest bit before she spoke. "It is not for me to forgive. It is for our son to do that, and he is lost to us both, he who was innocent, as Fionna never was."

"What will you do, then?" Ailill whispered, his voice barely audible.

"What I must," Morwyn replied, almost sadly.

"Not the Horn. Please, not the Horn."

Morwyn shook her head, laid a hand on the Horn at her side. "I do not trust this trinket," she said. "But I swore to have your death, and in that, at least, I will not be forsworn!"

"He is still under Lugh's law," Froech's voice sounded behind her, a he strode forward to prison her arm with one hand, even as he wrenched the Horn from her belt with the other.

The others were there then, shaking away their shock and the last of Ailill's binding, reaching out with still-sluggish muscles to augment Froech's grip as best they might: Alec, and Gary, and Uncle Dale—and a furiously wiggling Little Billy trying to help as well, by standing on the hem of the Fireshaper's robe.

"No!" Morwyn cried, as she tried to twist free of those hands. "It is my right! He slew my son, and kinslaying demands a stronger doom than Lugh has seen fit to deal!"

"You do not rule here," Froech snapped.

"Nor do you!" Morwyn replied, and began to wrap herself in Fire.

It came, burning from the center of her being, pouring out through her flesh to light the world, setting the air to throbbing with heat hotter than a furnace. The mortals fell back instantly. Froech cried out, raised one hand to shield his eyes; then he too backed away.

And as Froech released his hold, Morwyn moved, quick as only a Powersmith *could* move. With one fluid motion she stooped and grabbed the thing she had thrown to the ground earlier: the bone hilt of an iron-bladed knife. One moment she stood before Ailill, her flames raging about her, the next she had raised her hand and was drawing him toward her by subtle movements of her fingers.

Ailill fought it, or appeared to; but the flames were around him, and Morwyn was behind him, looping his arms behind his back with one deft twist of hand and elbow, while the other poised the blade above his heart.

"Not the Horn, Ailill," she said. "But perhaps a more fitting death: the same that you gave our child. The Death of Iron."

Froech started forward, but Morwyn's head came up. Fire flared out at him, forcing him back.

Liz squinted—it was hard to tell what was happening, so bright was the glare from the fire. Someone took her hand. She glanced beside her, saw Alec, grim.

Slowly, slowly—as Liz and her comrades looked helplessly on—Morwyn began to drive that point home between Ailill's ribs.

He screamed as the naked metal burned slowly into his body.

—And light filled the air, as, with a sound like canvas ripping, the scaled head of an immense wooden dragon pierced the Walls Between the Worlds beyond the precipice. An instant later the whole of the Ship of Flames appeared, sail redder than the sun, as its own eldritch glory came full into the skies of the Lands of Men.

In the prow of that ship stood a blond-haired boy, a jeweled curve of ivory in his hand. And that boy's eyes were opened wide in shocked alarm.

"I have brought you the Horn of Annwyn!" David cried. "But you no longer need it." He stared foolishly at the knobby object clenched tight in Froech's hand.

"I have brought the Horn of Annwyn," David called again, almost in panic this time, as the ship edged closer to the precipice. The low, sweeping sides brushed the granite. "And better news than that, even! I—"

He fell silent. Something was dreadfully wrong. What were Liz and Alec and Uncle Dale doing here? Not to mention Gary. And Little Billy and his—his *mother*, for God sakes—how had she got here? And who was that Faery boy? The one wearing Gary's old sweatpants?

And those figures wrapped in fire . . . was that *Morwyn?* what was she doing with—

Was that *Ailill* with the wrecked and ravaged face? What had happened to him?

"Morwyn, stop!" David cried desperately. *"Fionchadd's not dead!"*

Morwyn was staring straight at him from across Ailill's shoulder. With her left arm she held the dark one helpless. And in her right was a flash of shiny metal visible even within the flames that he recognized as Uncle Dale's favorite hunting knife. It was pointed right at Ailill's heart.

A chunk of cold fear dropped into David's stomach. He looked again at the glittering object in his hand.

"I no longer need the Horn of Annwyn to work this one's doom," Morwyn cried, as, with deliberate precision, she buried the dagger to the hilt in Ailill's body.

The dark Faery did not cry out, did not grimace. His body simply crumpled in Morwyn's arms, slid to the ground like a puppet that had lost its strings. A trace of its beauty yet remained, but it was an empty beauty, like the ravaged photo of a handsome man.

David stared helplessly at the shape sprawled upon the rough stone of Lookout Rock. His enemy, his great adversary, had finally been brought low; was dead by the Death of Iron, his spirit driven from his body by the fear of eternal torment. And he had been a moment too late with his news. Suddenly he felt very much as though he might be sick.

He paused at the railing, one foot on the Ship of Flames, the other on the rock of the Lands of Men.

The ship bobbed beneath him, and he leapt forward into arms that were suddenly around him, as Uncle Dale and Alec pulled him to the security of his own world. Strong arms that could only be Gary's locked around his chest in a bear hug. Little Billy tugged his shirttail gleefully. His mother was trying to kiss him.

And then *Liz*'s arms were around him, her lips on his cheek, on his mouth. "Davy!" she whispered through a rain of joyful tears. "Oh Davy, Davy! I thought you were dead!"

David closed his eyes, feeling an assault of emotions so intense he was nearly paralyzed.

"Yeah, well, I nearly was, I—"

A sound made him open his eyes: the sound of Morwyn weeping. He stared at the Horn he still held in his right hand. His lips drew back in a snarl of sudden rage, and he flung it away from him as if he had suddenly discovered he was holding filth.

A slim hand caught it, a hand which had no mirror twin to match it.

Two figures had joined them: a man and a woman of the Sidhe.

"Nuada!" Liz cried. "Where did you come from? *You're all right!*"

David stared at her. "What do you mean, all right? What the hell's going on?" He glanced at Nuada, saw how pale the Faery lord looked, noted the flimsy green robe that wrapped him, found his gaze wandering back to the Horn.

Nuada's eyes followed his. "This is *not* the Horn of Annwyn," he said with some amusement, "if it is the one that Lugh usually keeps in the vaults beneath his castle."

David lifted weary eyes toward the tall Faery. "I don't want to hear it!"

Nuada raised an eyebrow. "Oh, but you should, for you see, these multiple Horns seem to have involved your friends rather intimately during the last few hours."

"Horns? There's more than one? Oh, Christ!"

"Yeah, I'm a little confused there, too," Uncle Dale inserted.

"You're confused!" JoAnne broke in. "How in the hell do you think I feel? I've just seen a bunch of stuff that's flat impossible, and heard stuff that don't make a bit of sense—and David Sullivan, where'd you get them sorry longhandles?"

David could only grin. "I'll tell you later, Ma. Right now I think I need to hear about the Horn."

Nuada flashed his best smile at David's mother and began: "Lugh feared the Horn, David, and no sane being would not. But more than that, he feared for the *safety* of the Horn, so he had it split into three parts—an easy thing, for the Powersmiths had already made it so. One part he placed with two dummy pieces in the hilt of a particular sword, and another in the handle of a certain dagger, and the final part in a duplicate of the Horn itself, which he then stored in his treasure chamber. Thus, when Fionna winded the Horn—as I was certain she would eventually do, once she learned what she had—she was in fact winding only part of it. The Hounds were therefore bound only to answer, not to obey. Indeed, being summoned without proper control, their resentment turned them upon the one who had called them, for they do not like to be disturbed."

David's expression had clouded. "What're you talking about? What hounds? And who's Fionna? I was bringing the Horn to *Morwyn* to use on Ailill—though I didn't want to—and then, when I found out about Fionchadd, I—"

"You only know about that Morwyn lady," Uncle Dale interrupted, coming to stand beside his nephew. "But there'uz another'n, Ailill's sister. She was out to set him free, and to kill you. And she'd've killed all of us to get to you—maybe killed us in front of you, if she thought it'd hurt you more. But the joke was on her, as Mr. Silverarm just told you. She called the dogs, but she couldn't control 'em. Et her up, body an' soul together, so the Red Lady said."

Nuada smiled grimly. "There will be many tales to tell ere all the talk is done, I think."

"Yeah, like how'd you folks all get here?" David's eyes twinkled and he looked at Liz. "Liz, this is all your doing, isn't it?"

"I don't know where to start, Davy," Liz said, "but— Oh, look at poor Morwyn!"

Morwyn had risen from the ground where she had knelt by Ailill's side. Her face showed a strange mixture of joy, shock, and revulsion. Her right hand still clutched Ailill's, her fingertips twined with his, as if she could not bear to break that contact. Her eyes were glazed, unfocused—or focused on some sight none of the rest could apprehend.

"I followed his soul," she whispered. "It is no more. The Hounds were waiting in the Overworld. His sister and he shared one birthing; thus they shared one soul. And the Hounds were not yet sated, for they felt their hunting incomplete."

She paused, let go the hand, which fell heavily across Ailill's chest. "I have had my vengeance," she whispered. "But I think joy is lost to me forever."

David stepped forward. "Maybe not. I've been trying to tell you: *Fionchadd's not dead!*" He reached into the bloused front of his shirt just above his belt and gently withdrew something small and green and alive which scampered into his cupped palm.

The lizard darted a black tongue into the air.

Something buzzed in David's mind: thoughts, he knew now.

And then he saw Morwyn's face, saw joy banish the anguish that had taken dwelling there. Saw her eyes widen, and her lips curl, and saw the faint wrinkles of despair depart from her cheeks and brow.

"Fionchadd!" she cried. "Fionchadd, my son! I have found you!" She stretched forth a delicate hand, let a slim nail brush David's outstretched fingers, made a bridge across which the lizard scampered. With a flick of an emerald tail it made its way to the hollow beside her ear.

"But Fionchadd's dead!" Liz whispered. "David, what's going on?"

David flopped down against a convenient fallen tree trunk—solid wood, the real wood of his world. "Sit down, Liz," he replied. "I'm tired, and it's another of those long stories."

Wordlessly she sank down beside him.

"Fionchadd *was* dead," he began, "in the sense that his soul had left his body and couldn't return to it, what with the iron damage, and all. But at the point of his death, that lizard tasted some of the blood that had dripped onto the ground, so some of Fionchadd's essence was mixed with the lizard's, and he was able to link his spirit with it. Don't ask me how, 'cause I don't have the foggiest. And then for nearly a year afterward, it was like he was asleep, with his mind inside the lizard. He probably could have gone on like that forever, just fading further and further away until he forgot he was ever human—if Lugh's sealing hadn't awakened him—and even that wouldn't have done any good if he hadn't met me. Apparently there's some kind of bond between us, because he likes me, or something; and when he met me, he was able to draw on me to keep awake. He read my mind and knew I was his only chance, so he put everything he had into helping me fulfill my quest. But he's barely hanging on now, so if we don't do something real quick, he'll fade again. It's kind of a one-shot deal. Any ideas, anybody?"

Froech shook his head. "Such things are certainly beyond me. But what angers me is that I knew about the well, and I should have suspected there was more to it than was first apparent."

"Yeah, I don't understand that about the well, either," David said. "Fionchadd was just explaining that to me when we broke through the Walls Between the Worlds."

"What well is this?" Nuada asked, squatting down in front of them.

"It appeared after you went into the Lands of Men," Froech replied. "Scarcely a ten day ago, in fact. We had come to call it the Well of the Bloody Strand."

He returned his attention to David. "I did not think much of it—"

Nuada interrupted. "But you should have, Froech; such things are common where some disaster befalls one of our folk which forever breaks the link between matter and spirit. When that happens, the spirit flees; yet it cannot take its Power with it, or only very little, as Fionchadd evidently did. The Power that remains must go somewhere, or be manifested in some way. Usually it strives to imitate whatever active forces are nearby, in this case the running water of the nearby stream. It took so long because water is a very difficult thing on which to focus—a stream does not, as it were, stand still.

"What is *not* common," he added, "is that some other essence survives. I did not think Fionchadd strong enough, nor, of course, did I know of the lizard."

David nodded. "And when I drank from the well, Fionchadd was able to forge a link with me. That's how I could fight off Lugh's guards: Fionchadd was working through me. Good thing I took that drink, too, 'cause that's all that saved me! Not that it did any good," he added glumly. "I still couldn't keep Morwyn from killing Ailill."

"Nor could anyone," replied Nuada. "I certainly could not have. You see me whole, yet I am but lately healed."

"But still—"

"You did a better thing, David, for it was not simply your drinking of the well that made possible the link with Fionchadd—that sort of bonding is something only a friend of his could have made. It is through you alone that we know Fionchadd still lives."

Realization burned onto David's face. "Maybe he *was* my friend. I truly did like him—or would have, if I'd had the chance."

"And I imagine it explains something else," Regan inserted

smoothly, as if she had heard the whole conversation. "For if my memory serves, Lugh's vaults are guarded by a particularly fierce young wyvern, which, before its recent growth, was young Fionchadd's pet. Dylan, I think he called it. If the mortal boy met it in Lugh's vaults—which he evidently did—it would have torn him to pieces unless it recognized something of Fionchadd about him."

David's eyes widened, as he realized how close to death he had actually come. "He helped me," he whispered. "If it weren't for him I would never have escaped. I still haven't figured how he got out of the treasure chamber."

"Morwyn does not know as much as she thinks she does," Nuada confided cryptically. "Perhaps there were *other* exits."

"Or maybe *Lugh* released him," David suggested carefully, fixing Nuada's face with a keen stare. "In spite of all my trouble, I always felt like the whole bloody thing was too easy, like I was getting nothing but token resistance—and now it's all come to nothing."

"Not hardly," Uncle Dale said. "Not if somethin' good come out of it in the end."

"If anything did," David replied.

"We came out of it alive, anyway," Gary said. "We— Jesus, Sullivan, it's the old Gypsy lady!" He pointed toward the opening in the trees behind them where the trail from the logging road gave onto the clearing.

David twisted around, saw that it was indeed Katie. She was not looking at him, but over his head, to where the Ship of Flames still floated expectantly.

"Jesus H. God," he heard Gary whisper to his left. "Will you look at that!"

David whirled around again, saw the carved dragon prow, the slack red sail, the rows of shields of the Ship of Flames.

And then saw what lay beyond it.

Chapter XLVIII:
Fireshaper's Doom

(Lookout Rock, Georgia)

Clouds were forming: thick, heavy thunderclouds that cast a pall over the whole mortal vista of mountains and lakes, as though the storms that had watched Ailill into the world now gathered at his dying. Lightning flashed, and sharp gusts of wind whipped the pines. The smell of ozone filled the air, as bank after bank of sullen cumuli rolled over Bloody Bald. It grew rapidly darker, almost as if night were falling.

A breeze stirred David's hair, and he shivered, wishing for warmer clothes than his torn hose and stained shirt. He pressed closer against Liz, felt her respond, take his hand. It was good to be back in his own world with his friends standing by him, good to feel Alec's warm, solid presence at his back; so good to feel Liz's fingers lacing through his own that he almost couldn't stand it. They were watching the sky, all of them were—except his mother, who was over by the falls talking to the old Trader lady. He wondered what JoAnne Sullivan thought about all this. Not much, he imagined. Then someone whispered to his right and, glancing that way, he saw Nuada and Froech and Regan gazing skyward as well, their eyes wide in expectation. Morwyn alone seemed doubtful.

The clouds piled thicker, until they hung scant feet above the surrounding treetops. But there was something odd about those jumbled masses: they were *too* solid, *too* controlled in their movements.

A single red-gold shaft of light broke through that brooding darkness and cut a path to Lookout Rock that was like a spear thrust from Heaven. And riding that beam came the narrow shape of a mighty sailing ship—bright, almost, as the sun. One high, carved prow appeared behind it, and then another and another, until there were ten. Each was shaped like the Ship of Flame, each had a wide, square sail emblazoned with some fantastic beast or complex pattern, and every one bore outstretched oars that beat the air and moved them swiftly forward. They halted in triangular formation a little to

287

the left of the Ship of Flames.

In the vanguard was a ship of gold, its white sail ablaze with a golden sun in splendor.

A man stood in the front of that vessel, and he wore golden armor and a golden helm. Black was his hair and black the mustaches that brushed against his shoulders.

"The Ard Rhi!" David gasped, then said to Gary, "It's the king of the Sidhe himself!"

Lugh raised his arms above his head, then lowered them again. Arches of light sprang forth to bridge the space between the hovering ships and the rock of the Mortal World. The High King leapt from his ship and was the first to touch land. Behind him, a company of warriors followed, each man or woman coming to stand in disciplined array behind him.

Last of all came a woman dressed in red, with a black crow perched on her shoulder. She looked more than a little irate.

The High King of the Sidhe in Tir-Nan-Og ignored Nuada and the two Horn fragments he held, ignored Regan and Froech and Morwyn. Most particularly he ignored the mortals who pulled back into an awestruck group. He did *not* ignore David Sullivan.

Lugh pointed a gold-cased finger at David and curled it slightly toward him.

David gulped, stepped forward, found himself looking into the sharp angles of the Ard Rhi's face, into blazing eyes that he was certain could see all the way to a conscience that was far from clear. He took a deep breath.

Lugh said nothing at first, merely stared at David, and David could not read the emotion written there. Once Lugh's brows lowered and his eyes glittered so brightly that David feared for his life.

Finally the High King took a long breath and spoke. "It is almost a year since we have met, David Sullivan. And in that time you have learned many things, some of which you may even find useful—but I never expected you to number thievery among your studies. I do not think much of your recent visit, *mortal*, nor of my treasury being raided; though you *may* have performed me a service there—by showing me flaws in what I had thought unbreakable defenses."

David's lips quirked upward in an embarrassed, lopsided smile. "I'm glad you see it that way, sir."

Lugh raised a wry eyebrow. In spite of himself a ghost of amusement played around the corners of his mouth as well.

"I also realize that there were, ah, *extenuating* circumstances," the High King continued, fixing Morwyn with a meaningful stare, "so I suppose that leaves me with a single reasonable choice: to congratulate you for your skill at achieving the quest, and, more important, to acknowledge the honor you have shown by reuniting Morwyn and Fionchadd. A man who will do good for his enemy because it is a good thing for a *friend* is an honorable man indeed. And now," he added by way of dismissal, "I think I must speak to Morwyn."

David released the breath he had been holding, and rejoined his friends as Lugh motioned Morwyn forward.

The Fireshaper dropped on her knees before him, but Lugh raised her again to face him. Her body was taut as a harp string.

"Long has it been since we have met, Morwyn verch Morgan ap Gwyddion," Lugh said. "And the occasion of that last meeting was far happier than that which brings us together once more. But even then, I think, I had a foreboding of some mighty doom that awaited you—and now it seems that you have set it upon yourself. And that doom is *guilt*, Morwyn: guilt for the death of Ailill Windmaster. Whatever he did to you and to your son, yet I see that a shadow of love remains, and I fear that shadow will torment you. He need not have died, you know, had you waited but a little while. Though you have had your vengeance, Ailill's death was a thing in vain."

Morwyn's jaw tightened slightly. Lugh paused, his eyes narrowing before he continued. "And with the doom of that vast guilt must come another, Morwyn, which, though you may deny it now in your pride and arrogance, may come to haunt you even more as the seasons turn. And that is guilt for the anguish your selfishness has brought on a whole array of innocent folk, not the least two unfortunate lovers. *And*, Morwyn verch Morgan, there is one doom of guilt upon you that is greater than any other."

Morwyn raised her head and looked him square in the face. "And what is that, Lord?"

"The price that must yet be paid for the deaths of Fionna and Ailill. They had *kin*, Morwyn, mighty kin indeed. The King of Erenn was their half brother, and in more distant realms dwell others who might call them family. One slew herself through her own folly, though I know not whether her kin may see it that way, but you have slain the other by your own hand. And in that you may have helped bring war upon us: war between Erenn and Tir-Nan-Og. Think of it, Morwyn: All because you would not temper vengeance with mercy! All because Ailill's death—or your own pride—was more important to you than peace between the Worlds."

Morwyn's face went suddenly hard. She glared back at Lugh. "I swore an *oath*, Ard Rhi, and kept it. My soul holds no peace because of it, yet I know that in *that*, at least, I acted rightly. My duty was to avenge my son, and that I have done. The rest is for Dana to say; I care not."

"Not even if there is war?"

"I will return to the Land of the Powersmiths," Morwyn replied wearily. "War will sweep by me, and I will scarcely mark its passage."

"But others will not. You will come to know this, Fireshaper: that when war ravages Faerie, perhaps even breaks through to consume the Lands of Men, that every one who dies, man or Faery, will die cursing your name. *That* may be your doom, Fireshaper. I only hope it does not come to pass."

"But what about Fionchadd?" David interrupted desperately. "We've got to try to resurrect him, and soon—we're running out of time!"

"We are indeed," the Morrigu acknowledged unexpectedly, "but I think we may yet succeed—if we can enlist the aid of that mortal woman I see skulking about by the pool yonder."

Lugh followed her pointing finger, and nodded. "Bring that woman here," he commanded.

"Lord, help me," Katie whispered to JoAnne Sullivan, as she saw two warriors break ranks behind Lugh and start toward her. "What can they want with me?"

The younger woman could only shake her head and frown.

Katie cleared her throat expectantly. Whatever Oisin had chosen her for was about to happen. She was there, finally, the place where the cross had been. She'd been late—evidently something important had gone on that she'd missed. She had arrived in time to see the ships come sailing out of the clouds, though, and that was a wonder straight out of Ezekiel. But now they had noticed her, and were coming to get her. Did They want her to do something for *Them?* But what could Katie McNally do that these fine folk could not? She couldn't imagine.

A hand brushed her arm, gentle but firm. She looked up, saw a man there—or a boy. Which was he? She couldn't tell; they all looked like tall young men to her—except for their eyes. And the women . . .

"Come, Katie McNally," a gentle voice urged her, a woman's voice this time, at her left. A woman in what looked like solid gold armor. "You must come with us; the High King of the Sidhe has need of you."

Katie nodded, set her mouth, and stood up as straight as she could. "I'll walk of my own will," she said. "You do na' have to force me."

"Nor would we," the woman replied.

And Katie left JoAnne Sullivan standing speechless beside the pool and went forward to meet Lugh Samildinach.

Lugh looked her up and down. "Do you think she will do, Morrigu?"

The Mistress of Battles stared at Katie, and Katie felt as though something were pecking away at her fluttering heart; the woman's voice, when she heard it again, was like the cawing of a crow. "She will, Lord, if her doubts do not betray her."

"You are certain?"

"I know, Lord, that with battle comes death, but with the knowledge of death comes also the knowledge of life. And this one has lived a very long life, as mortals go. She has done many of the things we have done, and she has done one thing none of us will ever do."

"And what is that?" Froech asked.

"She has aged, boy," Lugh interrupted. "She knows the feel of mortality in her bones, as we never can. Death comes even to the Sidhe, sometimes, but we never see it approaching. To grow old and know it is waiting there at the end must take great strength indeed."

"So you need me for my old bones?" Katie snapped, feistier than she felt.

Lugh looked at her without emotion. "I need you for the Power age has horded within you."

"What power? I've got no power."

Lugh's face was impassive. "I need you to lead a ritual, to be a kind of priestess, as it were."

Katie's heart flip-flopped. A priestess! What did they mean by that? She wouldn't be involved in no pagan rites, no sir. That would be asking too much. She'd been a good Catholic woman since her birth.

"I'll not."

"But you must." Lugh smiled. "A life hangs in the balance, and you alone can help to save it—you and some of these other good folk."

"Why me?"

"Because this is your World. And because there is no time but now for the doing, and no one *for* the doing but you. Morwyn's son dwells in a body not his own. He cannot leave it, and yet that body will fail, it will die. He must have strength enough to claim another by then. Yet we cannot wait, for he battles the lizard's thoughts incessantly. He is awake now, but he must sleep again. He will not reawaken."

Suddenly the red-haired woman was on her knees before her. "Will you do this for me, Katie McNally?"

"Yer askin' me for my soul, Lady. I cannot help you."

"Let me talk to her," David interrupted. "Maybe I can explain—I've seen a little more of both sides."

Katie sighed and let the boy lead her back to the pool. If he thought he was going to convince her . . .

David grimaced uncertainly when he saw his mother still waiting there, took a deep breath, and slid his hands down his hips as though he sought pockets he did not have. Finally he folded his arms in frustration. "You've got to help them, Katie."

"And why would that be, young sir? I've helped them too much already."

David frowned. "But they *need* your help, Katie, it's as simple as that," he began slowly. "You asked why, and all I can say is because . . . because they're just good people, most of 'em. Because they're alive, even if it's not the same as you and me, and they've got a right to be happy just like us."

He paused, chewed thoughtfully on the side of his hand before continuing. "I *know* what's bothering you; it's the religion thing, and I'll tell you straight it bothers me too, sometimes; 'cause what I know, what I've seen, just don't jive with what you read in the Book. Hell, I was almost an atheist before I found out about all this. But it *is* real, Katie; it's all part of one creation."

He paused again, glanced around, locked gazes briefly with his mother, before looking back at Katie. "I know I must sound like I really think I know it all to be telling you this, but there's one thing I *do* know absolutely, and that's if you really do what you know is right, then you'll be okay in the hereafter. If you make people happy, that's a right thing. If you aid the sick, that's a right thing. I wish I had time to explain more, to try to make you see—that when they talk about you being a priestess, they're not trying to make you give up God, they're trying to make you *serve* God, just in a different way. I mean, it's all one world in the end—but you and me and just a few others know how much more to it there really is." He took another breath. "This stuff didn't cost me my religion, Katie. It helped me find my religion."

"Well, I ain't havin' any part of it," JoAnne said suddenly. "I'm gonna get Little Billy and get outta here. You better come on, too, if you know what's good for you." She began stalking away from the pool.

David's eyes flickered indecisively from Katie's uncertain face to JoAnne's rigid back. Finally he sprinted after his mother and caught her by the arm.

She looked around at him, her face a mask of uncertain indignation. "I can't go through with this, David," she whispered. "Do you *really* have any idea what's goin' on?"

"It's kind of complicated, Ma," David said, as he drew her back toward Katie, "if they're talking about what I think they are. I'll just have to tell you what I told Katie. These are good people here, getting ready to try to do a good thing."

"I don't want to hear about it. Tryin' to raise the dead an' all that! It's plain ol' satanism!"

"No it's not, Ma. Not at all." David released her arm and pointed toward the precipice. "I mean, just look out there! Look at those ships. You ever see ships floating in the sky? You ever see a man walk through the air like Lugh did about five minutes ago? You ever see *me* appear out of nowhere with a king's ransom in gaudy jewelry in my hand? Yet you believe in a man who's supposed to have walked on water and fed a multitude with loaves and fishes. This kind of stuff ought to make you believe more, not less, because it makes all that miracle stuff more likely. And anyway, what they're planning doesn't involve invoking powers or anything, it just involves one person's strength of will—he just happens to be wearing a lizard's body right now, that's all."

JoAnne's nose twitched. "Don't that make him a demon, though?"

David thought desperately. "No—of course not. Listen, I think the best I can tell you is that these folks are like angels, only not quite. Some folks say they didn't take sides when Satan rebelled, and were doomed to roam the space between Heaven and Earth. Don't ask me, I don't know. But we ain't got time to argue now. Talk to Katie if you don't believe me."

JoAnne's troubled stare shifted to Katie. The old woman smiled wanly and motioned her away. "You go on, child, I got to think by myself for just a minute."

JoAnne nodded slowly, as David led her back toward the waiting company. "I'm gonna be doin' some serious thinkin', too, let me tell you," she told him as they walked. "But that old lady's got some faith too, so I reckon if it's good enough for her, it's good enough for me. If she'll go through with whatever's goin' on, I will."

* * *

Katie looked at David's departing back. She'd heard every word: what he'd told her, and what he'd told his mother besides. But was he serious? Could he be telling the truth? It was too much, too complex. And he was so young. But he'd smiled; there'd been tears in his eyes, and his face had fairly glowed when he talked, like she'd only seen a very few people do in church. He believed what he said. She squared her shoulders and started forward.

"I'll do it," Katie said a moment later, as she stood before Lugh's splendid form. "And may the Lord forgive me. Now tell me what you need me to do."

"It will take six of you," Lugh said. "Six mortals, for we deal with the Powers of your World now, which even the Sidhe have almost forgotten."

"What do you mean?" Liz asked carefully.

"I mean that there are circumstances under which the laws that govern even life and death may be transcended—very particular circumstances, I might add. Circumstances that blur the distinctions between the Worlds, as they blur—or combine—all such distinctions: man and woman, youth and maturity and age!"

The Faery lord spared a sideways glance at JoAnne, who was glaring about distrustfully, apparently having second thoughts already. She was casting particularly disapproving looks at her older son, her younger one having already curled his hand happily in her own.

"Well, I don't see nothin'!" she announced flatly. "Just get it over and done with."

Regan laid a hand on her shoulder, which she tried unsuccessfully to shrug off. "You know it not, JoAnne Sullivan," the Faery lady said, "but together with Katie and Liz you embody one of the greatest confluences of Power in all your World. Indeed, men once worshiped one like you: the threefold goddess: the crone, and the matron, and the virgin maid. Goddess they never were, in fact, yet the three together are still a focus of Power. It is that Power we would draw on now."

"With," the Morrigu interrupted, "their consort, the threefold god: the sage, and the warrior, and the youth. They usually sacrificed the latter two," she added with a sly glance at David.

"By which you mean Uncle Dale, for sure, and . . . who else?" David faltered.

"There are several choices," Nuada observed, "but there is one particular requirement."

David looked at him dubiously. "Which is?"

"The maid and the youth must be virgins."

"Well, that lets me out, Sullivan," Gary chortled. He punched Alec's shoulder. "How 'bout you, McLean?"

Alec did not reply, though he blushed rather profusely.

"We could use Little Billy," David suggested. "He's sure to qualify."

Nuada shook his head. "No, he is too young."

"And is Liz a, er—" Gary found himself blushing.

"Damn right," Liz volunteered with conviction.

"So it's either Alex or Sullivan—if they're . . ."

David stared at the ground, kicked a stone. "I'm eligible," he mumbled.

"So am I," Alec ventured.

"But Liz and I make a better set."

"Well, there is that."

"And now for the warrior."

Alec and Gary looked at each other. "Flip you for it?" Gary said.

Alec shrugged. "*You* were the most heroic on the Tracks. I mean, you attacked the deer and the manticore—"

"Like a friggin' idiot."

"—and helped draw off the Watchers. I couldn't have done that."

Gary nodded. "Okay, okay, you've sold me. So what do I do?"

"Yeah," Liz broke in, "all this beating around the bush about threefold gods and goddesses and stuff is giving me the fidgets. Can we or can we not resurrect Fionchadd, and if so, how?" She whirled to face Lugh. "Well?"

"One word will say it," Lugh replied. "And that word is blood."

"Blood?" Gary asked, startled.

"Blood is the life," the Morrigu said, "the vehicle of Power. Without it, without the Power it contains, why, what is a man's body but earth and water? Even in Faerie it is the same. Now the first two things we have a-plenty in the water of yonder falls, the stones beneath our feet. But there are two other things that must be present also: Air and Fire: spirit and Power. Spirit Fionchadd has, and a life force of his own within the lizard. But more life force he needs, if he would shape himself anew: and that comes best from blood. Various rules determine whose, but in this World the threefold god and the threefold goddess would seem to do very nicely."

"I thought sex came into it some way," David muttered. "Or did I read *The Golden Bough* wrong?"

Liz raced his mother in shooting him a glare.

Morwyn looked amused. "You had your chance at that and lost it. Had I but known, this would be far simpler now. But however you work it, it still takes a certain amount of time and a certain amount of pain, and there are means both quicker and easier—if Fionchadd has the Power."

"So what do we do?" Uncle Dale asked, tugging nervously on his whiskers.

Lugh looked at the Morrigu. "This is really woman's magic," he said. "I think I had best defer to you."

"And about time, too," the Morrigu snapped. "I will need a cauldron, to start with. A pity Bran's was lost to us; it would serve very well just now."

"I have one on my ship here," Lugh replied, "though it is not enchanted." At his nod, two soldiers fell from ranks and quickly boarded his vessel, to return a moment later with, indeed, a cauldron large enough for a man to sit in.

"Looks like my old wash pot," JoAnne confided to Katie.

"Fill it with water!"

Two more soldiers brought water from the falls in golden ewers.

"Now add stones—bones would be even better." The Morrigu looked around. "I believe there is a deer's skeleton in the woods just to the right of those trees."

Two more soldiers broke rank.

A moment later the cauldron was full of a strange concoction of water and rocks, the bones of a dead deer, leaves from a certain tree . . . and a few things the Morrigu had not told them of.

Katie groaned and stood up. She couldn't delay any longer. Her time had come. It was her soul now: damnation or salvation, one, all in a couple of minutes. But she'd been praying while those other folks went on about high-sounding things. And she'd prayed again after the woman with the crow had told her what she had to do. She didn't like it, but she had no choice; too many folks were depending on her, too many *good* folks, good folks among even Those Ones, she guessed. Regan, at least, had never been anything but kind to her. So she had prayed and asked God's guidance, and then his forgiveness. She thought she had them. It was for a good cause, she'd decided. She didn't know if They really had souls or not. But they sure talked a lot about them. Maybe that was what made them so intense, so hot-tempered, so strange and perilous—they didn't truly know God's love. They were immortal, therefore they didn't need God, except that you needed God most when you were alive, not dead. Regan had told her about Dana, once, but Dana wasn't God. Regan was sure of that. What she was, Katie had no idea.

"Katie, it is time," Lugh said.

* * *

They stood in a circle, with the cauldron in the center. Uncle Dale was to Katie's left, and then JoAnne and David and Liz and Gary, back to Katie's right. Katie held her breath. She hoped she wouldn't forget. She hoped, one more time, that God would forgive her.

"Stretch out your arms," she commanded finally, in a stronger voice than she had known she had.

And six arms stretched above the water: Her own frail arm was there, soft-wrinkled as ancient silk. And the hard-knotted arm of Dale Sullivan, that had seen almost as many years, but showed them far, far less. And the firm, straight arm of JoAnne Sullivan, strong from ironing and hoeing. And the brawny arm of Gary the Warrior, forested dark with hair. And—touching eagerly when they thought no one was looking—the smooth young arms of Liz Hughes and David Sullivan, hers pale and lightly freckled, his muscular and tanned and almost hairless: the maiden and the youth.

The Morrigu stood behind them, her back toward the sun. From her belt she took a hook-bladed knife that had as its hilt the bone of a mortal man who had once been her lover—before she had had him slain. She handed it to Katie. "Do it as I told you," she said.

Katie looked at it sadly, but set her mouth. She reached out for David's arm, took it, nicked his wrist with her blade, then did the same with Liz. Gary was next, and then the reluctant JoAnne. Dale was last, except for herself. She set her teeth and finished it. And with each sure stroke, each careful narrow slit, twelve drops of blood welled forth: twelve only.

"Turn your arms over."

One by one those drops fell into the cauldron, veiling that still surface with a glaze of deepening pink.

"You can all go," Katie said. "I reckon it's up to Fionchadd now." The five nodded solemnly and backed away.

"Was that it?" Gary whispered.

"Guess so," David told him, "at least for us."

"Seemed like a lot of hassle over nothing."

"Silence," Nuada hissed.

Morwyn stepped forward with the lizard in the palm of her hand. She said nothing as she placed it upon the edge of the cauldron, but her eyes were clouded with dread.

Katie let it sit there a moment, emerald upon the black, its tiny sides billowing in and out as it drank in air. Its tongue flicked, and its eyes shone bright with fear. So pretty. She hated what she had to do. *Holy Mary, Mother of God . . .*

With one quick, sure stroke, she impaled it with the knife.

The lizard chirped once and fell into the cauldron, its mouth already spurting blood. Liz shrieked and buried her face in David's shoulder.

"It is better that the mortals do not watch," Regan said.

"I don't think I want to," JoAnne muttered.

"Nor I," came Katie's quiet echo.

"I do!" cried Little Billy. "Let me watch 'em rebuild ol' Fin'kid."

"No!" David said forcefully, and turned his back on the cauldron. The others did likewise—even Lugh and the Morrigu.

Silence fell upon them. As they waited, the clouds slowly faded, letting the sun blaze through. The ships of Tir-Nan-Og creaked and rattled in the morning air, but a ghostliness had settled about them, as the shapes of mountains and lakes and the scarwork of men's highways began to leak through their substance.

David wondered what they were waiting for. He half expected some sort of pyrotechnics—heat, or light, or at least the sound of bubbling water.

But there was nothing but the hush of expectant breathing. And eventually the sound of a harp plucked in delicate lament somewhere on one of the ships.

Someone else picked up a set of pipes and blew a counterpoint, the bass notes rumbling softly through the rocks of the mountain.

Nothing happened.

"It's not working," Gary muttered at last. "Something's gone wrong."

"Plain foolishness, if you ask me," JoAnne grumbled her disgust.

"Hush, woman," Katie whispered back. "After all you've seen this morning, that's a word you'd best be careful usin'."

The Morrigu sighed.

"It has not succeeded," she said with conviction. "Fionchadd was not strong enough."

Tears welled forth from Morwyn's eyes. "But we must have been. I could feel his Power. He cannot have failed."

Lugh turned and likewise stared into the cauldron. "There was simply not enough Power present. Earth and Water we added, Air we had in plenty from the blood of these fine folks. But of Power, which Fionchadd had to provide of himself, there was not enough."

"I should have used my blood," said Morwyn. "The blood of mortals is never strong enough."

"That makes no difference," Lugh replied sternly. "It is of Power we speak, not blood."

"Power?" Liz asked hesitantly. "What sort of Power?"

"Anything of Power around which Fionchadd could focus his strength, anything on which he could draw to work his rising!"

Liz set her mouth. "I know just the thing!"

David stared at her. "You *what?* You don't know anything about this kind of stuff, Liz."

"Want to bet, David Sullivan?" Liz replied with more than a trace of smugness.

And very quietly, very quickly she removed the Ring of Oisin from her finger and dropped it into the cauldron.

Nothing happened for a moment . . .

And then the cauldron began to glow, to take on an eerie translucence, as if it were in neither the Lands of Men nor Tir-Nan-Og, but a realm apart.

The brightness increased, then ebbed, as quickly as it had begun.

"I thank you, Liz Hughes" came a voice from within it.

The entire company turned as one to see, standing stark naked thigh-deep in the cauldron, the shape of a slender Faery boy whose bright hair and capricious looks and complete lack of apparent modesty were blessedly familiar.

Morwyn was the first to embrace him. "Fionchadd, my son," she cried.

David helped him from the cauldron. One of Lugh's soldiers handed him a cloak in which he wrapped himself.

He looked happy but dazed, as he sank onto a rock.

Something glinted above his knuckle, and he looked up at Liz, at David, whose fingers were twined with hers, even as older hands were twining shyly behind them. He smiled, though weariness shadowed his face.

"I can speak but little," he said, "for though I have returned to a body that seems to be my own, I am yet weak nigh unto dying. But for one thing I would not be here at all, and that is this ring." He withdrew it from his finger and handed it to David, who shook his head and passed it on to Liz.

"It has no Power now, I am afraid," Fionchadd added. "For I drank deep of it while I was a-borning. But thank you."

"Thank you all," Morwyn said, then paused. "I believe that is only the second time I ever said that to anyone of mortal lineage."

"See that it is not the last," Nuada noted wryly.

David went looking for Lugh and found him facing the lookout. The last of the clouds had vanished, and the High King was staring directly into the sunrise with unshielded eyes.

"I, uh, kinda need to ask you something," David said.

Lugh glanced askance at him. "Indeed?"

"Uh, yeah. I was kinda wondering about my escape and all. I mean, it really was too easy. You had the whole thing figured out and all, didn't you? You knew I was coming, and you didn't really have anything against Morwyn, so you just used me to be sure you gave Fionna enough rope to hang herself."

"Did I, now?" Lugh replied, not looking at him.

"Well, I would have. I figure you sent the first fake Horn to Nuada, knowing that there was a good chance Fionna would wind up with it, and then try to use it, only it would backfire on her, and rid you of at least one threat without you being blamed for it. But just to be sure, just in case she *didn't* wind up with it, you sent a second version with me, because you knew Morwyn would want to use it on Ailill face-to-face. And wherever Ailill was, Fionna wouldn't be far behind, and together the two of them could overpower Morwyn and get the Horn, and once again do themselves in. You didn't *want* me to fail, so you had to make it fairly easy to rob you—but you didn't want me to get too suspicious either, so you staged a halfhearted attack and pursuit." David folded his arms and looked very pleased with himself.

"I will let you wonder about those things for a while," Lugh told him. "Except to tell you that you are far more wrong than right. I never desired the death of Fionna or Ailill, for instance, if for no other reason than because their demise may well precipitate war between Tir-Nan-Og and Erenn."

David looked puzzled. "Hmmm, yeah . . . and suppose Morwyn had blown the Horn herself—that'd cause a war with the Power-smiths."

"I think *you* must do some more thinking."

"You're not gonna tell me, huh? Well, crap."

"Talk to your friends, learn their stories. Maybe you will have more answers then."

David shook his head. "And I bet we won't be able to talk to anybody else about this, either—right?"

Lugh laughed softly. "In that you *are* correct."

"And I'll just bet you'll play with the time, or people's memories or something, too, won't you? There'd be too many questions to answer otherwise."

"It is possible."

"And—"

"This is a fair land," Lugh interrupted absently, as he continued to scan the vista before him. "A land worth dying for, I think. I wonder on whose side you good folk will fight when the battle comes."

David shrugged, but did not reply.

Lugh sighed. "No answer? Well, I gave you none either, did I? Still, there will be other mornings in the Mortal World, though few as glorious as this." He turned, faced the group gathered around Fionchadd. "Let us away," he cried. "Morwyn, are you coming with us?"

The Fireshaper smiled sadly. "If you will have me, Lord; I would visit a while with my son."

She looked around, saw David looking at her. "Well, David Sullivan," she said. "It seems our quest has reached an ending quite unlooked for. You have brought me a gift beyond price, yet I have nothing with which to reward you . . . unless"—she glanced beyond the precipice—"you still have my ring, do you not?"

David glanced down at his finger. "Yep, sure do. I don't think I can work it very well. I had some trouble with it in Tir-Nan-Og."

Morwyn frowned. "Perhaps you did at that; its Power comes from the Land of the Powersmiths, and behind Lugh's barrier that might have been disrupted."

David flashed her an embarrassed grin. "Actually, I'm afraid most of the trouble was with me. I kinda got confused—scratched the wrong head the wrong number of times, I think."

"Gifts," Fionchadd interrupted. "You were talking about gifts."

"Gifts," Morwyn repeated. "Very well. How would you like a boat?"

David's eyes widened. "*That* boat? You'd give me that?"

Morwyn nodded. "And the ring that goes with it. I'm afraid, though, that it may cause you some problems."

"Well, I don't have anywhere to put it, and it is kind of big."

"The ring will take care of that," Fionchadd said.

David shrugged helplessly. "I really can't."

"You must, I insist. You do not want to make me angry. You know what I can do."

David backed away a step, but then he noticed the mischievous sparkle in her eye. "If *you'll* reduce it, I'll take it. It'll make a nice decoration, I guess." He handed her the ring, and she walked off in the direction of the Ship of Flames.

Fionchadd grinned, and extended a tentative hand toward David. "Thank you again, my friend. Or should I perhaps say 'my father'? I already like you better than Ailill."

"Not unless you say that to me and Uncle Dale as well," Gary laughed.

"Ahem," Liz interjected. "Some of us don't qualify—for fatherhood, anyway."

Fionchadd grinned again—and sweeping her into his arms, he kissed her firmly on the mouth.

Liz colored, glanced toward David, who burst out laughing.

"My first mortal woman," Fionchadd said.

"But not your last, I imagine," David cried.

"Fionchadd, we are going!"

"I come, oh hasty one, I come!"

Morwyn returned, handed David the toy ship and the serpent ring.

"Thank you once more," she said, and stepped upon the arc of light that led to Lugh's flagship.

There was a brightness in the air then, a rustle of feet and fabric, a clanking of metal, mixed with a glory of sunlight. And when it was gone, eight people remained on Lookout Rock: eight mortals who had seen the Sidhe.

JoAnne Sullivan was the first to speak. "I wonder what Bill'd think about a houseful of company."

Uncle Dale grinned and pinched her arm. "Well, it bein' Sunday and all, and without you there to wake him, I bet he's still a-sleep-in'."

"Then we'll get him up," Little Billy squealed.

"Probably have to." JoAnne sighed wearily. "That man could sleep through the Second Coming. Why I bet—" She paused, looking suddenly very shocked at herself. "Lord, lord, better not be sayin' things like *that* now, had I? Considerin' what I just seen. Maybe I better just think about other stuff for a while. I got a *bunch* of phone calls to make, for one thing. I expect the sheriff'd like to go to bed hisself. And then I gotta do me some *serious* thinkin'."

"Thinkin' goes a whole lot better on a full stomach, though," Uncle Dale said. "I tell you what, I'll fix us breakfast at my house. And you, Katie girl, can help me."

Chapter XLIX: Musing

(Tir-Nan-Og)

Starlight sparkled in the cup of wine Lugh Samildinach rested comfortably in his lap. So still was the night air, so fluid the High King's movements that one could read the constellations on its surface—or the future, if one had that dubious art. He wished someone had read his future some days ago. It would have spared him a great deal of trouble. He would have to summon Oisin back more often. Oisin was good at reading the signs.

He sighed and propped his feet on the low marble railing of the balcony outside his rooms. Beyond the sweep of white stone Lugh could gaze out over nearly half his kingdom—all the way to its limits, if he chose to strain his Power so. If he *chose*, he could pierce his own glamour and gaze into the Lands of Men. But he did not choose to do that. He had seen enough of the Lands of Men to last him quite a while.

He rubbed his left hand absently, feeling for a scar that was not there. He found himself wishing there *were* one, some blemish upon his perfect body to remind him of what had happened, of what it had felt like to be one with the land, to know, for a brief while, everything that passed within his realm. He had seen with more than eyes the walls of perilous flame he had raised about his borders, had known the weight of Morwyn's strange boat upon his waters. He had sensed with the land the tread of a mortal boy's feet on ground they should never have walked.

The Morrigu had been right, he decided, though he would never tell her that. He *had* acted hastily in sealing the borders, but Ailill's escape had touched him in his one point of vanity: his devotion to law and justice and the sanctity of his realm. Once he had set affairs in motion, though, he had had no choice but to follow through, knowing that eventually madness would claim his enemies if they did not give themselves up. He had feared the mischief they might perform outside, however, and that was why he had sent the sword to Nuada, because he needed eyes in the lands beyond and had himself cut off his usual sources.

But when Nuada had lost the sword, that had not been good at all, until Fionna had claimed it. He wondered what she would have thought had she known Lugh himself had followed her every move, had known her every thought from the time she had gained the sword. It was from her he had learned about Morwyn and her designs upon the Horn, which dovetailed rather nicely with his discovery of the newly awakened Fionchadd. And then things had unfolded rapidly: the Ship of Flames, the theft of the Horn itself—harmless that, in its various pieces, unless one winded it, and then, why, thieves got what they deserved. He wished Fionna had been less rash, though. Ailill he could perhaps explain. Fionna would be much harder.

He took a sip of wine. Ah well, there was one good thing at least; the mortal boy was shaping up nicely. He was brave, and resourceful, and lucky. Just the sort of person Lugh very much feared he would need, especially now that war loomed nearer. David Sullivan had passed his latest round of tests very nicely—not precisely as Lugh would have planned them, but they had nevertheless worked out well.

And Morwyn's son was coming along, too. Now *that* was a piece of luck. Had Lugh not become one with the land, he would never have sensed the ghost of Power that lay within a certain lizard, never would have been able to awaken it. That was another reason he had allowed David Sullivan to escape—that, and the weaponwork the mortal boy had engaged in as he fled Tir-Nan-Og, which had been contrived to keep Fionchadd's will awake and active. No, without his merger with the land, he would never have been able to orchestrate the one set of circumstances that would bring the boy back. And Lugh had plans for that one, too.

But would it be in time? he wondered.

He looked up at the sky again. *Gods, mortals called us once*, he thought. *Gods no longer. I play mortal against immortal like chessmen, but sometimes I feel someone else moving me. Perhaps I should summon Oisin—or Katie. Perhaps there is something to mortality.*

Chapter L: Coffee and 'Shine and Syrup

(Sullivan Cove, Georgia)

"Next?" David said, as he slipped out of the bathroom at Uncle Dale's house.

"Me, me!" Alec cried from where he lay sprawled across the bed in the old man's bedroom.

"Go easy on the hot water, huh?" Gary sighed. "I still need a go."

David flipped him with the towel he'd been using to dry his hair. "There's plenty."

"Better be," Alec muttered. "We've got the dust of half a dozen worlds to wash off." He glanced at his fingernails, frowning at the crescents of dried blood there.

"Would I lie to you?" David laughed, as he pushed through the door that led into the kitchen.

Liz was waiting at the breakfast table, hair wrapped turban-style in a snowy towel, wearing one of dead Aunt Hattie's bathrobes the old man had never had the heart to discard. Her face brightened when she saw him, and he felt his own grin spread across his face so quick and wide that it practically hurt.

"You look real silly," Little Billy giggled from behind a pile of pancakes as tall as he was.

"Not as silly as he did," JoAnne muttered beside him. "Leastwise he's got on normal clothes now."

Uncle Dale turned from where he was browning sausage in an iron skillet. "Don't give the boy a hard time, JoAnne, he's been through a right smart bit."

David blushed as he glanced down at the oversized khaki pants and shirt he'd borrowed from Uncle Dale, rolled up at both wrists and ankles.

"*I* think he looks just great," Liz said, as David snagged a cup of coffee from the huge pot and sat down beside her. Katie set a plate in front of him, and twin pans of bacon and sausage, and pancakes in front of that. David loaded his plate, applied a generous portion of maple syrup (the real kind), and cut a handsome wedge from the edge of the pile. It smelled heavenly. He took a sip of coffee—and raised his eyebrows in surprise. A second odor hid in the steam, an odor that warmed him and made him feel giddy at the same time. He glanced over his shoulder. "Is this . . . ?"

Uncle Dale nodded. "Shore is. I thought a little of the old squee-zins'd help mellow us out some."

JoAnne set her cup down with a thud. "Dale, you didn't!"

"Don't worry 'bout it, girl. You ain't likely to go to hell over a taste of 'shine."

"Yeah, Ma," Little Billy squealed. "He even gave me some."

"Good for what ails you," Uncle Dale said, and returned to the stove. David watched him, saw the looks he was giving Katie, who was busy scrubbing dishes at the sink, wished he could hear the phrases the old man kept mumbling in her ear.

Liz bent close and whispered, "Hey, you know I bet this stuff'd taste even better outside."

David nodded and picked up his plate. "See y'all," he mumbled through a mouthful of food.

He followed Liz to the front porch, joined her on the steps, look-ing across the yard at the road and the rumpled mountains beyond. Sunlight was playing there, dancing a sparkling dance across the trees, sliding along the fence posts closer by, prodding the world awake with beams of light. A yellow cat crawled out from under the steps and rubbed against David's bare feet.

Neither of them spoke.

"We'll have to be more careful when we go swimming," Liz said after a moment. Her voice sounded so serious that David looked up from his plate, but when their eyes met, and he saw them sparkle like green gems out of Faerie, he knew she had been teasing.

David laughed, and shook his head. "I'll have to be more careful about where I leave my clothes, that's for certain."

Liz plucked at one of the baggy sleeves. "Well, it's not quite *Esquire*, is it?"

David grinned. "Looks like there's something you need to be careful about, too."

"Oh? What's that?"

"Well, Liz, I don't know how to tell you this, but you've got syrup all over your face."

Liz raised questing fingers automatically, but David's were there before her. "I'll get it," he said. "There's some on your cheek"—he bent over and very gently kissed her there—"and on your nose"— another kiss—"and a great big gob of it right here!"

It took him a very long time to find all of the syrup.

TOM DEITZ grew up in Young Harris, Georgia, a small town not far from the fictitious Enotah County of FIRESHAPER'S DOOM, and has Bachelor of Arts and Master of Arts degrees from the University of Georgia. His major in medieval English literature led Mr. Deitz to the Society for Creative Anachronism, which in turn generated a particular interest in heraldry, historic costuming, castle architecture, British folk music, and all things Celtic. He began the story of David Sullivan and his friends in *Windmaster's Bane*, his first published novel, available from Avon Books, and intends to follow their adventures through several more volumes. Mr. Deitz is also a car nut and would like to build a small castle someday.

RETURN TO AMBER...

THE ONE *REAL* WORLD, OF WHICH ALL OTHERS, INCLUDING EARTH, ARE BUT SHADOWS

ROGER ZELAZNY

Coming in August 1988
The New Amber Novel

SIGN OF CHAOS   89637-0/$3.50 US/$4.50 Can

BLOOD OF AMBER   89636-2/$3.50 US/$4.50 Can
Pursued by fiendish enemies, Merlin, son of Corwin, battles through an intricate web of vengeance and murder.

TRUMPS OF DOOM   89635-4/$3.50 US/$3.95 Can
Death stalks the son of Amber's vanished hero on a Shadow world called Earth.

The Classic Amber Series

NINE PRINCES IN AMBER 01430-0/$2.95 US/$3.95 Can
THE GUNS OF AVALON   00083-0/$2.95 US/$3.95 Can
SIGN OF THE UNICORN   00831-9/$2.95 US/$3.75 Can
THE HAND OF OBERON   01664-8/$2.95 US/$3.75 Can
THE COURTS OF CHAOS 47175-2/$2.95 US/$3.75 Can